Oliver's Song

A Della Boudreaux Novel

Oliver's Song

Published in the United States of America
by
LINDELL PUBLISHING
P. O. Box 1005
New York, NY 10276
Lindellpubs@gmail.com
www.Lindellpubs.com

Cover Design and Illustration by Hannah Wilson
www.hbproductions.net

Printed in the United States of America
First Edition, 2017
ISBN 978-0-9984509-0-2

Oliver's Song is dedicated to book club women (and men) everywhere. There would be no writers without good readers who seek entertainment, enlightenment, education, self-help, and inspiration through books. Hats off to you! You are in the heads and hearts of every writer who sits—isolated and utterly alone—hour upon hour, and painstakingly creates worlds and characters who come to life on the pages of books. To book club readers north and south, east and west, this writer wants to say thank you!

A special *thank you* to James E. Robertson and Patsy Busby Dow—both attorneys—for some legal insights and some observations about Mardi Gras as well.   Thanks Jim, and thanks Patsy.

Oliver's Song

A Della Boudreaux Novel

Linda Busby Parker

Lindell Publishing 2017

New York, NY

Oliver's Song

1

Della Boudreaux leaned her shoulder against a cast-iron lamppost at the street corner in Bienville Square. Green and pink serpentine dangled from the lamppost and fluttered in the noon breeze. Mardi Gras was in full swing, and Bienville Square was ground-zero. The Square's wrought-iron fountain with acanthus leaves and fleur-de-lis proclaimed: *you're as far south as you can go without braving a ride on the Gulf waves. You're down here in ole Mobile, rubbing shoulders and elbows with coastal Mississippi and ole steamy New Orleans.*

On this February day, Della couldn't walk another step without adjusting the narrow strip of cardboard inside her brown, right-foot pump where a tiny crack opened in the thin sole this very morning. Now a speck of gravel wedged between the cardboard and the ball of her foot. Had the tiny stone not felt like a boulder pressing into the soft flesh just below her toes, she wouldn't have stopped next to Covey, the street musician who regularly set up shop on one corner of the square with his hand-scrawled sign resting against his plastic bucket—*Covey Says Thanks!* The little bucket brimmed with folding money, generosity of the lawyers who emerged from their high-rise offices in search of lunch or a noon workout at the downtown Y.

Della Boudreaux was not one of the high-rise high-rollers— at least not yet. Her office, two leased rooms on Government

Street directly in front of the old Bankhead Tunnel, was more than ample. In fact, her two rooms were greater than the sum of her current clientele, which was why she found herself leaning against the lamppost and slipping off her shoe. It was not yet noon, but already she had dined on dry chicken salad sandwiches and limp carrot sticks in a conference room at one of the big firms, getting her name on their list for any sideline legal jobs they might toss her way. She needed work and she needed it yesterday.

Covey ceased strumming his ukulele and watched her refit the cardboard over the hairline crack. "Mornin'," he said. "Benville Square's pretty today, huh?" He raised his index finger to his dirty gray beret and saluted her.

She glanced directly at his bucket. "Business looks good."

"Real good." He nodded his head and strummed Clementine. His ukulele pitched the notes high, but somehow Covey managed to achieve amazing volume on the diminutive instrument, the notes very clear—*Oh my darlin', oh my darlin', oh my dar-lin' Clementine* . . .

Della fitted the shoe back on her foot, rose to full height, and squared her shoulders. "I might purchase my own ukulele and join you if my business doesn't pick up," she said. She didn't tell him she was awaiting her first client.

"You got a place reserved right here." He pointed to his left.

With two fingers raised to her forehead, she saluted Covey and made her way to her own office where, in celebration of passing the bar, she had commissioned a sign maker to paint gold letters on a black shield—*D. Boudreaux, Attorney at Law.* Vapors from the fresh paint on the shingle or the identification of herself as an attorney (possibly both) made her feel slightly light headed, a not unpleasant feeling. To have earned the moniker—from Tulane Law, no less—in her early forties was no small achievement, and now all she needed was a few clients to pay for the sign and keep the doors open, not to mention keeping the bill-collecting sharks at bay.

Oliver's Song

Inside Della's office, Candy Sue rested one perfectly sculpted and bronzed leg on the desk while she painted her toenails an iridescent shade of purple Della had seen before on the inside of oyster shells. "Any clients?" she asked, hoping there had been a flurry of inquiries in her brief absence.

"Not one client walked through that door, Miss Della." Candy Sue nodded toward the front entry. "Phone's been quiet too." She feathered the edge of the brush across the tip of her middle toenail.

Candy Sue, a criminal justice major at the university, might have been a mistake, but Della knew she was fortunate to have a secretary at all. She had chiseled the secretary's salary so thin that had it been wood, it would have been transparent when held up to light. Besides, she was nearly a week late on Candy Sue's meager pay, which meant her secretary hadn't seen a nickel in nearly three weeks. Earlier in the day, she had politely reminded Della that she needed her pay for Mardi Gras expenses, namely a low-cut, rhinestone-studded evening gown for one of the Mardi Gras balls, and she needed a visit to the hair salon.

Della entered her office, closed the door, and sat at her desk where she withdrew her expense sheet. Rent on her little garage apartment, a studio with a bath, behind the main house of a Spring Hill matriarch, Mercedes Magellan, (her real name, honest to God), was past due by fifteen days. She still owed last month's repair bill at Coolee Automotive for her aging Dodge, which broke down and whined to be petted every time the old thing smelled an extra dollar. The Dodge, not smelling folding money, had purred lately. Rent on her two-room office was also past due by a full two weeks.

Immediately upon passing the bar, she had swallowed her pride and borrowed money from the State Bar Relief Fund for recovering lawyers, the fund being flush because few attorneys wanted to admit to past problems. Addictions—alcohol or otherwise—were not calling cards for successful attorneys,

3

although she had briefly toyed with the idea of scrounging business at AA meetings where she had seen more than a few members of the bar. The Bar Relief fund had come through, most of the money spent on office furniture and supplies. She had a small line of credit at the bank, already tapped once, and she knew the balance would have to be drawn down again soon—too soon.

She whispered a prayer for one or more clients to walk through her office door. She added an addendum—*more than one would be an undeniable God-send.* She added a postscript on top of the previous rider—for the client or clients to appear before the end of this business day. She needed a big case. Hell, a few small cases even—and she needed them now!

While she perused her list of debts, her ears were primed for the telephone to ring. At least she *hoped* it would ring. Her son Kevin and her daughter Josie were just down the street attending a Mardi Gras luncheon, both members of the Mardi Gras court—Josie a maid and Kevin a knight. Della had been excluded from the festivities because her ex-husband, Gaillard McElhenney, was paying the coronation expenses, and he had not invited her to the luncheon.

Josie had come into town from the University for the revelries, but had not yet contacted Della. Because of her past problems, namely her reliance on alcohol, Della knew she had some fence mending to do with her children—Josie, not Kevin. Actually, she didn't want to mend fences; what she really wanted to do was to *tear down* the fences.

Kevin would call in a bit. She'd just be patient and wait. Kevin would let her know what was going on down the street at the old Admiral Semmes Hotel. Meanwhile, she'd create a new spreadsheet based on the hopeful assumption that clients, and thus revenue, would be forthcoming.

Oliver's Song

***

A short distance from where Della Boudreaux sat at her desk, young Oliver Fitzsimmons, known as Ollie by his family and friends, looked around before he opened the driver's door of his ten-year-old Audi. He had the oddest feeling he was being followed. Night before last, a car parked in the curve just above his father's fishing camp on Dog River. A single beam of light searched across his backyard. He had stepped to the door and looked out but saw nothing suspicious. Maybe whoever drove the car was doing some early morning fishing, or maybe he had imagined the whole beam of light thing.

What he wasn't imagining though, was Billy Wong's enormous bass case and whatever that yellowish-white stuff was inside it. That was real. At this very moment, the bass case leaned against the wall in the front room of his father's fishing camp. Had he known then what he knew now, he would never have agreed to bring the thing to Mobile. *Would Billy Wong come to Mobile to get it as he said he would? Should he give it to him if he did show up?*

Bingo! He was right back to the question: What should he do with Billy Wong's bass, or more precisely, his case?

But . . . this was a question for consideration at a later date. For now, he was at the Radisson; old Mobile still called the hotel by its previous name, The Admiral Semmes, in honor of Admiral Raphael Semmes, Mobile's Civil War maritime raider. Ollie was here to enjoy lunch with the King and Queen of Mardi Gras and their royal courtesans. His sister, Kathryn D'Olive Fitzsimmons — everyone called her Kathryn Dee — would officially debut into Mobile's society at the Mystics of Time ball on Saturday night. Because his semester was in full swing at Florida State, he had missed all the other Mardi Gras shindigs, but he would not miss the MOT's, the big one — the Coronation Ball. *Laissez les bons temps rouler*.

Inside the hotel, a toast was underway when Ollie entered the ballroom. Waiters circled the room carrying trays of wide-mouthed champagne glasses brimming with a frothy orange drink. "What's that?" He asked an older woman sporting a black hat the shape of a medium-sized bowl turned upside down. Three hot-pink feathers shot out a full twelve inches from the brim, announcing: *I'm flashy and I don't give a damn!* She would have looked out of place except every female in attendance donned a hat (many of them also flamboyant). Early spring attire and snazzy hats were Mobile traditions—*costume de rigueur* for the Mardi Gras luncheon.

"Sur-gah, you mean these?" The woman's accent was heavy and distinctively Mobile.

"Those," Ollie nodded his head toward her glass.

"Mardi Gras kisses," she leaned in toward him. "Ummm! You've got to try one." The woman raised her glass as if in a toast. "Orange and passion-fruit juice mixed with vodka, served over crushed ice. Highly appropriate midday." She arched an eyebrow. "Respectable company can savor as many of these as desired. Get my drift, sur-gah?" She winked at him.

He got it perfectly. Ollie flagged a waiter, lifted a glass from the silver tray, and sipped his first Mardi Gras kiss. He had turned twenty-one several months back and he intended to liberally exercise his new status as a legal drinker.

His sister, Kathryn Dee, spotted him and made her way through the crowd. She wore a sky-blue suit and a fashionable straw hat over her deep brown hair. "Hey little bro." She kissed him on his cheek. "Mom and Dad are over there." She pointed to their parents.

"I saw Mom when I got in yesterday, but I haven't seen Dad yet." He took another drink of his Mardi Gras kiss—a slug, not a sip. He wiped his mouth with the knuckles of his left hand.

"You and Dad have got to get along. No hard words. I mean it!" Kathryn Dee smiled to soften her admonition.

Oliver's Song

"Small grievances." He grinned and waved his left hand in front of him as if to magically loosen any tension between himself and his father.

"They might be small grievances, but you two can sure get into it."

"Trust me," Ollie assured her. "This is your special time. I won't do anything to spoil it." He brought the Mardi Gras kiss to his lips again. He meant what he said. Kathryn Dee was a member of the Mardi Gras court. He was not. Besides, his older sister adored him, and he had every intention of maintaining her admiration.

He saw his father walking toward him. His sister kissed him on his cheek again. "Remember what I said," she raised her index finger, and turned to join a small group of friends nearby.

"Ollie," his father called when he got within earshot. Ollie extended his hand toward his father. Oliver Fitzsimmons Sr., Ollie's namesake, looked good for a man in his early sixties, lean and strong with shoulder-length silver hair, thick and abundant, and blue-gray eyes, sharp as a predator's.

"Guess you're all set up at the camp?"

"All set," Ollie raised his glass toward his father.

What kept the two at odds was Ollie's choice of profession. Over his father's objections, he studied jazz piano. His father wanted him to enter business school and emerge four years later with a degree that *meant something*—none of this jazz piano stuff.

"So how are those music lessons going?" The smile had left his father's steely eyes. He had gotten to the bones of the beast sooner than Ollie expected.

"Great," Ollie matched his father's stare.

"I know a couple of old black men right here in Mobile who can teach you everything you need to know about jazz piano. Great musicians." The senior Fitzsimmons took a sip of his drink and surveyed the crowd.

"Sure," Ollie said. "I'll remember that." But what he remembered was his promise to Kathryn Dee—he would be polite—so, he leaned in toward his father and asked, "how are things at Fitzsimmons Industries?"

His father's eyes lit up. "Couldn't be better! We've got our fingers in some s-w-e-e-t pies." He whistled between his teeth and took a half step back as if what he was about to reveal needed more space. "Even developing some high-end condos right here in the heart of downtown. Business is booming, son."

"Great, Dad. That's great."

Oliver Sr., looking like a preacher engaged in supplication, placed his left hand over the buttons on his jacket, just below his heart, "I've put the ball in play, son. All you have to do is step up to the plate and swing."

Ollie knew it had always been his father's dream that Fitzsimmons Industries would become a father and son enterprise. But he was not his father. He dropped his head toward his father's ear, "Dad, I love what I'm doing."

Oliver Sr. moved his head away from his son's mouth and looked him squarely in the eyes. "Remember that when you're playing *Moon River* out at the Country Club and sneaking a peek at the tip bucket." He smiled, but his smile didn't reach his eyes.

Patsy McNally Fitzsimmons broke away from two women who balanced enormous wide-brimmed hats on their heads and cut a path toward her family. She was all natural. Her shoulder-length dark brown hair was streaked with gray—natural gray. She wore a pearl-gray suit with a dusty-rose collar and on her head rested a small dusty-rose hat. Like her daughter, she also looked elegant, understated and reserved. Patsy Fitzsimmons was Ollie's ally. She was the one who had said *follow your heart, son. You're young only once.*

"Enjoy yourself," she said to him now. "Mingle. Kathryn Dee will introduce you. She knows all the girls." His mother's smile was warm enough to melt candle wax, and Ollie enjoyed being the object of her smile.

When his parents drifted into the crowd, he lifted another Mardi Gras kiss from a waiter's tray and surveyed the array of debutantes and other girls in attendance. He wanted the best looking girl for his lunch partner. Across the way, he spotted a girl with honey-colored hair, braided around the sides of her head and knotted in the back. She wore a straw hat that looked perfect on her. Little curls of amber hair escaped from the braids and accented her face. She looked like a portrait, or rather she looked like she should be the subject of a portrait. That was the girl he wanted to meet. He watched her as she leaned in toward a small circle of girlfriends—she was the one he wanted to sit beside at lunch. He was positive.

As he moved toward the girl with the golden-honey braids, he spotted three elderly black men, who looked sharp in military-style navy blue suits with gold epaulets on their shoulders; they were setting up their instruments on a raised dais. His group back in Florida should have applied for some of these gigs. A few Mardi Gras escapades would have been good medicine. He watched the bass player lift his instrument out of its giant case, and the sight of the bass brought him right back to Billy Wong.

Wong's bass case was a niggling worry, like a stalactite on the ceiling of his mind. He knocked it down and another worry grew. He had brought the case with the stuff inside it from Florida into Alabama. Should he ditch the stuff? What if Billy Wong showed up to get it? Maybe he should give the case to somebody official. Maybe the police. But . . . that idea was pretty scary. He might need an attorney to tell him what he should do, but he didn't want to talk with one of his father's lawyers. He was certain of this. It might take him a little while, but he'd get his head screwed on straight and figure everything out in a few days. All in his own good time.

For now, he knocked the ugly thoughts down one more time. This was Mardi Gras after all, and the Fitzsimmons family went belly to the rail when the time came to step up and slap down the cash necessary to maintain the oldest Mardi Gras celebration in the country. Along the Gulf Coast, Mardi Gras ruled, and Ollie had come home, at his father's behest, to assume his rightful place in the kingdom, which meant attending the luncheons, the balls, and all the rest of Carnival's revelry all the way through Fat Tuesday. He had social obligations and he intended to meet them. He would place everything else in a holding pattern, including Billy Wong. At least that was what he hoped to do.

2

In downtown Chicago, at the corner of Cermak and Wentworth, Chang Wu, owner of Imperial Transports, and also an importer of Oriental merchandise—Blue Dragon Trader—stripped off his workout clothes and made ready for his shower. He could have showered at the gym after his noon weightlifting, but Chang Wu, a meticulous man, enjoyed the luxury of his own shower in his own office. His secretary had placed a clean, white towel on the Asian garden bench beside the walk-in shower. His secretary knew what he liked. Every item was where Chang Wu told her it should be.

He adjusted the water temperature—hot. He liked his shower hot. He slipped the loofah mitt over his right hand and squeezed oil of peppermint blended with eucalyptus into the palm of his mitt. He worked the mitt in circles on his face, down his neck, across his shoulders. He lifted his face toward the hot water, allowing the heat to cascade through his hair and down his lean, muscular body.

Chang Wu knew he was in trouble. He had been in trouble since he first talked to the young men—three Asians and two Mexicans. The three Asians sported long hair pulled back in tails; one of the Mexicans had a shaved head, bald as an onion, while the other one had hair that flew out from his head like a thousand tiny birds in desperate flight. Each of the Mexicans carried a Bible, but Chang Wu knew they were the Devil's minions, not men of the Christian's Bible. Five young men.

One would have been sufficient.

He had done the bidding of these young men exactly as directed, but yesterday a Mr. Miguel Sanchez telephoned. Chang

Wu had listened to this man, Sanchez, but he gave none of himself away. He did not trust this Mr. Miguel Sanchez.

"Mr. Wu—you still there?"

Chang Wu cleared his throat. "I am here." He offered few words. That was all Mr. Miguel Sanchez deserved.

"Billy Wong has taken the load and left Tallahassee," Miguel Sanchez said.

"The transported goods?" Chang Wu asked, providing no more information.

"Yes, the goods. *¡Dios mío!*" The man hissed between his teeth. "Billy Wong got into a car with Alabama plates. Tag number began with two. Alabama—Mobile. I checked. I know this."

"Why do you think I have interest in this information?" Chang Wu asked, being as cagey as a beautiful blood pheasant, secreting himself from full view and away from the hunter's gun.

"We are on the same team. *Mismo equipo*," the man repeated. "My job has been to keep eyes on Billy Wong. I let him slip." The man cleared his throat. "Not yet ready to report this to the men who employ us. How about you, Mr. Wu?"

Chang Wu said nothing. He knew already something had gone wrong. Repeated calls to Billy Wong had gone unanswered. Chang Wu had not worried. Worry—*what senseless folly!*

"You still there, Mr. Wu? Hello. *¿Está allí?*"

Why was this man using Spanish? Chang Wu did not speak Spanish. *A man of limited wits*, Chang Wu concluded. "I am here," he answered, again keeping his words at a minimum.

"I will go to Mobile," Sanchez said. He fell silent for several seconds before his graveled voice resumed. "I will meet you there. We will locate Billy Wong. No point exposing lost sheep." The man surprised Chang Wu when he laughed. An explosion into the receiver.

A man of limited culture too, Chang Wu thought as he pulled the phone away, and then brought it back toward his ear.

"No need for a search party. Not yet." The man laughed again. "We can handle this. No one else will know. You with me, Mr. Wu?"

Chang Wu remained silent. He heard Mr. Miguel Sanchez breathe heavily.

"¡Dios mío!" the man whispered. "You still there? Mr. Wu, I was to keep eyes on Billy Wong. I would just as soon locate Wong and say nothing," he repeated this information, as if Chang Wu had not heard him.

"I see," Chang Wu answered.

He understood this man perfectly. If Billy Wong had indeed taken the transported goods and left Tallahassee, Chang Wu needed to locate him as much as did this Mr. Miguel Sanchez. He did not like the idea that someone had hired this man named Sanchez to watch Billy Wong. Had the Mexicans hired Mr. Sanchez? No one had told him about this. But . . . he had chosen to cover his eyes and keep his distance. He passed few words between himself and the tough young men with long hair.

"We both have interests here," Miguel Sanchez nudged into Chang Wu's silence.

"How did you get my number?" Chang Wu asked.

"Mr. Wu, I told you, we work for the same men. Get it! ¡De acuerso!"

Chang Wu recognized agitation in Miguel Sanchez's voice. Agitation would undo a man. Chang Wu knew this. "You work for the Long Hairs?"

Miguel Sanchez laughed. "Yes. Some of them have long hair."

Both men were quiet now until Sanchez broke the silence. "You don't want the goods returned? I'll get off the phone."

"I will be in Mobile, Alabama tomorrow afternoon," Chang Wu said. "Where will we meet?"

The arrangements were made. Now, Chang Wu would take charge as he always had. He would bring these current affairs under his own power. He would locate Billy Wong. Then, he was out of this business. He would enjoy the rest of his life away from all these forces.

Long ago he heard about a global village. He laughed when he heard this. Countries, separated by great distances and oceans, tied together by information and united enterprises. The global village had arrived before his own eyes. He lived and worked in this global village—although his was a village that operated in shadows. Mexicans, Asians, South Americans, North Americans tied in an enterprise he did not want to speak about. And now he was going to some place he had never been—this Mobile, Alabama. He would go, retrieve the transported goods, and then he was done with this global village. He was ready to live his small life in his own backyard, his home in the suburbs just outside the city. No more global village for Mr. Chang Wu.

He had come from China, an orphan of Mao Zedong's Cultural Revolution. Somehow, he was not exactly sure how, arrangements fell into place. His aunt and uncle got him out of Beijing. Just a teen, a political refugee, he arrived in Chicago with a sponsor providing a room, food, and little more. Chang Wu had done all the rest—a self-made man in the land of boundless opportunity. Yet, he maintained his Asian discipline. Often, he reminded himself he had an Asian mind, an iron-willed man in the midst of soft-bellied Americans. Iron willed because he had to be.

As the water in his shower rushed over his lean body, Chang Wu worked the loofah in circles down his arms, across his chest, and down his legs. He liked his body—not tall, average height, trim and muscular, even with age. A body to give its owner pleasure. He lifted his right foot, and while standing on one leg, he massaged tiny circles across the sole of his foot. His body tingled, alive and ready for whatever might happen. He would not have arrived in his own shower in his own office had he not maintained discipline.

His first job, a busboy in China Seas Restaurant; to this, he added presser in Liu's Laundry. He thought he had reached the pinnacle when he won his place tableside at Three Dragons, a Japanese chop, dice, and stir-fry restaurant on West 23rd — flashing knives, twirling them, slamming the stainless blades against the steel cooktop. He grew sideburns and chin hair, imagining he looked the part of a warrior, an oriental warrior. Then, Chang Wu mastered the best stunt of all, the one the other servers and tableside cooks could only envy.

He smiled when he thought of this. He, a regular customer at the House of Magic, a tiny place — a mouse hole, he liked to think — tucked into a corner off Archer Avenue. Painstakingly, he read, in his spare moments, every book on magic. He read at bedtime and while waiting for city buses on Cermak. Books on magic, his small luxury. He loved the dark arts, the black arts. He taught himself to eat the blue and yellow flame — a feat no one else at Three Dragons could master. He, Chang Wu, ate fire. His jealous comrades were acid-faced as pickled pig's feet, as stony as the clay soldiers of Xi'am. But. . . not to care. He, Chang Wu, in the land of plenty, had made his own way.

He learned English one word, one phrase at a time — adding, storing, hoarding the language that would sustain him in his new land. He stockpiled money too — a dollar, a five, ten, a hundred, which grew to a thousand, and multiplied to ten thousand, which transformed into a loan, and transposed again into a warehouse, which morphed into Blue Dragon Trader and Imperial Transports. Today he controlled a distribution and storage network that spanned the United States from California to Florida, from Mexico to Canada. He could transport and warehouse almost anything, almost anywhere. His trucks roared across the country with a blue dragon hunched on the side panel, a dragon spitting fire.

In building his empire, he had done a few things under the table, as the Americans said. A few things not in keeping with the letter of the law — another American way of speaking. The Asian Long Hairs knew this. He had paid for their silence by transporting their goods. His worry now was the Mexicans who had come with the Asian Long Hairs. *What did they know? What would they demand from him?* He did not want to surrender his import and transport business to the Mexicans for passage of certain goods that came into Mexico from Asia and spread across the United States from west to east, from south to north. All such business had been executed at arms-length, another phrase Chang Wu liked—*arms-length*. Even though he did their business, he had been careful to distance himself from the various transactions. They knew too much for Chang Wu to turn his back on them when they called, but this business with Billy Wong was his last compromise. After this run, he would no longer do business with the Long Hairs or the Mexicans. He had made that quite clear.

As the water cascaded down his back, Chang Wu remembered those long years of building his empire as tired years. He learned to sleep upright, holding to the rail on a bus. With the power of his own will, he blocked the noise, closed his eyes, and slept standing on his own two feet. He never missed his stop unless he sat. If he sat, he was doomed. *A hungry tiger in repose misses a mouse beside his nose.* His mother had savored a good proverb. He too carried her love of short, crisp wisdom. Chang Wu, a man made of magic and of discipline, would never be the sleeping tiger.

Billy Wong had deceived him. Had taken the merchandise and fled. But . . . Billy Wong was history. If a rogue dragon snorted fire at Chang Wu, he would eat that dragon's flame and break the dragon's back. He smiled when he thought of this. If Billy Wong had wronged him, Chang Wu would do whatever necessary. Billy Wong did not frighten him. Billy Wong was a dead man walking. He liked that phrase—*a dead man walking*.

He reached for his shampoo. The brand, Physical Man, ordered from a specialty spa, smelled of sandalwood and musk. He massaged his scalp with the pads of his fingers. He liked this smell—Physical Man. He closed his eyes. A beautiful woman, the swell of her breasts, the adoration in her eyes, her soft and giving touch. Physical Man—that was what this smell brought to his mind, a beautiful Asian woman.

Late afternoon he would be on a plane headed toward Mobile, Alabama. Al-a-bam-a, he rolled the syllables across his tongue, allowing the spray of water to wash over his lips— Alabama, a foreign place to him, a place he never imagined visiting. Billy Wong did not yet know what he had set in motion. Chang Wu, a man with the power of the blue dragon, would set everything right. Billy Wong would be an example to anyone who considered crossing Chang Wu.

From the hook in his shower, he reached for the loofah strip, a narrow band, five inches wide by thirty inches long. He had saved the best for last. He squeezed the blended oils of peppermint and eucalyptus onto the length of rough fabric. With the strip at an angle, he rubbed briskly across his back. He knew he would feel the tiny abrasions even as the airplane soared well above the clouds headed south. He would enjoy the stinging, the prickling—a reminder to himself of who he was.

For his final ritual, the one that reminded him of his manhood, he squeezed the peppermint and eucalyptus blend in a six-inch line on the length of the strip. He gently stretched the cloth between his legs, one hand in back, the other in front. He patted and massaged more than stroked, feeling his personal parts in the palm of his hand. He opened his mouth to let out his air of satisfaction. He held the cloth tight against his parts, his eyes closed and the flow of water rushed over his face.

After the last of his rituals, he turned off the water and stepped out of the shower where he reached for the clean, white towel. As he patted himself dry, he continued to reflect on the mission ahead of him. He had to set right this whole situation with Billy Wong. Chang Wu had his Lily to consider. Her picture, a framed 8 x 10, occupied the corner of his desk. Lily—six-years old, shiny black pigtails braided down to her shoulders, her two front teeth missing, her eyes alive with promise. The world belonged to his daughter. His Lily. He would give the world to her on the Americans' silver platter.

If he understood love at all, it was what he held for his Lily. He would do anything to protect her. He would take care of business in this place called Alabama and be back in Chicago by Friday night in time for Lily's dance recital. He would not miss that. Whatever problems Billy Wong had created would be put to rest before next Friday night—one week maximum. That was all the time Chang Wu would give this vexation.

He patted his arms dry and dropped his towel on the floor beside the Asian garden bench. He slipped his Hublot over his fingers, positioning the watch on his left wrist, glancing at the time. He dressed quickly now, tucking his white shirt, fresh from the laundry, into the black pants of his light wool suit. His driver would soon arrive or might already be parked beside the curb. After he was dressed, he combed his hair and kicked the towel he had used toward the small pile of clothes he had worn to the gym. This was his secretary's responsibility. She would take care of these after he left for the airport.

Chang Wu stepped from the bathroom, walked across his marble floors, the color of rich red wine, and he stood beside the window through which he saw his driver stop at the light near the corner. At that very moment, a cardinal cut a red line across the window where Chang Wu stood. The flurry of red brought a smile to his lips. A good sign. A good omen.

He walked to his desk, lifted his black notebook and wrote: *A beautiful bird causes the eye to sing.* This he would give to Lily when he returned from Mobile, Alabama. He and Lily composed proverbs for each other. When they enjoyed the luxury of rest and conversation, they opened their notebooks and read their collected bits of wisdom. *Lily's Songs* he called the proverbs he gave to her. *Daddy's Songs* she called the verses she gave to him.

Chang Wu's jacket hung on a teak coat rack. He reached for the suit coat and slipped his arms into the sleeves. After adjusting his cuffs, he slid his blue-dragon armband up his left arm and over his biceps. He wore it always, the Chinese-blue dragon embroidered on a black armband. *A military symbol? A secret society? Did you lose a loved one?* An elderly woman had asked him a few weeks earlier. *Yes, yes,* he said. *I lost a loved one.*

There was truth in this answer—he lost his mother when he was just a boy. He could still remember her face though, her lips smiling at him. But, he wore the armband, not because of his loss, but because of her gift. She had made his first blue dragon on a black armband. *Always wear blue, she said and a dragon too. The dragon will give you strength. The dragon will keep you safe.*

The dragon was fierce—mouth open, teeth showing. And he was living proof the dragon had kept him safe. Death and starvation had been all around him as a young boy in China— forty to seventy million had died in the Cultural Revolution. That was what he had read in historical accounts. Yet, in the midst of all the dying and all the turmoil, he had remained safe. He had been conveyed—perhaps on dragon wings—out of the country. He found himself in a new land where he had grown into a man of considerable wealth.

A man does not talk about things deep inside him, the place where he understands spirit and life, shadow and presence. Why should a man talk about these things? A man knows them, knows them through the core of his being. Chang Wu would never speak of what he knew, but he wore his blue-dragon armband. He wore it always.

Now, fully dressed, he wished he could carry with him one other possession—the little pistol locked in his personal cabinet. Only he had a key to the small rosewood cabinet with the bamboo lattice. If he could, he would tuck the fine crimson-trimmed pistol in the inside pocket of his coat. The pistol—a prized treasure— elegant in its proportion, the rouge-trim pleasing to his eye. He could not carry the little pistol—he knew this. Not to dwell on the impossible. He gathered his slim attaché case and reached across his desk for his airplane ticket to Alabama. His secretary opened his office door to announce his driver waited at the curb. She held the door for him as he walked past her.

3

"You are coming on Saturday night?" Kevin asked his mother when Candy Sue buzzed the call into Della's office. Della knew Kevin would call her because he telephoned every day and, for this, she was grateful.

"Of course I am," she answered, "but first tell me about the luncheon. What was on the menu and how did everybody look?"

"Can't tell you much," Kevin said. "I left early to run a few errands for Dad." He sucked air between his teeth—"actually, I didn't stay for lunch."

Ahhhh, Della got it. In order to run errands for his father, he had left the Mardi Gras festivities without eating. Meanwhile, Della's ex, and his new wife Dora, were still in attendance at the luncheon, savoring a delicious hot meal, while Kevin had left hungry in order to do his father's bidding. Kevin was always willing to sacrifice his own interests for his father's. Della had a hundred issues she could raise with Galliard over the way he expected their son to be his errand boy, not that she would ever raise or settle any of them.

And, if Galliard McElhenney understood anything about common courtesy, he would have included her in some of the Mardi Gras festivities. After all, Josie was making her debut and Kevin was a knight. Josie and Kevin were *her* children, not Dora's. But, Galliard wouldn't recognize a common courtesy if it appeared in brilliant neon colors inches from his nose. Della knew Galliard's reasoning: *He* was paying the expenses for the balls, the ball gowns, the booze, and the dining, and *he* would include whoever *he* pleased in the Mardi Gras activities. Della did not make *his* cut.

"Is Josie all right?" Della asked Kevin. "I haven't heard a word from her since she's been in town. I hate to call your father's house because every time I call over there Dora picks up."

"I'll remind Josie to call you," Kevin said. "She looked great at the luncheon. Her hair was braided and pulled back. She wore a hat that looked perfect on her and her suit, a green and rose-colored plaid . . ." He hesitated a beat—"I guess you'd call it a plaid . . . anyway, the green matched her eyes."

Della was glad Kevin had told her how Josie looked. Now she could close her eyes and picture her beautiful daughter. Josie had the same honey-bronze hair as Della and her eyes were green with tiny specks of gold. Green and rose plaid would be perfect on her. She just wished she could have seen Josie in person.

"Mom." Kevin hesitated again. "She should have called you. I'll tell her to call."

Della would not allow Kevin to feel responsible for Josie's failure to telephone. Already, he took too much responsibility for their family's dysfunction. She shifted their conversation back to Kevin's initial question. "You better believe I'll be at tomorrow's ball. I can't wait to see both of you walk through the tableaux."

She had purchased her own invitation to the MOT's ball. She would watch call-outs with the non-royal crowd in the viewing gallery, while family of the debutantes and knights sat in a special section reserved just for them—the best seats in the house. She would sit alone in the nose-bleed section, but she said none of this to her son.

"I got a new dress and new shoes too." She didn't tell him the size eight, stiletto, bronze torture chambers set her back a hundred sixty-five bucks. But the bronze shoes complimented her olive-green evening gown—two hundred and twenty-five bucks. It would take months to pay off her department store credit card, but the extravagance was worth the debt because she wanted to look her best when she watched her children walk through the tableaux. She wanted them to be proud of her. Lord knows she had acted her worst the whole time Kevin had been in high school and Josie in middle school. Back then their mother offered them little to be proud of.

Scenes flashed through her mind of all the times on their drive home from school, Josie, in an excited voice, tried to tell her about wonderful events in the school day but she was zoned-out, focused entirely on appearing sober and staying in her lane. Her efforts consumed every ounce of her energy and there was nothing left over for her daughter. Each day she vowed to herself that she would do better, yet she still craved a little buzz in the afternoon—nothing much, just a little. "Are you listening Mom," Josie would ask. She nodded her head, but she heard nothing.

Now, she was a changed woman—living, breathing proof that a life could be transformed.

"So, you got a new dress?" Kevin asked, bringing her back to the present. "Great. I can't wait to see you all dressed up."

Kevin wanted her to be at the Mardi Gras ball and this pleased Della more than she would ever tell him for fear of embarrassing him. Kevin had turned into a fine young man despite the fact that, as a teenager, he had raised himself. When Kevin went through the last of his teen years, Della had spent most of her days three sheets to the wind, and Galliard was gone at nights, climbing up the town's social ladder, accepting sympathy offered by single women and some married ones too. He was always on the lookout for another rung to mount. Reconciliation with her husband was not an option after the foundation of their vows eroded. While at Tulane, she had legally changed her name back to Boudreaux—Della Boudreaux McElhenney had never worked any better as a name than had the marriage worked as a union.

"Mom, it won't be too hard for you—going to the ball and all, will it?"

Della knew what he meant. Could she be around all that booze and not drink a drop?

"No, it won't be hard at all." This was an outright lie—although truthfulness was the motto of this new Della Boudreaux. Step four of the Twelve Steps—*make a searching and fearless inventory of self*. In the past, she had skirted the truth: *an afternoon nip won't do any harm. One more isn't too much*. After all the deceptions, the truth was finally this: while backsliding was always possible, she had been on the road of redemption for four long years, and she would not be shoved off the pavement by a Mardi Gras ball.

"Rocky Road double chocolate ice cream is the only intoxicating thing that has crossed my lips in four years," she told her son. And that was the absolute truth.

"Booze flows at these Mardi Gras balls, Mom. You know that."

How well she did know. There would never be a better occasion to imbibe than at the Mardi Gras Coronation. Two shots of bourbon mixed with a Coca-Cola would be just the ticket to take the edge off her aching feet and ease her precarious reentry into Mobile's social scene. She was always awkward at social events, not a *bon vivant* or a party girl in the least, a fact that had opened a sinkhole in the middle of her marriage, but there had been plenty of fissures all around the cave-in. Nonetheless, she reassured Kevin, "Son, you don't need to worry. I won't backslide."

She was proud of her sobriety. She had battled too hard on her road to recovery to backtrack. Every morning she got out of bed with pride, purpose, and promise. These three p's tasted better on her tongue than any drink ever had.

"I'm proud of you, Mom,"

"Of me?" Della cut him short. "No—no . . ."

But it was his turn to cut her off. "Don't deny it, Mom. I'm proud of you. That's a fact. You've made a comeback. A real comeback . . . and I mean . . . that isn't easy."

Oliver's Song

She had been gently upbraided by her own son, and how right he was. She, Della Rochelle Boudreaux, needed to learn how to accept a compliment. "Thank you," she whispered into the receiver.

"I love you, Mom. I'm glad you'll be at the coronation tomorrow night."

***

Several blocks away at the Admiral Semmes Hotel, Ollie Fitzsimmons nodded his head toward the girl he wanted for his luncheon companion. "That's the one," he said to his sister, Kathryn Dee. He had surveyed the room and, without a doubt, the girl with the honey-hair in the pink and green plaid suit was the girl he wanted to sit beside at lunch. He'd gotten close enough to see her green eyes. "She's hot!" he observed when Kathryn Dee looked in the direction his head nodded.

"That's Josetta Boudreaux McElhenney," Kathryn said.

"Whoooa. That's a mouthful."

"Don't worry, little bro. Everybody just calls her Josie." Kathryn Dee smiled at her brother as warmly as did their mother, and she patted him on his back. "You got lucky. She's a debutante and normally she'd sit beside her knight. But, she'll sit beside you today because her knight has his head hung over the rim of his toilet bowl. Mr. Escort over-partied last night. The idiot!" Kathryn Dee narrowed her nose, pursed her lips, and shook her head in mock grimace.

At lunch, Ollie sat beside the girl with the honey-hair, close enough to Josetta Boudreaux McElhenney to see tiny gold flecks scatter across her green eyes. The green lines in her linen suit matched the color of her eyes, and the little strands of her hair that had come loose from the knot at her neck curled next to her cheeks. Everything about her fit together perfectly, the color of her eyes and hair, and her creamy complexion with a few freckles sprinkled across her cheeks.

When Ollie surveyed the luncheon table, he was relieved to see white wine had replaced Mardi Gras kisses. The citrus-flavored kisses had begun to sour his stomach.

Josie lifted her wine glass and raised it toward him. "To my rescuer. I don't like a man who can't hold his liquor." She was obviously referring to her knight. Ollie grinned. He lifted his wine glass and imbibed.

"You're dealing with a man of great capacity," he boasted as he placed the glass back on the table, sloshing a bit over the rim and onto the white tablecloth. He could hold his liquor, and he was prepared to demonstrate this.

"So, why aren't you in the Mardi Gras court?" Josie picked at her salad, delicately raising a thinly shaved carrot curl to her lips. The rim of her hat sat at a slight angle, forming a halo around her face.

"My dad would have been on tap for the expenses. Acquiring royal status on my dad's nickel would have cost me too much." He cleared his throat and took another taste of his wine. "My dad and I don't see eye-to-eye. I guess you could say . . ." He hesitated and twisted his lower lip while he pondered. "I guess we're a little estranged." The word *estranged* felt peculiar sliding across his lips. He didn't want to tell Josie too much about himself but, at the same time, he wanted to maintain his end of the conversation.

She tapped the back of his hand with the pads of her fingers and looked squarely at him. "We have something in common. In my case, it's my mother. We're a bit . . ." She giggled. "I guess you could say my mother and I are a bit *es-tranged*." She placed heavy emphasis on the first syllable, toying with the word.

He could have melted into her eyes, green with those hot flecks of gold. He could still feel the four warm spots on the back of his hand where her fingers touched him. "Is your mother here?" Ollie looked toward the opposite table where parents had seated themselves.

"I have a mother here. Not my *real* mother, not the one I'm estranged from." Josie nodded her head toward a couple who sat directly opposite her, a short distance across the room at the parents' table. "That's my stepmother. That's my real dad sitting beside her, though." Josie grinned. "All this talk of real and not-real is funny. Actually, *not-real* fits Dora perfectly. My step-mom is totally *unreal*. Way over the top. She loves this Mardi Gras stuff. A fantasy queen."

The bone-thin woman with shoulder-length blonde hair sitting at the opposite table saw Josie nod in her direction. While still engaged in conversation with a woman directly across the table from her, Dora McElhenney blew a pretend kiss in a pretend hurtle toward Josie.

"Got it," Josie mouthed the words in Dora's direction and turned toward Ollie. "See what I mean. It's a fantasy world, and Dora loves living in it."

Ollie wanted to ask why Josie was estranged from her real mother, but he didn't want to pry, and he didn't want to upset Josetta Boudreaux McElhenney. No way! He had a few secrets to conceal about himself and he certainly wasn't going to pry into hers.

They chatted with couples around them and made small talk while lunch was served. Lubricated with enough Mardi Gras kisses and white wine, Ollie leaned toward Josie. Their shoulders touched. He felt the heat from her upper arm. "I want to be your knight in shining armor," he whispered in her ear.

She smiled and brought her wine glass to her lips.

✻✻✻

Shortly after Della got off the phone with Kevin, Candy Sue tapped lightly on her office door. "Someone to see you." The secretary rolled her eyes toward the reception area—a signal that Della might not want to see this someone. Della came from behind her desk and crossed in front of Candy Sue, careful not to step on her secretary's purple swirled toenails.

Covey, the street musician who performed at the corner of Bienville Square, stood by the door, crumpling his dirty gray beret in his hand, his ukulele tucked under his left arm.

"'cuse me, ma'am." His eyes watched his hands, rotating the hat band as if it were a string of prayer beads.

"Got any odd jobs? I'm real handy, Miss Boudreaux." Still, he did not look up.

"I wish I could offer you some work, Covey, but I'm looking for work myself. I'm going under faster than a shrimp boat in a hurricane," she said this to dash any hopes he might still maintain. "I've been giving more serious consideration to joining your act," she added to lighten the conversation.

Covey didn't lift his eyes, but he grinned. "Any time." His mouth opening no wider than the thickness of a dime. "Fifty-fifty," he said. He turned his back to Della and pulled out a roll of bills, sliding a twenty and then a five onto the edge of Candy Sue's desk.

Della realized Covey was leaving her money. He had seen the cardboard liner in her shoe—and now money on her desk. *Was this a sign of her desperate situation?*

She scooped the bills off the desk and handed them back to him. But, he turned sharply and walked out the door. She followed him out to the street, holding the twenty and the five in her right hand, ordering him to retrieve the money. "You take this back," she commanded.

"No ma'am. Nooooo ma'am." He shot an arm up to block her efforts to return his folding money.

A man in a Ford pick-up at the light just outside the entrance to the Bankhead Tunnel watched her. "Come on Covey, take it back." When he continued walking, she stopped and watched his gray beret and droopy jacket grow smaller and smaller. She had another method of returning his cash. She would drop the money in his bucket the next time she saw him strumming his ukulele at the corner near the Square.

***

When Ollie stepped outside the Admiral Semmes into the chilly afternoon air of mid-February, he knew he had to sober up before getting behind the wheel of his old Audi. The last thing he needed was a DUI. He decided to walk to the foot of Government Street, stand beside the seawall at Cooper Park, and watch the ships on Mobile Bay. The Navy ships were in port for Mardi Gras, and they were nothing short of majestic. He would stand by the water until he felt certain he could safely drive himself back to his father's fishing camp on Dog River. He needed to think, and no place was better for sorting things out than the bay. The smell of the rusty-colored water, a briny odor mixed with diesel from the work boats that cruised around the port, would sober him, and now the military patrol boats that protected the Navy ships also circled the bay.

As he walked toward the bay, he reviewed his current status. He had telephoned the number Billy Wong had given him. Billy said it was his cell number, but someone else answered—a young woman who sounded nothing like Billy Wong. He waited several hours and tried the number again, thinking maybe there had been some kind of screw-up. The woman was angry this time. She was not Billy Wong. She had never heard of Billy Wong.

He was convinced Billy had given him the wrong number—intentionally. *Would Billy Wong come through Mobile as he said he would? What should he do if Billy showed up?*

When he reached the water's edge, he leaned against the wall at Cooper Park and watched the ships. Sailors in white suits stood on deck and several waved at him. They appeared to be in fine

Mardi Gras spirit. He waved back and then he gave a salute. They laughed. He breathed deeply and wondered if he would have gotten himself into less trouble if he had found himself a job in the water trades rather than heading off to the university to study piano. He had piloted boats since he was ten years old—his father's boats, an old pontoon for leisurely surveying wildlife in the marshy Tensaw Delta and a speedboat for riding the Gulf waves. Immediately after high school, he had considered doing a stint as crew on a tug boat in Mobile Bay or maybe venturing a route on the Mississippi, but he abandoned that idea in favor of studying jazz piano at Florida State. Considering what he was facing now, the tug boat might not have been a bad idea. He breathed deeply, hoping the oxygen would cut through the Mardi Gras kisses and white wine.

The police station was only a block away. He could walk there and speak with someone—he wasn't sure who. But . . . he should not go to the police until after all the Mardi Gras festivities ended. Mobile would not settle down until Ash Wednesday, the day after Fat Tuesday swallowed the last of its glut and the faithful stepped solemnly into the first day of Lent. This was Friday afternoon. Four more days before the city settled back into its normal routine. He circled around to the same troubling question: *What should he do about Billy Wong?*

***

By late afternoon, no clients had walked through the door of Boudreaux Attorney at Law. Mardi Gras revelers passed Della's entry, but no one in need of legal assistance. She knew her game was up—no contingency plans remaining. She would go to the bank this very afternoon and draw down on the last of her loan. Then, she would return to the office before the evening parade and pay her secretary.

Oliver's Song

As she gathered her expense sheets, she heard Candy Sue speaking with someone else in the front office. She recognized his voice—her office landlord, Maurice Maple. She was behind in her rent, and she might as well meet this situation head-on.

In the tiny reception area, Maurice—everyone knew him as Moss—stood over Candy Sue's desk and smiled down at her. Moss looked relaxed, his graying thick hair combed casually behind his ears. His brown knit tie was no longer in style and had one spot of stain right in the middle—his lunch, no doubt. He was a handsome man with a strong resemblance to a young James Garner. He had all the slapdash devil-may-care attitude of a Garner character too. Despite his casual appearance, Moss Maple had plenty of money. Everyone knew this. When he saw Della, he flashed the same fleshy grin he had given to Candy Sue.

Della grasped his hand between both of hers and pumped like a bank loan glad-hander. "You need an attorney?" She tried to make light of his visit. Like her, Moss was also an attorney, but unlike her, he was one of downtown Mobile's biggest landlords.

"By the grace of God, I don't need representation this day. Never know what tomorrow may bring." He chuckled at his own wit.

Moss cleared his throat. "Miss Boudreaux," he stammered. "I … I think there might have been some misunderstanding on the due-date for rent."

"Not at all," Della bluffed. "I put it on my calendar. Two weeks from today."

Moss flushed. Della would have guessed his ruddy complexion could not have reddened any more. How wrong she was. He turned as red as school-house brick. "No ma'am. The due date was two weeks ago."

"My good Lord!" Della exclaimed. "Come on in the office with me and let me get the date corrected on my calendar." She glanced back toward her secretary who winked at her.

Moss accompanied Della into her cubbyhole of an office and sat across from her desk in the leather chair she had purchased with money from the State Bar Relief Fund. "I'll need to make a deposit before I write you a check." She lifted her pocketbook, opened it, and pulled out the twenty-five Covey had left on Candy Sue's desk. "May I offer you partial payment?"

The twenty-five was folded, and she hoped Moss thought she held out a clean hundred.

"No. Noooooo." He held his hands in front of him as if to ward off demons. "Monday's fine."

"Now that I've got the due date right on my calendar, I'll be on time next month." As she said it, her mind offered silent supplication for paying clientele.

"Got to get home and dress for tonight's ball," Moss said and brushed the right lapel of his jacket.

During the final week of Mardi Gras, a ball could be found on any night of the week, even Sunday and Monday—made no difference because Mobile was celebration central.

"Miss Boudreaux, I know you've just come back into town and set up your new business, but I hope you're taking a little time off to have some fun."

Della wanted work, not time off. But, she said what Moss wanted to hear. "You bet. I won't be at tonight's ball, but I will be at the MOT's ball tomorrow night. My daughter and son are in Saturday night's coronation."

"Grand," Moss said. "I'll see you there."

With that, he stood and Della escorted him out of her office. She glanced at her watch—nearly three. She needed to get to the bank, draw down on her loan, and come back to pay Candy Sue. They both needed to get out of the office before the crowd gathered for the parade, which would roll at 6:30, the first of a long weekend of nearly back-to-back parades. The Mobile P.D. would close the streets long before 6:30, and her office was right on the parade route.

Oliver's Song

Also, she had promised Mercedes Magellan, her apartment landlady, they would attend the performance of a chamber group at St. Joseph's Chapel on the campus of nearby Springhill College—a small and quiet event compared to the parade and the ball that followed it. But, one Mardi Gras ball was all Della could handle and that would be tomorrow night. Besides, Mercedes was looking forward to the chamber group and would be pacing the floor before Della could take care of her business, pay Candy Sue, and make her way home.

***

When he was certain the briny air had sufficiently sobered him, Ollie headed down Government Street toward his car. It was only a little past three, but a few people already claimed spots for the night parade. Several old folks and a couple of young children sat in folding lawn chairs, sipping Coca Colas and eating hot dogs. *Grandparents and grandkids out for a parade*, Ollie thought. *Sweet!* The little boy, who wore a Cat In The Hat top-hat, sat in a plastic webbed chair with his feet resting on an ice chest. Ollie winked and pointed his finger at him. The kid laughed and waved.

When he was directly across from the old Bankhead Tunnel, he saw the sign for D. Boudreaux, Attorney-at-Law. The gold letters glinted in the low afternoon sun. He wondered if the attorney was any relation to Josetta Boudreaux McElhenney, his drop-dead gorgeous lunch partner. At least Boudreaux was not a name he had ever heard his father use. Not one of his father's attorneys. That was enough for him. On impulse, he opened the door and walked inside.

A gorgeous blonde sat behind a desk. Another woman stood in front of the desk, her purse over her shoulder, her sweater across her arm.

He smiled at the women and tipped his head slightly. "I . . . I think I need an attorney."

The woman standing in front of the desk extended her hand. "Della Boudreaux, attorney. At your service."

"Oliver Fitzsimmons III," he said, taking the attorney's hand, "everybody calls me Ollie." He looked at the purse slung over the attorney's shoulder. "You must be leaving."

"I can wait. If you *think* you need an attorney, I'm sure you do." Della placed her hand under Ollie's elbow and led him into her office.

4

As the plane made its final descent toward the Mobile airport, Chang Wu thought of the young Asian men who had sat in his office with their long hair shading their eyes. They had smoked cigarettes, dropping ashes on the polished marble of his floors. *A horse's lips do not fit on a donkey's mouth*, his mother would have said. *You can't make a silk purse from a sow's ear* the Americans said. A donkey's lips, a sow's ear—no matter. These Asians and the Mexicans too—they were all bad business.

This time, he had agreed only to secure a route. Nothing more. Logistics. He, Chang Wu, understood logistics. He would not be in business with these rough, young men at all if they had not discovered some of his early transactions. Unfortunately, the Long Hairs had eyes on him, and they had come calling. He had purchased their silence by hauling their loads. But he had paid enough for his wrong-doing. They should leave him alone now. He had grown into an honest man. He would tell the Long Hairs to leave the next time they came. He would summon his courage, look them in their shaded eyes and say *Get out!*

He would transport this load only long enough to guarantee that every link in the route held tight. Then, it was all theirs. In fact, he had not asked what the young men wanted to transport. He did not want to know. He did not want the words spoken. *Silence evil, and bad spirits will not find you*, his mother had said this. He did not ask for information and the young men did not offer it. But . . . he was certain he knew what the Long Hairs transported from Mexico into California and on to Florida. Hundreds of years ago the Europeans had discovered the strong Oriental opium. Over the years, the points of distribution varied, but the appetite for the product endured. Always there had been a market.

The freight had come from the Far East and been loaded in Mexico. The product had never been stored in any Chang Wu warehouses. It had only been hauled from west to east. *Connect the dots*, as Americans said. But, one small dot in the connection disappeared—that lost connection was Billy Wong.

Trusting Billy Wong was Chang Wu's mistake entirely. He had some uncertainty about the man, and should have relied on his *gut feeling—rely on your gut* Americans said. On Chang Wu's behalf, Wong had resolved several issues with the Long Hairs and Chang Wu had trusted him. Billy Wong had long, slick, hair and he looked like one of them. *He speaks their language,* Chang Wu had thought. He had trusted Wong with matters in Florida, and that had resulted in the disappearance of the product. This he knew: Billy Wong had double crossed him.

Chang Wu sighed and reflected on his adversary who had smuggled himself into the States and purchased documents. As an illegal, he lived in fear of detection. Chang Wu offered him a job—in shadows, that was true, but a job nonetheless. A chance to make it. Wong, tall for a Chinese—tall and skinny—wanted to play some kind of musical instrument. Wanted to study music in the States. He wanted to play one of the big instruments Chang Wu thought. Not a horn. He would have remembered a horn. He had paid little attention when Billy Wong spoke of his personal interests. Now Chang Wu thought he should have paid attention to all of Billy Wong's words.

About his current situation, Chang Wu's mother would have said: *A fall into a ditch makes a man wiser*. Chang Wu knew he had fallen into a ditch. Now he would pull himself out by his own strong arms.

He watched out the airplane's window, observing green forests and waterways that cut through the dense trees like flowing ribbons. Twists and turns of water. Snakes of water. This Mobile, Alabama was a green and watery place.

Oliver's Song

Billy Wong was a vexation. Chang Wu despised vexations. Better to laugh at himself and move forward. *A fool stumbles while a wise man walks upright.* He had been the fool. Now his shoulders were squared. Iron ran down the spine of his back. *A clever man turns great troubles into little ones.* Locate the lost product and secure every link in the route. Then—bye bye to the tough young men he did not like as business partners.

He watched out his window. Neat lines of houses with swimming pools in backyards. Water, water everywhere. In the forests and in backyard swimming pools. He had read that rain falls in Mobile, Alabama thick as bamboo curtains. The plane descended to the edge of the dark green forests as the wheels touched the tarmac.

***

Della Boudreaux studied the handsome young man sitting in the chair opposite her desk, his thick sandy hair rested on the edge of his forehead, younger than her son Kevin, she guessed, but only by a few years. When young Oliver Fitzsimmons explained he had attended the Mardi Gras luncheon at the old Admiral Semmes, she told him he might have met her daughter, a debutante in the royal court.

"Probably not the one," he said, "but at lunch I sat beside Josie Boudreaux McElhenney."

"That's her!" Della exclaimed. She couldn't stop the broad smile that broke loose across her face. "That's my girl!"

"You weren't at the luncheon," Ollie said.

Della was uncertain whether this was a statement or a question. She decided it was a question. "No, I wasn't," she answered.

She did not tell him that Josie had not telephoned her since she had come into town to begin all the Mardi Gras activities.

Other mothers of the royal court had assisted their daughters in selecting satin gowns, beautiful shoes, and crystal-encrusted tiaras, but she had done none of these. Dora had taken her place.

"I see it now," Ollie said, "the resemblance. You both have those green eyes. A McElhenney equals a Boudreaux." He grinned. He did not tell her Josetta Boudreaux McElhenney was the most beautiful girl he had ever met, and he hoped for an opportunity to see her again. A worry slid through his mind — would discussing his problem with Josie's mother prevent him from seeing her again? Would her mother tell her to stay away from him? *Ollie Fitzsimmons is trouble!*

Nah, he reasoned. *They're estranged. Won't happen.*

"I changed my name from McElhenney back to Boudreaux," Della explained. "I wanted to use Boudreaux in my legal practice." She did not tell him she wanted to use her own name in everything else too.

Now, she must steer this young man in the direction of his problem because she needed to get to the bank before it closed so Candy Sue would have money for her new dress and for the hairdresser. She smelled the strong scent of acrylic and knew her secretary was applying a clear top coat to her toenail polish, the final touch. Della leaned in toward the young man who sat opposite her. "How can I help you?"

Her small leather journal lay open on her desk, ready for her to jot notes, but instead of explaining his legal problems, he continued talking about everything except why he needed an attorney. Against his father's wishes he studied piano. He was on partial scholarship at Florida State. "One of the finest music schools in the southeast," he added. He showed her his hands, wide, strong hands that reached an octave plus two.

She held up her own broad hands. The two matched fingertips to fingertips. "Me too," she said. "An octave plus two." Her large hands had once been a source of pride. She too could have been a pianist had her father not lost his job, at which time piano lessons ceased, and marriage to Galliard McElhenney some years later was the end of her pride in wide piano hands. *Peasant hands*, Galliard called them.

She glanced at her watch. The crowd had begun to gather on the streets. Mercedes Magellan was, no doubt, already dressed and ready for the concert at the college, but the young man in front of her rambled on about a bass player he had met at the university, a young Chinese man named Billy Wong. This man named Wong hung out in the courtyard between the two music buildings—"Kuersteiner and Housewright," Ollie explained, as if the names meant something to her. As Della understood it, Billy Wong wasn't a student. He hoped to get into the music program at the university. Until then, he hung out around the courtyard, talking with students as if he were one of them.

"He's tall and thin," Ollie said. "He's the kind of guy who doesn't look like he's eaten enough. Always has a cigarette dangling from his lips. He lights one cigarette with the butt of another."

Della wrote *Billy Wong* in her journal before she glanced at her watch and said, "Son, we're about to get boxed in by this parade. Did you come in here for something specific?"

"Yes ma'am," Ollie said.

She was trying to be patient, but the afternoon was rapidly getting away from them. Candy Sue tapped on the door and then opened it. "Miss Della, I'm going on," she said in a hushed voice. "We'll settle up next week. I got plastic to carry me through the weekend." She crinkled her nose, raised a MasterCard in the air, and grinned at Della.

"Della waved at her secretary. "See you at the ball tomorrow night."

Candy Sue's flip flops slapped against her heels as she left the building, still airing her toenails. Della turned her attention back to the young man. "Go for it," she said to Ollie, and again she leaned forward, waiting for the young man to tell her why he needed an attorney.

"When Billy Wong found out I was coming to Mobile for Mardi Gras, he asked me if I would bring his bass. I could keep it in my car and he'd pick it up on Sunday or Monday when he comes through Mobile. Right now he's at an audition in New York." Ollie took in air between his teeth as if cautious of what he would say next. "At least that's what he told me. He told me he has a friend there who lets him use his bass. If he carried his bass to New York, he would have to pay for an extra airplane seat. A bass is so big that it requires its own seat. He told me he couldn't pay for an extra plane seat."

Ollie took another breath. "You with me?"

"No," Della said. "Why did he want you to bring his bass to Mobile?"

"He's flying from New York to Mobile, renting a car and driving to Texas. He has another audition there. That's what he said anyway. Now I'm not sure anything he told me is true, but he said he had two auditions. The second one in Dallas, I think. Maybe Fort Worth. If I brought his bass to Mobile, it would save him the cost of an extra plane ticket to and from New York."

Candy Sue had left Della's office door open. Through the large plate glass window of the front room, she saw a balloon vendor walk past, carrying helium balloons in the shapes of fanciful animals—unicorns, purple spotted dogs, enormous black-eyed cats. She smelled the hot grease from the makeshift stand on the corner where the vendor was already selling corndogs and fried elephant ears heavily dusted with powdered sugar.

"I was just helping him out. I would have done the same thing for anybody else," Ollie said.

"What's the bottom line?" Della asked. Prodding him again, unable to wait any longer. They were both about to get stuck in

40

Oliver's Song

downtown Mobile for the parade that was nearly ready to roll, floats, bands, and masked horsemen lining up at the Civic Center.

"I'm almost there," Ollie said. He took another audible breath. "I brought the bass home where I'm staying out at my father's fishing camp on Dog River. I planned to leave it in the car, but I parked my car in the sun all day yesterday and I got worried about the inside of the case getting too hot. I wondered what too much heat would do to the finish on the bass. All those instruments are expensive. A musician will put money into a good instrument before he'll buy food. I didn't want Billy Wong's bass to be damaged."

Ollie slid forward in his chair, almost touching the edge of Della's desk. "I decided I had better take the bass inside and put it in my front room where it would be safe and protected from the weather. I remembered Billy had pushed the bass to the car on some kind of little wheeled platform. I looked in the back of my car, but Billy must have taken that little platform with him."

Ollie wiped the palm of his hand across his mouth. Tiny sweat bullets had formed above his upper lip. "Damned thing was heavy. I finally managed to get it out of the car. I wedged it out, inch by inch, because it filled the back seat. A double bass is heavy as all get out. I finally got the thing inside, and I decided to open the case to be certain the heat hadn't damaged the finish on the instrument."

The kid didn't need an attorney, Della thought. This situation should be on Judge Judy's docket. This young man would make a handsome defendant and Judge Judy would honestly and fairly adjudicate the case and set damages. He should help Billy Wong foot the bill to buff out the finish on the bass and all would be well. She was wasting time while Mercedes Magellan would be peeking out her front window waiting for Della to arrive. The old woman would be angry and bowed-up like an owl ready to swoop and snatch its prey.

"No bass in that case at all," Ollie said. "That entire case, the whole thing, is packed with yellowish-white powdery blocks wrapped in some kind of thick cellophane. Each block is about the size of two bricks, sitting on top of each other. Quite a few of them in there. Yellowish-white bricks." Ollie waved his hand in front of him as if trying to visualize the bricks, or maybe he was attempting to vanish them from his mental vision.

Della leaned forward in her chair. "Whoooa!" she whispered and raised her hand, narrowing her eyes to study the young man more closely. Now the conversation was moving too fast.

"How many of those blocks are in that case?"

"I didn't count them." Ollie pursed his lips while he considered. "Hummm," he drummed his index finger against his forehead while he calculated. "Hummm. I'd guess at least thirty, maybe thirty-five. Maybe more."

"Whoooa!" Della repeated—out loud this time.

"Funny thing is," Ollie said, "there's a violin in there too. The violin looks ancient. It's wrapped in a piece of old purple velvet and cushioned by some Styrofoam. That violin must be some kind of joke."

Della watched all the movements of the young man, wanting to observe his demeanor as he spoke. Could she count on him to tell her the truth? What did his body language say?

Oliver Fitzsimmons III locked eyes with her. "I think I need a lawyer," he said. His forehead and cheeks puckered like a six-year-old child. "I think I might be in big trouble."

Nothing in his demeanor indicated that Oliver Fitzsimmons III was telling anything other than the truth. Law school had taught Della to get past the initial surprises a client brought through the door, settle herself, and think clearly.

"First question," she said. "Did you open any of those cellophane-wrapped blocks? Do you know what they are?"

"No clue. I didn't open any of them. A couple fell out and I stuffed them back inside the case."

Oliver's Song

Della leaned back in her chair and folded her hands in front of her. *Never, ever jump to conclusions* she cautioned herself. The first error any attorney could make would be to leap to an erroneous conclusion. She had read an article about a man who was stopped by Customs because he was carrying a suitcase packed with a suspicious powder. Turned out to be a harmless substance used in some kind of quirky religious service. The guy was detained for hours while the powder was analyzed. Then, he was released, Scott-free. *No need to jump to conclusions*.

She sat up, her back straight, and she addressed her new client while looking him squarely in his eyes. "Is Wong a drug user?"

"Not that I know. I hardly know the guy, but he never looked like a druggie to me. He could be . . . but I don't think so."

"Does he seem like the criminal type? I mean, does he act odd or suspicious or hang out with sketchy characters?" She thought that covered all the possibilities. Maybe this Billy Wong was an obvious dealer. In that case, the police needed to be called and this stuff turned over immediately—even if the mission of turning the bass case and its contents over to the police took all night to accomplish.

Ollie looked down at his hands and thought about her question. Della hoped he was replaying everything he knew about Billy Wong. He raised his head and established eye contact before he spoke, "Honestly, as far as I know, he's just an ordinary guy. Loves music. A real music geek. Worst thing I've ever seen him do is smoke lots of Camels, one after the other. Tobacco seems to be his real addiction. Nothing else. I've never seen him hang out with anybody except the music students." Oliver Fitzsimmons III wrinkled his face again and looked like a kid.

"How about a prankster?" Della asked. "Is he known for mischief or a little tomfoolery?" *Tomfoolery*, one of her deceased father's favorite words.

For the first time, Ollie's face lit up. "I see where you're going with this. That could definitely account for that old violin too." He grinned at her. "That stuff might be corn starch or flour. Somebody's playing a big joke on me." He blew air past his lips and chuckled. "I just thought it was some kind of drugs. It's all a joke." He let out a half-hearted laugh. "I've seen Billy Wong clown around. I never thought of that." Ollie's smile grew broad. "That's it. A joke." He settled back in his chair and wiped his sweaty forehead with his open palm.

"I doubt it," Della said, and saw the smile ease off the young man's face. "But, that is a possibility. Where's that bass case now?"

"At my Dad's fishing camp. I'm staying there because my Dad and I aren't on the best of terms. I got the place to myself."

"Nobody else there?"

"Just me."

"It's Friday night," Della said, thinking out loud. Then, she settled into her own thoughts. The Mobile P.D. would have its collective hands full all the way through Tuesday—parades, crowd control, drunk drivers, mischief on the parade route, and God forbid that anyone get seriously hurt or killed during the long weekend's activities. The police would definitely be busy. Without a doubt, her young client would be booked and placed in a holding tank until someone had time to deal with him—Saturday or Sunday at the earliest.

Whatever this load was, her client had transported it across state lines. She needed to go straight to the U.S. Attorney, not to the local P.D.—let Ollie tell his own story, and have the U.S. Attorney accompany him to the police. Her client would agree to tell everything he knew, and she would negotiate with the Federal Office to keep her client out of jail.

But, what if she went off half-cocked and reported a huge drug shipment that turned out to be a harmless herb or a load of baking soda or talcum powder. She'd get her client arrested for nothing. She'd look like a fool and he'd sit in some interrogation room waiting—just waiting for his rightful exoneration. This would be an unfortunate introduction of D. Boudreaux Attorney-at-Law into the legal community, and it would be less than excellent service to her client.

Ollie said nothing, allowing her time to consider his situation. He read her Tulane diploma on the wall behind her desk. When he spotted a picture of Josie on a small wall shelf, he stood and lifted the tiny framed-picture, a close up of Josie in a black v-necked top, probably a high school graduation picture or a university sorority picture. Josie looked just as beautiful in the simple black v-neck as she did in the green and pink suit she wore to the Mardi Gras luncheon. Her amber hair rested on her shoulders in gorgeous reddish-bronze spirals. He placed the little metal frame back on the shelf and glanced at his attorney who was still in thought.

Della was certain Ollie had to take the powder to authorities, tell his story and have the stuff analyzed. If the yellowish-white stuff was an illegal substance, turning himself in would be critical to establishing his innocence and his lawful intent. But, the whole city was in party frenzy. Most offices were closed and would not be fully staffed again until Ash Wednesday.

When she looked up, Ollie was watching her. She rested both of her arms against the surface of her desk. "I don't want you to go to the police just yet. They most likely will book you." She drummed her fingernails against the desk top.

"Oh please!" Ollie said. "I'd ruin things for Kathryn Dee. That's my sister, and she's a debutante. I've always been the one to ruin everything in my family. My Dad would blow a fuse if I screwed this up. I absolutely cannot go to jail. *Cannot!* Couldn't we just drop that bass case somewhere? Anywhere? It's not mine." He lifted his shoulders in a shrug.

"We've got to report it," Della said. I'm concerned about you and the position you've been put in. But, I want to report it when we can get the U.S. Attorney on our side."

She didn't tell her young client, but she also wanted to circle around his situation a few more times and she wanted to check any relevant case law. For now, she reached for the telephone with one hand while she flipped through her circular Rolodex with her other hand. Over the past weeks of no business, she had plenty of time to organize and in seconds had the number for the U.S. Attorney at her fingertips. The attorneys were probably already in route to the Althestan Club for dinner before the parade. All she needed was to go on record. Leaving a recorded message would suffice. After all the floats, the riders, the funnel cake vendors, the spectators, marching bands, and Mardi Gras campers had abandoned the city, she would visit the U.S. Attorney's Office in person and negotiate on behalf of her client.

She dialed the U.S. Attorney's Office, and her call connected to the answering machine. Exactly what she had hoped. The recording stated the obvious: Office closed. Leave a message.

Okay. She would.

"This is Della Boudreaux. I'm a new attorney in town. I know we're in the middle of all this"—she wanted to sound friendly and not desperate, so she chose her words carefully—"all this Mardi Gras commotion, but I need to speak with you at your earliest convenience. One of my clients has some information that might be of interest to you."

She knew no one would call before Monday morning, possibly as late as Tuesday—and most likely not until Wednesday. That would give her time to gather all the information she needed and devise a game plan. She was officially on record and couldn't help it if Mardi Gras lent her a little extra time.

"There," she said to Ollie when she hung up.

Oliver's Song

"Last night," Ollie said, "there was a car parked not far from my father's camp on Dog River. That car stayed there for a long while—maybe an hour. Parked just above the house. Might have been somebody fishing, but it gave me an uneasy feeling. I think— but I'm not sure of this—I think whoever was in that car ran a light across my yard."

"Lock the fishing camp and leave everything just as it is," Della said. "Don't stay there again until we surrender that bass case. Can you stay at your father's house, not the fishing camp?"

"I don't want to. As I've told you, my father and I aren't on the best of terms." He shrugged his shoulders again, "but, I guess I can."

"Do it," Della said. "This is a time to let go of any small differences between you and your father. Do not go back to that fishing camp for any reason. Give me a number where I can contact you. There's nothing we can do tonight except sit tight. You've got to get out of the fishing camp and stay out. I mean that." She looked straight at Ollie.

"Okay. Not a problem," he said and shrugged his shoulders again.

"Do what I've told you and do it immediately," she cautioned her young client. She wanted to be sure he could not mistake what she had told him. She had laid it out clearly.

"I got it," he said, and they both stood.

"We'd better get out of here now or we'll be stuck downtown." She wrote her home number and cell number on one of her business cards and slid it across the desk, and then she pushed paper toward Ollie from the plastic caddy on her desk. When he returned the paper with his numbers on it, she slipped the paper into her pocketbook alongside the twenty-five dollars she had attempted to give Moss Maple.

"You call if you need me before tomorrow. Otherwise, we'll talk in the morning. You stay away from that fishing camp. Promise me."

"I've already promised." He raised his right hand like a Boy Scout.

Della and Ollie walked outside together, and when they reached the sidewalk, they parted in opposite directions.

5

Mercedes Magellan watched the aging Dodge move slowly toward the house. Della Boudreaux's car, Mercedes thought, was every bit as feeble as were her own tired legs. She would insist they get her Town Car out of the garage, even though they were going only two blocks to the college. Why look like paupers when they had a fancy new car to drive?

She also planned on giving Della a tongue lashing for being late but, in truth, she hoped her friend was running late because of improved prospects downtown. Della needed a break, but there wasn't anything Mercedes could do to boost her friend's legal business. She had provided the garage apartment at below market value, and still Della had been late on her rent every month since she moved in. Mercedes would have allowed her to live on the property rent free, although Della didn't know this, and Mercedes would never tell her. They were allies—Mercedes was Della's AA sponsor, and helping Della in her new life of sobriety helped Mercedes remain sober too. For Mercedes, Della's presence on the property also meant good company when company was in short supply for an old woman. It was best they maintain their established positions as landlord and tenant, because each understood her prescribed role. As the Dodge pulled into the driveway, Mercedes puffed her lips out and raised her shoulders, providing physical evidence of her annoyance over Della's tardiness.

Della saw the old woman sitting in a wicker chair on her front porch, which was not designed for sitting, but was intended only as a landing. *On the tiny front porch no less!* She had expected to find Mercedes peeping past the living room curtains, not sitting outside with shoulders bowed like a screech owl. Mercedes had an enormous tiled patio laden with pots of ornamental cabbage, and blooming pansies and mums. The patio, not the front porch, was designed for sitting. Her presence on what amounted to a front stoop, told Della — to put it in the vernacular — that Mercedes was pissed.

Della smiled when the word *stoop* popped into her head. Mercedes' home was one of the finest in Spring Hill. The word *stoop* would never have attached itself to the two-story Federal where a Mexican gardener came twice a week to manicure the grounds. Della parked in the driveway, got out of her car, walked to the front fender, and raised her voice when she spoke in Mercedes' direction. "Sorry I'm late. Need help to the car?"

"No," Mercedes shot back, her lips drawn tight. "You know I don't like to be pushed to the time limits when we're going someplace."

"Sorry. A client came through the door at the last minute, and the parade traffic had already hit downtown. It's a jungle out there." She smiled in a feeble attempt to soften the woman who did indeed look like an old owl — her body thick, her head resting on her shoulders with no sign of a neck, her lips puckered, and one eye closed to shield herself from the low afternoon sun.

"Better take my car," Mercedes said as she hobbled toward Della's old Dodge, her best mahogany cane, the one with an angel's head carved just below the curve of the handle, held snugly in her right fist. "We want to look good."

"Mine's fine. No need to get yours out of the garage."

After Mercedes lumbered into the passenger seat and closed the door, Della turned the key. The old Dodge made a clacking sound. She tried again. The motor refused to turn. The Dodge was dead as the proverbial doorknob. Mercedes snapped open her pocketbook and withdrew her keys to the Lincoln. Without a word, she held them out to Della.

Oliver's Song

"This damned thing thinks it smells a dollar," Della said by way of explanation. "It must think my client has money." She took the keys from Mercedes. On her way to the garage, she kicked the front tire to let the old beast know who was still boss.

Before she could seat herself in the Town Car, Della slid the seat back. Mercedes liked to drive with her belly touching the steering wheel. After adjusting the mirrors, she turned the key and the engine purred—a young thing with only 962 miles on the odometer, attributable primarily to two weekly trips to the grocery store and a trip around the corner to the hairdresser on Thursdays. Della looked over her right shoulder and maneuvered the Lincoln onto the grass because the dead Dodge hogged the driveway. She stopped and allowed Mercedes to painstakingly crawl inside and close the passenger door. The chamber group would begin playing in seven minutes.

"I don't like wheel tracks on my grass," Mercedes said, adjusting the angel-headed cane at her side.

"I'll rake over the tire tracks and throw some grass seed this weekend," Della said, wondering what Mercedes would have her do. *Shove the Dodge off the driveway?* She could imagine the two of them behind the old Dodge, pushing it. She almost laughed out loud envisioning Mercedes leaning her heavy body into the rear bumper, the angel's head staring out past her right hip.

***

Moon pie! Moon pie! Moon pie! Hundreds of people standing on the curb shouted at the masked men who waved their arms and danced around their posts on the giant paper mâché floats. The men, dressed in bright colored satin costumes, showered the crowd with beads, plastic cups, taffy kisses, stuffed animals, and all kinds of trinkets.

Chang Wu stood close to a tall woman dressed in a deep purple evening gown with a short white fur coat around her shoulders, while the man beside her wore black tails. Others in the crowd wore blue jeans and athletic shoes. *A mixed-up and crazy crowd!*

"What's moon pie?" Chang Wu politely asked the woman in the purple gown.

"You're not from here are you honey?" she said. Her blonde hair was piled high in tight curls on the top of her head. He liked her smell—something like sweet sandalwood. But . . . he didn't like the way her fragrance mixed with the odors of popcorn, roasted peanuts, and hot dogs from a nearby vendor's booth.

"No. I am not from here," he said and bowed his head.

"Moon pies are those little round cookie cakes with marshmallow in the middle. They come in chocolate or banana. Sometimes you get a strawberry. Me," she said, "I'm all for tradition. A moon pie should be chocolate." She turned to the man beside her in black tails. "Sweetie, we need to catch this man a moon pie."

Already the man's hands waved above his head. "Moon pie! Moon pie!" he shouted at the men on the passing float.

A long dragon, smoke streaming from its nostrils, slinked toward the crowd. Everyone darted toward the sidewalk laughing and screaming. The dragon was hinged like a prehistoric beast. When its head turned and spewed its steamy breath toward the crowd on the opposite curb, the belly of the dragon swerved toward Chang Wu. Masked men lined the belly of the dragon, tossing beads and trinkets. The crowd, in unison, bent to the pavement, scooping up the loot the men heaved out. Then the dragon's tail swished by, equally menacing as its fiery breath— the tail, lined with sharp red-foil barbs.

"Honey, we got you one," the woman in the purple evening gown said. She handed Chang Wu a round cookie cake wrapped in cellophane with Moon Pie written in red letters on the package. "We got you a chocolate one at that."

Oliver's Song

Again, he dipped his head in the slightest bow. With her white fur coat opened in the front, he saw her breasts, creamy skin against the deep purple of her gown. Large breasts—American sized. Maybe he should think blonde next time he chose a woman, one who was not his wife. This Mobile, Alabama opened his mind to new possibilities.

A tall, sinister European castle pulled by a Ford pick-up wobbled toward the crowd. From its dark portals, masked men threw handfuls of candy, beads, and more moon pies. A moat, lined with men dressed in black satin costumes and matching dark hoods, stretched to the ominous castle.

Ahhh! The dragon lived under the moat. This parade had a theme. *Beasts in the Courtyard?* Or maybe it was *danger in ordinary places?* Chang Wu understood. *He got it!*

"You got to have some of these," the blonde woman said. She stood a full five inches taller than Chang Wu. She bent her knees, dropping her large creamy breasts in front of his eyes. She raised her arms and surrounded his neck with strings of colored beads.

Again, he bobbed his head in appreciation.

"Now you're looking like a man who knows all about Mardi Gras." She patted his shoulder.

As he stood in the crowd at the corner of Government and Royal Streets, another idea came to Chang Wu. He had a warehouse full of miniscule pigeon whistles and panpipes. After he finished this nasty business on his current trip, he would return to this city ready to interest all appropriate parties in pigeon whistles and panpipes. *A Chinese addition to Mardi Gras tradition. Certainly,* he thought. This new century belonged to the Chinese. Every citizen should hold in his hand a tiny link to the Orient. Pigeon whistles and panpipes could symbolize Mardi Gras equally as well as could those little round cakes called *moon pies.* He smiled when he thought of this.

Another dragon sputtered toward him, this one with enormous glowing red eyes. He raised his hands, palms out, "Moon pie!" he shouted. "Moon pie!"

***

With Mercedes' handicapped shield attached to the rearview mirror, Della parked in a reserved spot close to St. Joseph's Chapel. But even the short walk proved hazardous for the old woman, who somehow managed to stumble. Della reached for Mercedes' arm at the same moment as the old woman staved her cane into the ground with strength equal to a young warrior. She righted herself. In proper balance again, she raised the angel's head in the air above her head. "Saved again!"

The chamber group—two violins, a harpsichord, and a viola d'gamba—had already begun their first piece when Della and Mercedes opened the door. They stood in the back of the chapel, allowing their eyes to adjust to the dim lights of the sanctuary, illumined by candles. When her night vision kicked in, Della slipped her hand around Mercedes' elbow and ushered her to a row midway down the aisle.

When Mercedes settled in her seat, she rested the cane on her right side with the angel's head pointing toward the performers, as if she wanted the carved cherub to *see*, not just *hear* the performance. Della breathed deeply and took inside herself all that was St. Joseph's on this night. The deep yellow windows of the chapel had transformed into translucent gold ingots.

This chapel, a lovely sanctum, could have been anywhere. She had never been to Venice, Italy, but while at Tulane, she had regularly spent her Friday evenings in a New Orleans bookstore, drinking coffee and looking at expensive books she could not afford to purchase. One of her favorites had been a picture book of Venice. One of the photographs showed a chamber group performing in a chapel much like this one, the light as amber-

54

toned as the illumination from the candles that graced St. Joseph's. When she graduated from Tulane, she had purchased the photographic essay of Venice with a gift certificate a friend had given her for graduation. The book graced her coffee table in the little apartment above Mercedes' garage. She loved chamber music because it allowed her to travel while sitting perfectly still.

Della's thoughts drifted to her new client, Oliver Fitzsimmons III, and to her son, Kevin, and to her daughter, Josie, and her ex-husband, Galliard McElhenney. Each needed special consideration, but those were concerns for later. For just these few moments, she sat, as if royalty, and rode into a magic world created by the harpsichord, the violins, and the mellow viola d'gamba that held a steady beat.

Inside the River View Hotel, Chang Wu waited in the lobby for Mr. Miguel Sanchez. "I'll be dressed in an orange athletic shirt with a red rose pinned to my collar," Sanchez had told Chang Wu when they spoke on the telephone. "I won't draw attention," he had said. "It's Mardi Gras."

Chang Wu waited and watched people coming and going across the wide hotel lobby. Women dressed in long gowns strutted arm in arm with men in tails and white ties. Other folks mingled in blue jeans and down-padded jackets. A jazz band played on the mezzanine. Chang Wu settled into the overstuffed cushions of the sofa. He should not allow himself this luxury, sitting deep in soft pillows like a sleepy old cat. He fingered the plastic beads around his neck and grinned. *Mardi Gras. Moon pies.* He slid his legs forward on the seat and propped his head against the sofa back. Yes. This Mobile, Alabama with its Mardi Gras might be his newest financial venture. He would relax and watch for this man named Miguel Sanchez in the orange athletic shirt with a red rose pinned to his collar.

***

In the best of worlds, Miguel Sanchez would find himself a counselor, maybe a psychiatrist, to explain to him why he did what he did. *¿Estoy loco?* He needed help and he knew it, but he suspected his possibility for help had long ago expired. He thought he might be in league with the devil, but he did not speak with the devil. He was careful not to acknowledge the devil at all, although he had done the devil's bidding. He knew this. His head was still screwed on tight enough to know this.

Sometimes in the night he woke in a cold sweat, his heart racing. He sat up in bed, his undershirt stuck to his chest. He made the sign of the cross in front of him and whispered, "get behind me Satan." When he could not sleep, he got up, went outside, and breathed the night air. Always this soothed him. Satan might trail him, but he crossed himself and repeated *get behind me. Keep your distance! ¡Apártate! ¡Apártate!*

To his credit, he was the father of three children. A good father. Two kids in college at expensive schools in the States. Another at boarding school in Argentina. He supported his wife well. He had his women . . . sure . . . but that was to be expected. No one could fault him for that. Yet he maintained his wife in good style, and they maintained their cordiality—for their children they did this. Was this not the sign of a good man? His children loved him. *They loved him.* A man who was loved could not belong to the devil. Love was not of the devil. Love was the very essence of God. He had learned this in the little Catholic Church in their neighborhood in Bogotá. He could see his mother, a lace mantilla like a fancy handkerchief on top of her head. She held Miguel with one hand and with her other she held his little brother, Dino.

Oliver's Song

His brother—now dead. They had both done the bidding of powerful men. Miguel had escaped encounters with death brought about by these powerful men. Dino had not.

As young men, Miguel and Dino needed work, and they had found work where it was to be had. On this earth—Miguel understood this completely—the devil has his hooves set firmly in some places. Unfortunately for them, they were in a place where the old evil beast—*diablo himself*—dug his toenails into the dirt. He and Dino did what they had to do. Looking back on it all, he knew they should have taken work on the banana plantations. They would have hacked with a machete until the abundant green bananas fell in bunches into their protective arms. But, they would have owned almost nothing. Maybe a modest roof over their heads, food on their tables, but nothing more. *¡Nada!* Nothing, but their souls.

Ahhh Miguel. Do not look back. Look forward! ¡Adelante!

He blew air out his lips and circled another floor of the parking garage. He would meet this man named Chang Wu. Surely the man had information about Billy Wong. He would gather information from Chang Wu, but he would hold his own information as close to his chest as if it were a hand of cards.

His position was tricky. No, not tricky—it was dangerous. *¡Peligrosa! Yes—peligrosa.* He had purchased the load from Billy Wong to save his own skin, to gain favor with The Boss. He was not the one who had double-crossed his employer. Billy Wong was the double-crosser. Wong had sold Mr. Wu's haul of drugs to Miguel, then he had double-crossed Miguel and had disappeared with all the money and all the drugs. Miguel was certain this load of pure Asian heroin—and the promise of future hauls—would have set him right with The Boss. He had botched his previous job for The Boss. He needed a score to save himself. His life depended on it.

57

The drugs were not the worst of it—the worst was that violin. For certain, that old violin would cost Miguel his life if he did not recover it.

He had led The Boss to believe he knew Billy Wong well. "A good man," Miguel told The Boss. "He is a musician."

"A musician?" The Boss questioned, admiration in his voice.

"Wong plays a big bass," he told The Boss. "He's a student at university. He studies music."

Miguel did not know if Billy Wong studied music or not. He did not know if Billy Wong was a student. He knew only that he had met him near the music buildings. Billy Wong did carry a large bass. That much was true.

"I will remove my instrument," Billy Wong had told Miguel. "I will put the goods in the case. In that way I will give the load to you. Then, it is payday for me?"

"You will have the money when I get the case with the goods," Miguel had said.

It should have been easy. One exchange—the goods for the cash, but The Boss had complicated things.

"Does Billy Wong know Hong Kong?" The Boss had asked.

"Billy Wong knows Hong Kong," Miguel told him. "He is from mainland China, but he has traveled to Hong Kong."

This was true. This is what Billy Wong had told Miguel. Sometimes Miguel had difficulty remembering what was true and what was not. He did know the difference between the truth and a lie, but sometimes it was easier to allow the two to merge, or to at least slide close to each other. But, this was true—Billy Wong knew Hong Kong.

"Good," The Boss had said. "You trust him with your life?" The Boss asked.

"I do," Miguel lied.

"If you trust him with your life, I need him to transport a musical instrument to Hong Kong—a violin. I will meet him in

Oliver's Song

Hong Kong and take the instrument back to Colombia for my personal use."

"Fine," Billy Wong had said when Miguel offered the job to him. The Boss would pay well for the service. Billy Wong had smiled.

What was so special about that violin? Miguel knew nothing of musical instruments. In truth—he didn't care. The Boss went nuts sometimes. No—often he had proven himself to be a crazy man. He had probably stolen the violin out of some performer's dressing room. Poor sucker! Who cared? A violin was a violin. *¡Violin estúpido!*

Problem was: Billy Wong had taken The Boss's money, had disappeared with the drugs, *and* had taken the old violin. The Boss knew none of this. *¡Dios mio!* Miguel rubbed his forehead where his eyebrow twitched.

"You have done well," The Boss said when Miguel was in Houston. "Our business is being threatened, our territory invaded, our income jeopardized. The Asians want our territory." *Not on your life,* The Boss had whispered, his back to Miguel. "You have made a good contact in this man, Billy Wong. With him, we will eat the Asians' lunch—and dinner too," he added. "One of their own will help us."

Miguel had taken the violin from Houston and driven it straightaway to Tallahassee. The violin was still wrapped in the old purple cloth The Boss had gently tucked around it. Miguel wanted the violin out of his hands and into Billy Wong's. He wanted no part in somehow accidentally damaging the instrument.

"I'll take good care of it," Billy Wong had said when Miguel handed the old thing to him.

"You had better," Miguel said, "or you will find yourself with no arms. I would not take any chances." Miguel had smiled at Billy Wong.

When the drugs arrived in Tallahassee, he had come early to the appointed location not far from campus to receive them. From a distance, Miguel saw Billy Wong load his bass case into an old Audi. He ran toward the car. "Billy. Billy Boy," he shouted, but Billy Wong fled, and the car pulled away from the curb. He had gotten a glimpse of the license plate—an Alabama tag beginning with the number 2. Mobile, Alabama—this he knew for sure.

Miguel was sitting pretty until Billy Wong disappeared with the goods—and the violin too. If The Boss found out, Miguel was a walking dead man. *Hombre muerto.*

He found a parking place on the third level of the garage. For now, he would meet this Mr. Chang Wu and see what he could discover about Billy Wong. He needed information that would save his life. Please God! *¡Ayúdame, Dios mio!*

6

Chang Wu almost missed him. Who would have thought a large man dressed in tan slacks, an orange athletic shirt with a red rose pinned to his collar could escape Chang Wu's notice? *Ten fat fowl dance across a snoring snout.* Chang Wu was the snoring snout. This man, Miguel Sanchez, had already passed through the lobby and was on the escalator when Chang Wu spotted him. He rose from where he sat and mounted the escalator a considerable distance behind the man. When he reached the mezzanine, Sanchez glanced around. He spotted Chang Wu and in several giant strides approached him.

"Wu?" Sanchez asked. "Mr. Chang Wu?"

"I am Chang Wu. Shall we speak in the lobby?" He asked this in a quiet and steady voice. He liked the hotel lobby. Anyone could become part of the crowd and disappear. He turned and rode the escalator down.

The South American stood nearly a foot taller than Chang Wu. Tan complexion. Dark hair. Broad chest. A very large man. He carried an odor with him—a smell of wet earth, moss, mushrooms decaying in late afternoon sun. A most unpleasant odor.

As soon as they had seated themselves on a sofa tucked in a corner of the lobby, the man, this Mr. Miguel Sanchez, licked his lips. "Think we can order ourselves drinks?" Before Chang Wu could speak the man raised his hand, summoning a cocktail waitress.

When the waitress came to them, Miguel Sanchez ordered a double scotch. Chang Wu ordered green tea. Only minutes earlier, he had allowed himself too much comfort. Now he would enforce his own discipline. Green tea to clarify his mind.

"What you got on your arm, Mr. Wu? Someone die?" Miguel Sanchez pointed to the blue dragon embroidered on the black armband.

Chang Wu would not share anything with this man. "Yes," he said, and offered nothing more.

"How long will you wear that thing?"

"Long time," Chang Wu said, and rubbed his fingers across the silk threads of the China-blue dragon. He would take charge as he always did. "You have information on Mr. Billy Wong?"

"I saw him with my own eyes," the big man said. "I watched Billy Wong load his bass case containing the goods into a car, an old Audi with Alabama plates." He did not mention that the old violin was in that case too. No reason for Mr. Chang Wu to ever know about the violin.

The man took a breath. "What do you know about Billy Wong? It's in both our interests to locate him."

Chang Wu lifted the Mardi Gras beads away from the front pocket of his white shirt and removed a small black leather notebook. Generally, he used the notebook for writing short pieces of wisdom he would perfect into crisp proverbs for *Lily's Songs*. Now, he wrote: *Miguel Sanchez. Billy Wong. Old Audi. Alabama license plate.* Chang Wu did not know why he wrote the note, but he knew it was good to write the facts. It demonstrated his discipline.

"Did Billy Wong get into that car?" Chang Wu asked.

Miguel Sanchez laughed and his eyes surveyed the crowd in the lobby. "I did not say I saw him get in that car. Billy Wong fled when I called his name, but he loaded the goods in that Audi. I saw that before a delivery truck blocked my view. The Audi pulled away before I reached it. But . . . ," Miguel Sanchez rubbed his chin. "I believe he got in that car. He is here in Mobile, and the goods are here too." He licked his lips again. "I need that drink," he said. "What contacts do you have here, Mr. Wu." He turned his head in search of the cocktail waitress.

Oliver's Song

Chang Wu said nothing. He had no contacts here, but he felt certain this Miguel Sanchez had connections here. He would squeeze the information from this large ox of a man who wore a silly red rose pinned to his orange shirt.

Miguel Sanchez turned back toward Chang Wu. "What can you tell me about Billy Wong? What do you know that might be of help to us both? We need Billy Wong."

Chang Wu was not certain he was on the same team as this Mr. Miguel Sanchez. He did not trust the man who sat in front of him, but he did not want to return to Chicago with empty hands. He did not want to discuss this situation with the Long Hairs. He did not trust them either.

"Who owns the car?" Chang Wu asked, his voice calm and steady. "Have you checked?"

"I have someone checking," Miguel Sanchez said. "I do believe the mother lode was placed in that car." He cleared his throat before he spoke again. "Mr. Wu, what do you know about Billy Wong?"

"Excuse," Chang Wu said. "Mother lode?"

"The smack, Mr. Wu." Sanchez grinned. "Little language barrier."

Chang Wu did not flinch, but he himself would not use any of the words—drugs, narcotics, smack, heroin, horse, mud, dirt, golden girl. None of these words would cross his lips. He would not name the transported load. *Sealed lips ingest no poison.*

The waitress delivered their drinks, placing them on the coffee table in front of them. Chang Wu paid. Neither man spoke for a long minute. Each man sipped his drink and studied the crowd lingering in the lobby.

"One damned crazy town," Miguel Sanchez said. He did not tell Chang Wu he lived in New Orleans. This Mobile Mardi Gras was family stuff compared to what could be had in New Orleans. Miguel liked this, a chance to catch his breath away from all the madness at the edge of the French Quarter where he maintained his small apartment.

63

Chang Wu smiled politely and took another sip of his drink. The odor coming off the South American was so strong, so musky, so dark, it interfered with the light fragrance of Chang Wu's green tea.

"Have you been in contact with the Asian community in Mobile?" Miguel Sanchez asked.

"I have only arrived," Chang Wu answered.

"What do you know about Billy Wong that might help us, Mr. Wu?"

Aahhhh. This Miguel Sanchez . . . insistent. Chang Wu did not like this man. The man had come to gather information from him. He had precious little to offer. But . . . he would give Sanchez something, some small pieces of information to nibble on. That would loosen the South American's lips. "I will find Wong's contacts," he said. "I will communicate with them." He folded his hands, one hand inside the other. "You will let me know about the car?" His voice was almost a whisper. "Who owns it?"

"I'll see what I can do," Sanchez said. He looked again toward the revelers in the lobby.

Chang Wu removed a business card from his pocket. On the back, he wrote his cell number. "Call tomorrow," he said as he handed the card to Miguel Sanchez.

Miguel Sanchez placed the small business card in the front pocket of his orange athletic shirt. He did not offer his number, and Chang Wu did not ask for it. "We'll meet again," Chang Wu said. The South American's face sweated. Chang Wu knew this man needed Billy Wong. Chang Wu had no doubt he would call.

"Tomorrow, mañana, mañana, it is." Miguel Sanchez saluted the air as if *tomorrow* was a command performance and he accepted the order to appear.

"I personally offer ten thousand dollars for anyone with information on Billy Wong," Chang Wu said, looking directly at Miguel Sanchez. "By Wednesday," he added, their eyes locked.

"Now you are talking, Mr. Wu," Miguel Sanchez winked. "That cash will buy us information. Won't take much. A few bucks and some guy will talk." Miguel Sanchez grinned and leaned in closer to Chang Wu. "We will work together," he said, hitching his left foot atop his right knee, forming a box with his legs.

Chang Wu studied the man who sat beside him—a block of a man. *Block head*, the Americans said. He did not like this man. He was not satisfied with the information he had gained, but he knew his business with this man was over—at least for tonight. Tomorrow he would offer some information and the man would bring information too. They would find Billy Wong before Friday.

Lily had told him she would be a flower at her Friday night dance recital. A lotus blossom he thought. He would be at her recital. He would use this man, this *block head*, to help him locate Billy Wong and complete his business here. Back in Chicago, he would have his secretary fill a basket with sweet Asian soaps— Monkey Pods, Lei-Lei Moons, April Flowers, and a handful of soaps shaped like little dragon flies. He had seen these in the window of a shop near his office. He would have his secretary add a pan pipe and a little pigeon whistle. He would tell her to fill the basket, wrap it in a plastic film, and tie it with a lavender ribbon. Lavender—Lily's favorite color. He would also have his secretary purchase pink roses. Before Friday night his business here would all be over. He would be home in time to see Lily dance.

"We will gather tomorrow," Chang Wu said again to the South American. He stood and nodded his head toward the man who still sat on the sofa, watching women in satin evening gowns and men in black ties and tails. Chang Wu turned his back and walked toward the elevator. He wondered if Miguel Sanchez watched him. The skin on the back of his neck bristled like the flesh of a prickly pear. *Goose flesh*, the Americans called it. He had goose flesh after talking with this Miguel Sanchez. Even in the elevator he could still smell the dusky odor of the man. Something dark and evil.

The dragon snorts magic breath, he reminded himself. Chang Wu eats fire. He knew the dragon's power—his own power. He would rid himself of the evil odor of this man. A night's rest and he would have a plan for completing his business in Mobile. He, a man of magic and of discipline.

What he did not tell Mr. Miguel Sanchez: he had a second load that would soon pass on the interstate just south of the city. A trusted ally would receive and distribute the goods in Florida. Even if Billy Wong had disappeared, Chang Wu would yet complete the links and secure the route for the Long Hairs and the Mexicans. He understood logistics. He did not like the Long Hairs, but they could count on him. With the help of this Mr. Miguel Sanchez, he would locate Billy Wong and put an end to the vexation that tipped his mind off center. *Almost done with the Long Hairs,* he concluded. He smiled. His mind at peace. A vision of Lily dancing across the stage in white satin scrolled before his eyes—Lily a lovely lotus blossom.

***

¡Qe ridículo! Miguel thought. The little Asian had offered ten thousand. *¡Diez mil!* What was his life worth? He had everything on the line. He had to locate Billy Wong, the drugs, and The Boss's old violin. Ten thousand was nothing! *¡Nada!*

He did not tell Chang Wu he was finished with him. He had others who would get information from this little man. They had methods of gaining information. Miguel Sanchez had no time for this small man with sealed lips. He licked the rim of his glass before tipping it and downing the last of his drink.

7

After the concert at the college, Della and Mercedes treated themselves to an ice cream at the Old Dutch Ice Cream Shop. When they returned home, the dead Dodge had been pushed to the end of the driveway. Kevin's Mazda Roadster was parked in front of it. Jumper cables extended from the Dodge to the Mazda, a Christmas present from his father. Galliard generously rewarded those who did his bidding. The engines of both cars idled. Della knew Kevin waited for her on the screened-in porch of her apartment. He came often and sat with her until bedtime, drinking coffee or fruit punch while the two caught up on the years they had missed when he was in his late teens.

Della maneuvered around the Dodge, pulled onto the grass again, and parked the Town Car in the garage. She walked around the car to open the passenger door for Mercedes.

"Need help?" Kevin called to them. He had come down the apartment steps and stood in the driveway.

"Any time from a good looking man like you," Mercedes called out as she and Della came out of the garage.

Kevin stepped forward and slipped his arm around the old woman's shoulder. She leaned in toward him and handed him the angel-headed cane, which he twirled like a drum major.

"You got to teach me that trick," Mercedes said.

"A tender roast with rice and gravy, and I'll teach you anything," Kevin said.

"You got a deal, mister," Mercedes answered.

Before he left Mercedes at her door, Kevin bent and kissed her on the top of her head.

"I do like me a good man," she said and patted his arm before bidding him a goodnight.

Della and Kevin walked back to their cars where he unplugged the jumper cables, but left the Dodge idling to build up the battery's charge. "I hope this does it," he said. "If it dies again, I'll take it to Sears and get a new battery put in."

"I'll pay for it," Della said.

Kevin ignored her. "See how it does tomorrow," he said. He put his arm around his mother—Kevin a full six inches taller—and the two walked up the steep stairs to the garage apartment where Della brewed a small pot of coffee. When the coffee was ready, the two took their mugs to the screened-in porch to enjoy the unusually warm February night. Della had new rocking chairs she had purchased with money she didn't have. The chairs were worth every penny she had put on her credit card however, because they provided a nice perch overlooking Mercedes' beautifully landscaped backyard, which was lovely even at night with accent lights illuminating trees and flowers. Here, she could sit with her son when he came to visit.

"This afternoon I met a young man, Oliver Fitzsimmons III, everyone calls him Ollie. He was at the Mardi Gras Luncheon with his sister Kathryn Dee who is in the court. My new client met Josie. Did you meet him too?"

"I left early. Business for Dad," Kevin reminded her. "I'm sure that's the fellow who sat beside Josie at lunch though. They were head-to-head talking. If he's a client, I hope it's nothing serious," Kevin said.

"We'll see," she said. *Legal matters stay in the office.* This had been drilled into her in law school.

"Want me to pick you up tomorrow night?" Kevin asked when Della offered no additional information about her client. Kevin sipped his coffee, leaned forward and placed his cup on the small wrought iron table positioned between the two rocking chairs.

"Thank you, but I'll decline. You've got to be downtown early. You're part of the royal court. I'll do just fine." She held her coffee mug between her hands. She liked the warmth that seeped from the surface of the cup into the skin of her palms.

"I'm sorry you're alone," Kevin said. "I know that gets hard sometimes."

Kevin was the kindest and wisest young man Della knew. How could she have raised him? In truth, she knew she had only half raised him. When he was a teenager, she was fighting her own demons. She leaned across the arm of her chair and kissed him on the side of his face.

"I'm not alone. I've got you. I only wish I had Josie too. If I haven't heard from her by tomorrow, I'll call her. I know she's busy. I've been putting off calling because I didn't want to trouble your father and Dora."

"Dizzy Dora," Kevin said.

Della could have so easily taken the bait. She had more than a few comments she wanted to make about Dora, who married Galliard on the rebound. Dora had also forced a wedge between mother and daughter, refusing to put Josie on the telephone when Della called, shopping with Josie for a prom dress before Della had the money to do so, and cautioning Josie to report any misbehavior on the part of her mother. Fortunately, there had been no misbehavior to report. She had remained as sober as a zealous Puritan. But, Dora never gave up.

Della suspected Galliard had taken a ribbing when he went from a Della to a Dora, but little Dora was everything Galliard had wanted in a wife. She fit the bill perfectly at slightly over five feet and barely a hundred pounds. Her shoulder-length blonde hair appeared heavier than the rest of her entire body. Dora lived to socialize—the quintessential hostess. Della had even received a few invitations to Dora's fetes. Della learned quickly that an invite from Dora must be opened over a trash can because glitter always cascaded out from the opened envelope. If a recipient of a Dora invitation ever forgot to unseal the envelope over a trash can, tiny tinsel moons and stars would twinkle for weeks on the hardwood or tile floors. Only a wet index finger pressed straight down over the sparkle could lift it.

"Dora must have helped Josie get everything she needed for the Mardi Gras balls because she didn't ask me for any help at all," Della said.

"Don't worry about it, Mom. Shopping and partying are Dora's specialties. That's not what you're about." Kevin sipped his coffee.

In fact one of the differences that finally separated Della from Galliard was his insistence that she entertain often and look like some image he had conjured that she never could get quite right. She held her hands out in front of her in the dim light of the porch—*peasant hands*.

Galliard had wanted her fingernails manicured—French nails with frosty, cream-colored tips, or red nails as rich as maraschino cherries. That had been easy, but Galliard wanted more. He wanted what she could not give. He wanted a petite wife dressed to the nines, and he wanted frequent, elaborate parties with Della serving as the toast of the occasion.

She hated the role. It was not her. She was not petite and never had been. She stood five feet eight inches tall, with generous round hips, and honey-brown hair. She was the daughter of a hard-scrabble, black-dirt farmer from coastal Louisiana. She hated the role of *bon vivant*. It simply wasn't her, and she couldn't live up to it. But the *role* grew in importance as Galliard's wealth increased. Della suspected Galliard's image-perfect wife had become a necessity because of his route to riches.

In the simplest terms, his route to new-found riches was *garbage*. His empire started with two roll-off trucks, hauling rubbish for a couple of building contractors. From such modest beginnings, he had signed a contract at a chemical plant that kept a fleet of trucks busy on a twenty-four-seven schedule for three years. From there he added garbage pick-up for small municipalities north of Mobile. Ultimately, he acquired the nickname, *King of Garbage*. The *Mobile Press Register* had even used the tag in an article on industrial clean-up and solid waste disposal. *Galliard McElhenney, Mobile's King of Garbage.*

Galliard visibly winced when one of his friends applied the moniker at a cocktail party. In order to allow the title to slide off as if he were Teflon coated, Galliard believed he needed a petite, blonde-haired, blue-eyed wife who knew how to spend money and entertain lavishly. With a wife who lived to entertain, no one would dare tease him about his status in the garbage industry, lest that unlucky person be cut off the party list at Galliard's estate in Mobile, or at his waterfront mansion on the bay.

"I guess I'm not much on shopping," Della admitted.

"For her Mardi Gras wardrobe, Dora took Josie to Atlanta and to New Orleans," Kevin explained. "They may have made one trip to New York. I'm not good at keeping up with details like that. I lose track of that kind of thing."

"New York?" Della asked, unable to keep her surprise out of her voice.

"I think so," Kevin said. "But, like I said, I'm not big on keeping up with Dora's shopping extravaganzas."

"I did well to get a gown from Dillard's," Della told him.

"You'll be beautiful, Mom. You always are."

"Let's see. I could use a complete body tuck, a face lift, and I could lose more than a few pounds."

"That's crazy, Mom. When's the last time you looked in the mirror? You're gorgeous. You always have been."

Della didn't hesitate a moment. "I needed to hear that, son. Truth or not."

"It's true, Mom." He reached across the wrought iron table and touched Della's hair. "You have the best hair in the entire world. I used to love touching it when I was a kid. All those little corkscrews."

She did indeed have nice hair. Even she had to admit it—a honey-bronze with red highlights, still vibrant, with only a hint of gray at the edges of her face. Her hair, a gift from her red-headed father and her brunette mother, framed her face in hundreds of small spirals. Where the spirals came from, no one was sure. As a girl, her mother teased her—*you stuck your finger in an electric socket when I turned my back*. As an adult, she had grown to love the warm amber spirals. Shampoo and go. In law school she had no time for fussing with her hair.

"You don't have an ounce of fat either."

"Now that's not true."

"Well, not much," Kevin said. ·

Not much was right, and Della knew it. *You could lose five, maybe ten pounds*, the doctor had suggested on her last visit. She wanted to take those extra pounds off, but at five feet, eight inches, she concealed them well. Generally, her self-assessments led down a path of condemnation, but with Kevin beside her, the path led to affirmation.

But now, she wanted to turn the focus on her son. "Are you surviving all right in your Dad's business?" A question she generally avoided when talking with her son.

"I try to be an eight-to-fiver," Kevin answered. "I do my time, and I cut out. That is, if I can," he added. "Dad gave me the accounts north of Mobile. Gets me out of the office. We got several new contracts brewing. Maybe I can turn the job into a five-day road trip."

"Good for you." Della knew her son liked to travel the Alabama back roads. She suspected he liked to eat his lunch in some small diner, reading his newspaper or with his nose stuck between the pages of a novel. Kevin, like his mother, was a reader, a quiet kid who excelled in literature and history classes in high school. He had read every book he could get his hands on about the Lewis and Clark expedition, and was now rapidly becoming an expert on the Civil War. He was building for himself little islands of knowledge where he could retreat from the world of industrial and municipal garbage.

She had retreated too, but her little islands had been in the bottle. Such innocent beginnings. A little drink in the afternoon soothed her nerves. All Galliard's suggestions for how she should look, the clothes she should purchase, the dinner parties she should host—it all went down better with a drink or two flowing through her veins. Then, a drink or three—maybe four. Then, less Coca-Cola or tonic water. Then, her shots of bourbon straight-up.

Kevin broke into her reflections. "I admire you, Mom," his voice a whisper in the darkness.

"*Me?*" She refused to point out to Kevin all the reasons why she was one of the last people he should admire. She, a middle-aged new comer to the legal profession with a struggling start-up practice, she who lived in a rented—payment over-due—garage apartment behind the big house, not to mention she who was an alcoholic and always would be.

"Yes *you*. Look at you. You've stood up to the forces that were about to pull you under. You have more courage than I've ever had."

Della knew what Kevin meant. She had refused to surrender her own style for whatever image of her Galliard had fantasized. But it had cost her everything. Now she was gaining back a little of what she had lost.

No—that was not accurate. She had Kevin, which was a huge gift. She also had her pride. She had not only survived law school, she had graduated with honors. She had survived the lonely nights in New Orleans, sleeping with the lights on, a law book at her right elbow for when she woke in the middle of the night and could not sleep. She lacked only two things to make her world complete—Josie, and enough revenue to pay her bills.

"I always wanted to study history," Kevin said. "When I graduated, I wanted to travel." He raised his coffee mug and took a sip. "I wanted to spend a year traveling out west. I'd have loved to spend an entire year working on a ranch in Montana or Wyoming or someplace like that. Keep a journal and write about it. Maybe get an article published or something."

"I remember that. You wanted to major in English or history, and I thought you would."

"I majored in business because that's what Dad wanted. I stayed here because that's what Dad wanted. I work in his business because that's what Dad wants. I wonder if I'll ever have the courage to figure out what I really want. Then, will I have the courage to do what I want once I've figured it all out? That's why I admire you, Mom. You have more courage than I've ever had."

Della decided the next time she browsed in a book store she would look for a photographic essay on Montana or Wyoming. Had anyone spent a year on a ranch and written a book about it? Kevin was on to something, she thought. A modern western. She'd love to read the story of a young man who set out on his own, found a job out west, and spent an entire year discovering who he was—locating the very core of himself. That was a book she wanted to read.

"I'm saving my money," Kevin said. "Maybe I'll strike out on my own someday. Meanwhile, tomorrow morning at eight-thirty I'm meeting a contractor who's building about eight high-rises on the Gulf. He'll need rubbish removal big time. I know it's Saturday, but Dad wants this job." He placed his cup on the wrought-iron table and stood. "I'll get it for him if I can." He stretched his arms above his head. "Better get some shut-eye now." He gave his mother a hug, and she latched the screened-porch door when he walked down the stairs.

Before going to bed, Della looked in the mirror—really looked at herself. She decided Kevin was at least partially correct. Her green eyes complimented her honey-brown hair and the little corkscrew spirals framed her face in a halo, both wild and warm. Okay. She had a few pounds to lose. That was for tomorrow. This night she would go to bed secure in her son's love and with the recognition that she was one of the luckiest women in the entire world.

Della slept so soundly that she struggled to decipher the ringing noise. Then she realized—*the telephone*. Her heart raced as she reached across the bed and nearly knocked the phone off its cradle before she answered it.

"Mama. I should have called you." Josie sobbed. "I'm sorry."

Della saw the glowing red numbers on her bedside clock which read 2:30.

"Josie, where are you?"

"I should have called. I'm sorry." Josie's words were heavy and thick on her tongue. Della heard music and voices in the background. "Where are you, baby?"

"I don't treat you right. I know I don't." Josie cried now and sniffed like a two-year-old.

"Where are you, baby? Do you need help?"

The temperature in Della's body shot up. A thin layer of sweat dampened her forehead as she swung her legs off the bed and stood. "Baby, I'll come get you if you tell me where you are."

"I love you," Josie said.

"I love you too." Then Della said what she had told Josie when she was a little girl. The last thing she said to her at night before she switched off the lights in Josie's room. "I love you from the bottom of your fleet feet to the top of your sweet head."

"Who's that?" a man's voice demanded.

"My Mama," Josie said, her words slurred.

"Your mama, my ass," the man said. "Your mama. Your mama," the man taunted Josie in a sing-song voice. The laughter grew louder.

Was Josie at a party or a bar? Della could not determine.

"Josie!" she shouted. "Where are you? I'll come get you."

The connection severed.

"Josie! Josie!" Della called into the receiver, but . . . with no response.

Her little apartment closed in on her like a sarcophagus. She placed the telephone back in its cradle, unlatched the locks on her door, and stepped out onto her screened-in porch. She breathed shallow at first and then deeper. She paced from one end of the small porch to the other. She would have set out on an epic journey from Mobile to China if that was what it took to have Josie beside her.

She paced and breathed deeply. She could telephone Kevin at Galliard's house and tell him about Josie's call, but there was no point in waking Kevin. He had to be up early to meet with the building contractor.

She would call Galliard's cell phone. He was never far from his cell phone. It would be on his nightstand.

She stepped back inside and dialed. The phone rang six times before going to Galliard's recorded message. She hung up, waited some seconds and dialed the number again.

"'lo," Galliard answered, sounding like a bear startled out of hibernation.

She told him about the call she had just received.

"She's at a party." The words stumbled off Galliard lips, annoyance in his voice. "She'll be on in soon."

"I think she's in trouble," Della said.

"She probably had a little too much to drink. That's all. She's young. She hasn't learned to moderate herself. She'll be on home soon."

"Tell me where she is. I'll go get her," Della's hands trembled from Josie's call, and also from the frustration of speaking with Galliard.

"I'm not sure exactly where she is," Galliard said, his voice sounding a little less scratchy. "There were a couple of parties tonight. She's at one or the other." He cleared his throat. "Tell you what. If she's not home within an hour, I'll go looking for her. You don't hear from me, you know she's home."

That was it. The end of their conversation. There was nothing to do but wait.

Della stepped outside again and paced to the rail that surrounded the screened porch. She leaned her hands against the rail and looked up at the night sky—clear, deep blue with millions of stars and planets.

Oliver's Song

"Lord God," she said. "I'm placing my little Josie in your care." She envisioned herself lifting Josie, carrying her like an infant. She placed her at the foot of the night sky, a tunnel of stars above her. "I can't take care of her. You can," she whispered. "I've placed her at the foot of your night sky."

She went inside, leaving the apartment door open to the screened porch. She poured the last of the coffee she had made earlier in the evening, heated it in the microwave, and took the mug of steaming coffee to the porch. She could not sleep and she knew it. She would be awake until morning.

How good one of those coffee drinks would taste—one with a shot of Crème de Cocoa or Crème de Menthe. But, no—and no again. She would drink hers black. No alcohol to sweeten the cup. The good news was that there was neither Crème de Cocoa nor Crème de Menthe in her apartment, nor any other liquor either.

She wondered if Mercedes was up. It would be nice to have someone to talk to about Josie's call. Mercedes had never had children, but she listened intently when Della spoke of hers.

Della placed her coffee mug on the wrought-iron table and stood. She walked to the porch rail and studied Mercedes' house. She saw no lights, with the exception of a small night light Mercedes always left burning in the kitchen. She was alone. Della Roselle Boudreaux, God, and the night sky. She sat in her chair again and sipped her coffee.

Gradually, the thinnest line of magenta tinged with gray cut through the darkness. She stood, entered her apartment, closed and locked her door. She could sleep now. Morning had made its way through the night. She had placed her Josie at the foot of God, just below where the gray and rose-colored lines entwined, breaking the night's hold.

Not long after she drifted into sleep, the ringing came again, waking her. Her hands trembled as she reached toward the nightstand. She dropped the telephone on the bed before she retrieved it and managed to get it to her ear.

"Josie! Hello."

"Miss Boudreaux. This is not Josie. It's Ollie. Ollie Fitzsimmons."

Della sat up and dropped her legs off the side of the bed. "Ollie. Yes."

"I'm in a whole lot of trouble," he said. "I'm in jail."

8

When Della walked into Mobile Metro Jail, her right hand covered her nose—a reflex action. The air reeked of cooked cabbage at least four days in the pot. The rancid odor mixed and mingled with the smell of full-strength Pine Sol, and the combination constricted her throat. The deeper she ventured into the confines of the jail, the thicker and more throat-constricting the odor. She kept her hand over her nose like a mask.

She would have placed both hands over her ears if the right hand had not been in service, shielding her nose. The jail had the roar and echo of a cave—as if a loud moan escaped from a man, perhaps years earlier, and that moan continued circling, bouncing off walls, gaining strength as it glided across vinyl floors, swirled around steel bars, and glanced off the backs of inmates. Della thought that constant roar could drive a man, confined in this place, crazy. The roar would lodge in his brain, eating one fibrous shred of gray matter, and then another. An angry voice somewhere inside the corridor of cells, sliced through the roar, but then blended into the circulating howl.

Della held in her left hand a copy of the booking report, which she scanned while she waited to be escorted to a small room where she could visit with her client. Oliver Fitzsimmons III was involved in a minor fender bender at the junction of interstates 10 and 65 where road construction was underway. His 1990 Audi Quatro was rammed in the rear by a second vehicle. A minor fender bender—*okay, no problem*. No problem until she continued to read: *a yellowish-white powdered substance spilled from the mangled trunk of the vehicle. Inspection of the trunk revealed a musical instrument case—the case severely damaged*. A handwritten note scribbled in the margin of the booking report read: *Per Fitzsimmons, the case housed a double bass. No musical instrument was found in the case. Thirty-five kilos of a powdered substance were found.* The powdered substance had been pressed into what the report described as bricks. When a K-9 unit was called to the scene, the dog alerted to the case containing the yellowish powder. Laboratory tests were ordered on the substance. Oliver Fitzsimmons III was booked at 4:25 a.m.

Della knew she had spoken clearly. She had told Ollie to leave the case where it stood inside his father's fishing camp and get out of the house. Transporting the case was the last thing he should have done. He had deliberately ignored her instructions. Legal training had taught her not to jump to conclusions. She would see what Oliver Fitzsimmons III had to say for himself. She knew this much—she would demand a full explanation.

A middle-aged uniformed officer stepped in front of Della and clapped his hands together. "Okey dokey," he said. "I'll show you back." He led Della down the hallway. "You here to see that kid from the drug bust? Right?" He glanced at her.

His gut hung over his belt a full six-inches. She wondered how he could run if required to do so, but concluded he had given up running some years prior and had opted instead for a desk job.

"Actually, I'm here to see the kid involved in the automobile accident last night," Della corrected the officer.

"Got it," the officer said and grinned. "Haven't seen you before though."

"I'm new. Just earned my law degree, passed the bar, moved back to Mobile, and hung my shingle."

"First case?" he asked.

Della sized up this man. An ally in the Mobile P.D. couldn't hurt. "Yeah," she said. "First real case." She smiled at him, and she saw that he immediately lapped up the attention.

He grinned. "Welcome home and good luck. Harold Eventide," he extended his beefy hand. "Easy to remember. *Even* as in balanced. *Tide* as in sea levels. Even-tide," he repeated. "If I can be of service, let me know."

Oliver's Song

Della lowered her hand from her nose and took Harold Eventide's hand. "Thank you, Harold," she said, deliberately employing *Harold*, not *Officer Eventide*.

He winked at her, signifying their new alliance.

Harold Eventide escorted her into a small room with a narrow, pressed-board table and several chairs. He pulled the door closed when he backed out of the room. Here in the little side room, the odor wasn't as strong, but the smell of stale cabbage still crept under the door and clung to the air. At least the roar was held at bay by the closed door. Della spread the booking report on the table in front of her, reading it more carefully this time.

While Ollie stretched his feet wide to keep the chains around his ankles from dragging the floor, his stride—if in fact it could be called a stride—was miniscule. The sound of his ankle chains scrapping across the floor made him think of himself as a victim in an Edgar Allen Poe story, one with chains, rats, and dark cesspools. With his legs wide and his steps small, he waddled. In his mind's eye, he saw himself bobbing like a manacled humpty dumpty as he made his way toward the interview room. He knew he had lost weight overnight, first from vomiting everything in his stomach, and then he ate little of his breakfast when it was slipped inside his cell—watery eggs, two strips of limp bacon, and a slice of burned toast served on a soggy paper plate. He managed to shove down the slice of toast and two bites of egg.

Although tears lodged behind his eyelids, he had plugged them. He would tell Miss Boudreaux his story fully and accurately. Then, he would hunker down for survival, no matter what he had to endure. He had already made up his mind to discipline himself—focus on survival. Narrow his whole world down to survival. This would all be straightened out. He hadn't really done anything wrong, had he? He wasn't a criminal. He had to maintain his faith in the legal process. What other option did he have?

When he stepped inside the small room, Miss Boudreaux looked down. He knew she saw the restraints around his ankles, and he felt his face turning red.

"Thank you for coming." His voice wasn't strong because he hadn't spoken for a while.

"I'm your attorney," she said, but offered nothing more.

She wore an auburn tweed pantsuit and was dressed formally even though it was Saturday morning. Her brown glasses almost matched the color of her suit. She looked all business and seeing her dressed for business—dressed for battle—gave him the first whiff of peace he had smelled since he arrived in this place in the wee hours of morning. She meant business and that was good for him. *She was on his side.*

"I'm glad to see you," he told her. "You can't believe how glad I am."

When he sat in the chair opposite her, he placed his hands on the table, the handcuffs still around his wrists. He had no pride left—*orange jumpsuit, restraints around his arms and legs. What pride?*

She reached across the narrow expanse and patted his arm. "Let's see what we can do."

"You got fifteen minutes," the guard said. "At eleven o'clock it's lockdown. All inmates have to be in their cells for lunch prep. No exceptions." He turned. "I'll be outside."

"Wait. You can remove the handcuffs." She tapped Ollie's wrists.

"We don't do that," the guard said. "Bracelets stay."

Ollie watched the guard as he closed the door but the burly man stood just outside the tiny room, his back to the glass panel. "He must think I'll try to go somewhere," he said. "Where could I go? Looks like a dead-end room to me."

Della Boudreaux ignored him. Her nose was buried in the paperwork she had in front of her. *Okay. She's on my side.* That was all he needed to know—someone was on his side.

Oliver's Song

Della looked directly into her young client's eyes. She pointed toward the booking papers. With her palms up and open like a supplicant in earnest entreaty, she asked, "What happened here?"

"I had to move Billy Wong's case. A car rear-ended me. That case broke open and spilled some of the powder all over the interstate. That's all there is to it."

"Why did you move that case?" Della strung out the question as if every letter in W-H-Y stood independently. She stared at him over the rims of her auburn colored glasses which rested halfway down her nose.

"I had to," Ollie said. "Dad called last night to say more family members had decided to come for the coronation. They all wanted to see Kathryn Dee. Dad's house is full. He planned to send the late comers to the fishing camp. I had to get Billy Wong's case off the property."

"Where"—she paused as if for dramatic effect—"were you going?" She was all business.

"To Dad's hunting camp. Near McIntosh. You know, just north of Mobile."

"I know where that is," Della said, "just past the Delta." Her eyes remained locked on his. "Your father has a hunting camp and a fishing camp?"

"Yes. Nobody was staying at the hunting camp. I wanted to get Billy Wong's case up there. I didn't call you because it was late—or early, depending on how you look at it."

"You're in serious trouble," Della said.

"What I did was stupid. I know that, but I was only thinking of my Dad and of our family. I didn't want family members at the fishing camp with Billy Wong's case. One of my cousins, he's about five or six, gets into everything. He would have opened that case for sure. I was going to leave the case at the hunting camp until you decided what I should do."

Ollie lowered his eyes to his hands. "I haven't seen my father yet. He'll believe I'm guilty. It's his nature. This should be my sister's special day. She'll be introduced to Mobile society tonight

83

while her brother sits in jail." His back pushed hard against his chair as he exhaled deeply. "What a bummer, huh?"

"Oh my God!" he yelled the next moment and slapped his manacled hands hard against the table.

The guard at the door turned toward them and looked through the glass. Della gave him a tiny wave, signaling everything was okay.

"Did this make the morning paper?" Ollie sucked air between his teeth while he waited for her answer.

"I've not seen the Saturday paper, but I'm sure the story isn't in it. The story will probably make tomorrow's paper."

"It can't!" Ollie said. "Poor Kathryn Dee!" He covered his eyes, both hands held together by the cuffs. The heels of his hands pressed against his cheeks, the tips of his fingers reached to his scalp. His stomach roiled audibly.

"Ollie. Look at me."

He lowered his hands and looked at her.

"When you moved that case, you deliberately did what I asked you not to do. Are you telling me the truth about everything? I can't defend you, and I won't try, if you don't tell me the truth, and if you don't follow my instructions. You can always find yourself another lawyer."

"Miss Boudreaux," Ollie's voice was low and steady. His demeanor changed entirely. He looked like a man now, not like a kid. His eyes stayed locked on her. "Every word I've told you is the truth. I should never have agreed to bring Billy Wong's bass to Mobile. It was stupid, but at the time, how could I have known that? I shouldn't have tried to move that stuff last night, but I thought I was doing the right thing to get it out of the fishing camp. I've done some stupid stuff, sure, but I'm no criminal."

He wanted to tell her that being in jail was already pushing him toward insanity. He wanted to tell her that stretched on the metal slab in his cell, he practiced mind-games to keep himself calm and sane. He envisioned himself as a prisoner of war, a man who survived by harnessing his mind. He wanted to stand up and shout at the top of his lungs, *I've got to get out of here!* He wanted to tell her that in the wee hours of morning when the guard had locked his cell, he had walked directly to the toilet and lost everything in his stomach. The man on the berth across the room with his back to him had said, "Flush it!" He had not rolled over. He had not looked to see who was in the cell with him. "Flush it!" An imperative, as in *I will roll over, stand up, and beat the crap out of you if you don't flush it. Now!* He did not tell his attorney any of this. His being here was his own doing. His own stupidity. His responsibility was to survive. He was a man now, or at least he was trying to be. His goals: hold himself together and survive.

"Miss Boudreaux, I want you for my attorney. I promise you, everything I've told you is the truth." He settled back, his hands calm now. "What happens from here?"

"You'll probably see a judge on Monday. That's when we'll learn the charges. It's Mardi Gras. That'll slow things down a little. I'll try to get bail set and get you out on Monday."

"Monday? Can't you get me out today?"

"Not a chance. They've got seventy-two hours to charge you. You've got to make an appearance before a judge before there's any hope of getting you out."

"I appreciate whatever you can do," he said quietly and studied his hands again. "I'm just two inches away from total madness in here."

"It's a tough place. I know that." Della removed her glasses and glanced at her watch to see how much time they had left. She pushed her chair away from the table and stood.

"Miss Boudreaux, I need to tell you one other thing. You may not want to take my case."

"Okay, Ollie, that policeman standing there with his back to the door is about to come in and call time on us. If there's anything else you need to tell me, it better be now." She sat at the table again.

"I want you to know I'll be paying for my own defense. This is not on my father's nickel."

Della dropped her glasses in a hard-sided case and snapped the lid shut. She gathered the booking documents. "I didn't suspect it would be," she said.

"I want to be sure you know I don't have any money. Not now anyway, but I will one day. I'll pay you as soon as I can. I'll pay every dime."

"This is on credit?" Della asked.

"I do have some compositions. I'll give you two pieces I've composed in the last year. One of them already won a competition. I made five hundred dollars, but I've spent that." He looked at her, his jaw squared, his eyes direct. "These two compositions are all yours until I can redeem them in cash. I don't have all the words to one of the pieces yet, but I've got the music down. Fairness requires me to tell you that this is all I've got. You might not want to continue as my attorney."

Now the ball was in her court. Della assessed her situation. She was broke, but better to be broke and busy than broke and idle. The young man was trying to pay his own way. She saw merit in that. And, maybe this client would lead to others. She might even have a couple of hit songs from those compositions. She doubted it . . . but might as well give it a try. She extended her hand for a shake. "Deal," she said.

The officer opened the door. "Two minutes."

"I'll see what I can do on bail. I'll let you know." Della stood again.

"Come back as soon as you can," Ollie said.

Della walked to the door and opened it. When the officer stepped in, Ollie stood and left the room walking in short steps. She followed him into the corridor and watched as he shuffled away from her, the hand of the uniformed officer resting in the middle of her client's back.

"Miss Boudreaux." Della jumped when she heard her name. She turned and found herself face to face with the U.S. Attorney.

"Sorry about that," he said. "Didn't mean to startle you." J.J. Ernest extended a business card toward her.

"Yes, Mr. Ernest, I know who you are." She fumbled in her purse for her own business card, which she handed to him. "I was coming to your office on Monday."

J.J. Ernest slipped Della's business card in his front shirt pocket and extended his hand. "Good to meet you."

Della shook hands and smiled. "Good to meet you too."

"I don't usually get straight to business," J.J. Ernest said, "at least not in a hallway at the Metro Jail, but a photographer is waiting to take a picture of me with the drugs. That's a big load we confiscated last night. I usually don't do photos of this nature. The Department of Justice frowns on that type of publicity." He raised his eyebrows and his forehead furrowed. "However ... this is an extraordinary situation. The public needs to be notified, so I called a press conference. I consider this a genuine public safety issue." He rubbed the side of his nose with the knuckle of his right hand, studying her as if pondering what he wanted to say next. "Your client's got himself into some considerable trouble."

A public safety issue—my ass, Della thought. She had heard talk on the street that J.J. Ernest had senatorial aspirations. Rumor was that his name would be on the ballot within a year.

"I'll be the first to admit my client's problems are deeper and wider today than they were yesterday," Della said and grinned in an effort to disarm J. J. Ernest who had probably come to the jail gunning for bear.

Ernest grinned back, his face now as round and blank as the surface of the moon, his abundant brown hair, thick as a bouffant. "Officer Eventide told me you were back here. I just wanted to meet you. Welcome to the bar, and welcome back to Mobile." His smile locked across his face.

"Thank you." She shifted her weight uncomfortably. This was not what she had planned for her first meeting with the U.S. Attorney—definitely not in a hallway of Metro Jail. He carried the aroma of herbal and mint aftershave, something expensive from the men's cosmetic counter at Dillard's or Parisian's. The spicy sweet smell cut through the rank odor of cabbage and Pine Sol.

He also appeared well rested. She, on the other hand, had slept no more than two hours the previous night and wondered if her lack of sleep showed on her face.

J.J. Ernest cleared his throat. "I want you to know we'll oppose release. Absolutely no bail. We're filing a motion to that effect."

"What?" Della's face drew into a question, her brows narrowed. "This kid thought he was transporting a bass—you know, one of those large stringed instruments. He hardly knew the man who owned the bass. He didn't even look inside the case until he got it to Mobile. And, I want to remind you, I did telephone your office and left a message. I hoped somebody would call me back. This could have all been avoided if someone had taken time to telephone me." She wanted to place the burden right back on his shoulders.

"Oh nooooo," he said. "That call wasn't nearly enough. You needed to tell us specifically what we were dealing with here."

"You know I couldn't leave that kind of information on an answering machine. I needed a call from your office." Della was insistent now.

"Let me tell you," he said, and pointed his index finger at her. "Your boy's tied to some Asians trying to introduce one more kind of hell down here. We won't have it. We don't normally get shipments of heroin like that here on the Gulf Coast. In fact, we never see shipments like that. Cocaine, meth—not heroin."

"Has the lab already sent a report?" Della questioned.

"Preliminary," he answered, "but they're rarely wrong."

Heroin echoed through her head, but she didn't flinch. "He's neither a dealer nor a user," Della cut Ernest short. "We're willing to give you full and complete information whenever you're ready. Meanwhile, the kid doesn't belong down here."

"I want him in jail. Nothing like a stay at Metro to clear his head."

"I don't get it. This is a little guy." Della held firm. "An innocent little guy," she added. "This is not any kingpin or dealer.

Just a college student who did a favor for a guy who hung around the music building at FSU. Trusting and naïve, but no criminal."

"Not the way we see it."

"Explain that," Della shot back.

"We think he's the last dog pulling the sled," J. J. said. "The sled starts in the Orient. The drug thugs there ship through Mexico and on to the USA. Got some South Americans in the mix too. Your kid is part and parcel of the big plan. He's a small player, but he knows more than he's saying."

He bit his lip and waited to see if Della had anything to add. When she said nothing, he continued, his features set firm, his dark eyebrows shading his face. "We think cartels want to introduce a whole new product here on the Gulf Coast. We have virtually no heroin down here now." His eyes remained fixed on her. "We intend to bust up this thing before the Asians, Mexicans, home boys or any other thugs get a solid toehold. We'll be tough on your client." With that, he took a step back, resting his shoulder against the wall still watching her. "Get it?"

"My client doesn't know anything about any of this."

"Sorry, Miss Boudreaux. He's directly tied to an Asian, a known drug associate." He pulled a small spiral-bound notebook from his shirt pocket and flipped several pages. "Mr. Billy Wong."

A wave of surprise washed through Della so suddenly it made her dizzy. How did the U.S. Attorney know about Billy Wong? She'd write her entire conversation with the U.S. Attorney in her own journal when she had time. *But . . . what else did this man know?*

She composed herself. "Anything else?" she asked.

"We'll talk at the proper time," J. J. snapped his little notebook shut. "After Mr. Fitzsimmons sits down here in Metro a day or two, he'll be ready to tell everything he knows. You can count on that." J.J. Ernest flashed a broad grin.

"I can't believe you'd use this tactic. What kind of justice is this?"

J.J. Ernest's broad smile faded. "That's the way it's played, Miss Boudreaux. Welcome to the real world of law and order. Not your law school cases. This is the real deal." His eyebrows raised. "Excuse me. I got a photo shoot with law enforcement in the evidence room. Thirty-five kilos. That's a big bust."

His index finger touched his forehead in a tiny salute. He turned and headed toward the rear of the building. "After this photo, I got to get on home and make ready for the parade and coronation tonight." He said this without turning back toward her.

Della's shoulder blades kissed the wall as she watched him leave. She did not tell him that her daughter, Josie, was in the royal court and so was Ollie's sister, Kathryn Dee. When Della inhaled deeply to steady herself, the spicy fragrance of the Attorney's aftershave was gone. What remained was the stench of Metro Jail. She straightened her blouse as if the U.S. Attorney's presence had ruffled her, and she headed in the opposite direction toward the double doors.

In the lobby, she raised her hand in a farewell gesture toward Harold Eventide, who sat at the main desk. She was tired now. Bone weary. Her two hours of sleep had finally caught up with her.

"Miss Boudreaux," someone called from behind her. This was her day. Everyone down at Metro seemed to know her name. She turned to see an older man, very handsome, tall and lean with thick gray hair. He wore an expensive sports coat. He extended his hand when he walked toward her.

"Oliver Fitzsimmons," he said.

"Ollie's Dad," she said and placed her hand in his.

"Mr. Eventide," he pointed toward Harold, "tells me you've seen my son."

Della peeked around the man's chest and spotted Harold Eventide. He waved. She knew if she ever wanted a story spread from one end of Mobile to the other, she would feed it to Harold Eventide.

Oliver's Song

"Yes, I've seen your son," she said to the man who stood in front of her.

"Well, I've hired an attorney," Mr. Fitzsimmons said. He raised his hand as if blocking a blow. "Don't think we don't appreciate what you've done, but I'll have my attorney take it from here. If there's a fee thus far, send your bill to my office." He reached in the breast pocket of his jacket and withdrew a business card, which he handed to her.

She took a breath, squared her shoulders, and raised herself another inch. She had been shoved around as far as she intended to be shoved this day. "Mr. Fitzsimmons, your son hired me. He's twenty-one. The legal age of majority. I'm his attorney until he fires me."

Oliver Fitzsimmons flushed. "Miss Boudreaux, no offense, but Bobby Jack Arnold has been in criminal defense for a solid twenty-five years. I believe this is your first case. From what I understand, we may need counsel with a little more court-seasoning."

Della held her position, shoulders squared and full height. "Until Mr. Oliver Fitzsimmons III releases me, I'm his attorney. Excuse me." With that she turned and headed toward the door.

"I'm not paying," Oliver Fitzsimmons said to her back as she went out the door.

He followed her outside.

"Your son told me," Della shot over her shoulder as she continued walking. Her first real case and she was working for two musical compositions. *Yes, she understood this. Working for two songs.*

"This had better not make the newspaper. If you're his lawyer, I'll hold you personally responsible."

She stopped, turned, and looked at Oliver Fitzsimmons who stood on the landing. "I don't control the free press. No attorney does. Rest assured, this story will make the newspaper. It's bound to." With that, Della walked toward the parking lot.

Oliver Fitzsimmons Sr. took two steps down the stairs. "What will you do then?" he snapped. "You'd better have a good plan. We need to keep this thing under wraps."

Della ignored him. She walked on and did not look back.

9

New Orleans was a beast of a town during Mardi Gras, getting a car into and out of downtown nearly impossible. Miguel Sanchez had come from Mobile back to New Orleans with a mission. Hire-out his dirty work. Why do it himself? After all, he would soon be a changed man. Make everything right for The Boss, and he was out of this life. He would surf the net for retreats—a monastery in Spain might be good. He had seen pictures of a monastery near Barcelona where anyone coming or going had to take a mountain tram. Yes—get the job done and he was off to a monastery. A silent one where he could redeem his soul. No chatter. ¡Perfecto!

He had paid ten dollars to several teenage boys who parked his Peugeot in the small side yard of a shotgun house. He saw no one coming or going from the house and wondered if the owners were out of town for Mardi Gras holidays. Had the boys hijacked the yard for the day, parking cars on ground that didn't belong to them and pocketing the cash? Miguel did not know and he did not care as long as the Peugeot was still there, unscathed when he returned.

For now, he sat outside of a tiny coffee shop on Magazine Street waiting for Cheever, The Snake—serpiente—and his friend, Fat Albert, also known as Tortuga. That was not quite right. Fat Albert had bastardized Tortuga into Tor-Tuba. Miguel laughed when he thought of this. He had suggested Fat Albert's nickname—Tortuga, the Spanish turtle because Fat Albert moved like a lumbering turtle and he tipped the scales at over three-hundred pounds—maybe three-fifty. On his feet he wore size thirteens, special orders, extra-wides. For comfort, he wore elephantine tee shirts and baggy pants that hung loose and low at his hips—all special orders from some big and tall men's shop.

One other fact distinguished the pet name Fat Albert had given himself before Miguel had suggested Tor-Tuba. Fat Albert was a white kid. He had named himself Fat Albert because that name placed him closer to the center of the circle, which was precisely where he enjoyed being. This was the new south where the black kids had the coolest rap and hip hop, the coolest language coded in urban slang, the clothes that hung loose and baggy, and the moves that looked impossible. Fat Albert or Tor-Tuba had been raised in African American foster homes and prided himself on being *accepted*, rare for a white kid. An achievement.

He moved slow, talked slow, thought slow. Miguel decided *Tortuga* was the perfect pet name. But Fat Albert actually thought Miguel had said Tor-Tuba. He cozied to the notion—his immense body, a large, low-pitched musical instrument. The last time Miguel had seen Fat Albert he shoved the sleeve of his tee shirt to the ridge of his shoulder, exposing a dark blue tattoo in the form of a beautifully shaped brass instrument, and below the horn, the word *Tor-Tuba*.

Miguel grinned. Poor Albert. He thought *tor-tuba* was actually a word—the Spanish word for brass horn. Miguel would not tell him. He would grant the slow giant the luxury of imagining his body a euphonium. What would he say when he saw the two? *Tor-Tuba or tortuga?* It would make no difference. Albert would hear Tor-Tuba no matter what Miguel said.

Cheever, The Snake, a different picture entirely. Miguel feared him, but he would never reveal this. Snake worked for him. Miguel had to remind himself of this. He was Snake's boss.

The coffee shop sold no liquor, but Miguel came prepared. He removed from the pocket of his trousers a small bottle of bourbon, a leftover from a recent airline flight. He broke the seal on the small neck and poured the contents into his steaming cup. Bourbon, the drink of Mardi Gras. *He was boss. He gave the orders. ¡Si! ¡Si! El es el jefe. Elda las órdenes.*

Oliver's Song

Miguel tipped his chair back and located a trash can directly behind him. He tossed the spent bottle into the can. He sipped his bourbon-laced coffee, inviting the analgesic to seep through his body, to the tips of his fingers and the nails of his toes. He would allow his mind the luxury of floating free while he waited for Snake and Tor-Tuba.

He had gotten out of Colombia—at least he had done that much. Who could blame him? His land was spoiled by the drug lords. He might have been a small part of the ruin, sure, but only a minor-league player in the big, ugly stuff. He now considered himself a Dominicano, the Dominican Republic his home.

He had constructed a ranch house in Puerto Plata—nearly paid in full. There he would run horses. In Puerto Plata, he would sit on his porch, cooled by three fans. He would watch the green valleys, the muted gold beaches, and the turquoise water below him. No, he would not simply watch the world below his feet, he would allow the beauty of the Dominican Republic, his Puerto Plata, to invade him just as the bourbon-laced coffee did now. *The fairest land under heaven*, Christopher Columbus had written in 1492 when he came ashore on the beautiful island. *Fairest land under heaven. ¡Paraíso!* He, Miguel Sanchez, was almost home—his adopted home. *He was almost there.*

Expenses for the ranch house he was building ran steep. He was doing things right. Good, solid construction, the metal and concrete pillars deep into the ground, the walls robust, the windows with solid wood trim. Soon everything would be paid and he would walk away from this life. Do penance in a monastery, come out clean, and read novels on his porch in Puerto Plata, where his children would visit, bringing grandchildren who would sit on his lap. Yes, he could see how his life would play out. He sighed audibly and sipped his bourbon-coffee.

He would establish a little law practice in Puerto Plata, mostly handling paperwork for the condominium developers. He wanted nothing else to do with drug money. None of it. His practice would be small. His office would be tiny. Just a little

95

abogado. The requirements for South American lawyers were not the same as in the U.S. He was certain he could place a little cash in the right hands and acquire a license. He would run his little office like a country gentleman. Everyone would say—*my-oh-my, lawyers do well here.* He would laugh when he heard this. He had spent a solid twenty-five years in this dirty business to get where he was. But soon everything would be paid in full. He inhaled. Instead of the heavy air of Mardi Gras—cotton candy, funnel cakes, hotdogs, and corn popped in reheated grease—he longed to smell the clean, fresh air of his Republica Dominicana. *Almost there!*

Miguel saw them coming. Snake's green eyes—green slits— hooded by dark shades. Even when the sunglasses were off, the man never opened his eyes fully, preferring to live in his own semi-darkness. Green eyes on a black man—unusual in the states, but not so in the Dominican Republic. This was how he recognized Snake the first time he met him, the green eyes. *His mother is a Dominicana,* he had been told. You can trust him. He has ties back to your land. But that was not so. His mother may have been Dominicana, but Snake had never been to the Dominican Republic. He was U.S.A. all the way. Snake had the dark skin and the green eyes of a Dominicano, but he lacked one ingredient. A broad grin—the Dominican smile—indicating contentment with the world. Such a smile had never crossed Snake's face. Snake scorned the world through hooded green slits, his eyes pissing on everyone.

Fat Albert grinned broad enough for both of them. "Boom-boom time," he shouted as he approached, referring to the drums of Mardi Gras. He extended his enormous hand toward Miguel. Then, in one quick movement, he shoved the sleeve of his tee shirt toward his shoulder. "Got to add a boom-boom here," he said. "Get the whole band right up here." He slapped his pale forearm.

Miguel laughed. "Tor-Tuba," he said, extending his hand.

Oliver's Song

Snake's back was to the sun, and he slid off his dark glasses—the green slits were now exposed, unnerving Miguel.

Fat Albert ordered two crullers and a hot beignet. Snake sipped his black coffee. Miguel explained their assignment. "Foreigners," he said, as if the South Americans were natives. "Asians and some upstart *Mexicanos*," he told the two who sat across from him, "men from the Orient and *campesinos sucios* . . . "

"What you say?" Fat Albert asked, his eyes large in his round pasty face.

"Peasants. Dirty peasants," Miguel laughed. "These Asians and dirt farmers from Mexico are invading our territory. We'll stop them." He shrugged his shoulders to show he was not overly concerned. The demise of these newcomers was certain.

"We know for a fact the outsiders have begun transporting drugs from the southwest to Florida. They cross our territory. Understand?" Miguel's voice low and steady.

"We hear you," Tor-Tuba said, and took another bite of his beignet. Snake said nothing.

"There is an Asian in Mobile, a Mr. Chang Wu. The man is from Chicago, a high-up in this would-be cartel. We need information from him. He knows the whereabouts of another man named Billy Wong." Miguel Sanchez tapped his index finger on the table. "Wong has stolen goods from us. First, we talk with Mr. Chang Wu. Then we find Billy Wong."

He did not tell them he had botched his last job. This was his last chance. Get it right this time or he was a dead man. He did not say this.

"You will be paid well. Understand?"

Snake grunted. "We got ears, man," his voice a rumble.

Miguel slipped a half sheet of paper across the table toward Snake, who leaned in to examine it. On the paper Miguel had written the barest bones of information.

--*Chang Wu—Riverview Hotel*
--*Must have information from Chang Wu on Billy Wong*

Miguel Sanchez retrieved the paper and added one additional note. *Find Billy Wong!* After adding an exclamation point, he slid the paper back to Snake.

Snake looked at the half sheet. "Our mode of operation," he questioned, his voice all gravel.

Miguel was certain Snake was or had been a high-up in a local gang. Miguel knew about gangs. Procedures passed from the USA to the South Americans—red bandanas tied around their heads, tattoos across their faces. From South America to the states, from the states to South America—Bogotá, Tijuana, São Paulo, Los Angeles, Hartford, New Orleans. Members did not shy away from undesirable work. He would give the two who sat across from him his dirty work. Snake and Tor-Tuba would understand Miguel's instructions perfectly. Miguel liked this arrangement. He would have clean hands. That's the way he figured it: placing an order was not pulling a trigger, not inserting a knife.

"No restrictions," Miguel said. "Your discretion. Do as you see fit."

"How we know this man, Wu?" Snake asked.

Miguel Sanchez raised his index finger in the air, and he smiled. He actually smiled. "Chinese man," he said. "Man wears a black armband with a blue dragon across the band. The dragon's tail circles the band. Blue dragon. Black armband," he repeated to be certain the two took this information inside them.

Miguel was never certain what Snake recorded in his mind because he gave away no information, his eyes like tinted windows on a car, obscuring the driver. With Tor-Tuba, Miguel suspected information came in and seeped out with little saturation. He placed his hand against the tattooed instrument on Tor-Tuba's enormous upper arm—"black band, blue dragon here." He removed his hand and again raised his bourbon-coffee to his lips.

Fat Albert slapped Miguel's hand. "Tor-Tuba will blow him away." He laughed, pleased with his own joke.

Oliver's Song

"Not until you get the information," Miguel turned toward Snake, who did not smile. With his long dark fingers, Snake folded the half sheet of paper and slipped it into his hip pocket.

"We need a bonus," Snake said. "How much?"

"Ten thousand," Miguel said.

"Over base?"

"Yes," Miguel answered. "Over base."

"Pay on return from Mobile?" Snake asked.

"If this mission is accomplished," Miguel assured him.

"When?" Snake probed again.

"Immediately upon return." Miguel looked directly into the green slits, as if he did not fear this man.

Snake stood. Tor-Tuba followed his lead.

"The intruders"—Miguel paused for a moment, pondering his adversaries—"these Asians and *Mexicanos*," he continued, "will be stopped." He looked at the two men directly now. "You will be paid well. Trust me." Miguel stated as his final words.

Snake cocked his head, considering all Miguel had told him. Miguel interpreted the man's silence as reluctant acceptance of the job.

Tor-Tuba extended his hand toward Miguel. "Boom-boom here, boom-boom there. We rollin'." He winked at Miguel.

Miguel watched them leave. Tor-Tuba sallow, wide, and squared at the shoulders like a man from ancient caves. Snake as long and lean as a lash, his venom poisonous. *¡Serpiente venenosa!*

Linda Busby Parker

10

Chang Wu spotted Jerry Jr.'s Pawn down by the water's edge, not far from the city jail. A couple of bail bond offices stood near Jerry Jr.'s. Mardi Gras activities did not extend as far as the pawn shop or the jail. Weeds grew tall. Chang Wu located a path that cut through the tall grasses. With his hands locked behind his back, he appeared deep in thought as he paced toward the pawn shop. He knew the shop would close soon, and might not open on Sunday. He needed to act now.

Miguel Sanchez had not called. Chang Wu had checked his cell phone, thinking he might not have heard it ring — but there had been no calls from Miguel Sanchez. He knew his second load should be in transit from Mexico, through Mobile, and on to Florida, but no message yet from his drivers either. This fact did not trouble him. His drivers would not pass through Mobile until late, maybe even Sunday morning. He had told them to call. They would. He was certain of this.

If everything had gone as planned, both the first and second loads would have been received by Billy Wong and delivered into the hands of the rightful owners. But . . . Billy Wong had crossed him. No doubt about that. This second load would be received by a man long employed and trusted by Chang Wu. What a mistake he had made with this upstart Billy Wong.

He had to focus. He understood this — one problem at a time. *Burdens on both shoulders break a man's back*, another piece of wisdom from his mother. The immediate problem was Miguel Sanchez. He did not understand this man; he did not know who paid him. *Why had Sanchez not called?* But, maybe this very minute, Mr. Sanchez gathered information about Billy Wong. For now, better to purchase a pistol than to worry.

Play the players Americans said. He thought of this when he opened the door to Jerry Jr.'s Pawn and stepped inside. "Let me know if I can hep ya," a big blonde with hair falling to her thick, broad shoulders shouted from the back. Chang Wu had never heard *hep ya*. But he understood. He smiled and moved on soft feet, quiet as a Siamese cat, toward a case of wrist watches.

He walked around the case, browsing the watches, and then he moved on to women's rings. He did not want to appear in any rush—a man casually examining the merchandise. Finally, he made his way to the pistols. He needed a gun, and he did not have time to wait for it. He would *play the players*. When he thought of this, Chang Wu held a smile within his cheeks, not wanting the woman who now stood in front of him to see it.

He spotted a gun—an ugly thing, a small caliber made of blue-green metal. He pointed to the gun. "Interesting," he said.

"Yep," she said. "Sure is."

"May I see it?"

The big blonde went to retrieve her keys. She wore blue jeans and a large purple tee shirt with deep green letters that read *Mardi Gras Happens*. Two gold crowns with ruby-colored stones framed the slogan on either side. When the blonde returned, she opened the case and placed the blue-green pistol on top of the counter.

Chang Wu lifted it. He turned his back to the woman and pretended to fire. "Nice," he said. "Good weight."

He cared nothing for the pistol. It possessed none of the elegance of his crimson trimmed pistol in the bamboo lattice case in his Chicago office. But . . . he needed a weapon.

"I am a collector," he told the blonde. "From Chicago. My plane leaves this afternoon. I'll give you all the information to run a check, and you can write the bill of sale for next Wednesday. What I want to do . . ." Chang Wu continued to admire the pistol. "What I want to do," he repeated "is pack this deep in my suitcase and take it back to Chicago with me."

Oliver's Song

The blonde folded her arms across her chest and picked at the skin on her elbows with the tips of her fingers. "Jerry Jr. would have to approve something like that," she said.

She turned her back to Chang Wu and spoke in a loud voice. "Jerry, come on out here. You'll have to handle this."

Chang Wu placed the blue-green pistol on the glass case. He did not want to appear overly eager.

"Jerry!" the blonde called again. "Come on out here."

A man, larger than the blonde, parted a curtain in the back of the store and came into the showroom. A red plaid shirt and denim overalls covered his expansive stomach. "Need hep, Chaunette?"

"You tell him," Chaunette said to Chang Wu.

"I am a collector," Chang Wu said. "This color," he pointed to the blue-green pistol, "I have not seen it before."

The man lifted the ugly little pistol. "It is nice," he said, his breathing heavy and audible.

"Yes," Chang Wu said. "I am from Chicago." He spoke softly. Every word spoken clearly. "I fly back to Chicago this afternoon. I will complete all the paperwork now. You can write the bill of sale after next Wednesday. That will make everything legal. I would like to take this pistol with me. I will pack it deep inside my suitcase. I like it." He spoke calmly. Casually.

The man held the straps of his overalls as if he rode a parachute coming in for landing. He pulled the straps out, both hands firmly attached, and he studied Chang Wu. "I'm not supposed to do that," he said.

"I've never seen a pistol like this one. I want to carry it back with me," Chang Wu stated again. He smiled at Jerry Jr. He stepped back, opened his arms, palms out and asked, "Do I look like a criminal?"

Jerry Jr. laughed at this. "No you don't. A business man, I'd guess. What's that armband all about?"

"This?" Chang Wu questioned and placed his right hand over his blue-dragon armband. "Martial arts," he answered. "I am a master. A special symbol in China."

He knew little about the martial arts, but suspected he knew more than these two. He stepped forward to show them the embroidered dragon on the black band. They ate this false knowledge as if it were something good.

"Well . . . I've learned something today," Chaunette said. "That's real nice."

Chang Wu took a step back and smiled. He was playing the players. Now he needed to close the sale and leave with the pistol.

"My interest in owning this pistol is only to place it in my cabinet at home. I will fire it one time—one time only—before I place it in my cabinet. I do that to make each gun in my collection my own." Chang Wu added this for authenticity.

"Hell," Jerry Jr. said. "If you take care of all the paperwork. I can go ahead and do the first level check. You got to pack it anyway. No other way to get it through airport security."

"That is correct," Chang Wu said.

Jerry Jr. pulled on the straps of his overalls again—gliding in for a landing. "Although, I would have to charge more." He twisted his lips.

"Fine," Chang Wu said. "That would be fine."

"Guess I can do it then," Jerry Jr. said. "What time's your plane leave?"

Play the player, Chang Wu thought. "Tonight," he said. "Early evening." He smiled—this time allowing the smile to come to his lips. He would have this ugly pistol here with him if he needed it.

"Come on up front," Chaunette said. "Let's get you started on that paperwork."

After leaving Jerry Jr's, Chang Wu checked his telephone twice. Still no call from Miguel Sanchez. When he returned to the hotel, he walked to the counter where two attendants—one male, the other female—stood looking at computer screens. The young woman, dressed in a navy blue suit, smiled warmly.

"Can I help you?"

"Yes, yes," Chang Wu said. "Is there an Asian community here? A large Asian community perhaps." He folded his hands at his waist and waited.

"Well, we don't have a China town or anything like that," the young woman said. "We have a few Chinese restaurants if you're looking for Chinese food."

"No. No," Chang Wu shook his head. "An Asian community where Asian families live and work."

Chang Wu had reasoned through Billy Wong's situation and determined that Billy Wong would need help getting his twice stolen load where he intended to take it. Inquiring within the Asian community would be a start. *Home plate, and maybe on to first base.*

"I don't know about that," the young woman said. She turned to her companion. "Bart, you know of an Asian community nearby?"

The gray headed man, who stood beside the young woman, looked up from his computer and scratched his head. He pursed his lips and his eyes rolled up.

Chang Wu understood he was taking mental inventory of the community. He rocked back on his heels. "Best place is probably Bayou La Batre. About twenty miles south of where we're standing right now. A little fishing community. Quite a few Asians there." He pursed his lips again. "You looking for any specific kinds. I mean Vietnamese, Thai? Anything specific?"

Then, the man laughed. "Well, you don't have to answer that question because I couldn't tell you anything about the mix out there. Quite a few Asians though. That I know for sure."

That was all the information Chang Wu needed. A lead. *Follow the bread crumbs,* Americans said. This place, this Bayou La Batre was a bread crumb. He would follow it and perhaps there were two or three more crumbs to be found in this place.

Linda Busby Parker

When he stepped away from the counter, he allowed his lips to form these strange words: *Bayou La Batre.*

11

Late Saturday afternoon, Mercedes busied herself watering plants on her back patio. When Della pulled down the drive, she placed the watering can on the patio tiles and walked toward the old Dodge. "I was beginning to wonder if you were going to stand me up tonight," Mercedes' hand rested on her ample hip, her left eye locked shut against the low winter sun.

At the last minute, Della had decided to ask Mercedes to accompany her to the coronation. A society matron of considerable standing, Mercedes knew every family who had a son or daughter in the royal court, and she relished the opportunity to attend the ball and offer ample commentary on all things from the royal robes to the canapés.

"We've got plenty of time," Della told her. "In fact, I'm going to take a nap before I dress."

"Come on in and I'll give you a manicure at the kitchen table," Mercedes said. She placed Della's left hand in her own and examined it. "You need it."

Della looked at her unpolished nails. "I do need a manicure, but I'll opt for a nap instead."

"You've been working long hours these past few days," Mercedes observed. "You must be making a pretty penny."

"Not exactly," Della answered her landlady. "I'm working for a song. A couple of songs, actually."

As Mercedes pondered this, the left side of her lips curled up in the direction of her closed eye. With her opened eye, she watched Della go up the stairs, onto the screened porch and into her tiny apartment. She had not argued in favor of the manicure—which Della needed for sure. But, she had seen the lavender half-moons below her friend's eyes and knew Della needed the nap more than she needed well-groomed nails.

Inside her own apartment, when Della looked into the bathroom mirror, she groaned. She headed straight to the kitchen where she filled a quart-size baggie with ice. She had heard that ice placed over the eyes would decrease puffiness, and it was worth a try.

As she stretched across the bed on her cool, clean sheets, she placed the baggie over her eyes and was almost comfortable when she remembered she needed to telephone Josie. She removed the ice pack, lifted the phone, and punched in the number of her ex.

Kevin answered. "She's not home, Mom. Josie, Dad, and Dora are staying down at the Riverview Hotel. It's too much trouble for them to come home, turn around and go back into town tonight. I got the house to myself."

Della started to tell him about the call from Josie in the wee hours of the morning, but opted not to trouble him. He seemed happy to be home alone.

"Mom, you sure you don't want me to come get you tonight?"

"Oh no," Della said. "I've got a date."

"You do?" Kevin asked with genuine curiosity in his voice.

"I do." Della paused to lend more impact to her revelation. "I'm bringing Mercedes."

Kevin bellowed a laugh into the receiver. "Never a dull moment. She'll have an opinion on everything."

"She'll keep the crowd at bay," Della said. "She'll bring her best cane for the occasion, the one with the angel's head on it."

"You be careful she doesn't deck somebody with that cane."

"I'll watch her every minute."

"I love you, Mom," Kevin said.

Della set the telephone on the nightstand, replaced the makeshift ice pack over her eyes, and removed it again. She stood and walked into the bathroom where she shook three extra-strength Tylenol into her fist, downing them with a palm-full of water.

She went back to bed, pulled the cover up to her chest, and once more placed the ice-bag over her eyes. The analgesic would relieve her headache and release the tension from her neck. The ice would take the swelling from her eyes. She relaxed, nested here in her little apartment in the beautiful backyard of Mercedes Magellan, and allowed her mind to drift in and out of past, present, and future.

She had entered criminal defense with a goal, a mission, and her young client, Oliver Fitzsimmons, fit the mold of clients she intended to help—those wrongly accused. She also wanted to help those who had made a mistake, and were, in fact, guilty as charged, but genuinely sought an opportunity to change their lives—people not unlike herself. Many of these unfortunates lived in society's margins. Few folks cared whether these margin dwellers lived or died. They lingered at the edges of life, ignored by mainstream America. She would reach out her hand and pull them toward the center if she could.

The future and her accumulating debts crossed her mind and sent a dagger of distress through her. She breathed deeply and meandered again into the past.

In a directed study with a professor at Tulane, she had been assigned an appeal for a prisoner in Angola, a death-row prisoner who claimed his innocence. She and two other law students worked with an attorney in New Orleans, reviewing the man's case and preparing legal documents for his appeal. She met with the man one time. Jimmy was his name.

She saw herself driving her old Dodge under the covered arch that read Louisiana State Penitentiary. She was so nervous that day her hands sweated. She had not wanted to see anyone behind bars, certainly not a man waiting for death—a man accused of killing another man in a drunken brawl. But here she was at Angola—a field study, an experimental course about law in action.

In her twilight sleep, Della saw Jimmy, dark as deep mahogany. His tooth decay was most likely exacerbated by drug use. She never asked. He sucked his lips through his missing teeth, which drew and puckered his face like an old man, although he was only in his late thirties. Jimmy claimed he had not pulled the trigger the night of the shooting. He had not even held the gun, which the police found in a pool of shallow standing water. His fingerprints were not on the weapon, but three witnesses identified him as the man who held the gun.

"Never put my hands on that gun," he said, his voice raspy. He looked at her, his eyeballs bloodshot.

She had written his bio for her fellow students to read. Jimmy Tucker, oldest of eight children. Raised by his maternal grandmother. Jimmy's mother had been in Tutwiler Prison in Alabama—bad checks, petty theft, prostitution, possession of narcotics, the driver of the get-away vehicle in an armed robbery. Della remembered counting the offenses of Jimmy's mother, making certain she had left nothing out.

Jimmy's I.Q. was at issue. At ten he had scored 78. In ninth grade, just before dropping out of school, he scored 82. The lower score had brought into question his ability to make reasoned decisions, the higher score made him more accountable. The judge had allowed the jury to weigh the impact of I.Q. at sentencing. But the jury's consideration didn't help Jimmy. As a dropout living on the streets, Jimmy had drifted from one backbone job to another— ditch digger for a plumber, a roofer, a carpet installer, a day laborer. He had been in and out of trouble—all small stuff until the fatal shooting.

No fingerprints on the gun, Della had written in the appeal. She had underlined the statement by way of calling attention to the fact. *No fingerprints*. The witnesses had consumed considerable quantities of alcohol and could be judged less than reliable, she had argued. The appeal went to the Fifth Circuit, but was denied. Jimmy was executed at midnight, April 12, 1999. She had failed. The New Orleans attorney had failed. Her fellow students who helped draft the appeal had failed.

"What would you do," she had asked Jimmy, "if you remained in jail, but were not on death row?"

He pulled his lips into the hollow spots where his missing teeth should have been. His bloodshot eyes looked past her. "I'd get me some education. That Baptist school comes here. I'd take me some of them courses."

His red-rimmed eyes closed, and he sucked on his cheeks as if he held a piece of sweet, hard candy.

Jimmy was dead.

She saw young Ollie too. His color was not good when she spoke with him at Metro Jail, and she had seen his hands quiver when he placed them on the table in the interview room.

Then, she saw Josie as a little girl, her hair in pigtails with red-checked ribbons around the braids. She saw Josie raise her arms. Della bent and lifted her, drawing Josie close. She smelled Josie's clean hair and the fresh scent of baby soap. She slept now, holding Josie close to her chest.

When Della woke, the little apartment was completely dark except for the soft glow of a single light at the porch entry. She looked at the clock on her night stand—6:30. She had plenty of time to dress and make ready for the coronation. She didn't need to be downtown until nine or even a little later. She got out of bed slowly and moved softly, allowing herself the luxury of slow motion and the extravagance of time. She laid her evening gown across the bed and placed her new spiked heels on the bed beside the gown. She showered and shampooed her hair—all in dim light, and in slow motion.

The Coronation Ball would be stressful enough—seeing her ex and Dora, smelling the liquor, which she would not allow herself to get too near. She would see all the social climbers, attempting to make small talk above the noise of the crowd and the music of the band. Yes, she would move slowly now and build a wall of calm around herself in preparation for seeing Josie and Kevin walk through the tableau. She hoped she would have the opportunity to wrap her arms around Josie and to hold her for a long minute, at least one long minute.

After she dried her hair and slipped into her olive green evening gown, she switched on the lights in front of the bathroom mirror and applied her make-up. The ice pack had worked wonders—the purple gone from under her eyes, the skin taut. A little touch of powdered rouge on the apples of her cheeks and she looked fresh. She was determined this night, the night of the Coronation Ball, to believe she looked divine. Attitude was everything. *Yes! She looked divine and would have a fabulous time!* She smiled at herself in the mirror when she applied her new lipstick, rose-orange, the perfect shade to compliment the muted green gown.

The telephone rang, startling her.

"Della? Della Boudreaux?" the man asked.

Della didn't recognize the voice.

"Harold Eventide," he said. "You remember me—from Metro Jail?"

"Sure, I remember. The front desk guard." Della sat on the bed.

"I got your number from the city directory," he said. "Hope you don't mind."

Della didn't answer.

Harold Eventide continued as if he had been encouraged to speak. "This is strictly on the Q.T.," he said. His voice went soft and low as if he whispered into the receiver or perhaps he had one hand covering the side of his mouth as he spoke, the receiver close to his lips. "It's all the talk down here."

"Yes?" Della said, now wanting to hear more.

"The booking report on your boy, that young client of yours. It's been amended. You'll get a copy. You won't get it until tomorrow, though. Thought I'd let you know tonight."

"Yes," Della said again.

"That was heroin in that music case. It's the pure stuff. The kind that comes through Asia or sometimes South America. Want to know the estimated value?"

Della thought of saying *No. No I don't want to know, Harold. I'll just wait until tomorrow when I'll get a call to come pick up that report.* Harold was flirting with her. He was risking his position to flirt. He was giving her something of value. Information. At some point he would expect his gifts to pay back. She would straighten that situation out when the time came. He was not the first man to pay her favors.

"Yes, Harold. What's the estimated value?"

"Says right here. Between six to seven million. Zoweeee!" he said. "Your client's in some big shit."

"Six to seven million dollars?" she questioned.

"Says so right here."

Della brought her left hand to her forehead. She was stunned, but she didn't want Harold Eventide to know. "I'm sure I'll get a call tomorrow," she said. "I'll come down and get a copy of the report. I appreciate the heads-up."

"Glad I was here, Della. Glad I could help," Harold Eventide said, obviously pleased with himself.

When Della got off the telephone, she repeated the figure out loud. "Six to seven million. Whoa!"

The thought raced through her mind, *could Ollie know more than he was telling. Okay* she reasoned. *Set that aside.* She would control her thoughts. Another thing she had learned in law school. Place tasks in mental boxes. Slide each box out at an appropriate time and deal with the contents — one box at a time. The secret to a successful woman or man, for that matter — know how to sort one box at a time.

The opened box this night was the Coronation Ball. She slipped the bronze heels on her feet and stood up, feeling like she was on her tiptoes. She stepped to the full-length mirror attached to the back of the bathroom door. She looked great. The dress was worth every penny. The heels seemed to take off most of the extra pounds she had gained in law school. Even her hair had cooperated, forming soft amber spirals around her face. She pulled several strands behind her ears and fastened those with tiny crystal barrettes. From her ears dangled long, sparkling, cut-glass baguettes. The effect was perfect.

Della came down the outside stairs slowly, holding the rail, not wanting her narrow heels to catch in any gap between the wooden steps. She tiptoed lightly across the backyard to keep the pencil-thin heels from breaking through the dirt. Then, she glided across Mercedes' patio with head high, back straight, and shoulders tilted like a model.

Mercedes opened the door before Della could knock. The old woman surprised her when she placed two fingers in her mouth and cat-whistled. "Whew-eeee. You do look grand!"

"I don't want to look grand," Della said. "For once in my life, I'd like to look sexy."

"That too. Turn around and let me look at you."

Della made a slow turn.

"You are perfection," Mercedes said.

"Olive green is my color."

"Nooooooo," Mercedes said. She wagged her stubby index finger with its bright red lacquered nail through the air. "We don't call an effect like this *olive green*. That's too common. Let's see." Mercedes placed her thumb on her chin, her index finger at the side of her mouth while she thought. "The color is olivine."

"*Olivine?*" Della questioned.

"Olivine," Mercedes affirmed. "Actually, it's a little more spectacular than olivine. The color of that dress is *viridescent olivine.*"

"Viridescent? Are you sure that's a word?"

"Of course, it is," Mercedes said, pretending annoyance. She ran the flat of her hand across the front of Della's skirt. "A divine color—viridescent olivine."

"Well, olivine—whatever that is—is my color. It goes well with my hair."

"Indeed it does," Mercedes said.

"And look at you," Della waved her hand in front of her as if she presented Mercedes in royal court. "I've never seen you look lovelier."

She spoke the truth. Mercedes wore a pale lavender gown made of satin. It suited her complexion perfectly. In her silver hair, she wore a rhinestone encrusted headband. She could have been the monarch of a small, but well-positioned, Old World principality.

"We need one final addition to complete our ensembles," Mercedes said. She brought forth a small bottle of perfume in a tiny decanter with a soft turquoise bulb extending from the neck. "I brought this back from Paris last time I was there. I'll mist the air. You walk through it."

Mercedes pressed the turquoise bulb, creating a cloud of light, sweet, floral mist, and Della stepped into the vapor. She closed her eyes, shimmied her body, and raised her arms, allowing the perfume to settle sparingly all over her.

"I think we're ready. Let me get my girl." Mercedes retrieved her angel-headed cane which rested in the corner.

At the Convention Center, Della parked Mercedes' Town Car in the parking ramp. From the raised crosswalk, she spotted Covey on the street corner below them. He sat on his stool, playing his ukulele, his bucket lined with folding money. She shouted his name and waved. When he looked up and saw her, he raised his ukulele in a salute.

"You shouldn't speak to street beggars," Mercedes said. "It's not safe."

"That's Covey." Della waved again. "He bankrolled me."

Mercedes squinted her eyes, examining Della.

Inside, they made their way through the bejeweled and satin-robed crowd toward the viewing area. Walking through the wide corridor offered Mercedes an opportunity to pass judgment on every evening gown they saw along their route.

"Orange?" she questioned. "Who wears orange?"

"She's young," Della said. "She can wear any color."

"Take a look at that, baby." Mercedes raised the angel's head on her cane into the air, giving the cherub a good view.

"A few years back, the official Mardi Gras captains wouldn't let you inside the coronation wearing an outfit like that," Mercedes observed when a young woman walked past wearing an ice-blue gown slit to the top of her thigh.

"I remember when every woman on the dance floor had to be dressed in a formal that dropped to her ankles. She could be drunk as a skunk, but that was a different story—the gown had to brush the ankles. The door captains would have sent that young woman packing if she'd tried to come in here wearing a cut-up thing like that." Mercedes moaned. "Where have the standards gone?" She kept the angel's face on her cane turned out toward the crowd, allowing *her girl* to see it all.

"Ho-leee smokes!" Mercedes whispered when a middle-aged woman, amply endowed, wearing a black gown trimmed in hot-pink lace and ruby-red rhinestones walked past them. "I believe I wore that very gown back in . . ." she raised her thumb to her chin, her index finger at her lips. "Back in '96," she said. "I donated it to the Senior Center for the old folks ball. The seniors must have sold it to a thrift shop. It lives and breathes anew."

"Impossible," Della said. "You would never have worn that hot-pink lace and those chunky rhinestones. No way. You've got too much class for that."

Mercedes' mouth opened. She closed her left eye and studied Della with her right. *A perfect owl. Whoooo. Whoooo.*

"Perhaps my memory did fail me." Mercedes straightened the bodice of her lavender gown. "Maybe that was not the dress I wore. Not at all."

Della turned her head so Mercedes wouldn't see her grin. Ahead of them, Della spotted Dora in a straight, tight-fitting gown that shimmered in a rainbow of colors, changing from pale blue, to pink, to mint green. Her shoulders were bare, a halter strap around her neck. The shifting colors made Della dizzy.

"Lord, I'm getting seasick," Mercedes whispered, watching Dora walk toward them.

"I've saved you seats in the family section. I asked Galliard to call, but I guess he forgot. I was watching for you."

"That was thoughtful of you, Dora." Della said and meant it. Of course, Galliard forgot. She and Mercedes would have had to sit in the nose-bleed section of the viewing gallery. Josie and Kevin would have been only dots, but in the family section, Della would be close enough to see the faces of her children.

Galliard stood when he saw them coming. Della allowed Mercedes to enter the row first. She followed Mercedes. Della sat beside Dora. When they were all seated, Galliard leaned across Dora's lap, his elbow on her thigh. Della noticed his black tie was off center. "How's it going? You got lots of business in that new law practice?"

"It's coming along," Della answered.

"I miss those parties at that Spring Hill mansion of yours," Galliard said to Mercedes, who had been friends with both of them prior to the divorce. "I hope I haven't been x-ed off the guest list." He winked.

"I've slowed down," Mercedes said. "Haven't thrown a big shindig in some time."

Galliard pointed his index finger like a gun. "Keep me on that list."

"Buzzard!" Mercedes whispered into Della's ear.

An entire row of Galliard's family sat behind Della and Mercedes. One by one, the family members tapped Della's shoulder and spoke. This is why she had girded her loins with rest during the afternoon. She had to face not only Galliard, but his family. She smiled sweetly, hugged, held hands, and greeted each one.

She would not allow this night to be like some from the past. She remembered several Mardi Gras balls when she had come unglued. After Galliard issued a negative critique of her gown and a scathing assessment of her hair, she had arrived at the ball ready for her first drink. And her second, and her third.

During the ball, she had drowned her pain, embarrassment, and anxiety in more booze until she had to step into the ladies room to vomit in the toilet. She remained locked in a bathroom stall until she judged everyone was gone. Then she staggered out, hoping only to go home, crawl into bed, and pull the covers over her head.

No, this would not happen tonight. She would do battle with the Devil's minions if she had to. This would be a night of sobriety. If Galliard's relatives thought ill of her, she could not change their minds, but she would take charge of herself tonight, this night when her children were in the royal court. She would make her children proud. She sat with Galliard's family and that was fine. She was an only child with both parents dead. She could have called her father's sisters who lived in north Alabama, but Mercedes was her family tonight. Galliard had his family and she had hers. She reached across her seat and patted Mercedes' hand.

Galliard leaned into the row to speak with Della again. His nose bulbous, his lips tight. "You'll be proud of Josie. She looks terrific. Dora designed her gown. I mean she drew it out in detail. Then she found a dressmaker."

"Not a dressmaker," Dora corrected him. *The dressmaker*," she said, letting Della know she had garnered the services of the most expensive and most sought after dressmaker to be found in Alabama, and Dora McElhenney was first in line.

"Cost me a fortune," Galliard said, his voice too loud. "But it was worth it. Dora has worked herself silly. She's attended every luncheon, every dinner, every dance. We both owe her big time," he concluded. He rubbed his hand across his wife's thigh.

How nice it would have been, Della thought, if Dora had shared some of those events. Galliard paid the expenses, and Dora served as stand-in Mom. But this was not the time to lick her wounds. That she could do later. Della smiled and nodded to acknowledge what Galliard told her.

When the call-outs began, the lights went down in the auditorium and the spotlights came up on stage. The tableau was Carnival in Venice. Della loved this. She had seen pictures of Carnival in Venice in the beautiful book that made its home on her coffee table. Here in Mobile, not Venice, a small canal filled with flowing water meandered on the left side of the stage. The water cascaded down the steps in the far corner of the raised platform and collected in a rock-lined pool on the dance floor where it recycled to the canal on stage, back down the stairs and into the pool again. Della recognized the stage design from her picture book—the Doge's Palace in the Piazza San Marco.

An accordion of stone arches spanned the stage, and open-flamed torches held by masked guards highlighted the central arch through which members of the royal court would emerge. The revelers who rode the floats earlier in the evening were everywhere in presence, dressed like guests of the Doge, the knights of the court in plumed hats and knee britches, cut-away coats, long stockings, and resplendent capes. Through one of the arches, the Adriatic Sea glowed, a brilliant turquoise blue.

"It's lovely," Mercedes whispered. "Nothing for us to do but enjoy." She stood the angel-headed cane beside her legs with the cherub's wide-open eyes watching the stage.

First to come through the arch were the King and Queen of Mardi Gras—white Mobile's Mardi Gras. Across town another royal pair was being introduced—black Mobile's Mardi Gras. Nearly a hundred and fifty years after the close of the Civil War, but integration had not arrived in the mystic societies.

"They have sailed across the Sea of Lemonade," the Master of Ceremonies announced. "They have arrived from the Isle of Joy. The Royal Pair, King Felix and his lovely lady, Queen Kathleen Ruanne Smith." The pair strolled down the red runway, paraded back toward the stage and sat in attendance over the regal court.

Two ladies of the court were announced. The ladies entered the stage from the right, their escorts entered from the left. Each name was pronounced in over-stated formality, as if Mobile's royal court was being introduced in one of the great halls of by-gone Europe. *The Doge's Palace*, Della reminded herself. *The Doge's Palace.*

Then, Lady Josetta Boudreaux McElhenney. Della leaned forward in her seat. She held her breath, wanting only to feast on Josie, who wore an ecru silk gown embroidered with star gazer lilies of beaded crystals. The gown tied at the back of her slender waist in an ecru bow etched with the same crystal florets. Her bronze hair was swept off her neck in a twist at the back of her head. Tiny studs sparkled in her hair. Like her mother, spirals of auburn-red hair framed her face from a central part that gave her face the shape of a heart.

"Look at my Josie!" Della whispered in the direction of Mercedes.

Galliard leaned across Dora. "Worth every buck!" he hissed. "Look at her! Dora busted her ass on this one." He placed his arm around his wife's shoulder and brought her under his wing.

Oliver's Song

Mercedes took Della's hand in her own and pressed it. "She is lovely," she whispered.

When Josie and her escort had taken their place in the line of the royal courtesans, Della sat back in her chair. She took a deep breath. Two more debutantes and their escorts walked through the arch, sashayed across the stage, walked past the waterfall, and paraded onto the red runway, but Della still held the image of her daughter, her Josie, in her head.

"Lady Kathryn D'Olive Fitzsimmons," the M.C. announced. Again, Della leaned forward in her seat. Kathryn Dee was as lovely as any maid in the court. Her gown, a dusky cream, draped her shoulders in rich satin folds. The gown was simple and elegant. Kathryn's hair, sandy colored like her brother's, was swept back and braided in a roll at the nape of her neck. She wore a single strand of pearls, and smiled regally, as if tonight she entertained not one worry.

Della sat back in her chair. She thought about how the Fitzsimmons family must actually feel this night. Their son in jail, accused of a crime that, if convicted, would send him to federal prison for many years. The story had not made the paper today, but most likely would be on page one tomorrow morning. No one could stop the press. On this night, which should be a carefree evening of celebration, the family was, no doubt, holding its collective breath, waiting for the other shoe to drop. The other shoe would hit the ground like a bombshell. Poor Kathryn Dee. If she could, Della would go to the Fitzsimmons family. She would stretch her arm around each of their shoulders. She would assure them of her commitment to Ollie. But, after her confrontation with Oliver Fitzsimmons Sr. this afternoon at Metro Jail, it was best to remain outside their territory. Tonight, they all needed to allow the shoe to dangle, pretending it would not drop with exploding force tomorrow morning.

Della was so deep in thought about Ollie's family, she almost missed the announcer's introduction of the next courtesans.

121

"Escorting Lady Bonita Brownwell Styles is Knight Kevin Allen McElhenney." Della sat forward again. She could not keep from smiling. Kevin, tall and lean, wore his cape, knee britches, and white stockings as if he were one of the original Musketeers. His pin-tucked shirt was so white it reflected light. He wrapped his arm through the bend in his lady's elbow and escorted her down the steps and onto the red runway. Della would have stood and shouted, "I love you, Kevin," if such behavior were acceptable.

After the call-outs, the dancing began. Della waved goodbye to Galliard and Dora, who were holding court, surrounded by a number of family members and business associates. She noted Galliard's tie was still askew, his pants slightly twisted, and his left pants leg was caught inside his sock, but Dora flashed in waves of color at his right elbow.

Mercedes leaned toward Della. "Once a garbage man, always a garbage man," she whispered.

With Mercedes in tow, Della made her way toward the dance floor where she hoped to rendezvous with her children. Hovering together at the edge of the floor, Della thought she and Mercedes looked like high school wallflowers—aged of course, but wallflowers still. She spotted Moss Maple, her office landlord, dancing cheek to cheek with a gorgeous blonde many years his junior. He must have rented his tails because, unlike his tweed jacket, the tux fit him perfectly. He spotted her and waved.

Candy Sue waltzed by, her arms wrapped around a good looking young man. "Miss Della," she called. "Miss Della."

"You're popular," Mercedes said, her lips pinched, her left eye closed against the strobe that shot bursts of light across the dance floor.

Della bent her knees and leaned toward Mercedes' ear. "Nope. That's just my secretary."

Before the dance was over, Kevin found them. "My date's getting more pictures taken. I think this one is for a portrait the family will have painted of her in her ball gown. It'll hang in the dining room, or the living room, or maybe at their bay house in Point Clear."

"A good idea," Mercedes said. "Maybe she'll invite you to the unveiling."

Kevin smiled. "May I have this dance?" he asked, extending his hand to his mother.

Mercedes looked more than a little crest fallen when Della and Kevin made their way to the dance floor.

Della loved dancing with her son, her son with the big and generous heart. She spotted Josie, who fluttered her fingers in a wave toward her mother.

"Dance toward Josie," she said to Kevin. He guided them in that direction, but by the time they made their way where they had spotted Josie, she was gone.

When the dance was over, Kevin escorted his mother back to where Mercedes stood. "May I have the next dance?" He extended his hand toward Mercedes, his knee bent in a slight bow.

"Yes, you may," Mercedes said. "I have always loved dancing with a good looking man."

"Miss Boudreaux," Moss Maple called as he made his way toward Della. "How about a dance with your landlord?"

Why not, Della thought. *It's Mardi Gras.* "I'd love to," she said. She glanced around, but didn't see the beautiful young blonde Moss had been cheek-to-cheek with during the previous dance. He slipped his arm around her waist, leading the way.

On the dance floor, Moss placed his hand on her back. He pulled her close to him, but she maintained an inch of space between their bodies, signifying the nature of their relationship — professional. He smelled of aftershave and whiskey — Scotch, she thought. He fumbled in the pocket of his pants, withdrew a breath mint, and with one hand maneuvered the mint free from its wrapper and popped it into his mouth.

"Miss Boudreaux, you are a vision this evening." He twirled her and pulled her back to him. "I hear tell the Queen is going to ask you to leave if you keep upstaging her." He spun her again.

Della threw her head back and laughed. The laughter felt good in her throat—she had not laughed like this in a long, long while. "She must not be too worried," Della observed. "The Queen hasn't thrown me out yet."

"Because," he said as he brought her closer, "I informed Her Majesty that in addition to your charms, you have a law license and won't hesitate to use it if provoked."

Della smiled. For a moment, she thought of her mounting bills and lack of cases. Moss must have read her changed expression. "As your landlord, and I hope as a new friend, I'm putting the word out that there's a fine new lawyer in town." He cleared his throat. "And," he hesitated, "your gown is lovely. Hell, you're lovely. Beautiful," he stammered. "I'm not good at expressing all the right things. But, you look terrific."

That was the closest to a real compliment she had received all evening. She concentrated on following his lead. She relaxed and surrendered the inch that separated them. She rested the side of her face against his. The warmth of his skin felt good against her cheek. *Yes. This was Mardi Gras after all and she would enjoy it.*

Moss moved with uncommon grace, unexpected in a man who generally wore a sample of his lunch on his necktie. Della closed her eyes and enjoyed following the movement of Moss' body, and she enjoyed the music of the band. She had not danced in a very long time and had forgotten how much she had missed it. One more encounter would make this evening complete. She wanted desperately to embrace Josie and hold her.

When the dance was over, Moss led her off the floor. "How about a drink?"

"A Coca-Cola," Della answered.

"A tee-totaler," Moss teased her.

Oliver's Song

Apparently, word of her past had not spread as far as she suspected. For this Della was grateful.

"It's Mardi Gras," Moss said. "Ash Wednesday's around the corner. You can repent then. What's your poison? Gin? Vodka?"

"Coca-Cola," she repeated.

He bent his arm and extended it toward her. She threaded her arm through his. They walked toward the nearest bar where he ordered a Scotch for himself and a Coca-Cola for her. When they stepped away from the bar, Mercedes and Kevin joined them, and so did the young blonde woman who had been dancing earlier with Moss.

The woman said not one word to Della. "Come on, bad boy. It's boogie time." The band had switched to a fast beat, hot and heavy. The young woman was already dancing a wild step at Moss' side as they walked away.

Moss turned and waved at Della. "Enjoy Mardi Gras."

She raised her hand as he entered the door leading to the dance floor.

"Mother," Josie called. Della turned to see her daughter, who now stood behind her with arms open for an embrace.

Della went to Josie. This was what she had craved. She wanted to feel Josie, the warmth of her, the flesh and blood of her. "You were so lovely when you walked down that red aisle, you took my breath away."

They separated, and then they hugged again. Della was grateful that Josie did not keep her at arm's length. "Turn around and let me look at you," Della said. Josie was even more lovely up close than she had been at a distance.

She wondered if Josie remembered the early morning phone call, or had her memory been erased by too much alcohol. "How are you?" Della asked.

"Fine," Josie said, not mentioning the previous night, nor the telephone call. "I'm tired though. Events night and day."

"Don't overdo it," Della said.

"I'm loving all of it," Josie assured her mother. "A dream come true."

"You look like a dream," Della said, "a beautiful vision."

"I hear you've got an office now. A degree and an office," Josie said. "Wow, that's something."

Della took Josie's hand. "Will you come see it? It's small, but I'd like you to see my office. Could we have lunch tomorrow?"

"Can't," Josie said. "I'll be up tonight until who knows when. Tomorrow I plan on sleeping in. There's another party across the bay tomorrow night."

"Well, how about the next day, or the day after that, or even the day after that?"

"Mother." Josie lifted her hands to Della's shoulders. "I've got Mardi Gras activities all the way through Tuesday night. Then I've got to get back to the University. I've missed a lot of school. I tell you what, I'll come home one weekend before long and we'll have lunch."

"That's fine, Josie. I'd love that."

Josie turned to her brother. "Kevin, get me a bourbon and Coke."

"May I give you one more hug?" Della asked.

"Ah, Mom," Josie said and put her hands out toward Della.

When Della embraced her this time, she closed her eyes. Her daughter. Her Josie in her arms. "I love you," she said.

"You too Mom, but my knight's going to be looking for me. I need to get back."

She pulled away and took the drink her brother had purchased at the nearby bar. "Thanks, Kevin." Then, Josie walked toward the double doors leading to the dance floor, and she was gone.

Della turned to Mercedes. "Old woman, are you ready to go home?"

"What do you mean?" Mercedes snapped. She straightened the bodice of her gown and stood as tall as a ceremonial soldier.

"*Old woman*," she mimicked Della. "Old woman—my rump," she said and lightly brushed the backside of her hip with her right hand. "I was thinking about having another dance with this young man." She patted Kevin on his sleeve. "Besides, I spotted a couple of older gentlemen in there who were about to ask me to dance. I'm certain of it. I think I'd better stay a while longer. I might be the belle of this ball before it's all over," Mercedes tapped her cane against the floor.

"You're not the old woman," Della said. "I am. I'm going on two hours of sleep last night and a short nap this afternoon." She glanced at her watch—nearly one a.m. "These shoes are now spikes digging into my heels. My toes are squeezed like Vienna sausages. It's time to go." She placed her hand on Mercedes' back.

"The party's just starting," Mercedes begged. "Can't we stay?" She pleaded like a young child, her lower lip extended.

Indeed, the party was just beginning. Della knew this. Most of the attendees would dance and drink until the wee hours. Della had never been good at extending the party. This had been another major source of conflict between Galliard and herself. In bygone days, she would have a couple more drinks, enabling her to stay an extra hour or two, but her tongue would become as flexible as rubber and her knees wobbly too, and her memory would shut down. The next day she would attempt to reconstruct what had happened and detested the fool she had made of herself.

Mercedes was different. She was a natural at parties. She loved to dance, gossip, schmooze, but she too had a weak spot for plenty of booze. Tonight they had both succeeded—a good party and no booze. "We've seen the call-outs, we've danced, and I've seen Josie and Kevin," Della said. She sang softly, "The party's over, it's time to go."

"I'll walk you to your car," Kevin said.

"This here your mother and grandmother?" A heavy set black police officer, who stood near the door, asked.

"Sir, I'm too young to be his grandmother," Mercedes said, pursing her lips and nodding toward Kevin.

The officer grinned. "Yes, ma'am. You go on back inside," the man said to Kevin. "Go on. Dance. I'll get your mother and this young lady here to their car. Come on ladies," he said, and he led the way.

Kevin blew a kiss to his mother. When Della and Mercedes crossed the walkway, Della looked down on Water Street to see if Covey still played his ukulele. He was gone. The city was quiet except here at the Convention Center where the revelry would continue until nearly daybreak.

It had been a good night. In her heart, Della gave thanks for dancing with her son, and for having the opportunity to hold Josie in her arms. She had even enjoyed dancing with Moss, an unexpected pleasure. A good night indeed.

12

In Biloxi, Mississippi, Miguel Sanchez took a dollar out of his wallet. He reached his hand in the pocket of his pants and found several quarters. He purchased the Sunday *Mobile Press Register* directly from the vendor who was replacing the Saturday paper with the Sunday morning edition. The Grand Casino and Hotel had quieted a little, but plenty of gamblers still dropped quarters in the slots and a few die-hard blackjack players still sat at card tables upstairs, their drinks on the house as long as the dealer placed a hand in front of them. Three a.m. meant nothing at the casino, where hours of operation were twenty-four-seven.

Miguel would sit, read the morning paper and watch others who, unable or unwilling to sleep, passed through the lobby. He had left New Orleans in early evening, weary of the Mardi Gras crowds, the noise, and the stupid chicanery. *¡Una locura!* Madness!

The Boss had called late in the afternoon. "Is the job finished?" he asked.

"Not yet," Miguel answered.

"What's the hold up?"

"Billy Wong is careful," Miguel had lied. "Taking his time before everything is final."

"What's the bottom line?" The Boss pushed back.

"Quadruple your investment," Miguel said. "Muy bueno!" He hoped his words set visions of dollars dancing into The Boss's open hands.

"Okay," The Boss said. "I have a buyer waiting. You got the account number. When the exchange is made, make a deposit into that account." The boss fell silent for a beat. "Understand."

"Right. Right," Miguel answered, no hesitation in his voice.

"What about my violin? I'll book my ticket to Hong Kong when I get word from you. Soon—right?"

"What's so special about that violin?" Miguel asked.

"Aaaahh," The Boss whispered. "It's old. I like an old instrument. Much sweeter."

The hour Miguel had spent driving from New Orleans to Biloxi made him feel as if he were doing something to improve his situation, although all he had done was change locations. He hauled all his trouble with him. The muscles across his back ached as if he had carried his load on his shoulders.

He ate dinner by himself, sitting at a table in the sunroom at Mary Mahoney's—prime rib over mashed potatoes, salad, and bread pudding with rum sauce. Southerners spoke of *comfort food. Alimento para el alma*—food for the soul—they would say in his República Dominicana. If there was such a thing as food for the soul, Mary Mahoney's served it. While he sat in the old place— the sign outside said the little French Colonial building had stood since 1737—he had felt comfortable. As soon as he stepped outside the old fortress, trouble settled again on his shoulders like cement weights. Nothing could or would comfort him until Billy Wong was found and the goods recovered. Then he would work with The Boss to complete the final sale. He would deposit the money, and he was done. Done with this business entirely.

His own neck stretched across the chopping block. As a boy back in Bogotá, many times he had watched his mother call gently to a chicken. With a little encouragement, the pitiful, dumb thing came to her. She eased its neck across the block of wood and stroked its feathers. The slow-witted bird extended its neck and closed its black eyes. He took his mother's place and with his index finger, he rubbed the neck while the bird lay contented. His mother raised the ax. "Step back," she said in a whisper as she brought the blade down with speed and accuracy. The chicken's eyes opened just as the blade struck—its head now severed from its body. The body flew into the air, wings flapping, feet scrambling. Two, maybe three brainless circles before the body descended, the feet still scrambling in the dirt. *Pollo estúpido*. Stupid, stupid! Unlike the chicken, he would not come easily for the slaughter. He would locate Billy Wong and recover the goods—the drugs and the violin.

He had personally paid Wong. Fifty thousand up front and promised a clean half-million on delivery. Wong's eyes bugged-out over the sum of a half-million. The Asians offered only thousands for Wong's services. Not a half-million. He could still see Wong's bubble eyes. Wong a goldfish, not a chicken—popeyes amazed at the sum, five hundred thousand. He could hear Wong's Asian sing-song. *Half-mil-lion. Half-mil-lion.* "Medio million," Miguel whispered.

He grinned when he thought of this. The kid did not know how fast a few hundred thousand spent. A dream house in Puerto Plata—a solid house with foundation set in bedrock. A sixty-eight-foot Maiora, sleek as a water serpent, and always hungry. The Maiora devoured way more than a half-million in one gulp—a berth to house her, a crew to maintain and operate her, a pilot who drew his paycheck whether the Maiora sailed or rested in port, and fuel. That beautiful beast could eat! Then, the hungry thing wanted more and more.

When, and if, Billy Wong ever put kids through college in Los Estados Unidos he would learn a thing or two. High-end, private schools—the costs soared steep enough to make a man stagger. *La plata se va como al agua.* Yes—money flows like water, in and out. Billy Wong was young. Let him learn for himself how fast a half-million came and went. But still he could see Wong's bubble eyes. *Half mil-lion! Half-mil-lion!*

Had Wong grown greedy? Maybe he figured it out—half-million, easy come, easy go. *Rapido! Rapido!* Miguel snapped his fingers at his sides. Gone in a flash! Maybe Billy Wong wanted all the money. Based on the evidence, Billy Wong had pocketed money from him, from the Asians too, and kept the brown sugar to boot.

Lento, Miguel. *Lento!* Don't leap to conclusions. Maybe everything is fine. Maybe Wong is not gone. Maybe he will bring all the brown sugar to Miguel. Maybe he is somewhere hiding— keeping everything secret as he should.

Miguel breathed deep, letting the stale air in the casino go all the way to his belly. He needed air to mix with the prime rib, and potatoes, and bread pudding with rum sauce. He needed air to mix with the red wine and settle his stomach. A troubled man should not eat. Miguel knew this. But, *comfort food*, the southerners said. *Comfort food*.

Miguel found a sofa in the lobby. He sat near a table lamp where he could read his newspaper. A young woman dressed in a red cocktail dress caught his eye. A beautiful young woman. *¡Fantástica!* One thin strap slipped down her upper arm. A hint. A suggestion. Up in a hotel room, the woman would slide that strap off one arm and then the other strap would slip down too. The thin, red dress would glide down her body all the way to the floor.

Ah!

He would hold that image for a better time when Billy Wong did not hang around his neck like concrete blocks. A young man joined the red-dressed woman. Miguel watched them kiss. He liked the way they kissed, their bodies touching—so hot Miguel imagined he smelled smoke. He laughed. He too would have time for this again after locating Billy Wong and taking possession of the goods. He opened the newspaper and stretched it across his lap, but still he watched the young couple.

The Boss would lose all faith in him if he failed again. One mistake—forgivable. Not two. Miguel took a deep breath and let it out audibly. Billy Wong should have been his salvation. Now he was—*be honest with yourself, Miguel*—most likely the weight that would sink him. *¡Honesto!*

Miguel ran his hand across his mouth. Then he massaged his forehead with the tips of his fingers. He brought his hands down and snapped the paper across his knees. He would read until morning. Surely he could sleep when the sun shined.

That's when he spotted the story. *Brother of Mardi Gras Royalty Arrested on Drug Charges.* He brought the newspaper close to his face.

Oliver Fitzsimmons III, son of a prominent Mobile family, was arrested on drug charges early Saturday morning. Another vehicle collided into Fitzsimmons' 1991 Audi Quatro at the juncture of I-10 and I-65. Mobile police found thirty-five kilos of an exceptionally pure grade of heroin inside a bass musical instrument case. Street value of the drugs is estimated at six to seven million dollars. Fitzsimmons was booked at Mobile Metro Jail, 4:25 a.m.

Miguel read the story again, his lips moving silently. *Oliver Fitzsimmons III . . . son of prominent Mobile developer . . . Kathryn D'Olive Fitzsimmons . . . Mardi Gras court . . . Della Boudreaux, attorney . . .*

"*Dios mio,*" he whispered, allowing the newspaper to rest in his lap.

Then, he stood and read the story a third time, standing beside the red sofa in the lobby of The Grand. That was his load and he knew it. *Who was this Fitzsimmons? How did he get what rightfully belonged to him—Miguel Sanchez?* He scratched his head. The police had the haul now. That was the bottom line.

The wine and bread pudding in his stomach roiled. A line of pain shot across his gut. He studied the newspaper article one more time.

No mention of the violin. "*¿Donde está el violin?*" His lips formed the question, but he held the sound inside him. Sweat beads popped out on his forehead and trickled toward his eyes.

If the drugs were gone, his only salvation was the violin. Even The Boss knew drugs could be replaced, but that violin. Miguel suspected that violin was one of a kind. Something special—but Miguel had not figured out what.

He scanned the article one more time for mention of the violin. The Boss had kissed it when he gave it to Miguel. *I trust you*, he had said. *Tell Mr. Wong I will meet him in Hong Kong where I will receive this sweet instrument.* He kissed the violin again before he wrapped it in that old purple velvet.

"It will be done as you say," Miguel had told him.

But nothing had worked as Miguel said. No Billy Wong. No sugar. No violin.

Now he knew who owned the old Audi he had spotted in Tallahassee. The Audi with the Alabama license plates. That car belonged to Oliver—he looked at the article to check the spelling of the last name—*Fitzsimmons*.

Miguel folded the newspaper and tucked it under his arm. He removed his cell phone from the pocket of his jacket, then walked toward the window facing the water.

On the other end, the phone rang ten times before going to Snake's message. *Snake say speak.* Cheever's low voice—a hiss. *La serpiente*, Miguel reminded himself.

He ended the call. He held the phone in a white-knuckle grip in front of him and dialed the number again, listening for each ring. *Cinco . . . seis . . . siete . . . ocho . . .*

"'lo."

"Tor-Tuba," Miguel said. "Put Snake on the phone."

After several seconds of silence, Miguel tapped the phone with his index finger. "Tor-Tuba," he said, his voice as precise as a boot camp drill sergeant. "Don't go to sleep. Put Snake on."

He heard rustling. The phone passed from one man to the other.

Snake did not speak. He grunted.

"Snake," Miguel said.

"Yeah."

Miguel could imagine him, running the flat of his hand across his face. "Yeah," Snake repeated.

"You seen the morning paper?"

"Ain't morning, man."

"Snake, you know someone in jail?"

"Easy or Mobile?"

Oliver's Song

"Mobile, Snake. You know anybody in Mobile jail?"

"Not offhand," Snake said, and yawned. "I can always touch somebody at da jail," Snake said. "Somebody know somebody."

"Good," Miguel said. "Make contact with that somebody in Mobile's jail." He glanced at the newspaper again. "Listen carefully, Snake," Miguel ordered.

"Who you talking to?" Snake asked, agitated by the tone of Miguel's instructions.

Miguel ignored him. "Have that somebody down at the jail make contact . . ." Miguel adjusted his shoulder to hold the phone in place while he read from the newspaper. "Make contact with Oliver Fitzsimmons."

"Black dude or white dude?" Snake asked.

Miguel glanced at the newspaper again. "I don't know. White guy, I think." He was almost certain the young man he had seen driving the Audi in Tallahassee was white. "A young white guy." Miguel added.

Snake grunted again into the receiver, acknowledging what Miguel had told him.

"Make contact with Fitzsimmons. Where is Billy Wong? That is the question for Fitzsimmons. Where is Billy Wong?"

"Whatever it takes?" Snake asked, his voice sounding more alert now.

"Whatever," Miguel answered. *"Lo que sea,"* he repeated

"Money for my man at da jail?" Snake asked.

"You got it," Miguel said.

"Get back wit' 'chu," Snake said.

"Wait," Miguel said. "Don't forget the Asian."

"Man named Wu?" Snake asked.

"Right," Miguel said. "Chang Wu. Same question. Where is Billy Wong?"

Miguel glanced at the newspaper again. "Might have you investigate the lawyer's office too. I need to locate some other merchandise."

"What's that?" Snake asked, his voice sounding sleepy again.

135

Miguel knew he could not overload Snake. He could not overload him. Simplify. That's what he needed to do—simplify the assignment. He wasn't dealing with triple digit I.Q. *Simplify!*

"Two assignments," he said. "You need to locate two men. Got that?"

Snake grunted.

"Oliver Fitzsimmons and Chang Wu. One question for each man. Got that?"

"One question," Snake said, his voice now heavy with sleep.

"Where is Billy Wong? That is the question. One more question for Fitzsimmons. Where is the violin? Got it?" He repeated both questions in case Snake had drifted off. "Where is Billy Wong? Where is the old violin?"

"Yeah," Snake said, yawning into the phone.

"One more thing," Miguel said. "Read the newspaper. Story's on page one."

"Mornin' paper for mornin'." Snake clicked off his cell phone.

Miguel tossed the newspaper on the red sofa. He went out the front doors of The Grand headed for the beach. Biloxi, the largest man-made beach in the world. He had read that somewhere.

He would walk until sunrise. Then, he would go to his room and sleep sitting in a chair. He could not rest fully until he located Billy Wong. If he stretched across the bed in his hotel room, his heart would race. Already he felt his heart, irregular in its rhythm.

The drugs were history, but where was that violin? *Stupid violin! "Estúpido violin,"* he whispered, agitation in his voice. He did not want that stupid violin to transform into a weight around his neck. He must retrieve the violin.

13

After her successful celebration at the Coronation Ball, Della awoke from a dead sleep and sat bolt upright in bed. She was sure she heard a sound on the steps leading up to her apartment. She could feel the weight of someone on the stairs reverberate through the floor of her bedroom.

Surely she had locked the latch on her little screened porch? Yes. She always did that. But, she couldn't remember doing it.

She eased back the covers and quietly stepped to the window beside her bed. She raised one slat on the Venetian blind. In the dim light before dawn, she recognized Mercedes at the very instant the woman began beating against the locked screened door with her fist.

"Della," she called. "Della," her voice raised.

Della tapped on the glass of the windowpane to let Mercedes know she saw her. Without putting her robe over her gown, she rushed to her door, unlocked the bolt, and walked in her bare feet across her porch. "My Lord, Mercedes. What's happened?"

Yes, she had indeed hooked the little latch on her screen door, which she now unhooked and allowed her breathless landlady to step up onto the porch.

"I don't often ask for help," Mercedes said. "But I need you to drive me to Montgomery. My sister's condition is worse. With these darn eyes of mine, I don't trust myself on the highway."

Della knew how difficult it was for Mercedes to admit she needed help. Always pretending to be decades younger than her actual age, Mercedes fought to maintain her independence.

"Come on in. I'll put coffee on. You can give me the whole story."

Inside her tiny apartment, Della steeped a pot of strong New Orleans dark roast and the two women laced the brew with heavy cream, Mercedes told her story while they sat on Della's porch, watching for sunrise. Mercedes' sister, her only sibling and a cancer patient in hospice, had taken a turn for the worse. The doctor thought her sister had several days, but he cautioned Mercedes to come as soon as possible. "The doctor said I don't have to rush," Mercedes said, "but I should come on. Her daughter just went home to California to take care of some urgent business, but she's coming back in a few days. I told my niece I'd get there today."

Three hours to Montgomery and three hours back. What Della wanted to do—no, what she needed to do—was to see Ollie again at Metro Jail. Visitors wouldn't be allowed until afternoon.

She remembered the concept of priority. *The key to success—open one drawer at a time.* The opened drawer was Mercedes, who sat beside her on the little porch, waiting for Della's answer. *Would she help?* Would she drive her to her sister's bedside for a final visit? That was the issue at hand—that was the opened drawer.

"Of course I'll take you," Della said. "Do I have time to go to church this morning and briefly see my client down at Metro Jail?"

"As long as we go today," Mercedes said. "The doctor said I didn't have to rush," she reminded Della. "I just need to get there."

"Get yourself ready. We'll roll out of here about three this afternoon."

"Well. That'll be okay," Mercedes said, obviously disappointed that Della had not decided the two of them would hit the road as soon as the sun came up.

Before Mercedes left the screened-in porch, Della draped her arm across the old woman's shoulder and pulled her close. "Don't worry. You'll be there by early evening."

Della wanted to sleep some more after Mercedes left, but she dozed fitfully, finally surrendering her quest for sleep shortly before six. The Sunday morning paper was most likely already in the driveway behind her old Dodge. She was sure the story of Ollie Fitzsimmons' arrest had made the *Press Register*. She winced when she thought of it. Dread of reading Ollie's story in print soured her stomach as if she'd eaten a large, bitter grapefruit.

She was flat-out exhausted and knew she would get through the day powered on New Orleans dark roast. She would not rush to get the newspaper. The newspaper could wait. She needed to construct her own emotional fortification before she read Ollie's story in print. She needed to face the story and the rest of her day with calm and studied objectivity. She owed this to her client. *Calmness and objectivity*—two essentials—would ensure her best job on Ollie's behalf.

She showered and shampooed her hair, dressed for church, and made her bed. At seven, she walked down her stairs, located the newspaper behind her old Dodge, unwrapped it, and carried it to a small bench near the back wall of Mercedes' garden. A Bradford pear surrounded by mondo grass stood tall above the bench. Della opened the newspaper cautiously. There it was. Page one. *Brother of Mardi Gras Royalty Arrested On Drug Charges.*

The bitter grapefruit lodged in the bottom of her stomach, but she read every word of the article. Unquestionably, the story beneath the story was this: Mobile Mardi Gras royalty is a sham. A brother of one member of the royal courtesans is locked up in Metro Jail, accused of transporting drugs. *See! Look! See! Money and social position do not protect a prosperous family. The Fitzsimmons family has fallen on hard times. A son in jail! Look!*

Bam! There it was. The shoe had dropped and then exploded.

Calm and objective, she reminded herself.

She breathed deeply, allowing the fresh air above the mondo grass to circulate all the way down to her toes. The last line in the article read, *Della Boudreaux, attorney for Oliver Fitzsimmons III, could not be reached for comment.* When had the reporter tried to telephone her? She had been available.

She folded the newspaper and slipped it back inside its plastic sleeve. She would have Candy Sue clip the article and begin a newspaper file. The stories might be important in Ollie's defense. For now, she would go through her morning just as she had planned. She would not be thrown off course. Everything in good time. The opened drawer was labeled Della's Time, at least for a short while.

She backed out of Mercedes' driveway headed to a little church north of Mobile, a rural community off Highway 43. An independent observer would have judged Della foolish to drive an hour and a half to attend church when almost every major denomination was within walking distance from her little apartment in Spring Hill.

However, had that independent observer, in drunken bravado, ever made a fool of herself at numerous parties in and around Mobile, she would understand. Della had done just that and she was not yet ready to face the upscale crowd of Spring Hill church-goers. Not just yet. She wanted to go where no one knew her and no one remembered her past. She wanted to sit on the back row and take in the gospel—anonymously.

Her first week after graduating law school, she had driven with Kevin—who was on an errand for his father—to a small community north of Mobile. Near that small community, she had spotted a tiny white chapel with long, dark green shutters beside its old wavy-glass windowpanes. The church was not affiliated with any national denomination as far as Della could see, and no one there would know her. Maybe, just maybe, she would feel perfectly at home sitting on the back row in the little white chapel. The service started at ten, not at eleven. She liked that too because she could grab a quick lunch at a roadside restaurant before returning to Mobile to see her client, and then drive Mercedes to Montgomery. She would beat the crowd and give herself a few minutes of quiet time over a good lunch eaten alone. For an insomniac, these little retreats constituted the equivalent of a solid eight hours of sleep and were as essential as potable water.

Oliver's Song

Della cruised her old Dodge along the interstate for nearly fifteen minutes before she exited onto Highway 43 where she would drive past chemical plants that rose from the piney woods like hideous, alien structures. Her cell phone startled her when it rang. She flipped her phone open and put it to her ear.

"Miss Boudreaux, J.J. Ernest here."

"Yes," Della answered. "Good morning."

"I hate to ask this, but could you come to my office today? I know it's Sunday, but I got a few things I need to share with you. Let's say about one-thirty."

"This must be something good," Della said.

To this, J.J. only groaned. "I just need you to come in."

"I can do it," she said, wondering what was important enough to bring the U.S. Attorney into downtown Mobile on a Sunday afternoon—Joe Cain Day, no less, the common man's day of parades and merry making. The crowd would be large and raucous.

First Mercedes, then J.J. Ernest. She wasn't earning a dime, but surely, on this Sunday morning, she was one of the most sought after attorneys in the entire city of Mobile.

Linda Busby Parker

14

Chang Wu gathered information about the community of Bayou La Batre, a small fishing village. *Seafood Capital of Alabama*, that's what his computer told him. Fewer than three thousand population. He looked at pictures of the Blessing of the Fleet. Shrimp boats with colorful flags and banners lined up in harbor while the Catholic Archbishop, in full ceremonial robe, hands in the air, prayed for safe passage and good harvest from the Gulf waters. Some reports listed the Asian population at twenty percent, others twenty-five, while some reports showed this little community at thirty percent Asian. As he scanned the information on his computer, he shrugged his shoulders and spoke aloud, "a start. Only a start." But he was proud of himself. As always, he was preparing for his mission. After he gathered his information, he asked the young woman at the hotel's front desk to rent a car for him. He would be ready for an early start in the morning.

He did not sleep late, and he did not sleep long. Only fools stayed in bed while the morning beckoned. *First birds eat first worms.* Something like that the Americans said. He ordered a light breakfast—whole grain toast, fresh fruit, and steaming green tea. While he ate, he sat at the desk in his hotel room, working numbers on a ledger page. The ugly blue-green pistol rested on the night stand, along with a small box of ammunition. He checked his cell phone several times. Miguel Sanchez had not called. This fact troubled Chang Wu, but he would not allow his mind to drift. Discipline. *A rod that does not bend cannot be broken.* Numbers. He must focus on the numbers in front of him. Regularly, he checked his own accounts. He liked to remind himself there would soon be no reason to do business with the Long Hairs.

For now, he needed to locate Billy Wong and retrieve his load. He needed to shoo his laying hens back into their pens and recoup his losses. *Do not count the speckled eggs until the hand slides past the chicken's leg.* Was that what his mother had said? Or was it: *Do not rest your hand near the chicken's beak and talon.* He laughed when he thought of this. Either way, his hand might be in danger.

To shake worry out from inside him, he reminded himself he worked logistics. *Only logistics.* He had not touched anything illegal. He did not know exactly what the Long Hairs carried. He did not want to know. *Just logistics.* Locate Billy Wong. Retrieve the product—wherever it was. Connect product with distributor. *Simple.*

He had one more shipment headed to Florida. The goods would soon slide through Alabama. The Long Hairs' own representative would receive the product in Florida. No payment for Chang Wu, they would say. You have not delivered *all* the goods.

He would locate Billy Wong. Place all the goods in the Long Hairs' hands. All other distribution points—including Florida—would be secure. *Know this,* he would tell the Long Hairs, *all the links are now tight.*

He looked at his numbers again before he closed his ledger. He stood and slipped the blue-dragon armband over the left sleeve of his white shirt—no tie. Then, he slid the blue-green pistol into his hip pocket. He was a man in charge, a man who ate fire and lived under the dragon's protection.

15

When Della pulled up to the little white chapel with the dark green shutters, the sign out front listed Stevie Knight as pastor. The sign also stated the topic of today's sermon: *Forgiving Number One*. Inside, the service had already begun, and she stood for a moment before she slid in on the back row. An African American church—she, the only white congregant. No. Two rows in front of her she spotted an elderly white woman, sitting alone.

The church, twelve pews on one side and twelve on the other, was three quarters full. Each window of the chapel had a border of colored glass, not stained glass with images of Biblical figures, but old tinted glass, the tints having been rendered from the blood of animals or the juices of plants. A bright rose—pigeon's blood, no doubt—bordered in five inches of sky blue—morning glories, perhaps.

An elderly black man stepped to the podium. "If you've not been here before, let me introduce myself. I'm Reverend Stevie Knight. Welcome," he said and smiled.

Della thought the introduction was for her. Surely, the rest of the congregation was his regular flock.

"I feel good this day," Reverend Knight said, enthusiasm in his voice.

Della thought about race relations in Alabama. When she was growing up, a black person could not walk through the doors of a white church. Now, most white churches were sparsely integrated, but few black churches were integrated at all. In general, Christianity in Alabama was still as segregated as night was from day, as sin was from salvation.

"I woke up this morning glad to be alive," the minister said. He raised his open palms toward the congregation.

She settled in to listen while Reverend Stevie Knight spoke.

"Look at us," he said. "The blessings of this life laid at our feet. Good water, good things to eat, good homes, good families, and most important, salvation through our Lord. Reverend Knight raised his index finger. "Let us give thanks and make our entreaties," he announced solemnly.

After the prayer, a quartet stepped to the front of the raised platform. The four ladies sang a cappella, a song Della had never heard before. The sweetness of their voices, the clarity of their pitch lifted from Della's shoulders the weight of an entire week of near sleepless nights. The singers tapped the beat of the song against the balls of their feet.

When Reverend Stevie Knight stood again, he stepped to the podium, opened his Bible and read to the congregation the story of the Lord in the house of the tax collector and the story of the woman beside the well. When he was done reading, he stepped away from the lectern and walked toward the center of the platform, where the singers had stood.

"I have a question," he said. "Has anyone here never—never ever—done anything you regret? If so, please stand now." He waited, his arms spread wide.

No one stood.

"Don't be shy," Stevie Knight teased his listeners. "Come on," he said. "If you have not done one thing in this life you regret, stand up now. Please."

No one stood. A hush descended upon the congregation as if each person feared making himself or herself visible. Della was glad she had chosen this spot on the last row. She suspected she carried more regrets than most.

"Well," Reverend Knight said, almost in a whisper. Then his voice boomed off the walls of the church. "I guess every one of us has done some things we regret." He paused a beat. "That's what I want to talk about today."

"I want to talk about forgiveness for number one— forgiveness for yourself. Generally, we think of forgiveness for our fellow man, forgiveness for the person who has wronged us.

Oliver's Song

Oh, we struggle mightily with that. It's hard to let go of that anger and grudge we feel toward someone who has done us wrong. But each and every one of us knows if we can ever forgive the person who did us wrong, a big burden lifts right off our chests."

He breathed deeply, his own chest rising visibly. "Oh my!" He placed his hands over his heart and brought them away, demonstrating the lightness of a man's rib cage once he has forgiven someone who has done him wrong.

"But the even bigger struggle," he said, "is forgiving ourselves when we do wrong. Just about impossible." Stevie Knight took a slow breath and looked across the congregation. "Some of us will go to our graves still feeling unworthy, embarrassed about ourselves, feeling like we have failed.

"I want to show you something." He took several steps away from the podium and pointed to a wooden cross that appeared to float in front of the podium, a cross secured in place by clear plastic wires.

"That right there is not just for the rapist, the thief, the murderer. Noooooo. This sacrifice was also for the good man and the good woman who slips into something he or she regrets."

He turned and faced his congregation. Then, his voice exploded. "Whoa! Goodness! This is good news!" He walked back to the lectern.

"What happens to a man who holds a grudge against himself?" Stevie Knight asked. "Come on," he encouraged. "Come on."

"That man gets mean," one old man sitting up front answered.

"That's right," Revered Knight said. "That man who has not allowed himself to be forgiven turns mean. He may take that grudge against himself out on everybody else—maybe his family, maybe the folks he works with. Maybe he takes it out on strangers. Maybe he keeps on pounding himself, beating himself over and over." With his fist Stevie Knight beat his chest—left, right, left, right, left.

"If that unforgiven man's not acting mean, he's going around with his head down, too embarrassed to let anybody see his face." The reverend stood silent again, looking at the small crowd.

"Here is the good news," he said. "You don't have to carry the burden of your past one step further. You can leave it here today." He silently paced back and forth before coming to rest again in the center of the raised platform. "I'm not going to ask you to walk down here and stand under this symbol of forgiveness. I'm going to ask you to do it in your mind's eye. Close your eyes," he said.

Della closed her eyes and listened. "See yourself walking down here," Reverend Knight said. "Come on now. You got a good mental eye. Come on, walk down this center aisle. See yourself standing right here."

Della opened her eyes to see Reverend Knight walk down two steps and stand in front of the small crowd, his back to them, his face lifted. Standing alone, in the sunlight shining through the rose and blue bordered windowpanes, Stevie Knight appeared to represent Everyman, standing at the foot of God.

"Lift all your regrets," the minister said in a quiet voice. "Lift all the things you have done wrong." He raised his arms as if holding packages above his head. He reached his hands behind his shoulders. "Take those regrets off your back too," he said. He raised his hands slowly as if he hauled a heavy load from the back of his shoulders to the front of his chest, his arms outstretched. He took the unseen box he lifted, bent, and set it down.

"We have been made new," he shouted, and he fell silent as shouts of amen echoed through the chapel.

Reverend Knight remained silent. He turned and Della saw tears on his cheeks. He removed a handkerchief from the inside pocket of his suit coat. "This is good news," he said. "When you leave this church today, walk out of here as a free man or a free woman. Hold your head high. Do not be embarrassed to look any man or any woman eyeball to eyeball. God gave us the gift of forgiveness. Forgiveness," he said, "a word sweet on the tongue. Forgiveness even for ourselves."

Della remembered all the times she had covered the bottles of hard booze at the bottom of her grocery shopping cart with loaves of bread and bags of macaroni only to be caught by a friend at the checkout who asked *where's the party?*

But here in the little white chapel—in her mind's eye—she lifted all the embarrassment off her shoulders and sat the load up front beside one of the blood-stained windows. Forgiveness was a process. She understood that, but she also understood she had come to this place today, and she was taking a first step. Yes, forgiveness of one's self was sweet on the tongue. Sweet through the body, and sweet within the soul.

Stevie Knight turned, walked back up the two steps, and sat tall in the pastor's chair in the middle of the raised podium. The four ladies of the quartet stood again and sang their own rendering of *His Eye is on the Sparrow*. They incorporated their own phrasing that made the old song new—rhythms broken, new directions set.

When the collection plate was passed, Della dropped in the twenty-five dollars Covey had given her, still folded in half. She would pay Covey back on Monday after she went to the bank and drew down on her loan, but today she could think of no better way to use Covey's bounty than to deposit all twenty-five in the collection plate.

After the benediction, Stevie Knight walked down the center aisle, his wife by his side. The two stood, shoulder to shoulder, outside the door as they said goodbye to worshipers. As Della left the little church, Stevie Knight took her hand in his and introduced himself. In turn, he introduced his wife, Evie. While Della thanked Reverend Knight for his sermon, the elderly white woman who had sat two rows in front of her came to them.

"You know why I come here?" she asked, looking directly at Della.

"No, ma'am," Della answered.

"This fellow's mother used to work for me," the old woman said. "She brought little Stevie with her. He was one mischievous boy." She wagged her crooked finger in the air in the general direction of Stevie Knight.

"If the Lord can turn Stevie Knight into a minister, a good minister like he is, then I know *all* things are possible. Virgin birth. Water into wine. Loaves and fishes. I can look at Stevie Knight and believe it all. He was one tough little boy," the woman said.

Stevie Knight laughed. "Mrs. Sexton, don't tell my secrets. I thought those things were between you and me." He winked at the old lady.

Della wished them all a good day and left to find a diner serving Sunday lunch. For a brief while, the drawer labeled *Della's Time* was still open, but it was about to quickly slam shut.

16

When Della reached the U.S. Attorney's Office and pulled on the door handle, she found the door locked. She had battled the Mardi Gras traffic, shelled out five bucks to park at the Civic Center, trooped through the Joe Cain crowd — a solid three blocks in high-heels. She had stepped in marshmallow from mashed moon pies, stepped on a smashed beer can, on broken beads, and only God knew what else. Now, she found herself locked out. She scrolled through the calls on her cell phone, hoping J.J. Ernest had telephoned from his office or from his cell, but she recognized the last number as a local exchange — his home phone, which would be of no use.

"You Miss Boudreaux?" The voice startled her. She turned to see a security guard approaching.

Before she could answer, the guard withdrew a ring of keys and unlocked the door. "Mr. Ernest told me to be on the lookout for you." His easy manner and his smile made her feel better about counting out the five bucks back at the Civic Center parking lot, and even her pinched feet inside her thin-soled shoes felt better.

"You don't get the day off?" Della asked.

"No ma'am. Not with this crowd down here. I'm state employed. Rest of the state don't know one thing about Mardi Gras."

"Certainly not about Joe Cain Day," Della said, and they both laughed. Joe Cain Day was "unofficial" Mardi Gras, a day when anybody could don a costume and parade around the streets on foot or on makeshift floats — no expensive mystic association dues and no traditions. Joe Cain Day was *just plain folks.*

When the security guard escorted her up the elevator to the office of J.J. Ernest, they found the Attorney's office door open. J.J. sat behind his enormous mahogany desk. When he heard Della and the security guard speaking, he looked up, stood, and walked toward them, his hand extended toward Della.

The security guard waved toward J.J. Ernest. "You have a good afternoon, sir," he said, and walked back toward the elevator.

"Let's meet in here." J.J. directed Della toward a side room with a small circular table in the middle. "Already got coffee on."

He dropped a file folder on the table. Della wanted to open the file and read the contents, but she knew she had to wait until J.J. Ernest was ready to share it with her—this was his file and his meeting. She settled herself at the table opposite the attorney's file.

"Cream and sugar?" He stood in front of a small coffee pot that rested on a credenza positioned in front of the window overlooking Bienville Square. The credenza matched the beautiful mahogany desk.

"No cream, no sugar," Della said. "Just black." This was step one in taking off those few extra pounds she'd gained.

Out the window in front of where J.J. Ernest stood, she saw the crowd lining the street, many sporting funny hats. One guy had on a grass-green cellophane top-hat that stood ten inches above his head. The hat looked like it had been resurrected from last year's St. Patrick's Day celebration. It reflected emerald rays when the sunlight hit it.

After J.J. Ernest stirred powdered creamer and artificial sweetener into his coffee, he brought the two mugs to the little round table, settled himself opposite Della, and drew the folder toward him. She withdrew a small notebook from her purse, ready to take notes about whatever he had to say. He had summoned her to his office on a Sunday, a Mardi Gras Sunday no less. She had not yet seen her young client, and this fact settled on her shoulders with some considerable weight. She needed to get to Metro Jail before visiting hours were over. She also had a roundtrip drive to Montgomery — three hours there and three hours back — all before she could call it a day. She was ready to get this unorthodox meeting underway.

"Well." J.J. Ernest cleared his throat. "I have one additional piece of information I think might interest you. I don't normally call defense attorneys to my office, certainly not on a day like this." He waved his hand toward the window and the crowd outside, waiting for another parade to roll through the streets.

"You're new, Miss Boudreaux. I want to be certain I give you every chance to understand what's happening."

Della clicked the tip of her pen, ready to write.

"We seized a white panel van on I-10, just this side of the Mississippi line. We believe the truck came from Mexico. Two Mexicans and an Asian were in the front seat. A large tool box inside that truck was loaded with blocks of heroin similar in content, strength, and packaging to what your client carried in that instrument case. The lab is conducting a full investigation. We'll have complete results next week. What we know at this time . . ." He glanced at the information in the folder. "It's heroin in a highly pure form. Federal authorities are analyzing it now in an effort to determine its point of origin. The DEA has sophisticated machines or some such that determine the chemical characteristics of this stuff. We'll pinpoint the origin of the drugs. I'm guessing it's from the Golden Triangle."

"Golden Triangle?" Della questioned. She had heard the term before, but wasn't certain of its exact meaning.

"One of the biggest opium producing areas in Asia," J.J. Ernest said. "Actually, it should be called a quadrangle because it includes parts of four countries in Southeast Asia — Burma, Laos, Vietnam, and Thailand.

"Opium based products are produced in Burma, brought out by mule and donkey and brought to the rest of the world by various Chinese. Sometimes Chinese living in Thailand or Hong Kong. Some of the stuff is transported on your regular airline carriers, and some is coming through Mexico. Breeching borders there is a joke. Hell, you don't have to worry about borders, just slide some cash across the right palm. We think these drug thugs are trying to distribute an old product into new territory, and I-10 makes the perfect corridor." He paused only long enough to breathe. His eyebrows raised when he continued. "It runs the width of this country from west to east, east to west. Anywhere along I-10 you can take your haul north, northwest, mid-west, northeast. If your Asians and your Mexicans get together, we don't know what's next. Down here, we've had heroin under control for decades. We intend to keep it that way."

"So . . . ." Della hesitated a moment, collecting her thoughts. "That's the premise of your case against my client?"

"You got it Miss Boudreaux. That's my premise." He closed the folder. "We think we're seeing a new pattern here. Somebody's trying to bring heroin across the southeast and on up into the Atlantic seaboard. If our suspicions are right, this is big news. In that van last night we found Asians, Mexicans, and heroin. Add it all up Miss Boudreaux."

"When was this . . ." Della glanced at the notes she'd made, "white panel-van seized on I-10?"

J.J. Ernest opened the folder again and sifted through several pages. "Three-thirty this morning."

Della wrote this information in her notebook.

"The Mexican who drove the truck and his partners are downtown," J.J. Ernest said. "We're trying to get some answers out of them. They don't speak fluent English, and they're pretending they know even less than we think they know. We'll do our best to find out who they're working for. We also want to know how they got into this country. We know the Asians came through Mexico. None of them has any identification or papers.

Oliver's Song

We got a translator with the Mexicans, and the FBI's sending a Mandarin language specialist for the Asians."

J.J. Ernest took a sip of his coffee, waiting for Della to speak. She said nothing. Uncertain where the conversation was leading, she thought silence was her best strategy. In law school, she had learned, when in doubt remain silent. She too sipped her coffee and waited for J.J. Ernest to continue. After all, he had called her. She would let him talk.

"What I want you to know, Miss Boudreaux, is this scenario is unfolding exactly as I predicted. This is a dirty little war fought on bloody terrain, the drug terrain. Let me tell you"—he pointed his index finger at her—"the terrain is a hellish place. I've seen lives ruined, homes destroyed, children damaged and placed in foster care, or deposited out on the streets."

Della still said nothing because she could not tell in what direction J.J. Ernest would steer. She agreed with everything he said, but she was sure he was barking up the wrong tree. Her client knew nothing—at least she believed that was the case.

"The battle is about who will run this damned drug trade down our way—across I-10 and through Texas, Louisiana, Mississippi, Alabama, Florida. Then, on up north. If this isn't stopped, we'll be the gateway to the rest of the country."

His voice was low and his fists clinched as he continued. "I stand ready to prevent that. So far we're on top of it. We're working in league with the FBI, DEA, state and local authorities. We'll defeat this before it ever starts." He looked at her, eyeballs to eyeballs. "We need your help, Miss Boudreaux."

He waited as if she should speak. But, still she said nothing.

"We believe your boy could help us," he continued. "We believe he holds some important information about the Asians. We need every piece of intelligence about this operation. Your boy has plenty tucked away in his head."

155

J.J. Ernest leaned several inches closer to Della. "You with me, Miss Boudreaux? Your boy cooperates and we'll work with him. Got me on this?" He fell silent.

"Mr. Ernest," Della said, "I've told you already, my client has little information to share. He hauled that instrument case thinking he was transporting a bass for an acquaintance—not even a friend, just an acquaintance—that Mr. Billy Wong you mentioned yesterday. This was a way of saving Billy Wong the cost of another airline ticket for his bass. He had an audition in New York and was going to come through Mobile on his way to Texas for another audition. That's when he was going to claim his bass. He would have had to pay for two seats if he'd carried the bass on the airplane to New York with him. At least that's what my client believed."

Della went through the explanation exactly as Ollie had detailed it for her—the audition, the trip to New York, the friend in New York who had an instrument Billy Wong could use. "We'll be happy to come in and talk. We want to cooperate. Believe me, we'll work with you in any way we can. I'm just afraid we have little information to share. My client knows nothing about a drug operation. He's a music major in college. He plays the piano and he composes scores." Her fists were clinched now, resting on the table on either side of her little notebook. "He'd only spoken with this Billy Wong a few times. The man hung around the music buildings and my client occasionally chatted with him. We're on your side, but we don't hold any crucial information." She wanted to tell him she hated the drug trade as much as he did, but she remembered her training and fell silent. She had stated her position as clearly and accurately as she knew how.

"Miss Boudreaux, get real. Your client was hauling millions in drugs. Do you really believe he was entrusted with that kind of cargo unless he's a player?"

J.J. Ernest didn't wait for an answer. He folded his arms across his chest. "I'll cut your client a sweet deal if he comes in and works with us."

Now, his elbows rested on the table, his hands folded beneath his chin. "Let me be frank with you. Your boy is facing big time. Probably life. He hauled a sizeable load. Not just any drug either. We're talking heroin. Our local judges won't be smiling when they dish out his sentence. They'll be intent on sending out a strong message. And if that doesn't get Mr. Fitzsimmons' attention, tell him we believe a turf war is coming down between the Asians and the South Americans. He'll be caught squarely in the middle."

He took another sip of his coffee. "Translation," he said, "lives will be lost. You tell your client I'll talk to him and cut him a sizable slice of pie if he comes clean before we have the first body. If and when the first body falls here in Mobile, I'll cut that slice of pie in half, and half again if there's a second body. Pretty soon that piece of pie will be cut thin enough to see light through it. After the first body, he can sing like a Baltimore Oriole and it won't make a whole lot of difference in the time he serves." J.J. Ernest leaned forward. "Got me on that? He had better come on over and tell us everything he knows. That's his best shot. In fact, I think it's his only shot."

"Mr. Ernest," Della began again. "I don't believe you heard a word I said. My client's happy to talk. He simply doesn't have crucial information because he isn't a party to this drug trade. He's innocent," she said to wrap up their conversation. She flipped her notebook shut.

J.J. Ernest stood and walked to the window overlooking Bienville Square. "You know, the murder rate in this community has declined, partially due to the efforts of the U.S. Attorney's Office. I've staked my reputation on that. I've about made up my mind to run for U.S. Senate."

There we go, Della thought. It was now out in the open. J.J. Ernest had his eye on a bigger pond—the U.S. Senate. Locking her client away would be fuel for his campaign. She slid her coat over her arms.

"I'll promise the citizens what I've always promised—a safe community where drug thugs are prosecuted to the max. Every year the *Press Register* does a story on Mobile and surrounding communities as a wonderful place to live. Here in this office, we're going to keep it that way. The citizens trust me," he added.

Della slipped the strap of her purse over her shoulder to let him know she needed to go.

"This is still the best country on the face of the globe, Miss Boudreaux. It's our job to keep the great U.S. of A. safe for our children."

She suspected J.J. Ernest wanted to use her client as part of his law and order platform that would catapult him to the U.S. Senate. He wanted to be the *Patriot Superior*—the number one advocate of country, home, law and order. He was unwilling to admit that while she loved her country, she also wanted justice to be served. She could not allow her client to be used as the scapegoat, earning another notch in the U.S. Attorney's law and order belt.

While J.J. continued speaking, Della sought the key of E above middle C. In her mind, she honed in on a clear pitch. When she had located the tone and established it in her head, she began.

God bless America,
Land that I love

J.J. Ernest hushed. He folded his arms across his chest, watching her. Her voice was strong and clear. She sang louder now, and with more confidence.

Stand beside her, and guide her

J.J. Ernest grinned and leaned against the window sill. On the last line, he walked closer to the round table and joined Della on the final refrain.

Oliver's Song

God bless America, my home sweet home.

He laughed out loud. "I guess I did get a little carried away." He placed his hands on his hips like a football coach. "But I meant every word I said. Sometimes I feel like it's me against them. And, it's going to be me. When you've been in this business as long as I have, you start to feel like you're Luke Skywalker fighting Darth Vader. I'm going to win because I've got right on my side, and you could be Leia." He grinned at this, his hands still on his hips.

"Mr. Ernest," Della said, her voice soft now. "I too love this great country. It's not a matter of who can out-patriot the patriots. I'm telling you the truth. My client knows nothing."

"I like you, Miss Boudreaux. You've got spunk. But . . . you're working on the dark side. Criminal defense is not where it's at. We got one attorney down here who'll retire soon. You should consider applying. Come on down here and join us on the side of truth and justice. Step into the light. Give up the dark side. Let's fight the Sith together. We could be the Jedi Knights."

"Sith?"

"You know, the bad guys."

Della dropped her little notebook in her purse. J.J. Ernest made her nervous with his talk of dark side and light side.

He walked with her to the elevator, but the security guard was not there to escort her down. "Please call me J.J. No more of this Mr. Ernest stuff."

"And it's Della," she said. "Not Miss Boudreaux."

"Deal," he said, and shook her hand before she stepped on the elevator to go down to Dauphin Street and fight the Mardi Gras crowd again.

On Dauphin Street, she glanced at her watch. She had just enough time to get to Metro Jail before heading home to drive Mercedes to Montgomery. She pumped the sidewalk hard, beating her way down the short blocks, walking a straight path to the jail, hoping Harold Eventide sat at the front desk and that he would expedite her visit.

The thought slid through her head — *Could I be wrong? Might Ollie Fitzsimmons know more than he's told me?*

Every man and every woman had to stand on one side or on the other. She believed Ollie. She stood on his side. She would hold her position, solidly on Ollie's side.

She leaned into the wind, almost running. Every lost minute worked against her now. She had nearly six hours of driving ahead of her once she got back out to Spring Hill and rounded up Mercedes.

When she walked into Metro, she spotted Harold Eventide. He saw her coming, stood, and extended his hand. "Miss Boudreaux." He leaned across the desk, sandwiching her hand in his paws.

"Harold, I ran three blocks through the Joe Cain crowd to get here." She withdrew her hand from his meaty palm. "I need to see Oliver Fitzsimmons or I'll be slap-dab out of time." She withdrew a tissue from her purse and patted the beads of sweat from her forehead.

"We may have you covered," Harold Eventide said. "His mother and sister are speaking with him now. Let's walk on back and see if we can piggyback off their visit." He summoned another officer to the desk and led Della down the hallway toward the visitors' rooms. In the hallway, Harold gave no fewer than three high-fives to anyone and everyone he met.

Midway he stopped and pointed toward a framed photograph of himself hanging inside a glass case. "Officer of the week," he said.

"Congratulations," Della said. Harold presented her another high-five.

Several doors ahead of them, an attractive woman with shoulder-length hair, peppered with fine gray streaks emerged from a doorway, a thin young woman stood beside her. Ollie, fettered hands and feet, shuffled from the room behind them.

Oliver's Song

"Whoa!" Harold shouted. "Wait up. He's got another visitor."

"Only two visitors a day," the officer said. These here," he pointed to the two women, "one and two."

"This is his attorney."

"But still . . ." the officer said. "Two a day."

"His a-t-t-o-r-n-e-y," Harold repeated as if the word carried final authority.

The officer shrugged his shoulders as if in reluctant surrender and led Ollie out of the visitors area and down the hallway to the small rooms where lawyers met with their clients.

The older woman who stood in the hallway opposite Della was striking in appearance. Her gray-blue eyes and creamy skin complimented her dark brown hair with fine gray highlights. The young woman beside her had been crying, her eyes red and puffy. She held a wad of Kleenex in her fist.

"Patsy Fitzsimmons," the woman said. "I'm Ollie's mother. This is my daughter, Kathryn Dee. You must be his attorney."

Della extended her hand. "Della Boudreaux."

"I'm glad you're on his case. My son has total confidence in you."

"I believe in your son," Della said. "He made an error in judgment, but he's no criminal."

"Might I speak with you over here?" Patsy Fitzsimmons asked, pointing across the hallway, some distance away from Harold Eventide.

"Don't worry about me," he said, "I'm heading back to the front desk."

"Thank you, Harold," Della said to him, and her gratitude was genuine. She would have been in a holding pattern had Harold Eventide not been there to run interference for her.

"Miss Boudreaux," Patsy Fitzsimmons said. "My husband wants to have his own attorney take this case and arrange some kind of plea bargain. My husband's attorney has convinced him

161

that Ollie will get off easier if he pleads guilty. As for me, I'm convinced my son is innocent."

"I know he is," Kathryn Dee said. "He's always gotten himself into trouble—even as a little kid. Always trying to help somebody out. Ollie can be a real sucker for his friends." She dabbed at her eyes with the wad of tissues. "It's big trouble now," she said. "I don't know how he can stand this place." Tears rolled down her cheeks.

"He shouldn't plead guilty if he's not guilty," Della said. "An innocent man should hold his ground."

"Thank you," Patsy Fitzsimmons said. "My husband means well. He likes being in charge. He's a good manager and he loves his family. He's worried Ollie might get a very stiff sentence. He's trying to cut Ollie's losses."

"He's miserable here," Kathryn Dee said. "We brought him a book to read, but they haven't let him have it yet. They've got to check all the rules to be sure he can have it. It's a biography of Beethoven. Who could object to that? Unless they approve it, Ollie doesn't have anything to do except worry and try to keep himself sane."

The officer down the hall outside the little room where Ollie sat cleared his throat. All three women got his message. He was tired of waiting.

"You do what you can," Patsy Fitzsimmons said. Tears filled her eyes too, but didn't spill over onto her cheeks.

"Josie Boudreaux McElhenney is your daughter?" Kathryn Dee asked.

"Yes, that's my girl," Della said.

"I like her," Kathryn Dee said. "We went to different high schools, but I've gotten to know her, and I've talked with her quite a bit. Ollie sat beside her at the Queen's Luncheon the other day." Kathryn sighed, "Now, I wish I weren't even in the court." Her fingers twisted the tissues she held in her palm. "I think my being in the court is making the press coverage harder on Ollie. I'm following through with all the Mardi Gras activities though. What else can I do? It looks worse for Ollie if I don't. What I really want to do is hide in a sandcastle down at the Gulf and pull Ollie in with me."

"Ah," Patsy Fitzsimmons said, "don't we all."

"Rest assured," Della said to the women, "I'll do everything I can on Ollie's behalf."

In recognition of Della's words, Patsy Fitzsimmons raised her right hand. "Thank you," she said. Now the tears spilled over onto her cheeks. "He's not the same," she said. "You'll see what I mean when you go in that room." She pointed down the hallway where the officer stood, watching them. "Do everything you can to get him out of here as quickly as possible."

The officer cleared his throat again, letting them know if anyone else wanted to see Oliver Fitzsimmons III, it had to be now.

"We'll go on," Ollie's mother said. She placed her arm around her daughter's shoulder and the two headed toward the double doors.

In the little interview room, Della gasped when she saw Ollie's face, his left eye purplish blue and swollen nearly shut. He held his jaws rigid, his lips drawn tight. He looked like an undernourished, abused, and defiant juvenile delinquent.

"What happened?" Della asked. She pulled out her chair and sat without taking her eyes off him.

"Two guys started going at each other. Fists flying like hammers. I tried to get out of their way. I got the backside of one hammer. It wasn't intended for me." His face remained expressionless. His jaws locked. His lips stretched tight across his teeth.

"You see a doctor for that?"

"I guess he was a doctor. It was someone here at the jail. The man took a look at it. Put some ointment on it. Said it would be okay." Ollie's face remained expressionless. "Don't worry," he added. "Dad's already threatened to sue."

Della told Ollie everything she had learned from the U.S. Attorney. She also cautioned him to keep his distance from any Mexicans or Asians he might see at the jail. She made clear to Ollie that the federal prosecutors were ready to barter. If he had anything to share, any information about Billy Wong or about the drugs, now was the time to talk.

Ollie looked at her, directly at her, his good eye nearly searing her, his swollen eye weeping from the corner. "Do you doubt me?"

She studied him, his face distorted from his swollen, red and purplish eye, his jaws, chin, and lips as tight as drum leather. This was not the Ollie Fitzsimmons who had stumbled into her office only several days earlier—a fun-loving kid who seemed to alternate in age between twenty-one and six. This Ollie was hard as gun metal.

"I believe you," she said. "I wouldn't accept two songs as payment for my legal services if I didn't believe you." She fell silent, her eyes still watching him. "Are you alright?"

"I'm making it," he said. His left eye watered beneath the bruised lid. He closed it and blew air between his lips.

"We should go before a magistrate on Monday or Tuesday at the latest. Then, we'll know the exact charges. You'll plead not guilty and we'll argue for a reasonable bail. With no prior criminal record, you should get bail and . . ."

Ollie interrupted her. "Should get bail? I've got to get bail. I've got to get out of this place." He took a deep breath and blew the air out again. "I mean—got to get out."

"As I said, we'll make a strong argument for reasonable bail. I'm expecting the U.S. Attorney will oppose bail, but I believe we'll come out the winner on that round. We should," she added to give him hope—an affirmation he could draw close to his heart as he endured another night in jail.

Oliver's Song

She glanced at her watch. Time was closing in for her drive to Montgomery. She was late already.

When she stood, she thought of hugging Ollie, pulling him to her, wrapping her arms around him for some long seconds. But, the metal in him held her back. His face remained intense, almost hostile. Instead of a hug, she extended her hand and patted his arm above the restraints—a distant compromise from the hug she felt he needed, but might reject. She turned to leave, making her way to the corridor when she heard him speak.

"I'm glad you're my lawyer," he said.

Della turned back toward him. "I'm glad too," she said.

***

Ollie watched her leave the room. He wanted to bawl. He employed every cell in his body to hold back his tears. Iron and steel had coursed through him all day. He had set the metal particles loose in his body when he knew his mother and Kathryn Dee would come see him. He wanted to weep on his mother's shoulder or hold her hand to his face and cry like a baby. He could not. He would not allow himself to do that. He was a man. He would prove this. He had locked himself shut—his mind, his body, his face, his lips, his eyes. All shut.

At least ten times he had told Kathryn Dee how sorry he was. She had wept—not him. "I'm so stupid," he had told her. "Always trying to do a favor for somebody. Stupid!"

"You're a good person," Kathryn Dee said. "I love you. You're still my little brother."

That's when he thought he might break down. He felt the tears behind his eyes. One tear did roll out the corner of his bad eye. He couldn't help that, and he couldn't wipe it with his hands cuffed. Kathryn Dee reached across the table and wiped the tear away with her fingertips.

"Thank you," he said to his sister and held the rest of his tears behind his eyes.

The only way he could survive here was to become the steel man—tough as iron. The eye, which was painful, had worked in his favor. Other prisoners cut him some space. His toughness, his resolve, had also worked in his favor, giving him an aloofness others did not violate. He knew he could make it through this day and through this night. Tomorrow was another day. Could he make it tomorrow, and the day after?

What he regretted most was not having the opportunity to hug his mother and Kathryn Dee. With restraints around his wrists and his ankles, how could he hug them? But he had pulled back when they tried to hug him. Had he allowed them to put their arms around him, he would have lost it for sure. That was the greatest of his crimes—wanting to protect himself from the love his mother and sister offered? Could he forgive himself that?

17

It would cost her a few more minutes, and Della knew she was already running later than she had told Mercedes. But, one quick stop by her office and she would have everything she needed. Earlier in the day, on her drive back into town from the little chapel, she had telephoned Candy Sue with a request, and despite her low salary, Candy Sue was always reliable. Della gave Candy Sue the names of several cases that might be useful in planning a strategy for Ollie's defense—depending, of course, on the charges J.J. Ernest decided to lodge against her client.

"I'm still downtown, Miss Della," Candy Sue said. "I'll go over and download those for you. Want me to deliver them to you too?"

"No," Della told her. "Just leave them on your desk. I'll swing by and get them."

"You sure, Miss Della? I don't mind bringing them to you."

"Positive," Della assured her assistant, and then she smiled— actually smiled. It felt good to have someone on "her team." No siblings, both parents dead, no husband, a daughter estranged, but she had Kevin, and she had Candy Sue, and Mercedes. They were all loyal and attentive. *My team*, she thought again.

She didn't know when she would have time to read the cases Candy Sue had located, but she suspected she'd be too tired to sleep when she finally got home from her roundtrip to Montgomery and back. Her mind would be spinning after the long drive. Reading over the cases would settle her down and ease her into sleep.

A parade had recently passed Government Street, now littered with spirals of serpentine in pastel shades of mint green, sky blue and pink. As she walked toward her office, a piece of taffy, spoiled loot from one of the floats, stuck to the heel of her shoe. She stepped to the curb, vigorously rubbing the heel back and forth to dislodge the taffy—another delay while Mercedes waited, probably sitting on her front porch, watching for the old Dodge.

Della unlocked the front door of her office, hurried inside, located the papers on her desk where Candy Sue had left them, shoved them into a manila folder, and was headed toward the door when she heard a rap on the glass. She looked up and saw a man dressed in a navy blue sport coat standing outside the door, his eyes watching her through the glass. To see a man at her office door on Sunday afternoon, Joe Cain Day no less, unnerved her. She took a quick inventory. The man was tall, middle-aged, his hair neatly combed. No street bum. People still lingered downtown from the last parade, and if for some reason she needed help, surely she could summon somebody. She had left the front door unlocked. The man could have pushed the door open had he wanted to do so. But, he stood and waited for her to answer the door. A good sign.

"Yes," she called out, looking the man straight in his eyes when she opened the door and took a single step outside. Whoever this man was and whatever his business, she preferred to meet him on Government Street, not inside her office where the lights were off and where she was alone.

"Ms. Boudreaux," the man said. "I'm Special Agent Sidney Winfield, FBI" He withdrew a small leather case from the inside pocket of his jacket. The leather case held his badge, which he offered to her.

She took the little leather case, which the man had left opened. The badge appeared official, FBI insignia clearly visible, and the inks appearing to be those shades of blue and magenta reserved for U.S. Government documents. Special Agent Winfield's picture also appeared on the badge. The photograph matched the man who stood in front of her.

Oliver's Song

Della looked at the badge and up at the man's face, down at the badge again, then back at Sidney Winfield's face. She wanted Special Agent Winfield to observe that she was no pushover.

"May I step inside your office?" he asked. "Won't take but a minute. I want to give you some names and numbers where you can reach me or someone else in my division should you need us."

"Why would I need the FBI?" Della raised her shoulders by way of saying *I don't get this.*"

"We think we've got a drug war brewing. You represent a young man who may be involved on one side or the other. We don't want to scare you, but we do want you to have numbers if you should need us. Day or night," Sidney Winfield added.

Della suspected J.J. Ernest and Sidney Winfield had chatted after she'd left the U.S. Attorney's Office. Otherwise, why did this agent stand in front of her talking about some drug war? Neither J.J. Ernest nor Sidney Winfield had a clear picture of her client—a scared young man who knew nothing of international drug wars. But, she had no time to explain nor to argue with Winfield while Mercedes waited.

She took a step back inside her office and allowed Special Agent Sidney Winfield to follow her. "I'll get you a piece of paper," she said. She did not turn on the lights nor did she offer Winfield a chair. She stepped behind Candy Sue's desk, located a piece of paper and handed it to him. He leaned forward on the desk, his left hand holding the paper in place. He wrote down names and numbers while Della watched him.

In a single flash of recognition, Della knew the man who stood in front of her. She came from behind the desk, switched on the overhead light, and stood beside Special Agent Sidney Winfield, studying his profile.

She had never done anything like this before, taking close scrutiny of a stranger's chin, imagining his hair unwashed and loose on his forehead, a dirty beret on his head. In her mind's eye, she saw him in a frayed gray sweater, not this well-cut, navy blue

169

sports coat with a crisp, pale yellow shirt underneath. She said nothing. She simply observed his face as an artist might.

Feeling her eyes on his face, he turned toward her. Like her, he remained silent, but the tendon of his jaw twitched.

"Covey," she said. "You're Covey."

Sidney Winfield froze. Even the twitch in his jaw stilled.

Della did a half-circle around the man. She studied his profile from the other side. "Covey?" she questioned.

Still, the man did not speak. Again, he leaned forward on the desk, his left hand holding the paper in place while he wrote. When he had finished, he folded the paper in half, stood full height, and handed the folded paper to her.

"You didn't answer me," Della said. "You're Covey. Aren't you?"

"Here's my name and number," the man said as if she had not questioned him about his identity. "Call me anytime. Sidney Winfield," he said. "If you can't reach me, there's the name and number of another agent." He lightly tapped the paper Della held. "You'll be able to contact one or the other of us. I've written all the information you'll need."

"This gives me some concern," Della said, folding the piece of paper she held in her hand. "I'm still uncertain as to why you think I need a direct line to the FBI. Is there something you need to tell me?"

"No," this man—Sidney Winfield or Covey—said. "We want you to have our numbers. That's all."

With that, the man turned toward the door and Della followed him. He stepped outside and so did she. Night was coming and already the automatic street lamps had come on. Downtown Mobile was a shade of light gray—the gray of late winter afternoons. The man waited while Della locked her office door.

"Always be observant," he said to her. "That's a rule for every day, all the time, but especially now."

Oliver's Song

"Are you telling me this because of my client?" Della asked. She did not say her client's name—Oliver Fitzsimmons III.

"Yes," he said, "I'm telling you this because of your client. Simply be observant."

Della wanted to press this man further about his identity. At Tulane Law, an undercover agent had made a special appearance in a class on criminal prosecution. *We never talk about our other selves,* the man had said. *Not to our wives. Not even to our mothers.* The students had laughed, but the undercover agent had not. *Those other selves hold our strictest confidence,* he had said. *It's a matter of life or death.* She suspected Sidney Winfield would never acknowledge his other identity. No point in pressing him.

"I'm always observant," she told him.

As she said this, she wondered if indeed she was on guard and attentive. Certainly she would not let Sidney Winfield— Covey, maybe—know she had any doubts. Sidney Winfield turned and headed toward Water Street. She headed toward Jackson Street, back to the Civic Center Parking lot. She'd get her car and drive out to Spring Hill as quickly as she could. Mercedes' feathers would be ruffled and raised on the back of her neck—the old owl ready to snatch her prey from the gray night.

✳✳✳

When Della pulled into the driveway, she was surprised when she didn't see Mercedes sitting on her front porch. In fact, the old woman had not yet turned on lights inside her house, despite the fact that night was coming on quickly.

Della glanced at her watch—more than an hour late. She braced herself for what Mercedes would say, took a deep breath, and got out of her car. She walked to the back patio where the outside light was on, but the house was oddly dark inside. She tapped on the kitchen door.

No answer.

She knocked on the back window with her knuckles, making a sharp clacking sound.

No answer.

Surely Mercedes heard her knock. The rap of knuckles against the windowpane was loud enough to be heard halfway down the street.

Perhaps Mercedes had gotten someone else to drive her to Montgomery. *Surely she would have called on my cell*, Della thought. She cupped her hands around the corners of her eyes and peeked into the dark house. She saw nothing. Maybe a note was taped to the door of the garage apartment.

Della stepped across the yard, walked halfway up the stairs and peered at her door. No note. She walked back to the big house and this time she knocked and shouted. "Mercedes. It's Della."

No response.

Apprehension bore through her body like a power drill— through her stomach and up into her heart. Something wasn't right. Mercedes should have been sitting on the front porch, bowed up like a bird of prey. Lights in the house should have been on. Mercedes' bag should have been packed and the old woman should have already set it on the patio in anticipation of their trip. She should have brewed coffee for their trip too, a strong New Orleans dark roast Della could smell all the way outside on the patio. The coffee would be stored in a large thermos. On top of the thermos would be two Styrofoam cups. But . . . no aroma of coffee, and darkness inside the house.

Mercedes kept a key on the east side of the patio, hidden in the dirt of an urn that held miniature calla lilies. Several times the old woman had shown Della where the key was concealed, digging her index finger into the loamy soil until she located it. "Everybody puts a key under a pot," Mercedes had said, "but this is a much better place. Somebody up to no good won't think to dig around in the callas."

Della only hoped she could locate the key now. The apprehension that had started in her stomach had not only bored into her heart, but had made its way down the backsides of her legs, and now her legs trembled.

She dug her finger into the loose dirt of the lily urn. She wiggled her index finger through the soil. No key. She stuck her finger into the dirt in another spot. No key.

On the third try, Della gave up on a finger search. With her cupped hand, she rooted into the dirt, all five fingers working through the soil. Her fingernails digging, the palms of her hands grabbing fistfuls of dirt.

There. There. Her index finger felt the edge of the thick gold key made at the hardware store around the corner. She lifted it out of the soil, brought it to her lips, and blew off the dirt.

At Tulane Law, one day an older student didn't show for classes. Several of her friends went to the woman's apartment to check on her. They found the woman dead—a brain aneurysm. *Don't go there*, Della said to herself. *Focus on the here and now.*

She brushed the key against her skirt to get more of the dirt off and slid it into the keyhole. The door opened easily. The house was dark.

"Mercedes. Mercedes!"

Della slid her hand along the wall by the window hunting for a light switch. She located a bank of switches behind the sink. She flipped one of the levers and illuminated part of the kitchen. Then, with the side of her hand, she flipped all the lights on at once.

Mercedes lay stretched across the sofa in the den. On the coffee table in front of her was a silver tray holding a bottle of bourbon and a small crystal juice glass. Mercedes' eyes were shut.

Della sprinted to the sofa. "Mercedes!"

She placed her left hand on her friend's forehead because her right hand was dirty from her exploration in the lily pot. Mercedes' skin was warm. Not dead! The odor of bourbon rode the air like a wave. The lid was off the bottle, and the juice glass still held a finger-full of liquor.

Della placed both of her hands on Mercedes' shoulders and lightly shook her. The old woman opened her eyes.

"Mercedes, how much of this did you drink?"

No answer. She looked at Della and closed her eyes again.

This time Della placed her hands—one dark from the dirt in the calla lily pot—under her friend's chin and gently patted her face.

Mercedes opened her eyes, brought a trembling hand to her mouth, and ran it across her lips. "She's dead," she whispered.

"What?"

"My sister. She's dead. We should've gone this morning."

This was not what Della expected. The doctor had not said to rush. "I'm so sorry," Della whispered. "So sorry."

Mercedes did not open her eyes in response to Della's contrition.

Della went into the bathroom where she dampened a washcloth with cold water. She returned to the couch, sat beside Mercedes, and wiped her face with the cool cloth. She wiped under Mercedes' chin and gently pressed the cloth under her eyes. She went to the kitchen sink, washed the dirt from her hands, ran more cool water on the washcloth, wrung it, and returned to wipe Mercedes' face again.

Failure. Big time failure! Della silently accused herself. She should have abandoned all her plans for the day and taken Mercedes to her sister straight away. She was angry with herself. She was also angry with God. She would have been perfectly willing to change her plans had God tapped her on the shoulder and said, *Wait a minute, Della. You need to go on and take your friend to Montgomery.* None of this cat and mouse stuff. None of this remaining silent. A tap on the shoulder and a message delivered straight up and down. That's all it would have taken.

She put this on her mental list to discuss with the Reverend Stevie Knight next time she saw him. Why didn't God just flat out tell a person what He wanted? *Della, go straight away to Montgomery.* He needed to speak loudly and clearly like a card drawn in Monopoly—*Go-to-Montgomery!*

Oliver's Song

Now she had to live with her failure. There was nothing else to do.

A little barb had shot through her head when the old woman stood on the screened-in porch as the day was just dawning. *Maybe you should take Mercedes first thing.* She had dismissed it. There was time—at least she thought there was time. Maybe she had received the message, but had decided to ignore it. Maybe she needed a slap on the side of her head, not a nudge. *Okay, Lord,* she mumbled, *you got something to tell me, hit me head-on, don't just tap me on my shoulder. I seem to be nerve dead.*

"I'm so sorry," she whispered again to Mercedes. She folded the washcloth and placed it across Mercedes' forehead.

Della screwed the cap on the bourbon, set the glass on the silver tray, and removed the tray to the kitchen. She poured the bourbon from the glass down the drain and then took the cap off the bottle and poured out the contents. She ran water in the sink to flush the liquor down.

In the pantry she found a can of chicken noodle soup. She opened the can, strained out the noodles, and heated the broth in a small pot on the stove. When the soup was warm, she took a cup of the broth to Mercedes. She tried to ease the old woman's shoulders onto a sofa pillow, but Mercedes did not cooperate. Della placed the mug of soup on the coffee table and, with both of her hands, she lifted Mercedes' shoulders and stuffed two sofa pillows behind her back. Mercedes opened her eyes. Della lifted the mug to her lips and now Mercedes sipped.

✳✳✳

On the drive to Montgomery, Della got all the details. Mercedes' sister died a little after three—the very time Della had made the quick trip to her office to pick up the legal cases, the cases she would almost certainly not read until tomorrow. She had tried to squeeze one more thing into her day, one more thing too many. The cases could have waited—hindsight provided perfect vision.

"My sister was afraid of dying alone," Mercedes said.

"I'm sorry. So sorry." Della repeated the empty refrain. If she could have replayed the day, she would have done things entirely differently. The day could not be withdrawn. It stood for what it was, as all failures did. They drove along Interstate 65 in silence, each sipping the strong black New Orleans dark roast Della, not Mercedes, had brewed.

18

Bayou La Batre, a small place, barely a town at all—a few restaurants, a gas station, a coffee shop, several churches, and a convenience store. Chang Wu drove right through the little community and found himself surrounded by deep green forests and lush yards with houses set a considerable distance from the roadway. When he realized he had gone beyond the community, he turned around and drove back into town.

Shrimp boats bobbed in canals on either side of him. He turned onto one of the roads beside the water and cruised slowly. This waterway was commercial—no yachts, no sailboats, no motorboats. Bayou La Batre provided the working man and working woman access to the Gulf. Shrimp boats with gigantic nets hanging from tall masts rested in harbor, some looking like they awaited repairs. A small freighter, puffing steam out its stock, berthed near a hoist, the freighter obviously in port for repairs. Several men walked on deck, repairmen or ship crew.

He passed two seafood processing plants and what appeared to be a small ship building operation. In his white dress-shirt with the blue-dragon band around his upper arm and his Oakley sunglasses over his eyes, Chang Wu looked out of place in this hard-scrabble working man's community, but he was comfortable in the compact Cadillac he had rented and received at the hotel earlier in the day. He looked left and right as he surveyed the canals that appeared to be at rest on Sunday, awaiting Monday morning when the shift workers would arrive early.

His exploration was fact-finding, and he prided himself in this. He, Chang Wu, worked hard and planned well. He, a survivor. Survivors gathered information and assessed what they discovered. Chang Wu, always a careful man. He smiled broadly and leaned forward, his chest touching the steering wheel of the small Caddy.

That was when he spotted them—five or six Asian men sitting in folding chairs, mending shrimp nets. He slowed the Caddy and watched them. All the men were old, red lines wrinkling faces that looked like clay masks. They wore light jackets because even though the sun was out, a chill breeze blew off the water. The men chatted, occasionally laughing at a funny line spoken by another in the circle. They were enjoying this Sunday, a day of no hard work, a day to sit beside the water and make ready for Monday morning, which would come too soon.

Chang Wu pulled the little Caddy onto the grass in front of the men, who stopped chatting and looked at him with suspicion etched across their red-clay faces. As he closed the door of the Caddy, which still smelled of new car, one man spat a stream of tobacco onto the dry grass. Chang Wu did not know what language to speak. He knew Chinese, of course, and a little Thai along with a smattering of Vietnamese, but these men did not look Chinese and he did not want to offend them by speaking the wrong language or the wrong dialect. He settled on English.

"Greetings," he said and dipped his head as he drew close enough to the men to speak comfortably. Not one of the men spoke in response, but several nodded.

"Is there a Chinese community here?" he asked, his hands folded at his waist.

The men glanced at each other, but continued to weave threaded shuttles in and out of the nets they were mending.

Chang Wu thought they had not heard him. He opened his mouth to repeat his question when one of the men asked—"Chinese?"

"Yes," Chang Wu said. "Yes, a Chinese community."

The men worked their bobbins in and out of the nets. "No Chinese community. Vietnamese, Thai, Laotian. No Chinese."

Chang Wu took one tiny step back. *What should he ask next? Did these men have any information at all that might be of use to him?*

Oliver's Song

That was when the man sitting directly across from where Chang Wu stood, looked up and spoke. "Two, three Chinese families," he said in a high-pitched, unhurried voice.

"Here?" Chang Wu asked, spreading his arms wide, indicating the entire community.

"No," the man said. "That way." He said and pointed his index finger toward the area Chang Wu passed when he ventured beyond the community.

Chang Wu listened carefully as the man told him where the little conclave of Chinese families lived beside a Catholic Church. As the man talked his fingers continued to work in and out of the net before he lifted the scissors and clipped several loose threads. "Church has plastic statue," he said.

At the mention of a plastic statue, grins flashed briefly across several faces in the circle. "That Mother Mary," a man sitting beside the chief spokesman said.

"Okay. Okay," the spokesman said. "Mother Mary." He waved his arm in front of him, dismissing the other man who had spoken. "They Catholic," the man said, demonstrating he too knew *Mother Mary* and *Catholic*.

"There," the spokesman said, and he pointed down the road. "Johnny, he Chinese. He keep his boat over there."

"There," Chang Wu asked, and he pointed in the same direction.

"Yes. Yes. His boat is *Johnny Boy*. Over there," he said.

"Saw *Johnny Boy* go out last night," another man said, the words rolling around like marbles in his mouth. "Don't think he's in." The man lifted his scissors, and he too clipped errant threads.

Chang Wu positioned his hands in front of him in a universal symbol of gratitude. "Thank you. Thank you." He bowed slightly.

"Had new Chinese man with him," the chief spokesman said. "Tall, skinny boy. Long hair."

Several of the men laughed. "Long hair," one man added.

"Yes, long hair," the spokesman said, and he too laughed.

"Crazy," another man said and shook his head.

Chang Wu placed his right hand over his blue-dragon band. "A Chinese man with long hair?"

"Plenty cigarettes," the spokesman said. "Long hair. Plenty cigarettes."

Chang Wu's heart raced, but he maintained his calm demeanor. "Did you hear his name?" Chang Wu asked.

"Name?" the man questioned. He fell silent and worked the shuttle through the net. "No. No name," he said.

Chang Wu bowed more deeply now. He backed three steps away from the men, his head still bowed. Then, he turned and went to his new Cadillac. In the car, he rubbed his armband. His mother and his blue-dragon armband still protected him. What had he to worry about? His mother had given him the blue dragon many years ago. In all his years, he had not abandoned his Asian discipline. He prepared himself well, and every day he wore his band. Every day he honored his mother. And, every day good things came to him, simply arrived within his grasp. Billy Wong would soon be a *bird in hand*—or as his mother would have said *a golden pheasant strutting in thinnest bamboo*. Just as he suspected, a man on the run would conceal himself in plain view with others of his kind.

He smiled as he pulled the car off the grass. One more time he Chang Wu would take control. One more time he would make right a bad situation. A donkey that falls in a ditch must right himself, dig his hooves in the dirt, and push himself out. *Johnny Boy*. He would find the *Johnny Boy*.

***

In a metallic orange Camaro resurrected from the 1980s with spinners that rolled even when the car was parked dead at the curb, Snake and Tor-Tuba pulled up to the front entry of the Riverview Hotel—Snake behind the wheel. On the ride, Tor-Tuba blasted radio stations from Memphis to Miami listening to a crazy

Oliver's Song

mix of Snoop Dogg, Tupac, and Ice Cube, demonstrating his knowledge of the rappers and hip-hoppers, and leveling it all out with a little Luther and Whitney. He prided himself that a white boy knew all the right jams. The orange bullet had swayed from the Big Easy to Mobile with hubcaps spinning and the entire vehicle bouncing as Tor-Tuba sang along and danced in his seat, the music blasting so loud that when they eased up to the hotel entrance, the doorman flung one hand over his ear and, with the other, he motioned for them to lower the volume.

Snake slipped a ten out of his pocket and handed it to the doorman for valet parking. With Mardi Gras in full swing, he suspected the parking garage would be packed. He had no patience for circling a damned parking ramp. He'd get agitated and might ram the orange bullet through a concrete wall—better to let the half-dead doorman do the circling.

When they entered the hotel, the lobby was nearly empty. A parade was in process down the street, and most folks were outside. Snake seated himself on one of the large couches. Just as he had no patience for circling a parking ramp, he also had no patience for chatting-up anybody, but . . . Tor-Tuba never shut his mouth. He did a white boy's shuffle as he jived, and messed with anybody who would listen. If information was to be had, Tor-Tuba would get it. The big man with a broad grin on his face bounced on the balls of his extra-large feet as he danced and spun his way to the front desk, a young white man with a cool vibe.

The young woman behind the counter laughed. "Somebody's in Mardi Gras spirit."

Tor-Tuba threw his hands above his head and executed a few dance steps, swinging his hips wide and working his feet—a big man's version of hip hop. Then, he hip-hopped his way to the counter, two steps forward, one tiny step back, two steps forward, one tiny step back. When he reached the counter the young woman was dancing too, her hands in the air. Tor-Tuba rested his elbows on the marble counter. "You good," he said. "We got to go dancin'."

Snake twisted his lips and watched. Sometimes he wanted to strap a concrete block on Tor-Tuba's back and shove the pale giant into the muddy Mississippi—for no reason other than the dumb kid could grate like a match whisked across grit-paper. But . . . they depended on each other. They worked a job well. Tor-Tuba could revert to white-boy when he needed to be—and that was now. Snake settled in to watch his partner work the woman at the counter.

"Lovely lady," Tor-Tuba said. "I need the room number of this man." He slid the paper Miguel Sanchez had given them out of his pocket and studied it as if he saw the information for the first time. "Let's see," he said and scratched his head. "I need the room number for a Mr. Chang Wu."

"Can't do it, big man," the young woman said. "Not allowed to give out room numbers." She raised her eyebrows and puckered her lips. "But, I can ring-up his room."

"That-a-be good," Tor-Tuba said.

"But, it won't do you any good," she added.

"No good?" Tor-Tuba questioned.

"Nope," she said. "Mr. Chang Wu's not here. "He got us to hustle up a rental car for him and he drove off to Bayou La Batre. I know that because he asked us all kinds of questions about that place. I rented the car myself." She folded her arms in front of her and looked a bit smug when she said this—she the keeper of information.

"Bayou La Batre," Tor-Tuba repeated.

"He wanted to find a place where he could be with some other Asians, I guess. Maybe he just wanted to find some authentic Asian food."

The Muzak that was being piped into the lobby shifted from easy listening for elevator rides to the real stuff—Gladys Knight and the Pips belting out *Midnight Train to Georgia*. Tor-Tuba couldn't help himself. He took a gigantic step away from the counter and began shaking his hips, his big feet moving up and down.

182

Oliver's Song

The young woman with several strings of Mardi Gras beads draped over her left arm, stepped around the counter and joined him. They danced, turning in circles and their hands rotating in front of them. When Gladys Knight hummed the last of the melody, the young woman stood on tip toes and slipped the beads around Tor-Tuba's neck. "You gonna have a good time at Mardi Gras," she said. "I can tell that already." She winked at him.

Tor-Tuba pointed his index finger at her and grinned.

She stepped back around and resumed her rightful place behind the counter before Tor-Tuba placed his elbows on the marble top again and asked one final question. "Mr. Wu's my friend," he said. "What kind of car did you rent for him?"

"I fixed him up good," she said, without hesitation. "I got him a Cadillac." She raised her shoulders. "It was a little Cadillac, but it was a Caddy. Kind of a funky color . . . sort of a pale lavender." She twisted her mouth, and her cheeks rose. "Guess that's why the rental company had it because most folks don't want to buy a lavender Caddy. But . . . it was a Caddy," she concluded. "Looked new too."

***

Night would descend early—Chang Wu knew this. Already, neon-pink rays of a low sun cut across the water, but still plenty of time to locate *Johnny Boy*. Chang Wu did not want to lay eyes on Billy Wong, at least not yet. He wanted only to find *Johnny Boy* and to locate the house near the Catholic Church with the plastic statue of Mother Mary. After he found these two, he would plan the perfect surprise.

In his Caddy, Chang Wu cruised beside the water where the man sitting in the circle had indicated he would find *Johnny Boy*. Shrimp boats lined the shore, but he had no idea if one of these was *Johnny Boy*. He passed the shrimp boats, turned and passed the boats again before he pulled the Caddy onto the grass, parked and walked along the shore where old wooden docks stretched into the water. He knew he had found the boat's slip when he spotted white letters on a raw-wood frame above the berth— *Johnny Boy*. But the shrimp boat was not in dock. Good. He needed time to think. He would walk beside the water, clear his head, and settle on a plan. Maybe the boat would come in while he waited. He rubbed his hand across his hip pocket to remind himself that he still carried the ugly blue-green pistol if circumstances required.

As he walked, he passed the men who had been mending nets a short while earlier. Now they loaded their refurbished nets into their pick-ups and tossed their folding chairs in the back. He nodded at them, and they nodded in return before they slid into their trucks and pulled away. With his hands locked behind his back, he ambled toward the thick weeds where the oyster shell road ended, but a path had been worn into the weeds along the water's edge beyond the road. He walked a short distance on the footpath and stood on the shore listening to the gentle laps of water tumbling toward land. He would watch for *Johnny Boy*. In his short walk, he had decided it would be best to locate Billy Wong here by the water, observe him, and look for his opportunity. While he waited, he would call his Lily, his precious child. Her voice would brighten his spirits and be a balm on his taut nerves.

***

"Nothing here," Snake hissed between his teeth and twisted his face in disgust.

"We got it," Tor-Tuba shot back in an attempt to settle Snake. "Wrote it down." He raised a note card with the Riverview Hotel crest on it. "See," he insisted. "We here." He rubbed his large hands together in anticipation.

Snake rolled the window on the driver's side down and spit.

They drove through the little community, turned around and drove back. Then, they turned onto every road that came off the

184

main highway and cruised, surveying the community, looking for a lavender Caddy or for something—they were not sure what—something, anything, that might be a clue to the whereabouts of this Mr. Chang Wu. They saw trailer parks and little houses and a few big houses set deep off the road. They saw children fishing beside a ditch and a house with a Mardi Gras flag flying out front, but they did not see a lavender Caddy. Each time they made a diversion, they gave up and returned to the main drag. They drove down an oyster shell road with a canal of water on one side, and all kinds of boats in dock, but—no lavender Caddy. They crossed the main drag and eased along the oyster shell road on the other side.

"Stupid," Snake said. "We screwin' ourselves over here. Screwin' ourselves in this little nothin' place."

Tor-Tuba said nothing. He snapped his fingers and rotated his head to whatever beat slid between his ears.

That was when they passed it. Parked beside the water. The pale lavender Caddy.

Snake braked the metallic bullet and backed up. Tor-Tuba's fingers stopped snapping and his head stood still. "That's it," he whispered. They pulled in beside the Caddy, got out, and looked inside.

***

Chang Wu listened to the rings. Three, four, five. He needed to hear Lily's voice. Had everyone abandoned him? Then . . .

"Hello."

"Lily. I thought you were gone."

"Dance practice, Daddy. We just got home. I ran to answer."

His precious Lily. She ran to answer his call. He needed to hear this. Lily—magic, like her father.

"No wind, no water," she said.

He smiled, his cheek pressed to the small phone. He could see her face, a top tooth missing, two shinny braids across the back of her shoulders. Her smile—the Christian's heaven. *Perfection!*

"Don't wrap a fire in paper," she said.

"Oh," he said. "And why not wrap a fire in paper?"

"It will all burn up!"

"I saw a dragon last night," he told her. "It curled through the streets shooting fire."

"A real dragon?"

"It moved," he said. "It breathed fire. Men rode its back and threw candy."

"Mommy," she shouted. He knew she had turned her back to the phone. "Daddy saw a dragon."

He heard her place the receiver next to her ear again. "Candy from a dragon?"

"Yes. Candy from the back of a dragon."

Next year he would bring Lily here to see this Mardi Gras. They would stand on the curb and watch dragons. They would raise their hands in the air and shout for these things called moon pies. They would stay in the Riverview Hotel where they could step to their window and watch the Navy ships in harbor. He would bring her here while she was yet young enough that ships and dragons would make her eyes sparkle. Magic dragons. Dragons that bent to let men step on their backs. Dragons that blew fire and smoke to amuse little ones who lined the streets.

As he talked with Lily, he walked back toward the oyster shell road. "Daddy," she said. "When you bow, bow low."

Not exactly right, he thought. *If you bow, bow low.* He did not correct her because her voice was excited, and he could see her beautiful face through her excited voice.

He could give Lily a proverb. Two proverbs came to mind. *A good heart does not fear the dark.* He could say, *Once on a tiger's back, hold on tight. It's difficult to set yourself aright.* These needed explanation. He would wait until they sat together in their living room in Chicago. He would give her these when they talked—her face to his face.

As he came around the tall weeks and established himself again on the oyster shell road, a car cruised toward him, a car painted metallic orange with an engine that roared. Chang Wu increased his pace. Night was coming quickly. He should be inside his car, watching for *Johnny Boy* to cruise in.

The driver of the car stopped in front of Chang Wu—in the path—its lights on bright, even though the sun was not yet down.

He had to create a new path to get past the orange car and get to his own car. He was alone here—just him and whoever was in that orange car. He increased his pace. Now, almost a jog.

"Lily," he said, panting into the receiver. "I will call tomorrow."

"I love you, Daddy," she said.

He did not answer back. He held his phone in his fist and increased his steps. He needed to get past this car. No reason to fear anyone in this car. *Calm*, he said to himself. Yet his heart raced. His feet pressed down weeds as he made his way toward the car.

When he drew near, two men got out—the engine still running, the headlights on, the doors open. One African man, the other a large pale man, squared as an enormous quadrangle. The odd word—*quadrangle*—echoed through Chang Wu's head. *Quadrangle*. The African man wore dark glasses. *Why dark glasses?* The moon would soon rise. This man with the dark glasses, tall and lean as a rope. *Once bit by a snake, a man fears a rope all his life.* His mother had said this. He remembered it now.

The two men waited for him beside the opened car door.

Chang Wu did not lope now because the men stood between him and his car. He walked. He wanted his demeanor to say. *There is no problem here.* Yet his heart raced. *These men want only some time by the water. Calm. No need to fear.*

Chang Wu lifted his fingers to his blue dragon armband. The pads of his fingers rubbed the silk threads, feeling the dragon's fangs and the curve of his fierce tail. Then he slid his hand into his pocket until his fingers rested on the ugly blue and green pistol. He was ready if these men intended trouble.

19

Ollie stretched out on his metal cot and read the paperback his mother had brought him. After careful inspection, the guard, dangling the book from its spine and flipping through the pages, had allowed this one book. One book and only one. A biography of Beethoven.

"I thought they might let you have it," Patsy Fitzsimmons had said to her son earlier in the afternoon. "Who would object to a biography of Beethoven?"

He was lucky to have the paperback and now he read it with his good eye. He closed his left eye, which was matted nearly shut. He would have placed a warm cloth over his bad eye—if he had a warm cloth. He had none, so he shut his eye. If he kept his injured eye open, the page in front of him blurred. He was taxing his right eye by making it pull double duty, but he had a book to read. A luxury he had not expected.

Several hours earlier the man who shared his cell had been removed. No one else had yet taken his place, but Ollie was sure that before morning, someone would be brought in. Mobile Metro Jail was bursting at the seams. While chaos reigned all around him, Oliver Fitzsimmons did his best to rest on his uncomfortable cot and read.

He had followed Beethoven through his early years in Bonn, through the awful years when his tyrannical father made life for the young Ludwig a living hell. Despite the differences Ollie had with his own father, he recognized his Dad's goodness by comparison to the senior Beethoven.

Yesterday, his father had sat in the visitation room with tears in his eyes. He had never seen his father like that. Yet, the two were still at odds. His dad wanted him to take Bobby Jack Arnold as his attorney and allow Bobby Jack to arrange a plea bargain.

"Problem is, Dad, I'm not guilty."

His father wiped his eyes with the backside of his hand. "I doubt you're telling everything you know," he had said.

"I've told everything, Dad."

Ollie suspected his father believed he was innocent of procuring or selling drugs—perhaps even innocent of using them—but had knowingly helped a friend, a drug user or seller and, in the process, had backed himself into real trouble. Ollie knew his story was difficult to believe, but what his father could not or would not fully process was that Billy Wong was not a friend, only an acquaintance and, in truth, he thought he transported only a bass. He knew nothing of the drugs until he opened the case at the fishing camp. He had explained this to his dad at least ten times and still his father said, "let Bobby Jack handle it. He'll know what to do."

In the life of Beethoven, Ollie was now at the part where the composer had turned eighteen, his father had died and Beethoven had assumed responsibility for his two younger brothers. Ollie figured Beethoven's eighteen years were pretty close to his own twenty-one. Actually, Beethoven might have been older at eighteen than Ollie would be at maybe twenty-five—a strange concept, but he had never had to earn all of his own living, nor had he had responsibility for raising younger siblings. Certainly Beethoven had suffered enough to be mature beyond his years. Ollie was determined that, like Beethoven, he too would grow into maturity. If this current trouble did not crush him, it would make him wiser and stronger.

He read on, blocking out everything around him. He could hyper-focus. He could narrow in so tightly until the only thing in existence was whatever was in front of him. As a boy, he had played Nintendo with both hands—left hand opposing the right. Controllers in both fists. His fingers gripped the joy sticks while Mario spun and jumped, avoiding all manner of booby traps— mines exploding around him, monsters rising out of nowhere. Ollie's parents watched him in amazement. Friends of his parents would come into the den after a dinner party and watch Ollie play Nintendo, left hand vs. right hand. Each hand performing nearly equally, each winning a fair share of matches.

"How do you do that?" his parents' friends had asked.

"He doesn't break focus," his father had said. "The kid zeros in on one thing and doesn't see anything else around him. We can call him to dinner six times and he won't hear us until we come in and take the controllers out of his hands. Then, he hears us," his father had said, and laughed.

This was what Ollie did now. He hyper-focused. The only place in existence was Bonn, Germany, the only years in existence were the 1770s. He was out of this place and into another. He read on as those around young Ludwig Van Beethoven began to realize he had been gifted with musical genius.

Ollie was not aware of the three men who had come into his cell—two white, one black—until the young white man, his head shaved and tattoos up and down his fingers, knocked the book from Ollie's hands. In rapid reflex, he shot up. His chest collided with the fist of the young black man who stood in the middle.

"We got a question," the shaved-head, the leader of the pack, said. He brought his face close to Ollie's.

"What's happening?" Ollie asked. "Guard!" he shouted. "Guard!"

"One question," the man said. Spit hit Ollie's cheek. The face of the man in front of him was so close, it looked as if he peered from a mirror that distorted shapes. The man's nose was flared, the skin of his cheeks pocked, his blue eyes enraged, his lips narrowed in furor.

In a flash, Ollie knew what these men wanted. They thought somehow he had been responsible for the fight earlier in the day— the little disturbance in which he had received a black eye. He started to explain that he had nothing to do with the earlier hassle. It was not his doing. In fact, neither man had intended to hit him. He got the back side of one of the men's fists as the man drew back to swing at the other guy. "I had nothing to do with it!" he shouted. "I was not involved!"

"One question," the narrow lips said. The two other men flanked him—one at Ollie's head, one at his feet.

"Question," the man in his face said. "Where's Billy Wong?"

"What?" Ollie asked. "Wong?" he asked.

With his balled fist, the man in front of him hit Ollie's chest so hard it sent him thumping against the metal cot. His head reverberated from impact with the metal slab.

"Billy Wong," the man demanded, his lips set tight.

"How do you know Billy Wong?" Ollie gasped. "I don't know where he is," he shot back so quickly spit flew from his own mouth. "Guard!" he shouted. "Guard!"

His feet kicked. Thrusting out. Pounding the air. The man at his feet grabbed his legs, pressing down on his knees. Locking his knee caps.

The enraged blue-eyed man in front of Ollie punched him in his stomach, snatching his breath away. In reflex motion, Ollie sat halfway up, unable to breathe. He opened his mouth to force air down his throat. The air stuck in his mouth. The man in his face struck him with an iron fist into the muscles of his upper right arm.

He had to fight or he would die. His only chance to save his life. Where were the guards?

Ollie thrust himself up, scattering the men around him. Then, he saw it coming. The enormous fist of the man closest to his head. He dodged, but the blow hit him solidly in his left temple. The pain deadening. Darkness came toward Ollie like the eye of a camera stopping down. He raised his arm, trying to close his hand into a fist, but his hand did not work. He ordered his hand to ball a fist, but it did not obey.

The man at the foot of the cot kicked Ollie's hip. A hard blow that thrust him against the wall. His head cracked against the concrete.

Oliver's Song

The eye of the camera grew smaller. Smaller. Blackness closed in until only a pinhole of light remained. He felt another blow on his leg—his thigh, he thought. Then, the pinhole of light was gone.

Linda Busby Parker

20

On the drive home from Montgomery, close to the Evergreen exit, Della's cell phone rang, startling her. She reached for the phone, but dropped it in her lap. When she finally got the phone to her ear, she was afraid the caller was gone.

"Miss Boudreaux."

Della didn't recognize the man's voice.

"Oliver Fitzsimmons here. Ollie's at the hospital."

"The hospital? Did his eye get worse?"

"Beaten up at the jail. Let's see—so far the doctors are concerned about a possible concussion, a cut under his eye, the blackened eye at that, and he has broken bones in his leg. Left leg. The cut under his eye took twenty stitches. They're still evaluating for other problems."

"Beaten up at the jail?" Della asked again, trying to make sense of what she was hearing.

"Beaten in his cell," Oliver Sr. replied. "They got an investigation underway already. I'm screaming bloody murder over this. Got my attorney, Bobby Jack Arnold, on it."

"How's Ollie holding up?" In her mind's eye, she saw Ollie as she had seen him earlier in the day—tough, and yet how miserable he had looked.

"Doctors are watching him. He's conscious. That's a good sign. They've put a cast on his leg. The eye looks bad. They've got an ophthalmologist coming first thing in the morning. He can't talk much. I forgot to mention he's got a cut, a real bad cut, inside his lower lip. His tooth must have cut into it. Lucky he's still got teeth," Oliver Sr. added.

"I'm driving back from Montgomery. I'll come to the hospital as soon as I get back into town."

"No. It's late. Under the circumstances, the brass down at the jail are letting me stay with him tonight. It's more than a little scary when your kid gets beat up when he's under lock and key, and the police are supposed to be guarding him."

"No explanation yet for what happened?" Della asked, the phone pressed tightly to her ear.

"Nope. None. They do have a guard outside the door here at the hospital. I hope he stays awake tonight. Nobody seems to know what's going on, but Ollie needs some protection. I mean with what's already happened."

"Are you sure you don't want me to come to the hospital tonight?"

"Not sure they'd let you in tonight anyway. You come tomorrow. That's soon enough."

Della punched her cell phone off and placed it on the passenger seat. What to make of this? *Why would Ollie have been beaten in his jail cell? How did the assailants get into his cell?*

The roadway was dark, illumined only by her headlights. An appropriate metaphor for her situation. She moved in darkness until she could cast some light on their paths—all of their paths. Ollie's father was as confounded as was she. If Bobby Jack Arnold was handling the situation at the jail, she would have to speak with him. So strange how life threw people together. Bobby Jack's reputation labeled him one of the most flamboyant defense attorneys in Mobile and he had an ego that went hand-in-hand with his reputation. She would talk to Moss Maple about him before she ventured into Bobby Jack's territory.

Why had Ollie been beaten—and at the jail, no less?

Her job tonight was only to get herself home safely and to sleep. Rest, so she could focus tomorrow and help her client. She thought again of the drawers. Open only one drawer at a time. Tonight the opened drawer was Rest. Tomorrow, the opened drawer would be *Oliver Fitzsimmons III*. Deal with the contents of one drawer at a time.

Oliver's Song

When Della pulled into the driveway of the big house in Spring Hill, she thought again of Mercedes. They had hugged awkwardly when Della left her with family in Montgomery to make arrangements for her sister's funeral. Truly, if she could replay the day and do things differently, she would. Mercedes had been kind to her, and she had let her friend down. "I'll come get you when you're ready to come home," she had told Mercedes.

"We'll see. Take care of yourself," Mercedes said just before Della closed her car door and headed back to Mobile.

"You too," Della said.

She took Mercedes' concern as one tiny step toward their reconciliation. Tomorrow she would call her friend to check on her. She would call every day. If Mercedes needed her, she would drive back to Montgomery. She only hoped her client, now in the hospital, and her friend, now in mourning, would not both need her at precisely the same moment.

She was glad she had remembered to leave Mercedes' patio lights on. It was nearly one a.m., but the outside lights illuminated the back yard.

Inside her apartment, she showered, and got into bed, but just as she suspected, she couldn't sleep. She got out of bed, found the cases Candy Sue had located for her, took those to bed and propped herself on her elbow to read. The opened drawer could be labeled Rest, but the body wasn't going to rest before it was ready. She read until she fell asleep, her bedside lamp still on, the legal cases beside her pillow, her reading glasses beside the legal cases.

The sound of breaking glass woke her. She bolted upright in bed, her heart racing. Had Mercedes stepped out on her patio and broken something? Maybe she had fallen. Then she remembered—Mercedes was not at home. Mercedes was in Montgomery. She was home alone.

She turned off the light on her bedside table, got out of bed, and stepped to the window. She got down on her knees and opened one slat on the Venetian blinds. The backyard was dark except for the light of the moon. The lights on Mercedes' patio were out. The light inside her screened-in porch still burned, illuminating the steps and a small area below.

Call the police? Or 911?

That's when she saw the shadow of a man below. The shadow made possible by her dim porch light and by a nearly full moon. The man's reflection stretched across the backyard. The gargantuan image hulked like a cave man, but it danced a slow-footed rhythmic rocking.

She did not stand. She crawled to her nightstand where she lifted the phone and dialed 911.

"A man's in my back yard. I'm positive. I see his shadow. He's knocked out the patio lights. I'm in the garage apartment. Not the big house. I'm here alone."

She gave the dispatcher the address, her voice trembling.

"Hurry," she whispered. "Hurry!"

She remembered Moss' address and telephone number were on a small slip of paper in her pocketbook. He had given her the information in case she had any problems with her leased office. She had glanced at his address and realized he lived only several blocks from Mercedes' home. "You're my neighbor," he'd said. He knew where she lived—behind the big house on Mercedes' estate.

Like the shadow in the backyard, she hunched over, not wanting to walk at full height for fear the man outside might spot her. Carrying the telephone with her, she crept to the dining room chair where she had left her purse. She squatted beside the chair, opened her purse and dug around for Moss' number.

Her hands trembled. *Where was that paper?*

She tipped her purse upside down on the rug, allowing all the contents to drop out. In the dim light filtering inside from the bulb on the porch, she found the folded piece of paper. At that very moment, she felt the weight of the shadowed man on her steps. He was coming up the stairs to the screened-in porch.

Della stood again at half height and moved swiftly back toward the bed, not wanting to be near the door. She lifted her reading glasses from the bed. Holding the small piece of paper at an angle so that it caught a shaft of light from the porch, she dialed Moss' number.

The phone rang.

No answer.

She felt the weight of the man coming closer. He rocked the banister back and forth.

Four, five, six rings. No answer.

Please Moss. Please!

"'lo."

"Moss. It's Della Boudreaux." She whispered, not wanting the man outside to hear her.

Moss cleared his throat. "Della?"

"Moss, a man is on my back steps. I'm here alone. I've called 911. The police aren't here yet."

"I'll be right there," he said. "I'll bring my pistol. Get on the floor and stay there. If you got a gun," he said, "don't shoot me."

"I don't have a gun," she whispered.

She felt the whole apartment sway. The banister squeaked as the man rocked it like the masked men who rocked back and forth around their posts on the Mardi Gras floats.

She heard a whiz. An explosion. Glass shattered at the same instant the light on her porch went out. Her entire body trembled. She was now in darkness.

She raised her gown above her knees and crawled to the far side of the bed where she stretched flat on the floor—the telephone still in her hand. The apartment no longer rocked. *Where was he? What was he doing?*

Her mouth was as dry as old wood. Still she clutched the phone in her right hand. Her ears—finely tuned to hear any movement on the steps. Darkness all around her.

199

She could call Kevin. Galliard lived in a new neighborhood in west Mobile. Kevin couldn't reach her in under fifteen minutes—maybe twenty. No point in that.

Where were the police? Where was Moss? Had it been seconds? A minute? Maybe two minutes. Maybe three. She breathed and counted. *One-one-thousand. Two-one-thousand. Three-one-thousand.*

Come on Moss! Four-one-thousand.

Where was the man? Would he shoot off the porch latch or rip the screen? She pulled air between her clinched teeth. *Ten-one-thousand.*

The telephone she clutched in her right hand rang, sending a pang of alarm through her body. Her heartbeat tripled. She lifted the receiver and whispered, "hello."

"I'm out here," Moss said. "I'm coming in the yard." She heard him breathe heavy into his cell as he moved. "I don't see anything suspicious."

"You be careful," she whispered, still flat on the floor.

"No car out here, but yours." Again she heard his breath in the receiver. "You stay down. I got my gun out."

"I'm down. You be careful."

"I see the police," he said. "I'll hang up and speak with them. You stay down until I get back with you."

She clicked off the phone. It rang again.

"Police dispatcher here. The police are at your residence. They'll be entering your property. When you hear a knock on your door, it will be the police."

"I'm in the garage apartment, not the main house."

"We got that. I'll stay on the phone until you hear the police knock?"

Della saw a beam of light sweep across the windows of her apartment. A flashlight. She felt the weight of the policeman on her steps. Then she heard the knock on the wood of her screened-in door. "Police," the man said.

She placed her hands on the edge of the bed and pulled herself up. She switched on the lamp on the bedside table and crossed her apartment to the door. Dressed only in her gown, she opened her apartment door and unlatched the screen door where she spoke with the police officer who flashed his light on the glass from the shattered bulb. Then, he ran the beam up the wall to the empty light socket.

His light focused on a bullet-hole just beyond where the bulb should have been. The police officer stepped onto the porch to examine the evidence more closely. Della spotted a second officer on Mercedes' patio, casting a beam of light on the pavers, up the walls and onto the empty light sockets there. The blue light from the police car flashed in eerie waves across the backyard.

The night air was cold on Della's bare arms. She went back inside her apartment to grab a robe and slip shoes on her feet. When she came outside again, the officer who had been on her porch, had joined the other officer on Mercedes' patio. Della lifted her robe above her feet and held the hem in her left hand as she came down the stairs. She too wanted to see the evidence.

A second police car parked in the driveway, its blue lights flashing out of sync with the other car's light. Mercedes' backyard was awash in flashing blue. That's when Della spotted Moss, dressed in deep maroon pajamas, his feet in leather slippers, his arms and legs spread out like a windmill, his body spread-eagled over the hood of the second police car.

"That's Moss Maple," Della shouted as she moved in fast steps toward the patrol car. "Moss Maple," she repeated. "He's my neighbor from around the corner. I called him for help."

"You know this man?" a black female officer asked. She stood behind Moss, holding a gun pointed toward the ground.

"Moss Maple," Della repeated. "My neighbor."

"Stand up," the policewoman said to Moss. She was no nonsense. All business.

Della stepped forward to give Moss a hug, but the officer threw her hand up. "Just wait a minute here. Did you ask this man to come over here with this pistol?" She pointed toward a small pistol that rested on a piece of plastic spread on the ground beside her squad car.

"I did," Della stammered. "I'm sorry. I was terrified."

"Good way to get yourself shot," the female officer said to Moss. She turned to Della. "Don't you ever call the police, then call somebody got a gun to ramble around in your backyard." She shoved her own gun into its holster. "Worse thing is, it's a damn good way to get me shot too. I ought to take him in for endangerment."

Moss slipped his arm across Della's shoulder and pulled her toward him. She was surprised at how comfortable she felt with Moss' arm around her.

"You got registration on this gun?"

"At the house," Moss said.

"Another thing," the officer said. "This man come out here, no identification, no permit, but he got a gun. What we supposed to think? This Robin Hood?" She waved her hand in front of Moss. "Damn idiot!"

"I'm sorry," Della said, the second time in less than twenty-four hours she had to apologize for her actions.

"Guess no real bad guy gone come out in purple p.j.'s," the officer said, casting her eyes over Moss. "Never know though." She turned to join her comrades on Mercedes' patio.

"That was stupid of me," Della said to Moss when the officer stepped away.

"Hush," Moss said. "Most of us don't have a game plan for this kind of thing. We play it by ear."

Della wrapped her arms around his neck. "Thank you for coming. I wouldn't have done anything to endanger you. I wasn't thinking straight."

"Forget it," he said. "I'm glad I wasn't any deeper on the property. They stopped me stone-still in the driveway."

A car pulled to the curb and stopped. Special Agent Sidney Winfield stepped out.

"Who notified you?" Della asked.

Oliver's Song

"Insomniac," he said. "I listen to the police radio. Puts me to sleep. But it didn't tonight." He grinned at Della and headed for Mercedes' patio.

Another police car pulled to the curb. With the blue lights flashing in neighbors' windows, a small crowd began to gather in the street.

Linda Busby Parker

21

Miguel Sanchez had not slept all night. He had walked on the beach beside the casino. For nearly two hours, he sat in a booth at a smoky Waffle House downing black coffee. While he sat, he imagined himself on a road trip across the U.S.A. Free. Thousands of miles ahead of him and only himself in the car. No hassles. No worries. *Sin problemas.* Time to think. Time to see the sights.

About 3 a.m. reality set in. Unless the violin could be located and delivered to The Boss, Miguel Sanchez was dead. Already he had screwed things up. The boss considered him on probation—not from a jail sentence, from a death warrant. Perhaps the police had the violin, but didn't know its value. He chuckled when he thought of this, but stopped when he considered the consequences. Even he did not know the monetary value of the violin, but it was worth everything to him.

As Miguel thought of this, his heart rate shot up—right there in the booth of the Waffle House. He thought his heart must be pumping 150, maybe 160 beats a minute. That was most likely the aerobic heartbeat for a man his age, but the problem was—he wasn't on a walking machine and he wasn't jogging.

Before he could pay the bill, he was sweating buckets. His shirt stuck to his back. His hands shook.

"You got a bad caffeine high," the cashier said to him when he handed her his ticket, his hands shaking.

"Yeah," he said. Maybe that was it. He had been up all night and had downed how many cups of black coffee? Hard to tell. The waitress topped off his cup every time she walked by. At least four cups. Maybe five.

That's it. A caffeine high. He crossed the divided highway. Busy in the daylight, but nearly void of traffic at 3 a.m. He

205

breathed deeply, conscious of his breath, filling his lungs all the way down into his belly. *Just a caffeine high.* "I'm okay," he whispered to himself. *¡Estoy bien!* He breathed deeply again. *¡Estoy bien!*

He would not go inside the hotel yet. He couldn't be boxed in by four walls, even walls as gigantic and tall as The Grand. He would walk this caffeine high off on the beach where the moon shone on the white sand and the water lapped gently against the shore.

The air off the water was brisk—even cold. He needed cold air. Let the cold air hit him in his face. This would settle him down. *¡Tranquilo! ¡Tranquilo!* He gave himself a stern order. Then a death warrant surfaced in his mind and his heart pumped overtime— 155 maybe 165. *¡Dios mio!*

Again Miguel breathed deep. Air into his belly. With his right hand he rubbed his heart. He would control his mind. He would not allow the ugly thought of the death warrant to enter his head. In fact, he would throw the warrant on the ground and walk on it. He would walk as far as necessary to rip the imagined warrant into shreds.

He walked the length of the beach. He saw himself on his porch in Puerto Plata. *Ah yes, the water so blue below him. A cool breeze. Not a cloud in the sky. He saw his last woman. Long black hair. Her waist thin, her breasts full. Her skin, an even tan. Her smell— berries and sun. His nose in her hair. He would have this again. Oh yes!* *¡Seguro que sí!*

Two miles at least, maybe three, until his heartbeat steadied. He walked to the water's edge, unzipped his pants, and pissed a quart. He felt better now. He could almost see it—the death warrant ripped in shreds. The sweat had nearly dried too. He thought he could sit in the lobby of the hotel now and wait for the sun to rise.

Oliver's Song

When Miguel entered through the enormous glass doors of The Grand, he smelled coffee brewing and bacon frying. The bellman gave Miguel a copy of Monday morning's newspaper. Sunday had turned to Monday. Even with the sun rising, he was not yet ready to close himself in his room. He would sit in the lobby, read the newspaper, and rest with his eyes open.

He settled himself into a large armchair and leaned his head against the soft cushioned back. He was spent. Shot. The black coffee, his pumping heart, the long walk, the entire sleepless night—all of this had left him an empty casing. He would have to sleep today. He could not go another twenty-four hours with no sleep. He pressed his index finger into his eyes, sat up, and opened the newspaper.

His cell phone rang, startling him.

"Yo, boss."

Miguel sat up. "Tor-Tuba," he said.

"We rollin', boss."

"You got it all done?" Miguel asked. The newspaper on the floor now.

He sat up in his chair. *Sweet relief.* He breathed deeply. Cleansing breath. Yes, the light shone at the end of his tunnel.

"We done it all," Tor-Tuba repeated.

"Where is Billy Wong?" Miguel smiled now. The grin felt good on his face.

"Whoa, boss. Slow down."

Miguel rubbed the heel of his palm across his eyes again. "Okay," he said, weariness creeping back into his voice. *Okay!*

"Dat boy down da jail. He roughed up. He at da hospital now."

"Not my concern. Tell me about Wong. Where is Billy Wong?" Miguel asked, sitting on the edge of his chair.

"Not panned out," Tor-Tuba said. "Da boys at da jail got little carried away."

Miguel stood now. "The point was to locate Billy Wong."

"Can't control da boys down da jail," Tor-Tuba explained. "Dat situation never a sure game."

"Okay." Miguel said, standing, pacing now.

"We got da little China man too. He not worry you no more. For sure."

"Where is Billy Wong?" Miguel repeated, his heart racing again.

"Dat little China man, he took off. Pull a gun. Not wanna talk."

"Bring him to me," Miguel said. "I will make him talk."

Tor-Tuba laughed. "Dat be difficult."

"Do it," Miguel ordered.

"Da little China man, he dead."

"What? You did get the information first?" Miguel asked. Even his hands sweated. He walked to the window where he rubbed the side of his face. His temples throbbed.

"We not get nothin' from him. We not stop though. We give a bonus. Dat lady lawyer in da news. We find her place. We mess a little wit her."

"She's not dead? Don't tell me she's dead." Miguel looked out into the rising sun, the water brown and placid, but a torrent exploding in his chest.

Tor-Tuba laughed. "She not dead. We scare her a little."

"Did she have the violin?"

"We never get inside. Car come down da street. Time to roll."

"Where are you Tor-Tuba?" Miguel asked this slowly, deliberately.

"We headed back to da Easy. Bout to Biloxi now."

"Turn around," Miguel begged, his voice pleading. "Go back. I got to have Billy Wong. Go back now. The job is not done. I've got to have Wong. Please." He could not believe he was pleading, but he repeated, "Please." *Por favor. Por favor.*

Miguel understood his situation. His life depended on this job being executed properly, but his partners were idiots. Chances of finding Wong and the violin were slim, but magic existed. He's seen it. In Haiti once he'd seen a man levitate. He'd actually seen it. Magic. *Magia.* He was reduced to two idiots and magic.

"Why you need this Wong?" Tor-Tuba asked.

"He's got that violin. Go back to Mobile. Locate Billy Wong."

"Jes checking, boss—violin, same thing's a fiddle?" Tor-Tuba asked.

This caught Miguel off guard. He had to think. "Yes," he answered. "A violin is the same thing as a fiddle. Turn around. Go back to Mobile. Find anyone who knows Oliver Fitzsimmons. Ask them about Billy Wong. Someone knows something. Please. Go back."

"Dat not much to go on," Tor-Tuba said.

Miguel heard Snake speak in the background.

"Snake say, what we got coming if we head back?"

"A hundred thousand," Miguel answered. No hesitation.

Again, Miguel heard Snake speak.

"When?" Tor-Tuba asked.

"You find Billy Wong or the violin today, you'll have your money tomorrow."

"For sure?" Tor-Tuba asked.

"It's yours," Miguel answered. "*Seguro.*"

"What you say?" Tor-Tuba asked.

"It's yours for sure—tomorrow."

"Think dat lawyer lady got da fiddle?" Tor-Tuba asked.

"Check everywhere," Miguel answered. "Billy Wong and the violin. I want them both. I've got to have them both."

Miguel heard Tor-Tuba's giant hand cup the phone. He knew the two discussed his proposal. He felt sick. Blood pounded in his temples. The black coffee churned in his stomach on top of the comfort food from the long night before. *¡Un tornado intestinal!*

"You got it, boss," Tor-Tuba said. "We go back. We got a idea. We be back wit' cha."

Miguel's stomach agitated in giant currents now. He would be lucky to make it to the toilet. He slipped the cell phone in his pocket and bolted for the men's room.

22

With the lit cigarette dangling between his lips and smoke drifting toward his eyes, he leaned over the side of the old boat and raised a crab trap from the brown, muddy water of Mobile Bay. Lights flickered on the bridge above the boat.

"Last one," he said to his cousin, Johnny, who stood at the wheel, steering the boat. "It's nearly dark, man. Last trap"

He brought the trap to the surface. Two blue crabs with hard-shelled spidery legs stepped gingerly across the wires of their cage. With a fourteen-inch pipe, Billy Wong tapped the latch and opened the trap. He shook the crabs into a refrigerated holding box, leaned over the side of the boat and dropped the cage into the muddy water again as the boat puttered toward the next trap.

"No more, man," Billy Wong pleaded.

"Two, three more," Johnny answered back.

With the tip of his index finger, Billy flicked his cigarette butt into the bay. He was ready to toss his cousin overboard too, if he did not head back to shore soon. With free help on his fishing boat, Johnny didn't know when to quit.

Billy Wong had met his cousin on Thursday morning. The perfect location—Bayou La Batre, a fishing community just west of Mobile, a place where one Asian blended in with the next one. At the close of the Vietnamese War, when Saigon fell to the North Vietnamese, thousands—those who were lucky enough to get out—fled to the States. Many of them had come to these little fishing communities along the Gulf Coast, places where Vietnamese, Cambodians, Laotians, and a smattering of Chinese, earned their living fishing, crabbing, shrimping, and hauling oysters. If the men and women weren't in their shabby old boats, they were in the seafood plants—shucking oysters, picking meat from crab legs and bodies, or processing the fish and shrimp they'd harvested from the Gulf.

Billy Wong knew Bayou La Batre was a place where he could fit in, and it positioned him not far from Dog River where that kid, that Ollie Fitzsimmons, cared for the bass case and for its contents. Ollie Fitzsimmons, a dumb, pampered and privileged American kid, would not exert the energy to lift the bass from the back of his old Audi. Billy smiled when he thought of this. The bass would be in the back seat, exactly as he had left it. Better to let Ollie Fitzsimmons store it in the back of his car than to have it at Johnny's house with his wife and kids. One of the kids would open that case for sure. Billy looked into the night sky and grinned when he thought of this. Ollie Fitzsimmons had transported the goods and was now storing them. Ollie was keeping that beautiful violin safe too.

On Thursday night Billy had stood on the road just beyond the house where Fitzsimmons stayed. He cast a beam of light into the back seat of the old Audi. There it was—the bass, just as he had expected. All Billy had to do now was get Johnny to head for shore. Back on solid ground, he'd borrow Johnny's old van and drive to Dog River. He would thank Ollie several times, even bow slightly. Then, he would retrieve his bass. Only problem was, his cousin Johnny still hauled in fish and crabs.

Friday night Billy had gotten no sleep at all. He and Johnny had taken the boat out after sunset. The idea had been to fish and gather crabs—work long hours, sleep, and be back on shore before dawn Sunday morning. But, that was not what had come down. Sunday and they were still fishing and crabbing. "Let's call it a day," Billy pleaded, proud of his American slang. "Knock off," he added.

"No," Johnny answered. "The fish are biting, man. Hold tight." Johnny too was proud of his easy words, a sure sign they were both well on their way to becoming full-fledged Americans.

Oliver's Song

"They're not biting. They're playing with us," Billy argued. Then something big took Johnny's bait. Johnny struggled with the fish for a solid hour, unable to land the thing. Johnny thought it was a large amberjack, the wide amber-brown stripe visible on the fish's body. The amberjack fought, but Johnny held his line and reeled him in a little closer while the fish struggled—east and west, pulling, tugging against the line. When the fish finally broke loose, Johnny baited his hook, ready to try again.

"No more fishing," Billy shouted. "Head for shore."

"No," Johnny fired back. "They're biting."

Billy gave up, baited his line, and sat beside his cousin on the back of the boat. Together they landed ten good-sized red fish. Johnny would sell some to a fish market in Mobile, while an Asian seafood distributor in Bayou La Batre would purchase the remainder.

"I'll throw you over if we don't head for shore," Billy said when the red fish stopped biting. That was when Johnny's old boat bobbed into a school of sea bass—small, but some measuring as long as twelve inches.

"Got a restaurant takes all these," Johnny said. So, they pulled in the small brown and yellow sea bass—one fish after another until they had completely filled another one of Johnny's refrigerated boxes. Finally, with his hands and shoulders aching, Billy went inside the little cabin, stretched out on a wooden slab intended for a bed and dozed. When he woke, he grabbed a boiled egg from a small woven basket, and went out to find Johnny still fishing.

Billy stood at the back of the boat and lit another cigarette. The insides of his shoulders still ached. The boat bobbed and puttered while Johnny continued to fish, crab, and scoop up oysters.

"Oh no," Billy said. "Look at that." He pointed to where the sun shot a tiny streak of pink toward the thin lines of gray clouds in the eastern sky. "We fished all night." Saturday had tuned into Sunday morning.

Johnny shrugged his shoulders. "Happens that way," he said.

Billy Wong knew exactly why he could not endure a life like this. His arms ached from the motion of tossing out and bringing in, tossing out and bringing in—the nets, the lines, the traps. The pain would grow worse over the next day, maybe two days, before his body settled into the fullness of its pain. When he was still in China, he had used his back and shoulders laboring for a few dollars. He knew pain. Many days, he had added soreness on top of soreness, added it on until he could not sleep at night from the pain. No way could he handle this kind of life. He had found an easier way. He would retrieve his bass case, sell the drugs, and keep the beautiful old violin. So much easier than tossing out nets, and lines, and crab traps. So much easier.

"We going in," Johnny said. "Give me a little more time. We'll check the traps again and I'll keep the lines out. No point in leaving if the fish are biting and traps are full."

Billy leaned over the boat, drawing a crab trap up so he could look inside the wire box. "Empty," he shouted to Johnny. "Turn this boat around. I got business on shore."

Johnny grinned at his cousin. "Your business is no good," he said. "Can't fool me."

"Least I got some business," Billy said, and lit another cigarette. Johnny grinned at his cousin.

They fished and crabbed all Sunday morning until afternoon. Then Johnny turned to his cousin and said, "we'll head back now." With that, Johnny turned the boat away from the bridge, headed toward the deepwater channel that ran to the Port of Mobile. He would then steer the boat south and west toward Bayou La Batre.

While his cousin maneuvered through the channel dodging barges loaded with coal and timber, Billy sat on the lid of a refrigerated box, brought his feet up and leaned his back against the front window of the boat. He watched the scenery — an old abandoned factory on one side and a dredging operation on the other.

Lazy American kids, he thought again, as he exhaled smoke that blew back into his face. Ollie Fitzsimmons included. Some people had opportunity given to them and some had to find opportunity — some had to steal it when they found it because it was the only way they would ever have any opportunity at all. The alternative was to do what his cousin Johnny had done. Johnny had dreams like everybody else, but Johnny made a settlement. His dreams had been sacrificed for his kids. This is what he and most of the Asians in Bayou La Batre did. They surrendered their own dreams, but held tightly to dreams for their kids, who would be second generation Americans.

DREAM BIG, Billy Wong had seen written in thick black marker on a piece of paper taped to the refrigerator in his cousin's kitchen. DREAM BIG, a sign made for the kids because now the greatest of Johnny's dreams was only to reach shore with his refrigerated boxes full to the top with food from the sea. This would never be Billy Wong. He had dreams for himself — not second-generation dreams he would pass to any kids he might one day have. *First generation dreams, not second.*

In the few days he had been at his cousin's house, he had not tried to conceal his business. In fact, he had involved Johnny — at least at the margins. Johnny had arranged a meeting with a new-identity man who prepared documents. Johnny had taken him to get a haircut too, no more long hair hanging to his shoulders and falling over his forehead. Now Billy sported a short cut, well-trimmed and parted on the left. Now he owned a pair of heavy black-framed glasses too. He liked the new man he saw when he looked in the mirror at the barber shop, new haircut and black-framed glasses. "Smart man," the barber had said out loud.

"Looks like a company man," Johnny said, observing Billy in the mirror. "Plenty intelligent. Plenty successful," he added under his breath.

Billy and Johnny drove to the mall in Biloxi where Billy had purchased new slacks and three new button-down shirts—white, yellow, and pale blue. Expensive shirts. Successful-man shirts. To his shirts and slacks, he added fine leather shoes and a brown leather belt, which he took to a shoe repair shop for extra holes so the belt would buckle smoothly around his narrow waist. In his new clothes, with his short cut hair, and black-framed glasses, Billy Wong was a different man.

The new-identity man snapped a picture of him in his new clothes with his hair neatly parted and smoothed down on the sides. *Handsome,* the man had said. *Very smart,* he had added. This picture would be used on all the new documents.

When Billy Wong arrived back at shore, his new identity would be waiting. Xi, he had told the new-identity man. He wanted his new name to be Xi. Try as hard as they might, Americans could not pronounce this name. When confronted with the X and the i, Billy Wong liked to watch the Americans' tongues tap the roofs of their mouths and thrust forward, touching the backs of their front teeth as they searched for the correct sound. *Where to place the tongue?* When they hunted and could not find the spot, they were thrown off balance. This was precisely what Billy Wong wanted. He wanted some airport security agent, some man or woman who checked passports to glance at his papers. He wanted the man's or woman's tongue to search from the roof of the mouth to the ridges of the teeth, hunting for Xi. When Xi could not be found, the embarrassed agent would look at the well-groomed, prosperous man who stood in front of him, see from the papers that he was a musician—a member of an American orchestra—and wave him through.

Oliver's Song

Billy Wong grinned when he thought of this. A violinist for the Cleveland Orchestra. That was what he wanted on his new documents. Yong Xi, member of the first violins. If questioned he would give reasonable answers. He had spent six months in Cleveland. He had stood in the back of the great Severence Hall, looked up at the beautiful gold of the ceiling and at the curves of the magnificent arches. He had listened to the great Cleveland Orchestra perform its music, each player holding a beautiful instrument. He knew the conductor's name too—Christoph Von Dohnányi.

During his months in Cleveland, he had lived in a one-room rental on Superior Avenue. He had slept on the floor because the narrow bed smelled of human urine. He had worked at a place called Ready Cash, running quick computer searches on men and women who came to cash checks, avoiding banks.

"You're smart," the owner had said. "Want a permanent job?"

But that was not what Billy wanted. He had not given up on his dreams. Eight dollars an hour to run computer searches? No way! DREAM BIG the sign read in Johnny's kitchen. That was exactly what Billy Wong was doing. DREAM BIG, BILLY WONG. DREAM BIG. He mouthed the words into the salty, silk air of Mobile Bay.

He dangled his feet down the side of the refrigerated box as the boat puttered toward shore. He could hardly wait to get his hands on that violin inside the bass case. He didn't know what he had, but it had to be something good. The man with the heavy Spanish accent—Sanchez, Miguel Sanchez—had given the violin to him wrapped in an old piece of purple velvet.

"This is important," Sanchez had said. "This instrument belongs to The Boss. When you receive the drugs, deliver those to me. I'll meet you. Then, you take this violin to Hong Kong. The Boss will meet you there. He'll take the violin from you. You will

217

be paid well," the man had said. "We like doing business with you."

Billy Wong was nobody's fool. Mr. Chang Wu had offered only fifty thousand to deliver the drugs to a man in Florida. But, the man with the Spanish accent had been willing to pay four times that. Still, Billy Wong suspected he could get more. He had made contact with a third party willing to pay nearly a million. Why settle for half a million when he could come close to a full million? He had Mr. Wu's ten thousand, down payment on the promised fifty, and the Spanish man had given him fifty thousand outright. That money with the money he would receive from the third party, and he would be set for life. And the violin. All the money, and he had that violin too. He could hardly wait to hold the instrument in his hands.

He had played the bass, but he could teach himself to play the violin. Always, he had been good with musical instruments. Back in China, in his Hubei Province, his aunt had bought him toy instruments—no money for the real thing. He had been fortunate to get the toys. All of those little instruments he could play. No problem. Music ran through his head. Give him any instrument and a few days to study it and he would make music. He dreamed of playing in an orchestra, a big American orchestra.

His bass was cheap. He had purchased it for two hundred dollars from a student at Cleveland State University, while he lived in the one-room apartment on Superior Avenue. The two hundred had come hard—money he had saved from his job at Ready Cash. But . . . now he had the special violin. When he took it in his hands, he would bring it to his nose and smell it. Then, he would bring it close to his eyes to see every fine detail. He remembered this about the violin, the wood on the back swirled in beautiful patterns and the violin shone with a luster set deep into the wood, a sheen, not a high gloss, not some cheap varnish. He would transport this beautiful violin to Hong Kong, but he would surrender it to no one. It was his. Soon he would have a million dollars and a special violin.

"We'll dock at the Service Mart," Johnny said. "I'll leave her there for fuel. Heard a knocking in the engine too. I want them to check that."

"Fine with me," Billy said. What did he care if Johnny docked in his regular birth or at the Service Mart. The knocking in the engine didn't bother him either. That was Johnny's concern, not his.

The cigarette in his mouth was almost spent. He removed the butt and held it between his fingers while he lifted a pack from his hip pocket. He thumped the pack against his hand and withdrew a cigarette with his teeth, lighting the new one with the butt of the old one. He stubbed out the spent cigarette against the lid of the refrigerated box and watched the channel open into wide water. The boat rocked as it crossed from the waters of the bay into the Gulf. Billy Wong hung the cigarette between his lips and held the lid of the refrigerated box with his hands, steadying himself. *Hold on Billy Wong. You'll be on shore soon.*

✳✳✳

"You like shrimp, Uncle Billy?"

"Sure." Billy tousled his nephew's hair—not actually his nephew, his second cousin, or was it his third cousin? Second cousin, third cousin—no matter. Mark's mother, Tuit, an immigrant from Vietnam and a new Catholic, had given the kid a saint's name. "I say his name and I think of Saint Mark." She smiled when she told Billy, as if a name made a difference. But, in Mark's case, maybe it did. Billy had to admit it—Mark was a good kid.

Johnny stood behind his son and placed both hands on his shoulders. "This boy wants to be a doctor."

"Straight A's in math," Johnny's wife Tuit said.

"A's in science too," Mark added.

"You boys peel these shrimp. Then we won't need to peel them at supper." Tuit turned to Johnny. "You want to read the Sunday paper?"

"Sports," Johnny said.

Tuit removed the sports section from the morning paper and handed the rest to Billy Wong. "Spread the newspaper over the table. Drop the shells on the paper. We'll roll it up and throw it out, shells and all. Clean and easy," Tuit brushed her hands together, illustrating her words.

Billy Wong took the paper and spread it over the table, glancing at the front page as he smoothed it. The name rose to his eyes *Oliver Fitzsimmons III*. He lifted the newspaper, snapped it to full size and brought it close to his face.

Oliver Fitzsimmons III, son of a prominent Mobile family, was arrested on drug charges early Saturday morning. Another vehicle collided into Fitzsimmons' 1991 Audi Quatro at the juncture of I-10 and I-65. Mobile police found thirty-five kilos of an exceptionally pure grade of heroin inside a bass musical instrument case. Street value of the drugs is estimated at six to seven million.

Billy Wong's lips moved as he read silently. When he finished the article, he went to the first words and read again, trying to make sense of what he was reading.

Johnny watched him. "Gonna read the newspaper?"

Tuit tugged at the paper in Billy's hand.

"Wait. Wait," Billy argued and scanned the words again.

"He wants out of shelling shrimp," Tuit said.

Mark laughed. "Come on Uncle Billy. Shelling shrimp's not that hard."

Billy folded the front page. "I like to read the news," he said. His hands visibly trembled. "Keeps me informed," he mumbled.

"This guy's Mr. U.S.A." Johnny laughed.

Billy folded the front page and placed it on the counter behind him. "I want to save this part. It's got all the news."

Oliver's Song

"He's serious," Johnny said and laughed again. "Mr. U.S.A."

Billy sat at the table, the boiled shrimp in a colander in front of him. *Ollie in jail. Drugs gone. Six to seven million the newspaper said.* He knew the drugs were worth a lot, but he had no idea they were worth that much. There it was in print. Six to seven million. He snapped the tail off a shrimp and peeled back the soft shell.

"Don't forget to de-vein those shrimp," Tuit said. She placed a nut-pick in front of each of them. "Use these to get the veins out."

What went wrong? What did the kid do? Where was the violin? He had to investigate. Do his own investigation to answer these questions.

"Could I have the van for a little while tonight?" Billy asked.

"You got to eat first," Tuit said. "I boiled all these shrimp."

"I'll eat," Billy said and snapped the head off another shrimp.

"You going to get the girls?" Johnny asked his wife.

Tuit looked at her watch. "Sure. They're done by now. I'll go on," she said. She pointed her finger at Billy and smiled. "Don't you think about going anywhere before you eat. I'll have the van for a while anyway. I want to run by the grocery store after I get the girls."

"Uncle Billy, next year I'll be old enough to go to church on Sunday nights."

"Good," Billy said to Mark, still thinking of the six to seven million.

"He's jealous of his big sisters," Johnny said, "but next year he'll be old enough for all the youth programs."

Tuit patted her son on his shoulder when she walked past, her purse over her arm, the car keys in her hand.

Billy pulled the colander close and reached in for a handful of shrimp. He placed these on the newspaper in front of him. *Where was the violin? The newspaper made no mention of the violin.*

"Hey, you're hogging the shrimp bowl," Mark teased. Billy pushed the colander back to the center of the table.

No wonder his third man was willing to pay nearly a full million. Old Chang Wu—the egg face—offered only fifty thousand. The South American offered a little less than half a million. But he had found a man willing to pay almost a million. Nobody gave Billy Wong credit for brains. He had brains. From fifty thousand to a fortune. Sums close to a million made him stagger. Yes, he had brains. *But . . . drugs gone, money gone. New plan. That sweet, sweet violin! Save that! At least save that!*

"What you doing Uncle Billy?"

Billy Wong's head jerked when Mark called his name.

"You put a shrimp you didn't shell in the shelled bowl. See." The boy pointed to a shrimp with head, tail, and shell still intact, tossed in the bowl with the shelled shrimp.

"He's thinking about the news," Johnny teased him.

"Not used to shelling shrimp," Billy Wong said, and lifted the offending shrimp from the bowl, snapping off its head.

"Look at you. Your hands are shaking," Johnny said.

"Too much work," Billy answered. "Feel it in my hands and arms." He held his hands in the air, palms out.

Billy couldn't tell them he was counting his lost money. *Now old Chang Wu was high and dry too.* Billy found no displeasure in this. Let the Long Hairs—that's what Mr. Chang Wu called them—deal with him. Old Chang Wu never thought Billy had brains. Let him see Billy Wong had plenty of brains. Old Chang Wu would suffer the consequences of Billy Wong's brains. Let the South American come up dry too. He cared nothing for the South American.

The third man had not yet given him a dime. The exchange of money would have taken place when Billy Wong delivered the drugs—which he would not do now. He counted in his head: minus ten thousand to pay the new-identity man, purchase clothes, cover the costs of an airline ticket and other small things, he had sewn the remainder of his money inside the lining of his suitcase. Gray thread. Nice stitches. Nearly forty thousand. *Smart, Billy Wong. Smart.*

Billy Wong raised his shoulders, releasing the tension drawing across his back like an iron bar. He stuck the nut-pick into the back of the orange shrimp and lifted the dark vein. He rubbed the pick across the newspaper to free the vein from the tip. He sighed when he thought again of the money he would never receive. He would have been sitting pretty when he arrived in Hong Kong. Not now. Forty thousand would ease him along for a while, but it was not a million. He drew a deep breath and let it out between his parted lips.

"You okay?" Johnny asked.

"You worked me hard," Billy grinned.

"Better stay in tonight. No carousing."

"Let me use the van," Billy said. "I need a night out."

"Too much trouble in some of these bars around here," Johnny said.

"I'll be okay. I need a little time off. Hey, look at me, I'm single." He spread his arms wide to say *look at me, look at Billy Wong.*

"Okay, man. After supper," Johnny said. "You take the van then. Got to have it back by early morning though. Tuit delivers the newspaper. Folks want their paper early."

"I'll be back by morning," Billy Wong said.

Johnny slapped him on his shoulder.

Billy would again find the little house beside the water where Oliver Fitzsimmons stayed. Surely the violin was there. Wherever it was, Billy would find it. He may have lost the money, but the violin was more than money. He could feel the wood, smooth as silk, under the pads of his fingers. He could hardly wait until he ran the bow across the strings. *What sound would it make? Sweet. He was sure of this. That violin would sing a sweet song.*

After he ate enough shrimp and Chinese noodles to satisfy Tuit, after he talked with his nieces about Sunday night church, after he examined Mark's model airplanes, they would give him the keys to their old Econoline van. He would again go to the house beside the river. If the violin was there, he would find it. He knew how to be gray as the night. Silent as the wolf. Swift as the lion.

He turned away from the table and lifted the front page. He read the story again to be certain it made no mention of the violin.

"You're funny, Uncle Billy. You really don't like shelling shrimp, do you?"

23

Early Monday morning, Ollie saw his attorney coming down the hallway toward his opened door. He hurt all over. Every time he moved, he found another sore spot he didn't know he had. He could still see the faces of the three men who surrounded his metal cot. Once in the night, here at the hospital, he had screamed in his sleep and struggled to flee. His father placed a hand on his shoulder. "You're alright son," he had said. "I'm here. I'm not going anywhere." Ollie had reached his right hand up—his shoulder hurt when he raised his arm—and patted his father's hand. This was the closest the two had been in what—maybe four or five years?

His father hadn't left his bedside until morning and then headed home for a quick shower. Ollie would not tell anyone this, but the beating was almost worth it. He and his father were a team, at least for now, and the beating had sprung him from jail. He only hoped the authorities would keep him here at the hospital, not send him back to jail in this busted condition. *They couldn't send him back. Could they?*

The guard outside the door took Della's driver's license and checked her name against the list he held in his hand. Ollie raised an arm and attempted a feeble wave. A sheet covered his lower body, but his left leg, in full plaster cast, rested on top of the sheet. When the guard granted her permission, she entered the room.

"'lo, Miss Boudreaux." Ollie spoke, his mouth open slightly, his lips barely moving. "Big cut inside lower lip. Hurts to talk." He squeezed the words out, his lower lip stretched wide to minimize movement.

"My goodness," Della said, looking at her client. Ollie's left eye was swollen shut. His eyelashes were matted and the skin above and below his eye was a purplish-blue. A row of tiny stitches in a diagonal zigzag crossed his cheekbone. His leg was sheathed in a cast.

"Leg's bad. Bones should heal. Cast keeps leg still." Ollie continued to use as few words as possible to keep his lower lip stiff when he spoke.

Della spotted a large round bruise on his upper left arm. She reached out and took her client's hand. "Wow! They did some number on you."

"Doozer," he said, his teeth clinched.

"Last night, your father mentioned a possible concussion."

"Still checking that. Blacked out. Seem okay. Some blood in ear. They asked for Billy Wong. What you make of that?"

"I don't know what to make of it. The U.S. Attorney thinks you're in the middle of a dangerous situation. Thinks it might be a coalition of forces or it might be a showdown. Mexicans, South Americans, Asians, and home-growns. A turf war or a new alliance. We're unsure of the alignments. Regardless, this is big trouble."

"Could be," Ollie whispered. "Guys beat me were home-growns. Couldn't believe they asked for Billy Wong."

"I'm sorry about this, but I'm going to have to press you for every detail you can remember," Della said. "I need to know everything." She sat on the bedside chair, took her notebook out of her handbag and began asking questions.

Ollie answered every question slowly, careful not to drag his lower lip across his teeth. He told her everything he remembered, down to the page he was on in the Beethoven biography when he looked up and realized the three men stood beside his cot. He told her too about the final blow that sent him into darkness, his vision stopping down like the lens on a camera.

"Dad's got Bobby Jack Arnold on this. One of his attorneys." He opened his mouth too wide and winced from the pain.

"That's good," Della said, although she wasn't at all certain that was good. She wasn't sure Bobby Jack wouldn't try to walk over her. For now, she would let it rest. Ollie didn't need anything else to worry about.

"Dad stayed last night. He'll be back. Mom's on way too."

Ollie slowly turned his head toward the nightstand. "Water. Could I have water? Not supposed to raise head yet."

Della lifted the large plastic bottle on the nightstand and carefully placed the straw between Ollie's lips.

"Sir," the guard outside the room spoke.

Della looked toward the door. Oliver Fitzsimmons Sr. handed his driver's license to the guard and turned toward another man standing next to him. "This is Bobby Jack Arnold," Ollie senior said. "His name ought to be on that list too. One of our lawyers."

The silver-haired man standing next to Oliver Fitzsimmons stood well over six feet. He sported a light brown western jacket complete with fringe. In his hands, he held a western hat, buff colored, with a narrow scarlet rope around the band and a large, red bead on the lower part of the crown.

He's a nut case, Moss had told her. *Used to come into court with a holstered pistol under his jacket. That was before metal detectors and courthouse shootings. Tried to wear the empty holster in court after the gun got axed, but the judges put a stop to that. Bobby Jack is one piece of work. Smart man though. Idiosyncratic as hell,* Moss had said and whistled between his teeth.

Della placed the water bottle back on the night stand and studied the man in western dress while the guard returned his license. *Yes, this Bobby Jack Arnold was one piece of work.* His high-heeled boots clacked against the tile floor as he followed Oliver Sr. into the room. When he crossed the threshold, he extended his right hand toward Della.

"Miss Boudreaux," Oliver Sr. said, "I want you to meet Bobby Jack Arnold."

Bobby Jack took Della's hand and dipped his silvered head.

"Ollie tells me you've begun an investigation of what happened down at Metro," Della said, wasting no time. She had a full roster of events planned for this day. Not the least of which was to speak with J.J. Ernest about her client, and she had to make a quick trip to the bank to draw down on her loan. She'd been trying to do that since Friday. She wanted to have a check ready for Candy Sue.

"Just like you'd expect," Bobby Jack said. "Nobody wants to take responsibility. Two guards walked the cells together last night. Both swear Ollie's cell was locked. Secured — shut, and tight as a drum." Bobby Jack placed his hat on the chair beside the bed. "Fraternal Order of Police is all over this. One guard is sticking up for the other one. Both swear up and down, the cell was locked. Didn't hear a thing until it was too late. A camera should have picked up some of it, but the camera was turned off. What do you make of that, Miss Boudreaux?"

"Well, somehow the thugs got into his cell. There's the evidence." She raised her hand toward her client, who watched them.

"Guards are on suspension with pay. Fraternal Order of Police is saying the guards did nothing wrong. They were short handed down at the station last night because of Mardi Gras. I'm going back today. Keep the pressure on. Truth of the matter is," Bobby Jack said, "lots of prisoners get injured down at the jail. Some serious. Rarely gets reported. Most of the boys down there don't have families with any resources. Some of them don't have families that check on them at all." He raised his shoulders, his hands clasped in front of him.

"Unbelievable," Della said. She didn't tell Bobby Jack Arnold she had spoken with Harold Eventide, the front desk officer at Metro Jail. He wasn't on duty when Ollie was beaten, but Bobby Jack had echoed what Harold Eventide said: *Lots of the boys down here have big old chips on their shoulders. Sometimes somebody knocks the chips off. Know what I mean? But, I wasn't here,* Harold had said.

"Black eye," Ollie reminded them that he had gotten caught in a crossfire before his beating.

"Wasn't much the guards could do about that," Bobby Jack said. "I was already squeezing my grip on the P.D. about that when this happened."

"Thugs should not be allowed to run roughshod at the jail," Della said.

"We'll stay on this case," Bobby Jack said. "See if we can't shake something loose, but I'd be telling you all a lie if I said I knew we'd find all the answers. In fact, I know we won't ever have all the answers."

"Something strange happened to me last night too," Della told them. "Someone entered my property and shot-out the outside lights. I think it was an attempted break-in. Somebody probably saw me load my landlady's suitcase in the trunk before we rolled out of the driveway yesterday. Probably thought nobody was home."

"You be careful, little lady," Bobby Jack said when she had finished. The police report stated this boy transported blocks of pure heroin. Somebody wanted that cargo and wanted it bad." Bobby Jack raised his hands. "Our boy's innocent, I know that. But still, he's in this thing up to the hairs on his chin."

"Ollie had no idea what he transported," Della said with authority, but she didn't want to get into it here and now with Bobby Jack Arnold.

"I'll be sure the feds know what happened at my place last night, but I doubt it's related," Della added quickly to redirect the conversation.

"What happened to you probably isn't related to this, but what happened down at the jail is," Bobby Jack said. "The men who beat him asked about that Chinese fellow named Billy Wong. Same fellow who set our boy up for his fall. Pretty peculiar they'd be asking for Wong."

"You're right. Obviously others know Billy Wong." Della did not tell him she knew other Asians were somewhere down at the jail, incarcerated in the wee hours of Sunday morning for transporting drugs across Interstate 10. This information she'd keep to herself—at least for the time being. She'd speak with J.J. Ernest today when she told him about the attempted break in at her apartment. Give him a little new information and see if he shared any more information with her. She wasn't sure she trusted Bobby Jack Arnold. For now, she'd ease out of the room and return when she had time alone with her client.

She took Ollie's hand and held it. "I'll come later today," she told him.

"Dad's got something," Ollie said, his lower lip stretched and pulled away from his teeth.

"I almost forgot," Oliver Sr. said. He reached down to the seat of the empty chair where he had placed a manila folder. "Ollie tells me he wants you to have these two compositions. He'd left them at our house for safe keeping last time he was home. As I understand it, that's your pay until he sells these works and pays you in cash."

She opened the folder and saw handwritten pages of music, the notes neatly scribed with a #2 pencil on paper with the music staff already printed on it.

"Haven't written titles yet. I think that one will be Oliver's Song," he said about the piece of music Della held in her hand.

She closed the top flap on the manila folder and offered it to Ollie. "No," she said. "These are valuable to you. I can't take them."

"They're yours," he protested. "Payment. Keep them 'til I can sell them. I'll give you cash then. Just wait."

"He wants you to hold them," Oliver Sr. said. "He's an artist. I wanted him to go into business, but he plays piano and writes music. Artists use their works as cash."

"Are these the originals?" she asked.

Ollie nodded.

"Make me copies." Della again offered the folder to her young client.

Oliver's Song

"No," he said. "I got copies. You hold originals. More valuable." Again he spoke as few words as possible, protecting his busted lip. "You working hard," he added.

Della could have kissed him, but she didn't. She patted his hand. "I'll be back," she repeated. At the door, she raised the manila folder in the air, "I'll take good care of these."

***

On a sofa in the lobby of The Grand, Miguel Sanchez woke himself when he jerked. In his dream, a man had been at his throat with a knife. The sharp blade pressed sideways against his windpipe, almost blocking his air passage. He hadn't exactly seen the man's face. He saw a bushy brown mustache and smelled the man's foul breath.

Miguel wiped the flat of his palm across his face and looked at his watch. Ten o'clock. He had slept a solid three hours. He glanced across the lobby. Used bar glasses were stacked on the end table beside him when he dozed off. Now they were gone. If a housekeeper had cleaned around him, he had slept through it. He stood and walked to the large glass windows to see the new day, the sun bright, a pelican perched on a lone post that jutted out of the muddy bay water.

What he wouldn't give to be on his Maiora right now, cutting through the turquoise water of the Gulf—none of this muddy brown muck of the Mississippi Sound. He could feel saltwater spray brushing the side of his face as he looked over the edge of the boat, searching for some exotic water creature at the azure surface—maybe a sailfish.

Puerto Plata. He should have never left. *Don't look back Miguel. Look forward. That's the trick. Look forward.* His ranch house was nearly complete. He had only to get back there where he would sit on his porch. He could see it as he looked out the enormous glass window of the casino. His Dominican Republic, the blue-green water below him and the golden beaches.

231

Three hours rest had calmed him. He could think straight now. Everything would be alright. Snake and Tor-Tuba hunted for Billy Wong. Snake had an evil eye and would locate his prey. As soon as Snake telephoned, Miguel would drive to Mobile. For now, he would shower. Clean himself up. Even he could smell his raw odor. Nothing else to do but play this hand out. *Everything will be fine. Fine!* He looked out the window one more time before he walked to the elevator. Yes, now he could make his way upstairs. He could enter his room and close the door behind him. Tight spaces would not suffocate him. Morning and three hours sleep had refreshed him. A whole new day. That was all he needed—for now at least.

As he made his way to the elevator, he saw a load of old folks stepping off buses and coming into the lobby of the casino—old folks, laughing and carrying on. For the first time in his life, he wanted to be an old person like those crazy senior citizens cavorting as if they were elementary school kids on a field trip. Their worries behind them, cruising around on a luxury coach. He laughed when he thought of this—he, an old man. No way! When Snake and Tor-Tuba located Billy Wong, and when he had the violin safe and sound in his hands, he would celebrate with wine and a woman. This is what would refresh his body—Billy Wong, the violin, good wine, and a good woman. In that order. After he had these things, he would sleep some long hours.

While the seniors swapped stale jokes and guffawed loudly, Miguel pressed the button and waited for the elevator to arrive and take him five floors up.

24

Like the Mardi Gras throngs who had come downtown for the Monday parades, Della shelled out five bucks and parked at the Civic Center. Two days and Mardi Gras would be over for another year. She was ready to get back to normal. Generally, she parked in a small lot near her office, but for Mardi Gras, the lot's owner rented the spaces at a premium. He had printed the proviso right into the yearly contract—he reserved the right to resell the parking spaces during Mardi Gras.

Get through Monday and Tuesday and the city would step into Ash Wednesday, somber as a mute monk. She'd get her parking space back and the whole city would slow-walk for a while, everybody recovering.

She still held the manila folder containing Ollie's music. She had plenty of respect for her client's work. Original compositions—heady stuff—even if the composer was a young man, falsely accused, beaten, and flat on his back in the hospital.

She didn't know if Candy Sue would be in the office. She'd told her secretary to set her own hours today. They'd staff the office for a short while and tomorrow the whole place would be shut down for Fat Tuesday's finale. She wanted to put the folder on her desk, leave her purse in her office, lock up if Candy Sue wasn't there, and step back out on the street for the King's and Queen's parade. Josie and Kevin should both be on one of the floats. On Sunday she hadn't seen her kids at all. The drive to Stevie Knight's church, her visit to the jail, and to J.J. Ernest's office had consumed the day—not to mention her round trip to Montgomery. She'd wave at her kids on the float when she spotted them and she'd talk to each of them later in the day. At least she'd talk with Kevin. Josie might make herself unavailable.

When Della crossed Government Street and walked past the entrance to the Bankhead Tunnel, the sight before her made no sense at all. A crowd had gathered in front of her office. Candy Sue stood on the sidewalk, a pistol in her right hand, her left arm bracing her right. A very large young man, his feet splayed wide, his baggy cargo pants down around his lower hips, his enormous pale derriere exposed, stood with his arms spread-eagle on the plate glass window—just below the sign reading *D. Boudreaux Attorney at Law.*

Like the young man who stood spread-eagle, six feet from the muzzle of Candy Sue's pistol, Della's secretary also stretched her legs wide in a cop's stance, but instead of spit-shined police brogans, Candy Sue wore smart looking patent-leather crocodile-print flats. The expression on her secretary's face was one Della had never imagined for Candy Sue—a bared-tooth bulldog with hot-azalea-pink lipstick.

Della looked back at the heavy-set young man, the palms of his hands against the plate glass. The young man's backside—and front side too—had come out of his cargo pants. He wore no underwear. Yes, his derriere was indeed fully exposed, the skin on his backside as pale as late afternoon sun in winter. There he stood, wide as a windmill, bare as a newborn. Fortunately, he pressed the front side of himself close to the plate glass window in a modest effort to shield some of his private business from public view. Della was glad she wasn't inside the office. The outside view was more than sufficient.

She shook her head to be sure her vision wasn't cloudy and stepped toward Candy Sue. "What's going on?"

Candy Sue still held the pistol on the young man flattened against the plate glass. She spoke without turning toward Della. "He picked the lock. Came right into the office. Thought he'd get any cash we had."

"If he was looking for loose change, he sure picked the wrong place," Della said.

"This mama mean business," someone in the crowd said.

"Got this man where it hurts," someone else added. The crowd hooted.

"Look at his boo-dy," a child's voice said. "That's not nice." The crowd laughed again.

"Step back!" an officer ordered when he broke through the crowd. "Step back!" A young police officer followed an older officer.

"Put the gun down," the older officer said to Candy Sue. She lowered the pistol, the muzzle facing the sidewalk.

"Hands up!" the officer shouted to the young man who dropped his hands toward his pants. "Hands up!"

The young man raised his arms again, his pants still below his derriere.

"I was in the office there," Candy Sue pointed with her left hand to the entry door of Boudreaux Attorney at Law. "This idiot picked our lock and walked in. I hadn't turned any lights on. He must have thought nobody was in and thought nobody would notice what he was doing in a crowd. I heard him picking and scraping at the lock. When he walked in, I was ready. He tried to run. You see how far he got."

"I sure do," the officer said and grinned. "Pat him down," the older officer said to the young officer standing beside him.

"Not me!" The young officer pleaded, and winced when he looked at the exposed derriere.

"You're the rookie," the older cop said and raised his shoulders.

The younger officer groaned and stepped to where the heavy-set man stood. Standing at arms-length and keeping his head above the large derriere, the officer patted the pockets of the cargo pants, lifting out the contents and placing the man's possessions — including a small, slender ice pick — on the sidewalk.

Another patrol car pulled to the curb. "Rookie gets the tough stuff," the officer said as he stepped out of his car, his eyes on the pat-down.

The officer, who had just pulled to the curb, snapped on rubber gloves and brought a plastic bag from the patrol car. "Awh man!" he said when he squatted just below the large derriere. The crowd laughed in approval.

"Man, it's Mardi Gras," someone shouted.

"Stinky butt," someone else said.

The officer grinned and played to the crowd by fanning his gloved hand several swipes in front of his nose. Then, he gathered the evidence.

"Pull your pants up and put your hands behind your back," the young officer said after the contents from the pockets were placed in the plastic bag.

"So you work here?" the older officer questioned Candy Sue.

"I'm the secretary. Here's the boss," Candy Sue nodded toward Della, who stood beside her.

"I had no idea you packed a pistol," Della said to Candy Sue, who had again transformed from a bared-tooth bulldog with hot-azalea-pink lipstick to a gorgeous blonde, every hair in place. "Can you shoot that thing and control it?"

"At this range, I could split the threads on his shoelaces," Candy Sue said, pointing at the massive tennis shoes worn by the young man being led away. "You're looking at the state champion skeet shooter. In high school, that is." She shrugged her shoulders. "I love a moving target. I'd probably try to graze his ass."

"You got a permit for that gun?" the older officer asked.

"In my purse, inside the office," Candy Sue answered.

"Permit to carry?"

"I do. I work part time for a security service on weekends," she said and caught her bottom lip between her teeth. "I hope you don't mind, Miss Della."

A whole new side to Candy Sue—one Della had never envisioned. She always felt a little off-center when someone totally surprised her. Well, maybe this surprise wasn't bad. Maybe it was a good thing to have a secretary who was also a sharp shooter.

236

Oliver's Song

"No," she managed "I . . . I don't mind." She was glad Candy Sue had an additional source of income—but security guard? Candy Sue in uniform? Gray? Maybe even drab blue? Security guards were generally beefy. She looked at Candy Sue, her frame slender and shapely.

Covey stepped out of the crowd with his ukulele in hand. He leered at Candy Sue, an odd grin on his lips. "Pretty good," he said, rocking his head up and down as if it were connected to the rest of his body by a coiled spring—a bobble-head doll.

Della glanced at the edge of his chin to determine once and for all if the man in front of her was Special Agent Sidney Winfield, but Covey had the collar of his dirty jacket pulled up over the line of his jaw and she could not determine if these two men were one and the same. All she knew for sure was that Covey had changed his location. Instead of playing his ukulele at the corner of Bienville Square, he had, of late, set up shop near her office.

"Back up," the officers ordered everyone standing around the squad car as they pushed through the crowd, the big guy in tow.

Before the officers left, Della wanted them to know about the attempted break in at her place last night. Two in a row—her home, her office.

"You file a report?" the officer asked.

Della nodded, but before she could speak, the officer closed his squad-car door. The crowd had gathered around the patrol car. The officers wanted only to get the handcuffed miscreant locked up and get back to their duties, patrolling downtown during Monday's Mardi Gras celebration. No point in trying to explain further. She didn't want to sound like a woman in a state of panic, but she would call J.J. Ernest later in the day and tell him about both events.

If she wanted to see the King's and Queen's parade, she had just enough time to place the folder with Ollie's music in it on her desk, leave her pocketbook inside a desk drawer, and run to the corner. Maybe she'd get a glimpse of her kids. Already she could hear drum beats from the marching bands approaching the bend in front of the tunnel.

Candy Sue came into the office as Della was going out. The secretary carried her pistol, muzzle down, in her right hand.

"I'm going to try to catch a glimpse of Kevin and Josie in the next parade," Della said.

"You go on, Miss Della. I'll be here, but I'm going to lock the door. When you come back, tap and I'll let you in."

Della wrapped her arms around her secretary and hugged her. Candy Sue put her left arm around Della's shoulder, but kept the pistol straight down in her right hand.

"You were something!" Della said. "I mean, really something."

"Go on, Miss Della, or that parade will be gone."

When Della reached the corner, the parade had stalled a block away. She didn't know which side of the float her children would be on. Across the street she spotted Stevie Knight, the minister from Highway 43, and his wife, Evie. Mardi Gras crowds always yielded familiar faces. A young boy stood beside them. She squeezed between two pieces of portable metal fence—essential crowd control for Mardi Gras—and crossed the street. Stevie Knight and his wife Evie saw her coming and they both waved.

"We didn't expect to see you so soon," Stevie Knight said.

Only yesterday morning, she had sat in the little chapel, but it seemed like a week ago. She was ready to make the drive north of Mobile again, sit on the back row, see the light coming through the old wavy glass windows bordered in rose and sky blue, and listen to Stevie Knight speak to his congregation in words as rhythmic as poetry.

"This is our nephew, Tyrone," Evie said, both her hands rested on the boy's shoulders.

Tyrone looked up and grinned at Della, his two front teeth missing. The child had a face that literally shone light, filled with hope and promise, and pure joy to be downtown, out of school on a Monday morning, seeing a parade, complete with floats, bands, and police, some mounted on horses and some on bicycles.

With the parade stalled, Stevie Knight and little Tyrone had stepped toward a balloon vendor who set up shop on the corner.

"He wants to look at every one of those balloons before he makes his decision," Evie said. "It's big stuff for him. He wants to get the best one."

Evie Knight was impeccably groomed in a soft blue wind breaker over a navy blue pant suit. Her hair was cut short and curled in tiny, tight rings close to her scalp. Small patches of gray mixed with the black. She wore large gold earrings, like ornate medallions flat against her ears.

"Your nephew is a precious boy," Della said, a little envious of the Knight family, who were on a lark, a day of good spirited revelry that little Tyrone would remember as part of his childhood. She too had once enjoyed a day like today with her own children. Now she hoped only for a glimpse of Kevin and Josie—maybe a wave—as they rode by.

"He's like our own son," Evie said. "We've raised him since he was three. We'll probably have him until he's grown and goes off to college. We don't have children of our own. We love Tyrone, but if we could control what happens in life, we'd never have written this script."

Della, unwilling to ask any questions—*Is his mother dead? Has something terrible gone wrong?*—looked at Evie, who must have recognized Della's concern. "Last time we saw his mother, she was skinny as a rail, her eyes glazed over. She's on some kind of dope." Evie raised her right hand to her chest, "'bout this tall. Smart girl. Always did well in school." Evie glanced toward Tyrone, who was still circling the helium balloons.

"Miss Boudreaux, why do you think a smart girl, a good looking girl, would get herself messed up like that?" Before Della could offer any kind of assessment, Evie drew her own conclusion. One Della could not dispute, even if she had wanted to do so. "Dope is the scourge of our time," she said, shaking her head.

Della knew all of this. She could have told Evie about her client in the hospital somehow tangled up in the drug trade—not of his own doing. She could have told Evie about J.J. Ernest who saw every day the magnitude of the drug problem, and was being consumed by it. She had so much she wanted to share with Evie Knight. Women unburdened their troubles by sharing them, splitting the weight of their loads. Della also wanted to tell Evie about her own struggles, about her own addiction that had severed her from her daughter. She wanted to tell her how only now she was rebuilding her relationship with her own children. But, the parade began to move forward, the horns now joined the drums in spirited rhythm. Della and Evie stepped back to the curb and stood next to Tyrone, who had settled on a blue octopus with bouncing legs. They all leaned forward, looking down the street, watching for the first float.

***

After the parade, Della made her way back to her office, a little disappointed she had not spotted Kevin or Josie on any of the floats. She must have selected the wrong side of the street. Kevin and Josie were on the other side of the float, but she had gotten to stand beside Reverend and Mrs. Stevie Knight and meet their little nephew—an unexpected blessing.

When she walked into her office, Candy Sue held the telephone out toward her. "I saw you coming. It's your ex. He says he has to talk to you. Now!"

Della rolled her eyes.

"I'd have taken a message, but he was insistent," Candy Sue said.

"He's always insistent. I'll take it in my office."

Candy Sue buzzed the call in just as Della sat in her desk chair. She placed the phone against her ear. "Galliard."

240

Oliver's Song

"Della, there's no way to break this easy. Before I tell you, let me just say . . ." He took a breath. "Don't get upset. Everything'll be alright. She's already in recovery mode."

Della stood now. "Who Galliard? Who's in recovery mode?"

"It's Josie. Got a call about six this morning. She was brought by ambulance to the hospital. She's on a drip. On some oxygen too. She's opened her eyes a couple times." Della heard Galliard breathe deeply again. "It's what they call alcohol toxicity. Nothing huge," he said. "She just partied too much. Sometimes you have to learn a lesson the hard way. She won't ever do this again. I'm sure of that."

"You didn't even bother to call me." Della felt heat rising up her neck.

"Whoa Della! Don't you do that to me!" His voice was filled with anger and accusation. "I been trying to call you ever since we got here and I figured out what was going on. I couldn't reach you. Your cell phone must be turned off. I even sent Kevin out to your apartment. We didn't know where the hell you were. I never thought you'd be in your office on Mardi Gras Monday."

Della slipped her cell phone out of her purse. She'd turned it off when she visited Ollie in the hospital and had forgotten to turn it on again.

Her baby in the hospital! Alcohol toxicity. She pulled a yellow sticky pad from the dispenser. "I'm coming," she said. "What hospital? What room number?" Her hand trembled as she wrote the information.

As soon as she turned on her cell phone, the message ring sounded. Okay, Galliard had tried to reach her. She gathered her purse on her shoulder and bounded out of her office.

"Josie's in the hospital," she shouted toward Candy Sue. "I'll call you as soon as I know more."

"Mr. Moss Maple's been trying to reach you," Candy Sue said.

"Later. Tell him I'll reach him later."

241

For now, the only important thing in the entire world was to be beside the bed where her daughter rested. Her daughter who took care of herself through her teen years, who had been forced to provide her own counsel. Della needed to be beside her bed now, waiting and ready for whatever Josie needed.

25

As Miguel Sanchez stepped out of the shower, his cell rang. Buck naked, with only a towel wrapped around his waist, he stepped to the bed, lifted the phone, and looked at the incoming number. One he did not recognize.

Should he answer? *Think positively Miguel. This is a new day. Un nuevo diá. It's Snake. He's got the violin. Billy Wong is dead. Even sweeter—he's bringing Billy Wong to you.*

He flipped open his phone and answered.

"Miguel." Not the hiss of Snake. The Boss's voice.

"Yes," he answered. The towel slipped from his waist. Miguel paced to the window where he stood naked to the world.

"I know about the drugs. Gone. My man got word to me."

His man. ¿Que hombre? The man who had brought Wong to Miguel in the beginning? The man Miguel could not reach now? Jack up the ante, and any man in this business would turn his back on his brother. His man—my ass!

"Yes," Miguel said. "The drugs are gone."

"Wong does have the violin. Right?"

"Si," Miguel answered. He shook his head in the affirmative as if The Boss stood in front of him.

"Is Wong with you?"

"Yes," Miguel lied again.

"Who will get the violin to me?"

"I will," Miguel answered. "I will personally deliver the violin back to you. A change in plans. I will explain everything when I see you."

Sweat trickled down to his elbow. His heart marched double time.

"We will settle on the drugs later."

"I know," Miguel said. "There must be a settlement."

"You will drive the violin to me? I want to lay eyes on my violin one more time before you take it to the Dominican Republic."

"Me? The Dominican Republic?" Miguel questioned. "Not Hong Kong?"

"Santa Domingo," the Boss said. "You know Santa Domingo, right?"

"Si, si," Miguel answered.

"You will do this for me, Miguel. Right?"

"I will do this," Miguel answered. "You can count on me."

His heart raced. His whole body now wet with sweat. He had to get out of the hotel room. His breath drew shallow.

"Tell me when."

"Let me make proper arrangements," Miguel answered.

"Soon," The Boss said.

"Pronto!" Miguel assured him.

He was gone. Miguel heard silence on the other end of the small phone he held in his palm.

He snapped his cell shut, threw it on the bed and stepped to his closet. His heart running fast. The beats pounding like a runner's feet sprinting hard against pavement. His hands shook. He slipped his pants over his feet. He reached for a shirt, his hands trembling.

The shirt clung to the hanger by a top button. Miguel ripped the button free. The button dropped and rolled across the marble floor.

He slipped his shoes on his feet—no socks. His head dripped water. He ran his fingers through his hair. No time for a comb. On the third try, he slid his wallet into his side pocket. *Should he take his cell? Yes! Yes! Snake would call. Surely Snake had Billy Wong and he had the violin. He would need his cell phone to give Snake directions.*

In the hallway, Miguel couldn't decide what to do. He could not get into the elevator. He couldn't ride down five floors in a small box. A coffin. ¡Una caja! He had to take the stairs, although the stairwell was not nearly large enough for his racing heart. His heart needed space. Lots of space. He would run down the stairs. Make his body match the rhythm of his heart. That would settle him.

Miguel placed his hand over his heart. He opened the door to the stairwell and, with his other hand, he held the rail, took in as much stale air as his shallow lungs would hold, and began his descent to the ground floor.

Hurry, Miguel! ¡Rápido!

Linda Busby Parker

26

When Della walked into the hospital room, she stopped in her tracks, allowing her eyes to adjust to the darkness.

"We had the lights on," Galliard said. "Josie didn't like that. So we turned them off."

Galliard stood beside Josie's bed. Kevin stood on the other side. Dora sat in a chair beside the window, the blind drawn shut.

Della felt her body tremble as she approached the bed. She had run to the parking lot, fought downtown traffic, and raced to get to her daughter. Galliard stepped back and stood beside Dora, allowing Della to assume his spot.

Della gently brushed her daughter's auburn hair away from her forehead. She cupped her hand and placed her knuckles against Josie's cheek. Never in her entire life had she been so glad to feel human heat, the heat that said *alive. My beautiful daughter is alive.* Tears filled her eyes. She wiped them with the pads of her fingers. Kevin pulled several tissues from the box on the nightstand closest to him, came around the end of the bed, gave his mother the tissues, and stood beside her. Della bent and kissed Josie on her forehead.

"How bad is it?" she asked without turning toward Gaillard.

"Not nearly as bad as it could have been." Galliard spoke to Della's back. "Kevin's the one we need to thank. He was at the party. He knew she'd had too much. When she blacked out, he called the ambulance."

Kevin put his arm around his mother's shoulder. "She was out, but she was still throwing up. I kept her head bent over so the stuff would run out her mouth, not back into her throat."

"That's the biggest danger," Galliard said. "A person blacks out, the body tries to get rid of all that alcohol, and the person chokes."

"Will she be okay?" Della asked, not taking her eyes off her daughter, still stroking Josie's hair.

"Should be," Galliard said. "First twenty-four hours are crucial. She had her last drink eight or nine hours ago. She has to be watched the whole time though. Like Kevin says, we don't want her to throw-up and get the stuff back down her windpipe or into her lungs."

"Did they pump her stomach?"

"They didn't have to," Kevin answered. "Soon as we got to the hospital, they put her on a drip and gave her oxygen."

"Glad they didn't have to pump her stomach," Galliard said. "I don't like the idea of them shoving a tube down her esophagus."

"Sit down, Mother." Kevin pulled a chair close to the bed, but Della didn't sit. She clung to her daughter's hand.

A little past noon, Galliard and Dora went downstairs to the cafeteria for lunch, but Della and Kevin remained by the bedside. When they returned, they tried to persuade Della to take a short break, but she refused. If Josie woke, she wanted to be beside her daughter's bed. She had been gone so many times when Josie needed her. She would not go this time.

Twice she and Kevin had raised Josie into a sitting position when she heaved. Each time, Della had wiped her daughter's face and mouth with a clean washcloth, cooled with fresh water. Each time a nurse had come into the room, repositioned the oxygen mask, checked the drip, taken Josie's blood pressure, and checked her heartbeat. Each time, the nurse had assured them Josie was doing well.

Once, Josie had opened her eyes. Had looked at Della. But she closed her eyes again and slept in a post-alcohol stupor.

At Della's insistence, Kevin went home for a quick shower and a bite to eat. When he returned, he brought a sandwich for her. In the hallway, she ate a few bites of the sandwich with soggy bread, and threw the remainder in the trashcan because her stomach still churned, and she knew it would until Josie completely recovered.

When Della returned to the room, Galliard was pacing—to the door and back to his daughter's bedside. To the door and back. To the door and back. Dora again sat in the chair beside the window and appeared exquisitely bored. She closed her eyes and napped sitting up.

Della wanted to tell Galliard their daughter had a drinking problem, but there was no point in telling him here and now. Surely he recognized Josie had a problem for which she needed treatment. To rid her body of toxins was only the beginning. But for now, they all needed to focus on the immediate problem—see Josie through the crisis hours and into tomorrow, a new day when the issues could be addressed calmly and examined carefully. Della had removed her shoes and stood barefoot on the tile floor, watching her daughter, unwilling to take her eyes off Josie.

Mid-afternoon, Dora, who still sat beside the window, stood, stretched, and looked at her watch. "It's been over twelve hours. I'm going home. Four of us here seems a little wacky."

"Go on," Della said. She turned and faced her ex-husband. "You go on too, Galliard. We need to divide our efforts. I'll be here. I'm not going anywhere."

"You sure?" Galliard stretched and raised his arms in the air above his head.

"Positive," Della assured him.

As Galliard and Dora were leaving, a heavy-set, black nurse came into the room. "Are you Della Boudreaux?" the nurse asked.

"I am," Della answered.

"Same man's called here three times. Says he needs to talk to the patient's mother. I told him, if you were here, I'd get you the message." She handed Della a small yellow note. "Here's his name and number. He said just tell you to let him know if you need anything. Says he's standing by."

Della glanced at the note. Moss Maple. Two telephone numbers followed his name.

"Might as well check everything while I'm here," the nurse said.

Della watched her. She lifted the oxygen mask, looked at Josie's face, and repositioned the mask. She placed Josie's wrist across her large palm, gently pressed her fingers against the vein, and counted. "I'll tell you the same thing that man there said," she pointed to the note in Della's hand. "You let me know if you need anything."

She turned toward Kevin, "we got cookies at the nurses' station. Come on down and get some. Your mother too."

"I'll do that," Kevin said.

Della didn't want to leave Josie's bedside. She handed the note to Kevin. "While you're down there, would you please call this number? It's a friend of mine. Tell him we're all fine. Josie's recovering. Tell him I'll call him later."

Kevin looked at the name and number on the little yellow paper. He looked up at his mother, but he didn't question her.

When he returned, he brought two large, chocolate chip cookies and a bar stool with a round wooden seat. "The nurses found this for you. They say you need to sit down. That last nurse says your feet are swelling."

Della looked at her bare feet. They were cold from standing on the tile. Sure enough, the top of her left foot was puffy. Kevin positioned the stool close to the bed. Della sat and reached between the bars of the bed rail, taking Josie's hand.

Josie opened her eyes and spoke. "Mom. Mom."

"I'm here," Della said. "I'm not going anywhere." She gently brushed Josie's hair, the spirals fanning out on the pillow like an angel in flight.

Josie closed her eyes again.

"After those cookies, I need coffee," Kevin said. "When I get back, I want you to go downstairs for a little while. Take a few minutes for yourself." He looked at his mother. When she frowned, he said, "Let me put that another way. When I get back,

Oliver's Song

I'll insist you go down for coffee and a little something to eat." With that, Kevin turned and left the room.

Just as Kevin left, the heavy-set nurse entered again. She placed her hand on her hip and grinned at Della. "Lady, you sure are popular. Another man called. He doesn't want to call the room, but he wants me to give you this message." She handed another yellow note to Della. "If you don't want to use the phone in the room here, we got one outside you can use."

J.J. Ernest's name and number were in large handwritten print on the note. *Call as soon as possible.*

Was J.J. calling to check on her daughter, or did he have information to share on Ollie's case? Maybe he had decided on official charges. If so, he needed to state his charges today — Mardi Gras or not.

"You need anything? We got a fresh pot of coffee at the nurses' station."

"I'm fine," Della said. "I'm going down to the cafeteria when my son gets back."

"You need to take care of yourself." The nurse pulled the door nearly shut, leaving Della in semi-darkness. Della stuck the note in the pocket of her skirt and closed her eyes. The sounds outside the hospital door were like the yellow lines on an endless roadway, soothing her and blending together into background noise.

When Kevin opened the door, a sharp beam of light from the hallway cut across Della's face. She woke with a start and nearly fell off the stool. Kevin lurched toward her, grabbing her shoulders. "I'm not sure this stool is such a great idea. One of us will fall asleep in this darkness and fall off." He helped his mother down from the stool.

When Della slipped her shoes on her feet, they fit snugly. She had to slip her index finger into the backs of her shoes to ease them on. She needed to walk, to get her circulation going again.

Kevin slid the stool away from the bed. "I'm not going to sit down for a while. I'll stand. That'll keep me awake. I've got my coffee too." He raised his Styrofoam cup for Della to see.

"I won't be gone long." Della pulled the door nearly closed as she eased out of the room. Her first mission—to telephone J.J. Ernest.

"I heard about your daughter," J.J. said, his voice a reedy drawl. "I'm sorry."

Della wondered what news about Josie had circulated through the Mardi Gras societies. Would her daughter now be a pariah? A bad influence, banned from the "good girls?" Even worse—would this make the newspaper? Her heart sank when she thought of the effect this might have on Josie. She knew too well the alcoholic's painful loss of self-esteem, and the slow rise to reclaim the previous self. She did not want to discuss any of this with J.J. Ernest.

"She's doing well," she said, then narrowed the conversation to professional matters. "You must have some news about my client."

"Unfortunately," J.J. cleared his throat. "We got our first body. An Asian found by the water in Bayou La Batre. Been dead about twelve hours."

"Whoa," Della said. "How do you know this body—this man," she stammered, "is tied to my client?"

"Let's take it from the beginning," J.J. said. "Name's Chang Wu. Owns an import and freight business in Chicago. Checked into the Riverview Hotel on Friday night." Della heard him flip a page, probably a page in his little pocket notebook.

"The Asians we got down at the jail haven't given us much information. They're pretending they don't speak much English, and they claim they don't know a thing about what they carried in that van. One piece of info they did give us was the name of the man they worked for." He paused. Della thought the pause was for effect.

252

Oliver's Song

"A Mr. Chang Wu." *Wu* came out as a puff of air. "Say they're only the drivers. They take cargo from one place to another and never ask questions. Talk to Mr. Chang Wu they say. Well, what they don't know is, Mr. Chang Wu's right here in our city, but we can't talk to him. He's in the morgue."

"Are you sure this Chang Wu isn't Billy Wong, the fellow my client needs to locate?"

"Doesn't fit the description," J.J. said. "We did find Billy Wong's name in a little black book inside the pocket of Mr. Wu's shirt. All kinds of little sayings in that book too. Crazy stuff like, a beautiful bird causes the eye to sing. Stuff like that. Probably drug code."

"What do you make of all this?" Della asked, hoping to get as much information from J.J. Ernest as she could.

"That's what your client needs to tell us. I know he's down there at the hospital. I understand the boy's got a busted up leg and he's banged up pretty good. He can still talk though. If he's going to talk, he needs to do it soon. One body so far. I'll be less lenient now than I would have been yesterday."

"I'll say the same thing I said yesterday," Della reminded him. "My client's told all . . ."

J.J. cut her short. "Mayor Dow won't like a body found downtown during Mardi Gras. And, for me, I've staked my reputation on a safe city. My patience is nearly rubbed raw. My nerves are exposed. I highly recommend your boy sing like a young male mockingbird." J.J. was on a roll now and barely paused for air. "I filed charges today. Transporting a controlled substance with intent to distribute. Enormous street value. Your boy's in for big time."

"I'll review the charges." Della said. She wanted to get off the telephone fast now. She had nothing else to say. She had a plan. "If my client has anything else to say, I'll call you."

"I'd have him consider what I've told you. One more body, and there's no talking. He was caught red-handed with the goods. He's headed to prison."

253

"Thank you for the information," Della said. "By the way, there's one thing I need to tell you too." She told J.J. about the attempted break in at her apartment and about the entry at her office.

"See what I told you," J.J. said. "This whole thing's getting serious fast. Too fast. Your client knows a whole lot more than he's owned up to. I have a feeling he's going to need protection to save his skin, inside prison, as well as outside. You might need protection too. Sounds like you've become a target."

"Wait a minute," Della said. "Both the attempted break-in and the entry could be coincidental but non-related. You remember Logic 101—just because one thing happens in close proximity to another thing doesn't mean they're related."

"True, but I have my suspicions. I'll have the P.D. watch your office and put your apartment on cruise-by tonight." She heard him take a bite of air. "Lady," J.J. said. "I'm afraid you're a duck out of water. You don't know what you're dealing with here." With that, he said his goodbye and hung up.

Della placed a quick call to Candy Sue. After seeing her secretary—pistol in hand, pit-bull stance, miscreant subdued— Della had new respect for her assistant. This woman had talents beyond directing calls and painting her toenails.

"Pack an overnight bag," she said when her secretary answered. "Fill your car with gas and stand by. I'll be back in touch."

"You got it, Miss Della."

27

On the Biloxi beach, Miguel moved swiftly. His feet spun sand into his shoes. The sand ground against the skin of his heels. He didn't care. He leaned his body into the stiff breeze off the Gulf and trudged forward. *He was the rooster with its head on the block.* He saw the downy neck feathers, iridescent green and blue, highlighted in sunlight. The bird's eyes closed while Miguel stroked the gorgeous neck. He saw again his mother. Her arms raised above the bird's head. The ax in her hands. *Whack! ¡Hombre muerto!*

He lifted his arms to waist height and pumped, walking faster. *Fast! Fast!* His heart pounded. He would leave the pounding behind him. He cautioned himself: *Calm Miguel. Calm!*

He breathed deep. *Again, deep. Deep. Let it out. Deep. Let it out.* The pounding slowed a little. He slowed his pace.

He turned his head to watch pelicans searching the water for prey. One of the pelicans spotted its kill and dropped straight down, breaking open the water's surface. Miguel stopped and watched the bird when it rowed its wings and rose from the water, a long fish wiggling in its beak.

He walked slowly now, filling himself with sunlight and the heavy salt-air off the Gulf. *Calm! Tranquilo. T-r-a-n-q-u-i-l-o.*

He saw his beautiful Puerto Plata. He could actually feel the sun of his Dominican Republic on his face.

But—he was here in Biloxi, not in his Puerto Plata. In the distance, Miguel spotted the remains of a pier. Pilings with some cross boards still attached. He would go there. Sit and stretch his body across the boards, close his eyes, and feel the sun's warmth on his face.

As he walked in the breeze toward the pier, his cell rang. He fumbled for it in the pocket of his pants, glancing at the number before he answered. It was Snake. Tor-Tuba would do the talking. Snake rarely spoke on the telephone. Snake rarely spoke at all.

To block the wind coming off the water, Miguel pressed the phone tightly to his ear. He cleared his throat. He was in no mood for formality.

"Tor-Tuba. Do you have Billy Wong?"

"Not Tuba," Snake hissed. "Tuba in jail."

Miguel stopped in his tracks. "Tor-Tuba in jail?"

"Picked up snooping 'round that lady attorney's office."

"What about the violin?" Miguel asked. "Do you have that?"

"Headed back to da Easy," Snake said, ignoring the question. "Meet you there. Two-thirty. Little coffee place. Like before."

"Snake, do you have Billy Wong?" Miguel asked his questions slowly—deliberately. "Do you have the violin?"

"No Wong. No violin. Collection day. Tuba need money for bail. You be at da coffee place. On time."

"Job's not done. I need Billy Wong. I need the violin." Miguel closed his eyes, his left fist pressed to his forehead. *¡Carajo!*

"No violin. No Wong. All over, man." Miguel heard Snake suck air. "Cash," he said. "Hundreds be best." With that Snake hung up.

What surprised Miguel the most was that his heart did not pound now. He was a broken man. The tense rod down his back split into pieces. He had no explanation for it, but he was calm. He remembered the old priest back in Bogotá who talked of a peace that passes all understanding. When the rod was broken, it could no longer strike. When the old man was crippled, he could no longer run. With acceptance, came peace. *Tranquilidad.* He saw the rooster stretch its beautiful neck across the block—so calm, it closed its eyes. He looked toward the water. In the bay, the pelican perched on one of the pilings to down its wiggling prey.

No Billy Wong. No violin. He stood and watched the other pelicans hunt above the water, hoping for prey as large as their brother had captured.

Oliver's Song

All over. No money for Snake. No violin for The Boss. No Billy Wong. If he tried to run, where would he go? His legs were crippled.

He looked over the water, as far as his eyes could see. He knew what he would do. He would go to his Puerto Plata. He would again sit on the porch of his beautiful ranch house. He would sit and wait. They might not come for some long while. They would find him—sooner or later—he knew this. While he still had time, he would sit and look down at the water, his water. There was no blue like it anywhere else in the world. The same blue Columbus must have seen when he sailed into the Caribbean. The blue he could see from his chair on his own front porch—nothing more beautiful under the heavens. *Mi pedazo del cielo*.

Linda Busby Parker

28

Before going to the cafeteria, Della wanted to stop by Ollie's room and tell him about the call from J.J. Ernest. She also wanted to ask him a few questions. When she stepped off the elevator, she saw the guard across the hall, his back to Ollie's door, sipping coffee and flirting with the nurses. She walked to the door, stood and waited for the guard to turn and see her.

The door to the room was nearly closed, but she heard two voices inside the room. She recognized Ollie's, his words tight, coming past his stiffly held lower lip. But whose was the second voice?

"Son, you're not fooling anybody. You think this is bad? Wait 'til they send you to Federal prison. The inmates there will use you for sport."

"Nothing," Ollie insisted, his voice a note higher than normal. "I know nothing."

"You got everybody scurrying around trying to save your ass. At some level, you're guilty as sin itself. You know it and I know it."

Ollie moaned. The guard still sipped coffee and flirted with a blonde-headed nurse.

"Stop!" Ollie ordered, the sibilant sound coming past the edges of his clinched teeth.

Della charged into the room—permission no longer an issue.

Bobby Jack Arnold, Oliver Sr.'s silver-haired attorney, had his fist balled around a hunk of Ollie's hospital gown, pulling the young man toward him.

"What in hell is going on here?" Della asked, her voice raised.

Bobby Jack flung open his hand, releasing the fist-full of gown.

Ollie glared at his father's attorney.

259

The guard was in the room now. "You don't have permission to be in here." He looked directly at Della, his index finger pointed at her face.

"This man's harassing my client," Della snapped.

"There's some kind of misunderstanding," Bobby Jack said. His silver tongue had returned to match his silver hair.

"This is my attorney," Ollie said. He pointed at Della. "This man is not," he said with a nod toward Bobby Jack.

"Don't matter who's who," the guard said. "Nobody comes inside this room without my permission." He turned toward Della and lifted his index finger again. "I can arrest you on the spot."

"I can't stand outside while this man verbally and physically batters my client."

"Noooo," Bobby Jack said. "Nothing like that's going on. I'm afraid you've misunderstood me."

He turned toward the guard. "I'm leaving, sir." He glanced at Della. "I'm sorry you misunderstood what was going on." He nodded his head at her and dipped slightly, his cowboy hat in his hands.

Della stepped outside the room with the guard, who questioned her before he allowed her to enter again. He wanted to be certain she understood his authority. When she again stood at Ollie's bedside, she explained what she had learned from J.J. Ernest.

"No kidding! Ollie blew a shrill whistle between his teeth, keeping his lower lip stiff. "This thing's heating up."

"You got it. One man dead already. Can you think of anything that might help us? Anybody who knows Billy Wong? Anybody who might have heard your conversation with him in the courtyard at F.S.U.?" Della pulled her small leather journal and her pen from her shoulder bag—ready.

"Same people hang out in the courtyard all the time. Spend part of every day there. Go there and you'll see them all. I know Wong's got a girlfriend—or he did have a girlfriend. I think

Vietnamese or Thai. She works at a nail place close to campus. She paints fingernails or puts on artificial nails or something like that."

"What's her name?"

"Don't think I ever knew name." Ollie brought his hand to his hurt lip. "I know name of shop because I heard Billy Wong say it. Funny name." He tried to smile and winced from the pain. "Tips and Toes. She picked him up from university a couple times. Has gold crown on first molar. Shows when she talks." He offered as few words as possible, protecting his lip.

Della jotted everything down. "I'm sending an investigator to Tallahassee."

"Good. That's good. Maybe somebody heard Billy ask me to carry bass to Mobile."

"That won't get us out of the water," Della told him, "but it's a start."

What she didn't tell him was that she would send Candy Sue, the pit-bulldog. Now that she saw her secretary in a new light, investigation might be where she would shine.

"If that Bobby Jack Arnold comes in here again," Della said, "I want to know."

Before she left, she told him the story of her own daughter, one floor below him. She might as well be straight, tell the truth — alcohol overdose. Truth was her manifesto.

Ollie took her hand. "I'm sorry. Anybody can make a mistake. She'll be okay."

What Della didn't tell him was that she suspected Josie was in for a battle, an alcoholic's battle. What she said was: "You're right. I know she'll be fine."

She raised her palm. Ollie lifted his palm and touched hers. A high five. "Later," she said. She tucked the little notebook back into her purse and left the room, speaking to the guard on the way out to let him know she acknowledged his authority. It would be best to remain on his good side — after all, he was the gatekeeper.

Outside the cafeteria, she placed a call to Candy Sue. "Is your bag packed?" she asked. "You're going to Tallahassee to do some investigation."

"Miss Della," Candy Sue said, "I knew this job would turn into something good. You know how sometimes you just get a feeling about things. The pay was low. Real low. But the whole situation had good karma."

"Great. I think you'll be a fine detective."

"This could be my big break," Candy Sue said.

Della pulled her small journal from her bag and gave Candy Sue the information she had received from Ollie—the students who hung out in the courtyard and the young Asian woman with the gold crown on her first molar who worked at a place called Tips and Toes. Candy Sue would be on the road well before sunset.

In the cafeteria, Della got a salad and a small bowl of strawberry Jell-O. Funny how certain foods looked better in the hospital than they looked anywhere else—namely, the strawberry Jell-O. She also poured a cup of black coffee, which she took to a small table overlooking the courtyard.

She had taken a bite of the salad and a sip of the coffee when someone placed a hand on her shoulder. She turned to see Oliver Sr. standing beside her.

"Mind if I join you?"

Della raised her hand toward the empty seat. "Please."

Oliver Sr. placed his coffee and his sweet roll on the table, pulled out a chair, and seated himself. He had presented himself to her; she didn't have to go looking for him—the time was right to speak. "Your attorney's been badgering my client. I caught him in Ollie's room a few minutes ago. He was way out of line."

"He was trying to help. That's all. Man-to-man stuff. Trying to determine if Ollie knows more than he's saying."

Della leaned in, her arms on the table. "I'll file a complaint with the bar if he doesn't stop badgering my client. He knows full well Ollie has representation."

Oliver's Song

"Pshhh," Oliver said, blowing air between his teeth. "I've known Bobby Jack for a good thirty years. He didn't mean any harm. Just trying to help."

"It's help like that I don't appreciate and won't tolerate." Della kept her eyes dead-on Oliver Sr.

He took a bite of his sweet roll and wiped his mouth with his napkin. "Something I should tell you too. Our relatives left town today, and I've got a business client wants to use the fishing camp. Before I came back to the hospital a while ago, I took our maid out to clean the place up. Soon as I opened the door, I saw it wasn't right. The place was torn up. Somebody had busted the back door, looking for something to take, I'm sure." He took a sip of his coffee.

"Everything out of closets, furniture upturned. The place was wrecked. Funny thing was, they didn't seem to take anything. I have several shotguns in a cabinet. The cabinet was busted open, but the guns were still there. All three guns in their places—not even touched, far as I can tell. Some expensive mountain bikes in the garage too. All those were still there. Whoever came in was looking for something else. I called the police. They came out and I filed a report. What do you think this means, Miss Boudreaux? Why would somebody break into the camp and tear the place apart?" Oliver Sr. looked out the window toward the courtyard. He brought his coffee mug to his lips again, pondering his own question.

Della told Oliver Sr. about the attempted break-in at her apartment and the entry at her office. "And now the fishing camp," she added.

"Something big is going on. I'm worried about my son. I wish he would come clean. Tell us everything he knows. That's all Bobby Jack was trying to do. Get the truth out of him."

"I believe he is telling the truth. I think he's told us everything he knows."

At that very moment, she remembered something. A detail Ollie had told her about the contents of the bass case. "Come on," she said to Oliver Sr. "Let's go have a chat with your son." Oliver Sr. took one final slug of his coffee and left the mug on the table. He followed Della to the elevator.

"Dad tell you someone broke into the fishing camp?" Ollie asked as soon as Della and Oliver Sr. walked into his hospital room.

Della nodded. She stood on one side of Ollie's bed and his father stood on the other.

"When you first came into my office," Della said, "you told me about a violin in that bass case. I don't remember seeing that listed on the police report."

"A violin?" Oliver Sr. asked.

"Yeah, Dad. Was a violin in that case too. When I tried to move bass case out of fishing camp," Ollie brought his hand to his chin in an effort to ease his pain. "Couldn't fit violin back inside case." Again, he kept his words to a minimum. "Don't know how Billy Wong got it in there. Wasn't worried about violin. Wanted to get bad stuff out of camp before family came."

"The violin," Della asked "what did you do with that?"

"Put it in closet. Closet in room where I slept."

"Is it still there?" Della looked up at Oliver Sr.

He shrugged his shoulders. "Haven't a clue. I looked around with the police. We glanced in the closet. Saw my son's clothes and his suitcase. Tell you the truth though, when the guns and the bikes weren't taken, we decided the burglars might have run before they had time to take anything. We didn't look for a violin because we didn't know any violin was there. Why would someone break into the place for a violin? Those things aren't worth much are they, son?"

"Depends on violin. Really good violin could run fifty thousand. Stradivarius might be over a million. But can't find those for sale."

"I've heard of those violins," Oliver Sr. said. "Italian," but he pronounced it *Eye-talian*. "Don't remember the century."

"Stradivarius," Ollie said "mid-sixteen to early seventeen hundreds. Took a class in music history."

"What kind of violin was in the case?" Della asked.

"Don't know. Was old. Looked very old. Didn't think much about it. Didn't look like cheap student violin though. Not kind Billy Wong would have. Had nice trim around edges, chain like pattern. Never seen anything like that. Pretty. Violin was golden brown."

"Okay," Della said, and she divvied up the next steps between herself and Oliver Sr. He would head out to the fishing camp to check inside the closet, and on her way to her daughter's room, she would telephone J.J. Ernest.

"Hello," J.J.'s reedy voice spoke into the phone.

"Hi, J.J., Della here."

"Della Boudreaux? Two times in one day? Mardi Gras Monday no less. Must mean your client has something to say."

She had no time to waste pawing or clawing at J.J. Ernest. She needed to get back to her daughter's room.

"I told you there had been an attempted break-in at my apartment last night and a man picked the lock and entered my office this morning. Add one more to that list—the fishing camp where Ollie Fitzsimmons was staying. Burglars tore the place up. Oliver Sr. was out there with the police about noon today." She grabbed a quick breath and charged ahead, not wanting J.J. to gain verbal footing in the conversation.

"An old violin was in the bass case along with the drugs. On Friday night, Ollie Fitzsimmons placed the violin in his closet before he moved the bass case. The violin wasn't on the police report, because it wasn't in the case. The burglars didn't appear to take anything from the camp. Oliver Sr. is in route to the fishing camp now to check the closet. We need to determine if the violin is still there. Bottom line is—J.J., you might want to head out to the fishing camp."

"More drugs in the violin?" J.J. questioned.

"No. The violin's the only thing we can think of the burglars might have been looking for. Guns and expensive bikes weren't touched."

"What are you trying to tell me, Della? What we got here? You telling me this is some kind of expensive violin? You trying to get my hound's nose off the scent of your client? The boy's a mule. Caught red-handed transporting. Can't get a hound dog off something that stinks like this."

"J.J., I got no time for this. I have a daughter here at the hospital. I need to get back to her. I'm handing out information I think might be valuable. Take it, or leave it lay." She stopped right there. It was his decision. She had no time for shenanigans.

"I'll give you one thing. You sure know how to mess up a perfectly good day off. We're both supposed to be enjoying Mardi Gras." J.J. strung out the words—*Mar-dee-Grawww.*

"No sweat," Della said. "Take it or leave it." With that, she snapped her cell shut.

29

"Look at you!" Tuit said when Billy Wong walked in the side door, holding a violin in his right hand and a bow in his left. "This the man who would have my van back before I needed to deliver the morning paper. Sure! You lose your route if you can't deliver the paper." She glanced at her watch to be certain Billy understood the magnitude of his error. Then, she turned toward the kitchen sink, her back to Billy Wong. She rinsed dishes and stacked them in a draining tray.

Sorry," he said in a soft voice. "How'd you deliver the paper?"

Tuit looked over her shoulder at him. "Borrowed the neighbor's car."

"I screwed up," Billy said.

"You stay in some bar all night?" Tuit asked, accusation in her voice. She turned the water off, dried her hands on her apron, stepped to the counter and faced Billy. "You drunk?"

"No. Not drunk. I had to get this violin. Took longer than I thought." He held the violin in front of him so she could see it.

"You win that violin in cards or something?"

"Nope. Bought it."

"Where? I don't know any stores around here that sell violins. How far'd you drive?"

"Pawn shops got everything," Billy said.

"You bought that in a pawn shop?" She puckered her lips, assessing Billy and his violin. "Nice!"

"Sorry about the van," he said again.

"I guess it was okay. I got the papers delivered." She said this in a voice of resignation—a woman used to disappointments. "Johnny's in the shower. He slept late."

267

She came around the end of the kitchen bar, her eyes on the violin. "Let me look at it."

She put her hands out to take the instrument. Billy placed the bow on the coffee table and held the violin out. He let Tuit look at it, but he didn't let her hold it.

"Can you play that thing?"

"I can play anything," he told her. "Give me a musical instrument, and I'll play it. Just have to learn to hold it and speak its language. "Bass, cello, a horn, a violin. I could be a whole orchestra, if there was enough of me. Not enough Billy Wong to go around," he shrugged his shoulders.

"A whole orchestra? You're something." She laughed and folded her arms under her chest, studying him.

"Honey," Johnny called from down the hall. "I need a towel. There's none in the bathroom."

"Coming." Tuit lifted a stack of folded towels from the bar and headed down the hall.

She didn't believe him. Billy knew this. He wouldn't bother to give Tuit an explanation, but he knew he had a special gift that had passed through the ages and slid through his shoulders to his heart. He understood musical instruments and always had. He could hear almost any instrument play itself before the instrument sounded its first tone.

He was convinced that a spirit had placed this talent on his shoulders. He didn't even think the spirit had been one of his own relatives. He had never heard talk of good musical ears in any of his ancestors. The peculiar thing was, the spirit had to be European—not Asian. Maybe some old fellow with no children had died, and just for the fun of it, the old goat decided to give this special gift of music to an Asian kid. Billy knew the spirit was European because he could hear a piece of the white man's European music one time and the notes locked in his head. He had every note almost perfect after listening to a piece one or two times. The spirit might even have been some crazy European playing a joke—give the white man's ears and the white man's

Oliver's Song

European music to a poor kid in China. *Funny! Funny!* But, what he had told Tuit was all true. Musical instruments spoke to him. Not only that, he could hear a piece of music and know the next notes before they sounded.

Only question was — why would so special a gift been given to a baby born in rural China? That's why he thought the spirit that had touched him was some real prankster. Some real joker. But then — he also understood what probably happened. He grew up in Hubei Province, that had to be the reason the old European spirit had placed special musical ears on him. Maybe the old spirit had come to live in the mountains of Wudang. Everyone knew spirits lived in the old monasteries that lined the mountains.

The Chinese said the Hubei lived between heaven and earth. People from Hubei Province were Nine Headed Birds, head strong, aggressive and hard to kill.

In the sky live nine-headed birds.
On Earth live cunning Hubei people.

The old spirit had found a Hubei child on whom to place special musical ears and the love of music flowed all the way to Billy's heart.

Had he been born not in Hubei Province, but in the United States to some rich parents, he would be performing in Carnegie Hall right now. He knew it. He would be touring Europe. China would be calling. His only problem would be deciding which instrument to play and which engagement to accept.

No — that would not be a problem. His rich parents would have settled on the instrument when he was just a boy. By now, he would have had lessons on the instrument with the finest teachers. He would be set. He would be smiling from the pages of newspapers all over the world — a musical prodigy.

But — no. That was not the way it had happened. Rural China. A gift, but no education. No lessons. No instrument. He had worked in a small tea processing plant. Hubei — all hills and

269

mountains growing tea. He had hauled great sacks of tea as if he were a mule. Then he had found his own passage to the states and made his way to Mr. Chang Wu.

Selling Chang Wu's drugs, not once, but two times—he grinned when he thought of this again—would have been plenty of money for lessons had Ollie Fitzsimmons not ruined things. Give a job to a rich U.S. kid and somehow, one way or another, the job would be spoiled. The spirit had not failed him though. This beautiful violin had landed in his hands. This violin was meant for him. The old spirit had sent it to him.

He sat on the couch, brought the violin close to his nose and smelled it. Beautiful smell—old and mellow. Now he had an instrument to match his talents. He wasn't sure what he held, but he knew it was something special. When he got to Hong Kong— he had his ticket already and he would use it—he would have time to study this violin, to find out what treasure had fallen to him. He would lose the old Billy Wong and would be Yong Xi, a new man with a beautiful instrument. He sniffed the violin again, allowing the violin's fragrance to seep into his lungs. *This belonged to him.* He was sure this violin would speak to him in the sweetest voices. His hands sweated with anticipation.

Johnny came down the hall, his socks in his hand. "Hey, Billy. What you got?"

"Look. Don't touch. Your hands might still be damp from your shower." Billy held the violin out, allowing Johnny a close examination.

"Looks old. Hope you didn't pay too much." Johnny lifted his foot to the edge of the couch, slipping his sock over his toes.

"Got a good deal. Didn't pay too much." Billy tucked the violin under his arm, close to his chest, holding it as all the great players held their instruments.

"I need to leave today. Can you drive me to Atlanta? I'll pay you well." Billy added this last sentence by way of enticement.

"Today?" Johnny questioned.

Oliver's Song

"This afternoon," Billy said. "I'll be ready." He did not tell Johnny where he would go after he reached Atlanta and Johnny did not ask. Johnny was cool.

30

Josie was sitting up in bed when Della opened the door. Kevin stood beside the bed, holding Josie's water bottle. The Venetian blinds were opened and late afternoon sun cut narrow shadows across the tile floor.

"Look at you," Della said.

"I told her you'd been here all day. I made you go home for a few minutes to refresh yourself," Kevin said. Della knew how hard her son was working to smooth out creases in the relationship between mother and daughter. She loved Kevin for who he was and for all he did.

"I had to get some comfy shoes too." Della raised one foot, showing her canvas shoes. "My feet were killing me."

"Good." Josie licked her lips. She reached for the water bottle Kevin held, and she drew on the straw. "My lips are parched," she said when she pulled the straw away from her mouth.

"You were dehydrated," Kevin said.

Josie looked at her mother. "Thanks for being here. I was stupid."

Della patted her daughter's hand, which felt cold and trembled. "We've all done things we regret."

The paleness of Josie's skin and her green eyes made her bronzed hair appear deep gold in the low light of late winter. "I feel rotten." She rubbed a shaky hand across her forehead.

"I can tell you all about that," Della said. "Least the room's not spinning. Right?"

"Not much. I was so stupid," she whispered in utter disgust of her situation. "Guess I pulled a Della Boudreaux."

"Wait a minute," Kevin said. "Josie, you shouldn't take things out on . . ."

Della cut him short. "That's exactly what you did. You pulled a Della Boudreaux."

Rebuilding her relationship with her daughter would not be smooth sailing. There would be plenty of rough seas.

"I really do feel awful." Josie leaned back on the stack of pillows.

Della stepped to the bathroom to get a cool, damp cloth for Josie's neck. She knew from experience a cool cloth under her daughter's neck would make her feel better.

But, instead of slipping the cloth under Josie's neck, she handed the moist cloth to her daughter. She knew Josie would recoil if she attempted to touch her. She also knew—a gut-level understanding—she could not push their relationship too far too fast. Being here with Josie was a crack in the door, the first tiny opening. Della had to measure every inch, making certain she didn't overstep the space Josie allowed her.

Josie took the cloth, wiped her face and draped it across her throat, just under her chin. "Thanks," she said without opening her eyes.

Della heard her cell phone ring inside her purse. She stepped to the window to answer it.

"I heard Josetta drank too much and is at the hospital," Mercedes said without so much as hello. "Is she okay?"

"Dear Lord," Della said. Josie opened her eyes and looked toward her mother. Della wanted to say, *Mercedes, you heard about Josie all the way in Montgomery? My dear God—how fast does bad news travel?* For fear of alarming Josie, she held these questions inside her mouth. "Hold on a minute," she said.

"Darling, I'm going to step outside to take this call, so you can rest." Josie nodded her head slightly and moaned, which Della took as acknowledgement.

She walked half way down the hall toward the elevators before she spoke. "Mercedes, how did news about Josie travel all the way from Mobile to Montgomery?"

Oliver's Song

"I got friends you know. Lots of friends in the old societies. These new societies are a different animal altogether. Most of their members are transplants from somewhere else. I've had two or three calls as a matter of fact. Of course they were checking on the situation here with my sister's arrangements and all, but then they told me about Josetta." Mercedes always called Josie by her given name, *Josetta*.

"Oh my!" Della muttered, wondering if her daughter would now truly be off limits for the *good girls*.

"When an ambulance is called to rush a girl to the hospital, Mercedes said, "a little ole girl like Josetta with a great big blood alcohol level, there *will be* some talk. Not to worry though, everyone's just thinking it could have been their own child. You know young people don't always make the best decisions."

Della heard Mercedes sigh. "Old folks don't always make the right decisions either. Anyway, let me get back to my original question—how's Josetta?"

"Doing fine. An I.V. drip and time are making her whole again. She's talking a little and sitting up, but she's still shaky."

"We both know how that is."

"Yes. We both know," Della said. "And how about you, how are you doing?"

"My sister's daughter is here from California. She's made all the arrangements. There'll be a memorial service on Tuesday. My niece will bring me home later in the week."

"It's good to hear your voice, Mercedes," Della said. "So good," and she meant it. She did not tell Mercedes about the attempted break-in at her house, about the shattered light bulb on the back patio, about the bullet that grazed the wood and left a permanent skid mark on Mercedes' door casing. These things could wait. No need to worry her when she still carried the emotional burden of burying her sister.

"I'll feel good to be home. Everybody fits best at home," Mercedes concluded.

"Yes. I'll be glad to have you home. Let me know if there's anything I can do. I mean that."

"See you soon," Mercedes said.

Della pressed the off button on her cell phone and was nearly back to Josie's door when her cell rang again. "Della here."

"Glad I reached you." She recognized J.J. Ernest's drawl.

"I need to get back with my daughter," Della said. "Did you and Mr. Fitzsimmons locate that violin at the fishing camp?" She wasn't going to waste any time.

"No violin," J.J. said. "This case is taking a strange turn. Why would someone want a violin? You sure there was a violin in that bass case?"

In her mind, Della could see J.J.'s face, his lips puckered, his eyes squinted in consternation as he tried to put the pieces together.

"That's what my client told me. An old violin was tucked inside the case. He couldn't get it back inside, so when he moved the other stuff, he placed the violin in his closet."

"No violin there now," J.J. said. "I've called the FBI to see what they make of it. I still don't think your client is telling us the truth—all the truth. I'm not a hundred percent sure there was a violin in that case. I'll be adding years to your boy's time for failure to cooperate." J.J. took a breath. "I hate to see a thing like this. A young person who's gonna spend all his best years in the penitentiary. Looks like that's what he'll do if you don't talk some sense into him."

"Look. Piece it together. Someone broke into the fishing camp and tore the place apart. They didn't take guns, and they didn't take expensive bicycles. In fact, they didn't take anything." Della paused here for effect—"except the violin. My client is telling the truth. You didn't find anything else missing did you?"

"Not that Mr. Fitzsimmons can identify."

"There you go," Della said.

"Well," J.J. Ernest said, "like I told you, I've called the FBI We'll see what they say."

Oliver's Song

Inside Josie's room, the friendly nurse stood beside the bed. "Hey Mama, I told your girl here I know something that will make her feel real good. A nice sponge bath. You and your son want to step out? Nothing gives a body a new lease on life like a bath. Even a sponge bath," the nurse said. She patted Josie's arm.

Josie moaned. "I'm not so sure. My head still hurts." She licked her dry lips.

"Come on. Let's get you cleaned up. I've got a fresh gown for you."

"We'll wait down the hall," Kevin said.

"Little lounge down there," the nurse said. "Got a coffee machine and a coke machine. Coffee's not much good, but those little chocolate covered doughnuts in the goodie machine are my favorite. You'll probably like them."

In the lounge, Kevin inserted a dollar bill and hit the coffee button. Powdered instant coffee dropped into the cup and then the machine dispensed steaming water. "Doesn't look too appealing." He peered at the grayish-brown liquid in the Styrofoam cup, and handed it to his mother before sliding another dollar into the machine.

"Want to try those chocolate doughnuts?" Della asked. When he nodded, she dropped three quarters into the slot.

She and Kevin took their coffee and doughnuts over to the window and stood looking out at the late afternoon traffic on the street below. "Interesting how something like this changes everything," Kevin said. "This killed my Mardi Gras activities. Can't say I regret not attending the last of the parties and balls. I'd had about enough."

"You can go on. I've got it covered here. No need for you to miss tonight's ball."

"No. I'm serious. I've had enough."

They sipped their instant coffee and watched the cars below them stop at the traffic light. "I need to tell you something," Kevin said. "I'm sorry I didn't tell you sooner."

Della sensed the conversation had grown serious.

"This isn't the first time something like this has happened with Josie. I don't mean being in the hospital. There have been other instances, but I think this is the first time she's come seriously close to overdosing."

"Why didn't I know?"

"You didn't know because no one told you. I was sworn to secrecy and damn me—I'm not proud of this, mother—I raised my right hand and swore. Dad pretended it was a joke, but he had me raise my hand and swear." Kevin lowered his head and pressed his fingers against his eyes.

Della sat at the table now. She felt dizzy. What else had been concealed from her?

"I don't know all the facts. But, I'll tell you what I know." Kevin pulled out a chair and sat at the table across from his mother.

"Last semester Dad got a call from somebody in administration at the University. Josie had checked out a lab to complete a project at night—a recording lab, I think. She was taking a course where she had to produce some kind of recorded program—I believe that's right."

Kevin shook his head as if trying to clear his memory. "Anyway, every time Josie used the lab, the next morning the professors found liquor bottles in trash cans outside the building and inside the building too. Somebody at the university talked to Josie and she claimed she was innocent. They called Dad. He went there and threatened to sue the university if they didn't have evidence that the empty bottles were actually Josie's. Apparently the folks at the university just wanted Dad to talk to Josie and see if there was a problem. He told them there was no problem. He didn't want to hear anything else about it."

Oliver's Song

Kevin took a sip of the weak coffee. "Dad asked me not to tell you. No—that's not quite accurate. Dad *told* me not to tell you and I went along with it. You know, good old go-along Kevin."

He balled his fist and pounded the table. "I'm sick of playing these games! Don't tell this person this and don't tell that person that. There were a couple of other situations too—drinking too much at sorority parties, I think. I was sworn to secrecy about those too."

Kevin slammed his fist against the Formica tabletop again—hard this time. Their coffee cups wobbled and coffee splashed on the table. "When will I ever get some guts like you have, Mom? Go-along Kevin," he said, condemning himself once more.

Della placed her hand on top of her son's hand. "Thank you for telling me."

Kevin pulled away and reached for several napkins from a dispenser on the counter. He wiped the table. "I should have told you before. I should never have let Dad ramrod me into silence."

Della wanted to console her son, but she was angry that these previous problems with Josie had been hidden from her. She thought it best to say nothing until she could put things into perspective, until she could bring some wisdom to bear on the situation.

"There you two are," Galliard said as he entered the lounge. "The nurse told me you'd be down here. She's giving Josie a sponge bath." He looked around the tiny room with the vending machines. "I didn't know this little lounge was here."

Neither Della nor Kevin had yet spoken to him, but this didn't seem to bother Galliard.

"Coffee any good?"

Before they could answer, he deposited three quarters and pushed the button. The powdered coffee and steaming water flowed into the Styrofoam cup. Galliard brought his cup to the table, pulled out a chair and sat. "What are you doing here?" he asked Kevin. "There's a ball tonight. You need to get yourself dressed and get back to town."

"I didn't think I'd go. Not tonight."

"No. You gotta go. Our little Josie here took a fall. You don't go to the ball tonight and it says she's down and out. You got to go to protect your sister. You go on and when folks ask you how's your sister, you tell them she's fine. Just had a little too much to drink. Tell them she's new at this drinking stuff and hasn't yet learned how to regulate the booze."

Galliard laughed and glanced at Della before he turned to his son again. "You go on now. Takes a little time to get that monkey suit on?" Galliard waved his hand in Kevin's direction, indicating *go on. Go on!*

Della held her silence. She watched her son to see his reaction. This was Kevin's decision.

He looked at his mother and then at his father. "You think I need to do this for Josie?"

"I do. Your sister made a little mistake." Galliard pursed his lips and exhaled. "We can't let it cost her. Dora's home dressing now. If Josie's doing okay, I'm going to go downtown tonight myself. I'll say the same thing I told you to say. She's okay. She just went a little overboard. Young people do that sometimes. Not-a-problem." Galliard opened his hands, palms wide. He grinned. "Go on." he ordered.

Kevin stood. He kissed his mother on the side of her face. "I'll come back to the hospital later. If we need somebody to stay the night, I can do it."

"I've got it covered," Della said.

Kevin dumped his coffee cup in the trash can as he left the lounge to do his father's bidding.

Della turned to Galliard. "You know it's not that simple. You know we got a problem here. Pushing it under the rug's not going to help Josie."

"Like I said—anybody can make a little mistake. That's all Josie did." He took a sip of weak coffee. "Good God that's bad," he said and shoved the coffee cup across the table.

Oliver's Song

"Alcoholism runs in this family," Della said. "I can tell you all about it."

Galliard slapped his palm on the table so hard Della jumped. The Styrofoam cup tipped and coffee spilled across the table. "Damn it!" he said. "I won't let you start doing this. Because you have a problem, you want to transfer that problem to our daughter." He leaned in toward Della and looked her eyeball to eyeball. "Because you got a problem doesn't mean Josie's got a problem. She hasn't. Case closed!" With that, he sprinted toward the sink and grabbed a handful of paper towels. The coffee had already begun to drip onto the floor.

Della drew a breath. She wanted to tell him she knew about the other times—the ones Galliard wanted to sweep under the rug. She didn't say this because she wanted to protect Kevin's confidence. She too grabbed a handful of paper towels and began sopping up Galliard's mess.

When they had blotted the coffee from the table and the floor, Della summoned the courage to speak again. "Josie's current situation is only a sign of the problem, Galliard. It needs to be addressed before it gets worse."

"Hell, Della, I won't get into this." He pushed his chair back and stood abruptly. The chair tipped over and made a crashing sound against the floor.

"Damn!" he shouted.

"You folks sure are making some kind of noise down here," the nurse said when she stood in the doorway of the little lounge. "Probably best to save that kind of stuff for later." She paused a beat, and then grinned at them, releasing the tension. "You can go back in the room any time. I got your baby all cleaned up."

Della's knees trembled. She wanted to stand on top of the table and yell at Galliard. Covering up Josie's situation was the worst thing he could do for their daughter.

"Come on," Galliard said in Della's direction as he charged out of the room.

Instead of standing on top of the table and shouting, Della, like Kevin, did what Galliard told her to do. She followed her ex-husband down the hall toward their daughter's room.

31

In twilight, just before night descended fully, Miguel pulled his Peugeot in front of his small yellow apartment, a walk-up duplex divided into two shotguns with their front doors nearly on the sidewalk. The duplex stood in a beam of dying sunlight. The old wood, painted yellow, appeared to glow. He liked his apartment because it reminded him of Santo Domingo. He liked all of New Orleans for this reason. He felt at home here. He would be safe here.

Cars lined the street. He had a small garage in the back, but he never used it. The garage was so old, it leaned. He would be here just long enough to grab a few things—his passport and the cash he kept hidden beneath a loose floorboard under his bed. He grinned when he thought of his hiding spot. Better than a bank box. He could access his holdings anytime.

Miguel looked through the front window of his Peugeot, studying the cars ahead of him. All the cars empty. He had circled the block twice, looking for anything or anyone suspicious. Everything appeared to be as it should be.

He knew Snake had long since come and gone from the little coffee shop. Even if he had money to pay Snake, he would not have shelled out the cash. Snake had failed him. As for Tor-Tuba, he could rot in jail. Fat idiot! Both men, miserable failures. Worthless—which was precisely why Miguel had to get out of town. No Billy Wong. No violin. Snake and Tor-Tuba had hung a noose around his neck. Why would he hand out cash for this kind of failure? Besides, he would need all the cash he had hidden.

For a long minute, he looked behind him. *Check your backside,* he reminded himself. *¡Cuídate la espalda!* He had no one to cover his back but himself.

He opened his car door and stood beside the Peugeot, appreciating his duplex bathed in a swath of low winter light. He stood for just a moment in the last sunlight of this day, feeling the light against his face. A good sign. Miguel Sanchez bathed in sunlight, even though night was bearing down hard.

Inside, he lay flat on his belly beside the bed to retrieve his passport and his cash. The loose board was just under the edge of his bed. He pried the board up with his pocketknife, lifted the wood, and placed it aside. From the narrow pocket in the floor, he retrieved nearly five thousand in cash. He would hide the money before he went through customs in Miami. For now, he stuffed the money and the passport deep inside his right hip pocket, and replaced the board, concealing his makeshift strongbox. He pushed himself up from the floor. Since he was in his apartment, he might as well pack a few shirts, two pairs of shoes, and dress slacks.

No doubt Snake had waited a solid hour or more for him at the coffee shop before he gave up and realized Miguel wasn't coming. Their business was over. He would drive to Miami tonight, one step closer to his beautiful Puerto Plata. A night drive would be good. Maybe the moon would shine on his path—a full moon. Tomorrow he would book a flight and be on his way.

His plane would stop in Haiti before going on to the Dominican Republic. Maybe he'd get off in Haiti. Stay there for a while. No one would look for him in Haiti. He could go into the mountains. Hide there. Or he might go to the mission hospital in Port Au Prince. He had met the missionary doctor when the man had come to Santo Domingo for a couple of days of rest.

If he got off the plane in Haiti, Miguel would say to the doctor: *I've had a conversion. Let me work. I need to cleanse my soul. He would come out a new man—un nuevo hombre.*

He felt satisfied when he thought of this. Maybe that was exactly what he would do.

If he got off in Haiti and decided not to stay, he would have to be quick to get back on the plane. The plane did not stay on the ground long. As soon as the gate opened, passengers ran to the plane, some carrying their belongings tied in strips of cloth. No suitcases. They would come to the plane dressed in faded khaki pants and shirts a size too small for them. They would run for fear the plane would leave without them. The peasants would be headed to the sugarcane plantations outside of Santo Domingo.

Miguel had been on flights that lifted off the ground with peasants still standing in the aisles, clutching their belongings. They sat down on the floor, sat down in the aisle because seats were not available. Total violation of all flight rules and regulations. But he had seen it.

The mission hospital was not a bad idea though. He could see himself sitting in the chapel of the hospital, engrossed in morning prayers. Maybe he would assist the doctors. Take blood pressure or something like that. He could help one of the doctors roll a bandage around the leg of a child—strips of gauze or strips of bed sheets. He remembered the old women at the little Catholic church in Bogotá ripped bed sheets into long strips of bandages for hospitals. He could help others while he helped himself. He would start all over again—a new life, a new beginning.

The last thing he gathered was his 9mm pistol from the drawer of his nightstand. He slipped it in the pocket of his pants. He would place the gun on the passenger seat of the Peugeot until he was well outside of New Orleans.

He opened his front door cautiously. The duplex, no longer bathed in dying beams of sunlight, now stood in the gray of early evening. Everything appeared as it had before. He'd be out of town long before anyone realized he was gone. In the street, he opened the back door of his Peugeot and slid his small suitcase onto the seat.

They must have stood at the side of a nearby house, watching him. He did not see them coming. They were on him quiet as creeping lions. The gun in Snake's hand pressed hard against Miguel's ribs.

"Money," Snake hissed.

Miguel could not see who stood beside Snake. Two of them—this was all he needed to know. He flailed his arms wildly upward, knocking the gun away from his ribs. He ducked and lurched for the handle of his Peugeot.

He arms shot out in furry. Like a super hero with extraordinary powers, he flung his arms and hands into the air. ¡Invencible!

The first bullet caught his shoulder. The second entered the side of his ribs. He grabbed a mouth full of air, pain like a siren drilling his heart. A crack of pain in his left knee caused his legs to buckle. A rocket of pain up his body. ¡Dios mio! Qué agonia!

The other man—not Snake—caught him. The man did not drop him onto the asphalt. He put him down easy. Snake removed the pistol from Miguel's pocket. He dug his fingers deep into the right hip pocket—Miguel felt the fingers working, locating his roll of cash.

Tears rolled on his cheeks. Tears dripped onto the pavement. Such pain!

Miguel watched as Snake took the suitcase from the back seat of the Peugeot and looked inside. You got it all. You got it all, he wanted to shout. But he said nothing.

He raised his right hand, palm open. The universal symbol. Mercy. Have mercy! ¡Ten piedad!

He wanted to be still—to sit in the mission chapel, his head bowed. Here on the street, his body quivered, a dying animal, something primeval, not human. Short breaths.

He wanted to sit in the chapel at the mission hospital for just one minute. One minute to look at the small stained glass window. What was it? Jesus in the Garden of Gethsemane? Jesus, ten misericordia de mi alma.

32

"Aw man, you're not leaving," Mark said when he saw Billy Wong's suitcase standing in the center of the den.

"Yes, I'm going tonight," he said, but it was getting late and Billy was growing anxious. It was Tuit. She was the problem.

"You can't go until tomorrow afternoon," she had said to Johnny when he told her he would take Billy to Atlanta.

"The children are out of school tomorrow. You promised you would take them to the parades. It's Mardi Gras Tuesday," she said.

Tuit and Johnny were in the bedroom negotiating. Johnny wouldn't stand up to his wife. That was the real issue. Earlier in the day, she had given him a long list of chores that needed to be completed before he took Billy to Atlanta. Small stuff. Billy had helped Johnny do everything on her list. Now Johnny and Tuit were behind closed doors still negotiating about when Johnny could back the old van out of the carport and drive Billy to Atlanta.

Billy and Mark stood in the living room, facing each other, but they did not talk. They listened to the voices down the hall.

Had it not been for the thousand dollars, counted out in hundred dollar bills, Johnny would never have agreed to drive Billy to Atlanta.

"What are these?" Johnny asked when Billy handed them to him.

"Look at them." Billy said.

Johnny held the bills with both hands. "Are these counterfeit?" he questioned.

"They're real."

"Can't be," Johnny said, still examining the cash.

Billy tapped the corners of the bills. "These landed in my hands."

Johnny looked up now, his eyes on Billy. "You kill somebody for this?"

"No. I did well in Florida. It's yours for a ride to Atlanta. The money is between us. Don't tell Tuit or the kids."

"Am I going to get arrested when I try to use these somewhere?" Johnny asked, still looking at the bills.

"Use them anywhere. They're good. I promise." Billy shrugged his shoulders and watched Johnny open his wallet. Billy noted the wallet was empty. He watched Johnny place the bills inside.

Billy knew he had a ride to Atlanta. Just a matter of waiting for Tuit to come around. She was angry, judging from the tone of the voices down the hall. She wanted the Econoline parked in the driveway, not on the road to Atlanta. But Johnny had kept his word and not told her about the thousand dollars.

Finally, Johnny emerged from the bedroom.

"We got it worked out," he said when he came into the living room. "Tomorrow's Fat Tuesday. Kids are out of school. I'll take them to the parades tomorrow morning and come straight home. We'll pull out of here about three tomorrow afternoon."

"Come on," Billy said. "I need to go tonight."

"Can't do it," Johnny said.

Billy remembered his over-long stay on Johnny's fishing boat. No point in rushing the man. He would not be budged.

"Tomorrow," Johnny said and raised his hand as if he kept the lid on a tempest.

Mark charged forward and wrapped his arms around Billy's waist. "I'm glad you're staying."

"What's that?" Mark asked. He pointed to Billy's violin case on the sofa.

Billy had purchased the case earlier in the day. Except for when he took a quick shower, the violin had not been out of his sight.

"Come here," Billy said.

Oliver's Song

He sat on the couch. Mark sat beside him. "I'll show you, but you can't touch it."

Billy removed the violin from the case and held it so Mark could see it. The boy didn't try to touch it. That's what Billy liked about this kid. He listened. He was careful. He respected his Cousin Billy.

"Can you play it?"

Billy tightened the bow and checked the strings for tone. Sweet, sweet sound.

He remembered a piece he had heard in the halls of Florida State University when he walked through the practice areas and listened to the students, his ear pressed next to a closed door. Beautiful pieces. The notes locked in his head even though he didn't know the names of any of the pieces and had never seen a score. He played one of the pieces for Mark just as he remembered it. He closed his eyes when he played, allowing the notes to pass through him. That was all he had to do—close his eyes and the notes were there.

"Wow!" Mark said. "How'd you learn to play like that?"

"I don't know," Billy said. "I just play."

"Will you teach me?"

"I've got to catch a plane soon. But, don't worry. I'll give you lessons someday. Maybe your parents will send you to Hong Kong. You come stay with me for a summer. I may even let you play this violin."

"Can I touch it?" Mark asked.

"Here. One finger. Here." Billy showed Mark the spot where he could touch.

The boy reached his index finger out and tenderly touched the violin. That was another thing Billy liked about the kid—he had great respect for something so beautiful as this old violin.

"Can I smell it?"

"Yes," Billy said. The kid wanted to inhale the old-wood fragrance just as Billy had.

He brought the violin close to Mark's nose and let him smell the centuries hidden inside the instrument. Yes, he would teach this kid. When he was established in Hong Kong, he would telephone Johnny and Tuit. Have them send their son. He would purchase the plane ticket because this kid would take pleasure in such a treasure as this old violin.

Just then the girls ran into the room. They spotted the violin and charged toward Billy. He stood and held the violin above his head. "Hands behind your backs," he ordered. "If you keep them behind your backs, I'll let you look at it." Cautiously he brought the violin down, but when one of the girls brought her hand around to grab the instrument, Billy raised it again.

"Come on, girls," Tuit said. "Supper's ready."

Billy was relieved when the children sat at the counter shoveling fried rice into their mouths like open-beaked birds. All of his life would be like this. All of his life, he would shelter and protect this violin—his violin. This instrument had been destined for him.

Billy Wong knew he was in a holding pattern, waiting for tomorrow afternoon. Everything he needed was already packed. His new identity. His new clothes. His black-framed glasses. When he reached Atlanta, when he saw the Econoline pull away from the terminal, he'd become a new man—Yong Xi, violinist with the Cleveland Orchestra.

He walked to the counter and ran his fingers through Mark's hair. For now, he would sit in the bedroom and get to know his old violin. He would close his eyes and remember how he had seen others hold an instrument like this. How did the hand fit on the bow? Where did the elbow reside when the violinist pulled a long, slow note? He would close his eyes and think of all these things. Then, he would allow music to flow through him. He and the violin would become one.

33

A deep green Jeep Cherokee was parked at the curb beside Mercedes' house when Della arrived home from staying with Josie at the hospital. She pulled to the side of the road, studying the SUV. It had been a very long day, and she had not expected to be home tonight, but both Josie and the nurse insisted she come home. Josie wanted nothing more than to sleep. The nurse would be there to check on her and would call if there were any problems.

Who owned the Cherokee? She'd seen it before, but couldn't place it. Maybe someone visiting a neighbor? Della looked around and saw no likely prospects. No one appeared to be entertaining.

Then it hit her. Moss Maple's SUV. What was he doing at Mercedes' house?

She pulled her old Dodge into the driveway, stepped out of her car, and followed a swishing sound to the back patio. Moss, dressed in navy slacks and a buttoned down light blue shirt, pushed a broom, corralling glass fragments into a small heap. He looked up when she came around the corner. "I replaced your lights. Tomorrow I'll go to a hardware store and see if I can match the lamp covers." He picked up the dustpan beside the door and bent forward, holding the dustpan in his right hand as he pulled the broom with his left.

"You hold the dustpan," Della said. I'll sweep."

"I got another bulb to replace out there." He pointed toward a light in a bed of mondo grass. "That one wasn't shot out, looks like it just burned out. I'll replace the one on your porch too."

It felt good to have Moss here, cleaning up the mess and making sure everything was in order. "It would have been awfully dark here tonight without those lights," Della said.

"No it wouldn't. I wasn't going to let you stay here in the dark."

She liked that too—Moss thinking about her. She swept the last of the glass fragments onto the dustpan and Moss stood. He dug his hand into his pocket. "Here, I got this for you."

Della looked at the small black plastic cylinder. "What is it?"

"Pepper gas. Actually, it's a combination—gas and paint mixed. That gas will stop any attacker and the paint won't wash off. The varmint will have the evidence right on his face when the cops pick him up."

Moss dumped the glass pieces in the trash can. Della studied the small canister.

"Whoa!" Moss said. "Don't turn it toward your face. That's the same gas New York street-cops carry. Has a quick release." Moss took the cylinder from Della's hand. "See." He slid the small lever to the right. "You're ready to fire. It's that easy."

"Good thing I didn't have this when I pulled up. I didn't recognize your SUV. I would have come around the house with the trigger in the ready position."

"Good," Moss said, "that's what you're supposed to do." He picked up the bag of light bulbs and headed toward the mondo grass. Della followed him.

"How's your daughter?" he asked as he unscrewed the bulb.

"Much better. She'll probably go home tomorrow."

"She'll have to learn how to pace herself with the booze. Takes a while." Moss stuffed the old bulb in his pocket. "We better get that light on your porch."

Della led the way and Moss followed. Even with him behind her, she got another whiff of his aftershave—something spicy and fresh smelling.

"I'll switch the light on inside so you can see to change the bulb out here," Della said.

In the dark, she fumbled with the key. Moss came and stood beside her. "I got a pen light on my key chain." He leaned in close, directing the tiny light at the keyhole. He stood so close, she could feel the warmth from his body.

She opened the door, turned on the light, and came back out to watch Moss carefully work his fingers around the shattered bulb, unthreading it from the socket. "We need to sweep up out here too," he said. "The numb-nut that did this left a mess."

Numb-nut. A Moss-ism.

Della got the broom and again Moss held the dustpan in place. She swept until all the glass pieces—even the slivers—were in the pan.

Moss followed her inside to empty the dustpan and remove the spent bulbs from the pocket of his pants. "You had any supper?"

"No. I haven't had time to think about it," Della said.

"Me neither—no supper that is. But I've had plenty of time to think about it. I'm hungry. It's not too late to go out for seafood. Let's go over to the causeway and grab a bite on the bay."

Della looked at her watch. Nearly eight. "Let me make something here. Something simple. How about scrambled eggs and toast?"

"Fine with me," Moss said.

Della slipped her shoes off beside the refrigerator. "Feels good to have my shoes off. You can take yours off too. Make yourself comfortable."

It felt odd to have someone else in her apartment—especially a man. The garage apartment was just a studio, one large room with multiple spaces. The queen-size bed against the south wall, a rice-paper screen partially separating it from the living and dining area—a Formica table with six oak chairs around it. Della kept the table dressed in a linen cloth she had purchased from a local antique shop. She had one other touch of elegance on her dining table, an old silver candelabra with three arms. This too she had purchased at the antique shop. The dining area opened to the tiny galley kitchen. The little garage apartment was fine for her, but Moss seemed to fit in the small space as tight as an extra sardine squeezed into a roll-top tin.

"I think I will take my shoes off," he said, "if you're sure you don't mind."

"I'm sure. If you're going to have supper with me, I want you to make yourself at home."

He slipped off his loafers and placed his shoes beside hers, next to the refrigerator while Della cracked four eggs into a small bowl.

Standing beside the refrigerator, Moss looked around, taking the whole place in. "I like it," he said. "Comfy." He stepped to the coffee table and lifted Della's picture book of Venice. He brought it to the dining table to examine the pictures more closely.

"Got a beer?"

Della mixed three tablespoons of milk into the eggs and beat them with a fork. It was time she made clear to Moss who she was and where she came from. Honesty was the best policy in any friendship. Besides, it would be a burden off her mind to come clean with him.

"I don't have any beer. I don't have any wine. No scotch. No vodka. No bourbon." She stopped whipping the eggs. *Give the man a chance to run if he wants to.* "I'm an alcoholic. I probably could have all those drinks here and I wouldn't touch any of them. It's just easier if I don't."

Moss was silent for a long minute while he watched her beat the eggs again. "You're not really an alcoholic. You may have had a little drinking problem, but that's behind you. An alcoholic's somebody who gets drunk, can't stop, and repeats the same mistake over and over."

She knew he was attempting to make her feel better, but she was having none of it. "I've done that plenty of times. Once an alcoholic, always an alcoholic. You need to know I have a past and it's not a hundred percent good. Far from it."

Moss Maple had been good to her and she appreciated that. She needed to be honest with him and that meant going one step farther. "There are plenty of women out there without lots of baggage, but I'm not one of them."

294

Oliver's Song

They were both silent now.

Moss got up and walked to the counter beside the sink where Della stood. "Would it bother you if I kissed you?"

"You mean if you'd had a drink, would it bother me if you kissed me?" She thought for a second. "You know it might. I just never thought of that."

"No," Moss said. "I mean now."

He eased close to her, put his arms around her and buried his nose in her hair.

She didn't push him away. She felt his nose nuzzle her neck, and still she didn't push him away.

She tilted her head back for more. She closed her eyes and felt his lips on the front of her neck, working his way around to her left earlobe. His lips sent a tingle through her like contact with a live electrical wire.

How long had it been? No romance in law school—three years. No romance in recovery—six months. No romance the last six months she was with Galliard either. *Had it been four years? Four long years!* Her whole body pressed against Moss. She reached her arms up, circled his back and pulled him tightly against her.

She laughed now. This giddy feeling was fun. She had been married to Galliard for nearly twenty years and in all that time, she had known no other men. Galliard had been the one and only. Then, four years without any relationship that even vaguely hinted of romance. Relationships had not been on her mind. Recovery, studying, reclaiming herself. These things had been dominant. Now, how good it felt to be so close to Moss that his heat became her own.

Moss pulled back and looked at her.

"I'm sorry," she said. "I think I've forgotten how to . . ."

Before she could finish the sentence, Moss kissed her.

Her heart beat faster. She felt a crazy spiraling motion in her stomach. Nerves? No. This didn't feel like nerves at all. This felt unsettled, but Moss' kiss felt and tasted delicious. Like something good she had missed.

She didn't intend for her first kiss in four years to be passionate—but it was. Moss kissed down her neck again, and this time she did pull away.

She placed her hand on her forehead and felt her fingers tremble. "I'm not the person you're looking for," she said. "I'd almost forgotten how to do that. I'm out of practice. I haven't sought an intimate relationship and one hasn't come looking for me."

Moss started to speak, but she pressed her fingers over his lips. "This has caught me by surprise." She took a deep breath. For the first time since Moss had stepped close to her, she could breathe. She had told him the truth. He could leave now, or eat scrambled eggs and then leave. "I'm not the woman you're looking for," she said. "In the last four years, I guess you could call me celibate."

"Easy to rid yourself of that label," Moss said. "I haven't forgotten a thing. All you need is a little recall." He placed his hand on the back of her hip. "Want a lesson?"

"We need to get these eggs scrambled."

"Okay, we don't need to rush things." He turned toward the refrigerator. "How about milk?" he asked. "No beer—but you got milk?"

"Want me to stay?" Moss asked after they had eaten eggs and buttered toast with jelly. "What with Mrs. Magellan gone, I don't want you to be afraid here alone. I can sleep on the couch. You can trust me. I won't try to get into your bed." He raised his hands in a defensive manner. "I'll stay on the couch. I promise."

His lined face was straightforward and honest. He stated exactly what he meant. Della knew this. This was a man who could be trusted. He would stay the night and sleep on the couch if she wanted him to do so. He would do this to keep her comfortable—to keep her from being afraid.

"No," she said. "I'll be fine. I'm sure there won't be a repeat of last night. Someone thought Mercedes was gone and it was a good chance to break in. With the lights replaced, they'll think she's home again."

"I'm around the corner. You need me, you call. I'll be here in two minutes." Before he left, Moss drew her to him and kissed her again—long and passionate.

How could she have forgotten this?

She stepped to the front porch and watched Moss leave. She latched the screen door on the porch and double-locked the door of her apartment. She had lied to Moss. She would not rest easily tonight. She would sleep with the proverbial one eye open.

After she showered, she sat at the table in the dining area and opened her Bible. Tonight she would read Ecclesiastes. This would calm her. Old King Solomon's words would ease her into sleep.

Vanity of vanities! All is vanity.
A generation goes and a generation comes,
but the earth remains forever.
The sun rises and the sun goes down,
and hurries to the place where it rises.
The wind blows to the south,
and goes round to the north;
round and round goes the wind,
and on its circuits the wind returns.

Beautiful. This poetry soothed her. The fellow who wrote this thousands of years ago nursed as much anxiety as she often felt in the very core of herself, as much uncertainty as she felt tonight. The wee hours of morning would come and she would be alone.

She arrived at the third chapter and she savored every word, every play on an opposite. Opposites, the very essence of life.

For everything there is a season,
and a time for every matter under heaven:
a time to be born, and a time to die;
a time to plant, and a time to pluck up what is planted;

a time to weep, and a time to laugh,
a time to mourn, and a time to dance.

She could see herself, hands held over her head, dancing in the moonlight. She, Della Boudreaux, dancing in the open air of night because she had lost everything, yet so much had been returned to her. Her daughter had allowed her to stand beside her bed in the hospital, her son, loyal and handsome, loved her. She had a new law practice—and now—now a man had rekindled passion in her. She didn't know how far her relationship with Moss would go. She didn't know how far she wanted it to go. But, she liked being desired. She had forgotten how good it felt to be desired.

She read the last lines again—*a time to weep, and a time to laugh, a time to mourn, and a time to dance.*

That was when she heard a car pull into the driveway. She closed the Bible and listened. Had she really heard a car? Then she heard the door slam. She was positive—a car had pulled into the driveway. She retrieved her cell phone from the nightstand. She also found the little cylinder of pepper gas Moss had given her beside her purse. With her thumb, she slid the lever on the little cylinder to the right. A tap of her index finger and the gas would release. She began dialing Moss' number when she heard a voice from the foot of the stairs.

"Mom. Mom." Kevin didn't shout, but his voice was loud enough for her to hear him. She placed the pepper gas on the table and ended her call before it had begun. She released both locks on the inside of her door, unlatched the little hook on the screen door, and Kevin walked inside still dressed in his tuxedo—his collar open, his bow tie abandoned somewhere.

Della looked at her watch. Barely midnight. "I thought you'd still be at the ball."

"No. I left there a long time ago. I've been standing at the foot of Government Street, watching the Navy ships in port and thinking."

Oliver's Song

"What about your date? Where is she?"

"She hooked up with somebody else. She didn't miss me. And, actually, that was okay by me. I needed time to think."

"Want me to put some coffee on? I've got some decaf."

"No. I won't stay long. I just wanted you to be the first to know. I've made up my mind. I'm leaving."

Della studied her son. Tall. Handsome. His hair smelling of salty wind off the Bay. "Leaving?" she questioned.

"I've made up my mind. I'm going to Wyoming. I'm finally going to cut the cord—not the cord that attaches me to mother, but the one that attaches me to father. It's time for me to go it alone."

She felt a knot in the pit of her stomach. She was not ready to see Kevin leave. "When?" she asked.

"It'll take me a few weeks. I want to leave Dad in good shape. I've got some deals to close for him. I'll train someone to take over my job. Then, I'll leave. I've always wanted to spend a year in Wyoming. You know that."

"I remember." Della opened her arms and Kevin came to her. She pulled him close. He lowered his chin and rested it on the top of her head. "I need to do this, Mother. I need to get away."

"Promise me you'll keep a journal, send me letters, and call often."

"I'll keep a journal every day, send a letter once a week, and call as often as I can. How about that?"

"That's great," Della said, and hugged her son again.

Kevin looked around the small apartment. "I'll stay tonight if you want me to. After what happened last night, I know you might not be comfortable here alone. I'll sleep on the couch."

"No. I'll be fine."

How wonderful it was to have two men offer to sleep on her couch. Two men who wanted to stay over to give her peace of mind. But—no. She would rest now.

Linda Busby Parker

She stood on the porch and watched Kevin walk to his car. She latched the porch screen. Inside, she secured both locks. She turned off the lights and got under the covers.

The sun rises and the sun goes down,
and hurries to the place where it rises.
The wind blows to the south,
and goes round to the north;
round and round goes the wind,
and on its circuits the wind returns.

34

A plate of grits and scrambled eggs rested on the hospital tray in front of Josie. She picked at the eggs and brought a small bite to her lips. "I'm out of here today," she said as soon as her mother walked into the room. "Can't wait."

"Hospitals are no fun," Della said.

"Right about that." Josie twisted her mouth in disapproval. "These grits need salt." She tore open a small paper tube of salt and then a tube of pepper and stirred both into the grits with her fork.

In truth, Della felt a little remorse about her daughter getting out of the hospital. This twinge of remorse embarrassed her. She wanted her daughter to be fully recovered, but once she was back to her old self, Josie would be an isolated island, and Della would be at sea, circling the island for a safe place to come ashore.

"So, Oliver Fitzsimmons is in this same hospital?" Josie asked, bringing Della out of her thoughts.

"One floor below."

"What's wrong with him?" Josie continued to eat her grits and eggs in tiny bites. "I mean I know somebody beat him up in jail, but how bad was he hurt?"

"His eye is a mess, bones in his left leg are broken, his lip's cut, and he's bruised up pretty badly."

"I'm going down on the elevator to see him today." Josie said. "The nurses said I could get up. In fact, they want me to walk around."

"A guard's at his door. I'm not sure they'll let you in. Might be just family and his attorney."

"Doesn't matter," Josie said with the abandonment only youth could so quickly muster. "If I can't go in, I'll stand at the door and wave. You will get him off, won't you?"

Josie removed the plastic cover from the cup of black coffee, held two packets of sugar between her fingers, ripped open both packets in the same movement, and dumped them into the coffee. She opened a short, squat carton of milk and dumped in as much milk as the cup would hold, stirring the coffee with her teaspoon. With both hands she brought the cup's rim to her lips.

Della noted her daughter's hands trembled. "Actually, he'll get himself off because he's innocent."

"He might be innocent, but you'll have to prove that—won't you?"

"Yes. I have a detective working on the case right now."

"Wow!" Josie said, resting the cup on the tray. "A detective? That's impressive."

Okay, so she stretched the truth a little. She was using Candy Sue's new title. In fact, Candy Sue didn't even know detective was her new title. Next time they talked, Della would tell her. For now, she wanted to impress her daughter, at least a little, and this was all she had.

"You'll get him off?" Josie asked again.

"I believe so," Della answered.

Josie rubbed her forehead and closed her eyes. "This is Tuesday, isn't it? Mardi Gras Tuesday?"

"That's right. Fat Tuesday. Last day of Mardi Gras."

"What a bummer! I'm stuck at this frigging hospital." Josie massaged her forehead with the tips of her fingers. "I'll be glad when Dad comes. He'll get me out of here. I'll bet he even lets me go to the ball tonight."

They were right up against the issue now. Della could speak or hold her peace. Once Josie went home with Galliard, it was anybody's guess when she would again have an opportunity to speak with her daughter in private. She took a deep breath, set her head to the proverbial wind, and pushed forward.

"Sweetheart, I think you might have a drinking problem. You know I do. Drinking problems run in families. My father had a drinking problem too."

Oliver's Song

"Don't you do that to me!" Josie cut her short, metal in her voice. "Don't you project your problems on me. I'm no drunk. You are. Or were. Or whatever." Josie attempted to lift her coffee cup, but her hands trembled, her emotions were at the surface of her skin. She placed the cup back on the tray.

"I'm not saying you're a drunk or an alcoholic or anything like that, I'm just saying maybe you want to read a little about drinking and find out why people drink too much. That sort of thing." Della's mouth went dry. The last thing she wanted was a confrontation. She wanted to talk. She wanted to hold Josie close to her. No arguments.

"Why didn't *you* read all about it?" Josie asked. "You'd drink until you fell asleep. I missed soccer practices and piano lessons because you passed out—a drunk sleep," Josie added. "Then, just when I needed you, you were gone. Flash!" Josie raised both hands, held her fingers together and snapped them. "Flash!" she said again. "Gone to some dumb recovery program."

Josie pushed the rolling tray away from her bed. "Daddy hired a nanny. What kind of deal was that?" Josie's face blotched with color. She pushed the rolling tray again, sending it halfway across the room. "I'm no drunk! And, I don't want to ever hear that again!"

Della placed the flats of her palms against the bed to steady herself. She wouldn't—she couldn't—deny anything Josie said. Why had she done it? *Pour a little more and a little more until she was relaxed, so comfortable she nodded off. She would say nothing in her own defense. She had no defense.*

"I'm sorry," she said. "I've always loved you. But because of my drinking, I missed out on a lot of wonderful things."

Josie tried to speak, but Della added quickly, "And, I did it to myself. I was totally at fault." Her voice was almost a whisper.

What else could she say? *I couldn't control myself. I have an addictive personality.* These excuses seemed paltry when she stood beside her daughter, who had suffered for her mother's failures.

303

Observing her mother, Josie's anger eased and the steam leaked out. She held her hands together and rested them on the folds of the sheet.

Della made a deliberate decision to remain silent. Any more words about a drinking problem and she would be banned from the room—a *persona non grata*. Galliard would, no doubt, want Josie to attend the ball tonight. The final Mardi Gras ball would be a way of saying *I'm okay. I was a little stupid, but . . . that's youth.* Josie would be lovely and old Mobile would welcome her back into the fold with open arms if she behaved herself and courted them. Sure, she had taken a fall, but she would be up and on her feet—not a bad girl at all.

Josie patted her mother's arms. "We got that behind us," she said.

"Yes," Della said. "We got that behind us."

Galliard exploded into the room and startled them both by clapping his hands together and pointing his index finger at Josie like a loaded gun. "You're out of here," he said. "The nurse says when the doctor comes he'll check you out. Free as a bird," Galliard grinned at his daughter.

"Let me help you get your things together," Della said, still feeling off balance when she lifted her hands from the bed.

"No. Dora's coming. She'll take care of it." Galliard waved his hands in Della's direction, dismissing her.

He turned his attention back to Josie. "Dora's got some appointments for you this afternoon. At the beauty shop I think."

Della knew for sure—Josie would attend the ball tonight. Still a little unsteady on her feet, but Galliard would guide her through the evening—allowing her to drink just a little to show she had learned her lesson. *A little does it.*

Della wanted to scream. She wanted to stand in the middle of the room and tell both her daughter and her ex-husband the way it was. An addictive personality beats her head against a cement wall over and over, despite the fact it hurts like hell. She was willing to admit all her faults and accept all her downfalls—but

God knows she wanted her daughter to avoid the same pitfalls. She wanted to roar at the top of her lungs. But . . . if she ever wanted to see her daughter again, she would remain silent. At least the topic of alcoholism had been broached. She would maintain her silence while Josie still held the door open to their recovering relationship—at least a tiny crack.

Josie put her arms out and embraced her mother. Della could have remained in that embrace all day. When Josie released her hold from around her mother's shoulders, Della pulled back and looked at her daughter, her beautiful Josie with the auburn spirals—now looking a little tarnished and in need of a shampoo, but her green eyes with the gold flecks sparkled with the prospect of getting out of the hospital and taking charge of her life again.

"I love you," Della said. "I'll check on you later."

"Tomorrow," Galliard said. "She'll be at the dance tonight."

"Don't get too tired," Della said to Josie.

"We won't let her. She needs to show her face though," Galliard added.

Always worried about appearances! Della thought.

At the door, she blew her daughter a kiss.

Her cell rang on the way to Ollie's room. "Glad I reached you," J.J. Ernest said when she punched the green button and answered. "One more body. A man found shot in the French Quarter. We got a call from the detective over there."

With her right hand, Della rubbed her forehead. "How does a dead man in the French Quarter have anything to do with my client?"

"Detective called because the man had a matchbook from the Riverview Hotel. On his person, he also had the name of your client and his Alabama tag number. Also had the edge of a cocktail napkin where someone had written the names Billy Wong and Chang Wu. Course Mr. Wu's deceased. The man killed was Hispanic. Bingo, one Asian, one Hispanic," J.J. said as if he called out a winning card. Then, he fell silent, waiting for Della's response.

When Della didn't speak, he continued. "No way around it. We got ourselves an international situation here with players from Asia, South America, Mexico, and your boy, a homie."

Della hesitated, not knowing what to say. Then, her repartee arrived on the tip of her tongue. "J.J., this is all interesting. It's clear my client has backed himself into something dangerous here, but he's as baffled as we all are. My client has been beaten and is flat on his back in the hospital. We've got an innocent victim here."

"I sure hate to see a young man draw big time," J.J. said and blew air out his mouth in apparent exasperation. "But two bodies. I won't be easy on him. I can't."

"We stand ready to tell you everything we know, but we can't create information. We'll tell you the truth, but we won't fabricate what we don't know." Exasperation rode on her voice too.

"Use your best judgment here, Della. There are serious consequences."

"Thank you," she said, as if she didn't already know.

She got off the elevator when she reached Ollie's floor, but before entering his room, she decided to check with Candy Sue to see if she had discovered anything in Tallahassee. She stepped into a little lounge close to the elevator and opened her journal, ready to jot down any information, but before she could place her call, her cell rang. "Miss Della," Candy Sue said.

"Well, we're great minds on the same wave length, or something like that," Della said. "I was just about to call you."

"I've got some information. That's why I called," Candy Sue explained. "What do they say? Something like a woman's scorn can burn the heck out of you?"

"That's close enough," Della said. "What'd you find out?"

"I got everything we need, Miss Della. Just left the Tips and Toes Salon. Had a long chat with May Lin. She's been scorned, and she's hotter'n hell about it. She said Billy Wong told her he was going to buy her an Audi TT—you know, one of those cute little sports cars. She could pick her color. He was going to marry her too and take her on a big trip."

"Where was the money coming from?" Della asked.

"According to May Lin, he said he was about to come into some big money. When he did, he'd let her pick an engagement ring. Well. No ring. No TT. The man disappeared. May Lin thinks he went off with another woman. That's what has her so steamed up."

"What about drugs? Did she know about Billy Wong and the drugs?"

"Didn't let on she knew a thing about that. I asked her if she thought his money might be coming from something illegal. Said she didn't know. I wasn't going to push too hard. She was digging around my toenails with that little pick.

"Oh! Here's some more real good news. I found a kid at Florida State who heard the conversation between Ollie and Billy Wong. I hung out between the two music buildings and talked with a lot of folks. This one guy said he was sitting outside drinking a Coca Cola and taking a smoke when he heard Billy Wong ask Ollie to carry his bass to Mobile. He sat right there and watched Billy Wong load the bass in the back seat of Ollie's car. He heard the whole story about how Billy Wong was going to New York and coming back through Mobile to pick up the bass on his way to Texas for another audition. The kid said Ollie didn't even want to take the bass, but Wong pleaded. Wong said he was broke and couldn't afford money for an extra seat to put his bass on an airplane."

"I'd give you a raise if I had any cash," Della said. She thought, but didn't say *I'm praying I can pay your next paycheck.* What she said was—"you *deserve* a raise."

"Thank you. I sure do like this detective work. I think I've got a good nose for snooping."

"Let's change your title to Detective and Administrative Assistant. At least maybe there will be some money for a Christmas bonus." She thought that was a fairly safe bet, since it was only February.

"Good," Candy Sue said. "I like the new title and a little spending money at Christmas sounds good too. Hey," Candy Sue said, changing the subject abruptly. "May Lin gives a good pedicure. Great color too. Pistachio."

"Here's a new assignment for you," Della said, thinking about what had transpired in Candy Sue's absence—a dead man in Bayou La Batre with Billy Wong's name in his notebook and another dead man in the French Quarter with Ollie's name and the name of this Mr. Chang Wu on a napkin, or something like that. "On your drive back, stay on I-10. Go out to Bayou La Batre and do a little snooping there. This is a long shot—a hail Mary," she added, thinking of an impossibly long pass in football. "Check around. See if anyone's heard of Billy Wong."

"Gotcha covered, Miss Della. I'm on my way."

"This whole thing's getting weird," Oliver Sr. said as soon as the guard cleared Della and she stepped into Ollie's room.

"Sure is," Ollie said. "Detectives are swarming."

Della noted Ollie seemed to be speaking easier this morning. He moved his lower lip more comfortably.

"Let's see," Oliver Sr. said. He picked up a note pad from the bedside table where Ollie kept notes. "Last detective in here was Sidney Winfield."

Covey gets around, Della thought. She wondered if he would be playing his ukulele near her office today. Mardi Gras Tuesday would be a great day for watching the crowds and, in general, keeping an eyeball out for miscreants.

"Winfield said the FBI is sending in a special investigator. They think that old violin might be a Stradivarius."

"You're kidding!" Della gasped.

Oliver's Song

"Can you believe that?" Oliver Sr. said. "Even I know a little about Stradivarius." He looked at his son. "Tell Miss Boudreaux what you told the detective about that violin."

"Had a reddish sheen. Looked like repair work had been done in the center between the F-holes where the sound comes out."

"That damage around those sound holes seemed to be a clue to the investigators," Oliver Sr. said.

"Had old pegs too," Ollie said, "and a real fancy curve to the scroll. I keep rubbing my hands together. Maybe these hands have touched a Stradivarius." He raised his hands, palms open.

"Those Stradivarius violins have names," Oliver Sr. said. "There's one missing up in New York and it's called . . ." he hesitated. "You tell her son. I've forgotten."

"They think it might be Le Maurien. There's a big reward for it. Le Maurien's the one with the reconstruction between the F-holes. Unbelievable." Ollie opened his palms again and looked at them. "Yep, maybe these hands have touched a Stradivarius."

Della raised her hand for a high-five. "Now my hands have touched the hands that might have touched a Stradivarius."

Oliver Sr. slapped his son's open palm. "Me too," he said and laughed.

"I have some good news." Della was eager to tell them of Candy Sue's discoveries. "I put my detective on the case" — she loved saying those words, *my detective* — "and she found a couple of good witnesses."

She told them about May Lin, and the student who had heard Billy Wong ask Ollie to transport his bass to Mobile, and she told them about the student seeing Wong load the bass into the back seat of Ollie's old Audi. "I'll call the U.S. Attorney again. This should give us more leverage."

"You think it might keep me from going back to jail?" Ollie asked.

"I'm going to use this new information for all it's worth. It corroborates everything you've said."

Ollie brought his hand up and touched his swollen lip. "I wonder where that violin is now? Do you think Billy Wong has it? I'm thinking he's the one who broke into the fishing camp." He shrugged his shoulders. "Maybe not." He threw his hands up. "I don't know. This whole thing about the violin maybe being a Stradivarius has thrown me for a loop. If that violin is a Stradivarius, how'd Billy get a thing like that?"

"I'm in deep water here too," Oliver Sr. said. "I prefer keeping my head above the waterline so I can see the terrain and understand where I'm heading, but I'm dog paddling below the surface. I know one thing," he said. "I'm impressed you put a private investigator on the case. That was smart."

Pat yourself on the back, Della thought, *and kiss Candy Sue*. She could hardly wait to speak with J.J. Ernest—again.

35

Tuesday morning. The first day of his new life. Billy Wong showered and shampooed his hair. He toweled his body and put on fresh underclothes. He parted his short, black hair and combed it toward the right side of his head. He put on his black-framed glasses and studied himself in the mirror. Next, his expensive new trousers, and a blue oxford shirt. *Yong Xi. Yong Xi. Yong Xi.* With every step, he repeated his name. *Yong Xi. Yong Xi.* Violinist with the Cleveland Orchestra.

The house was quiet. He had slept late. Tuit and Johnny had the kids at the parades downtown. Billy—*no, Yong Xi*—was packed and ready to go. As soon as Johnny returned, they would hit the road. On the drive to Atlanta, he would answer to his old name, but in his mind he would repeat: *Yong Xi, Yong Xi, Yong Xi.* As soon as Johnny let him off at the airport terminal, his mind would be ready to answer the world as Yong Xi.

It wasn't so much the documents in his new wallet that brought Yong Xi to life. It was the violin. This old instrument exuded karma as sweet as ancient perfume. A rich perfume to be rubbed on dead bodies, preserving them in perfect form. That was what this old violin was—a balm. Through it, Yong Xi lived. The old musical spirit that had set great talent on Billy Wong's shoulders had also given Yong Xi the violin. Yong Xi held the musical case in his right hand. He could see a ring of light—blue light—circling his hand. *Was he the only one who would be able to see it?*

No matter. He hoped he was the only one who could see the light. When he held the violin under his chin to play it, the nimbus of light would enter his heart. The magic belonged to Yong Xi. One day he would actually play in an orchestra, not just pretend he played in the Cleveland Orchestra. This violin was insurance backing up his dream.

At security, the officers would treat him like royalty. Mr. Yong Xi. Violinist. Oh yes! Cleveland Orchestra.

"I've even heard of the Cleveland Orchestra," the security guard would say. "I'm sorry, but I've got to look in that case."

Yong Xi would carefully place the violin case on the counter.

"Open it," the security guard would say.

Yong Xi wondered if the light from the violin would shine a blue beam into the guard's eyes. He would open the case cautiously.

"Take it out."

Yong Xi would carefully unstrap the musical instrument from the case. He would lift it so the security guard could see.

"I need to hold it," the guard would say. "I'll be careful."

Yong Xi would hand the violin to the guard. "Hold it here. You see where other hands have held it." The neck of the violin showed wear where long-dead hands had held this sweet instrument.

"This must be some special instrument," the security officer would say.

Yong Xi would smile, the gracious smile of a well-educated man. He would speak in a soft voice, a sophisticated voice. "Every professional violinist thinks his instrument is special," he would say.

He would hesitate just a beat, "In point of fact, this one is special," he would say. *Point of fact*. He liked the way Yong Xi spoke.

Money in his pocket. The old violin in his lap. A ticket in his pocket—Atlanta to San Francisco, and on to Hong Kong. Make no mistake about it, Yong Xi would play in a great orchestra. Yong Xi had been given life. Billy Wong had only to wait for Johnny and they would be on the road, on the way to all the good things that awaited Yong Xi.

36

Despite the continuous string of Fat Tuesday parades, Della made her way from the hospital to her office. The day had turned brittle cold, but not a cloud in the sky—the kind of day that forced Mobilians to haul out coats that spent more time hanging in closets than on backs. On Government Street, the Mardi Gras crowd stamped their collective feet on the asphalt to keep their toes warm.

Della heard the drums of a high school band beat a smart-stepping rhythm as the marchers turned the corner and headed west. She pressed the phone hard to her ear as she dialed the number for J.J. Ernest.

"It's Della Boudreaux," she said when he answered.

"Please don't tell me you need me for anything today. My plans are set. I'll be at the Athelstan Club for lunch."

Della listened while J. J. listed the items on his itinerary. She had not yet asked him for a single thing.

"Then, I want to catch a little of the Comic Cowboys' parade. I hope they don't zing the U.S. Attorney's Office too seriously. They got a little rough last year." J.J. cleared his throat. "I'm still thinking about running for U.S. Senate."

He was about to drone on when Della interrupted him. "Okay. We won't meet today, but I'll need to see you first thing tomorrow. We've found a couple of witnesses. I think you'll want to hear what they've got to say before you go any farther with this case."

"You must think you've got something good," he said.

She didn't reply.

"Della, you certainly know how to drop big boots down hard on a perfectly good holiday. All day I'll be thinking about what you've got up your sleeve. We should be sipping a little Mardi

Gras relief and enjoying the revelry, and you got business simmering on the back burner."

"Tomorrow morning," she said. "First thing. Your office." She slid the phone into its cradle.

She made a note in her journal—the time of her call and the date she was to meet with J.J. Ernest. When she closed her journal, she stood and walked to the large plate glass window in the front room. She looked out at the crowd gathered on the corner. A parade would soon turn in front of the Bankhead Tunnel and head west on Government Street. She held her hands behind her back and lifted her face toward the sun, allowing the sunlight coming through the window to warm her. Outside it was cold, but in this spot of sun, she was warm and the world was bright.

Ever since she left the hospital she had felt a spike of anger pierce through her. She tried to ignore it, but the anger surfaced and jabbed her again. She was furious with Galliard, but she had not told him. One way or another—either confront Galliard, or swallow her anger—she wanted to put this bitterness behind her.

She thought of Reverend Stevie Knight and wondered if he would be in his office today. When she had attended church at the little chapel, she observed a small addition built onto the east side of the sanctuary. The small addition had green shuttered windows like the church. She suspected the added-on room was Stevie Knight's office. She envisioned Reverend Knight at his desk, a battered old desk resting on a patterned rug. She envisioned a small bookcase stood against the wall.

She decided to telephone the church office and ask Stevie Knight for advice. She had to rid herself of this anger before it consumed her. She found the number in the phone directory.

She didn't expect the minister to pick up the phone—in fact, she thought she wouldn't reach him at all. But, to her surprise, he answered.

"I'm mighty glad you're in your office today. This is Della Boudreaux."

Oliver's Song

Stevie Knight laughed. "Another case of the Lord working in mysterious ways. Evie just stepped over from the parsonage, asking me to invite you to lunch after church next Sunday. I told her I didn't know how to reach you. She walked back to the parsonage disappointed. Then, what happens? The phone rings, and it's you."

"Does the offer for lunch on Sunday still stand?"

Stevie Knight laughed again. "Evie would wring my neck if I had you on the line and didn't ask you to join us for Sunday dinner."

"I accept the invitation," Della said, pleased to have been invited.

She got straight to the point, explaining her situation with Josie and Galliard. If she protested too much about Josie's drinking, her daughter would shut her out. She had just begun to rebuild their relationship and didn't want to compromise even one building stone. But Galliard was closing his eyes to Josie's problem. He was enabling her to walk straight into a danger zone, and was winking, pretending everything was fine. Della was angry and the anger was eating her up.

"I've got one question," she said to her new spiritual mentor. "How do I control this big ole ball of anger that's lodged in my chest and in the pit of my stomach?"

"Well." Stevie Knight was quiet for a long moment. Della envisioned the minister looking out his windows into the brilliant, cold day, rubbing his chin with the palm of his hand. "Anger's not always bad," he finally said. "In the presence of evil even the Lord grew angry. We just need to know when to allow ourselves to get angry and when to stroke the old angry beast and settle him down."

"I'm trying to save my daughter," Della said.

"Maybe the time's come to get angry and fight. I fought for my niece last year. I mean—I fought. I went into an old house trailer at the edge of the woods up in Monroe County. A bunch of vipers were holed-up there using drugs. My niece was there

315

among them. One of the young men said, 'you can't take her. She can't go.' He tried to hold her back. I brought my hand up and broke his nose. That young man bled profusely. I took my niece's elbow and led her out. I thought they probably had guns in that trailer. I prayed to the Lord to keep us safe, but I told the Lord if they were going to shoot us, they'd have to go ahead and do it because I was taking my niece out of there."

Stevie Knight audibly sighed. "I'm not proud of my behavior. I didn't mean to come down so hard on that fellow's nose. But, I had to rescue my niece. She didn't stay here with us long, though. She's gone again. We got her son. You met him—our little Tyrone."

The preacher fell silent. Della waited until he spoke again. "What I'm saying to you is this—if you're angry and you're trying to save your daughter, you need to tell your ex-husband exactly what you're thinking. Lay it out. Say a prayer before you open your mouth that the Lord will help you control your tongue, and keep your head screwed tightly on your shoulders. It should all work out fairly well."

She thanked Stevie Knight for his advice, but before she hung up her office phone, her cell phone rang. She ended her conversation with the minister and answered her cell.

"Mom, where are you?" Kevin asked.

"In my office, catching up on a little work." She didn't tell Kevin no one had invited her to any of the celebrations this last day of Mardi Gras, and work seemed an attractive option to sitting at home alone. Besides, she did have work to do. At least here she was near the crowd and the boom, boom of the drums.

"I'm downtown too," Kevin said. I've got to attend a reception, and I've got to board a float a little past noon. Could I stop by your office? It won't take long. I'm just around the corner."

Kevin rapped his knuckles on the door and Della let him in. When she opened the door, she heard Covey's high-pitched ukulele *this land is your land, this land. . .*

Kevin pointed in Covey's direction. "That guy's not half bad."

Kevin wore the outfit of a Seventeenth Century dandy. Lavender satin knee britches over white tights. The knee britches were trimmed in fluffy white fake fur. He held a large deep-purple and lavender hat in his hand—the kind a Halloween witch might wear, but this one was trimmed not only in fake fur, but was loaded with sequins and studs. Kevin brushed his hat against his knee and held the hat out in front of his body, as if formally presenting himself to her.

"I look ridiculous. This is the prescribed costume for the afternoon's events. Dora had this one made for me."

On his head he wore a long dark wig—something between a swashbuckling pirate and a court partisan. He looked so miserable in his fancy satin britches and ruffled shirt with puffed sleeves, Della couldn't help but laugh. Then, Kevin started laughing too, and they both laughed until Della wiped tears from her eyes.

"Is this another Dora original?" Della asked when she stopped laughing long enough to speak.

"Check the label," Kevin said, turning the back of his neck toward her. "I'm sure it says Dumb Dora Designs."

Della lifted a Kleenex from the box and wiped her eyes. "Come on in." She moved toward her office where she had brewed a fresh pot of New Orleans dark roast.

Kevin settled himself into the new office chair opposite his mother's desk. When she handed him a mug of coffee, he blew steam off the top and took a sip.

"I've told Dad I'm leaving. I'm going in two weeks. Dad also knows that I've told you about Josie. I can't abide family secrets anymore. I hate that feeling that comes from keeping something from one person and something else from the other person. I can't live like that."

"Thank you for telling me about Josie," Della said.

"I didn't tell you everything. There were a couple of instances with Josie and drinking in high school too. To be honest, I don't remember all the details. Dad and Dora knew, but they thought the drinking was typical high school stuff."

"That's okay. I got enough information to draw my own conclusions."

"I think Josie needs help. I don't think Dad's accepted the fact that there's a real problem."

"I'll see what I can do," Della said. "I'll talk to your father about Josie."

Kevin rubbed his fur-lined cuff across his forehead. "At least now you have the facts." He took another sip of his coffee and placed the cup on his mother's desk. "I'd better go. We'll be lining up to get on the floats soon."

Della came from behind her desk to walk outside with her son.

In Candy Sue's small reception area, Kevin stopped in front of the desk. "Oh, I didn't tell you the good news. I've worked out most of the details for my trip. I'll be working on a ranch about a day's drive outside Laramie. Also, I'll be a part time teacher's aide in a little elementary school." He took a deep breath and drew his lips tight. "I suspect I'll get lonesome, but I want to spend a whole year finding out who Kevin McElhenney really is. I want to write down everything I see, everything I do, and everything I feel."

"I'm glad you'll be keeping a journal," Della said.

"Daily," Kevin answered her. "I want to write out all my questions and I want to find as many answers as I can. I also plan to do a considerable amount of reading. I'm taking fifty books." A shadow of doubt cut across his face. "Do you think fifty books will be enough?"

"You read the first fifty, and I'll send you the second fifty," Della told him.

"Good deal," he said and grinned.

Cold air hit them in their faces when they opened the door. Della walked outside with her son. "Damned cold day for Mobile," Kevin said as he he donned his Mardi Gras hat and held it in place with both hands, struggling against the brisk air coming off Mobile Bay.

Della folded her arms across her chest and tucked her hands under her arms to keep them warm. She watched Kevin in his ridiculous lavender satin costume fight the wind. "I love you," she said to his back. He turned around, still holding the hat with one hand, and blew her a kiss with the other.

When she went inside her office, her cell phone was ringing again.

"Miss Della, I'm almost to Bayou La Batre. I'll do some snooping and let you know what I find out."

"Good. I've got one stop to make, and I think I'll join you. Maybe two noses will be better than one."

"Come on whenever you're ready," Candy Sue said. "Call me and I'll give you my exact location."

Della liked the sound of that—*give you my exact location*. Somehow it sounded official—like a genuine sleuth, not like a secretary turned into a part time P.I.

Before she met Candy Sue in Bayou La Batre, she would drive out to Galliard's house in west Mobile. She had remained silent too long. She had gone along to get along. As Kevin had put it— the time had come to move past all the deception.

***

When she turned onto the cul-de-sac, she spotted Galliard's house—his mansion—set on a solid acre of well-tended Bermuda grass. The ornamental trees in the front yard stood on their own well-landscaped islands planted in perennials and surrounded by mondo grass. The old Dodge whined when she pulled into the circular driveway. The pitiful thing was way out of its class in this neighborhood—a mutt in a pedigreed kennel show. Della patted the dash. "Hang in there, baby," she encouraged. "Hold your own. I won't be long."

At the beveled glass doors, she rang the bell and heard Westminster chimes echo through the wide halls and spiral up to the rafters of the vaulted ceilings. Dora opened the door. Seeing Della, she took a sharp intake of air. Her face said *what the hell are you doing here?*

She quickly gained her composure and said sweetly, "Why Della, come on in. You must have come to see Josie. She's home from the hospital, but she's taking a little nap right now."

Della stepped onto the shell-pink marble floor of the foyer. "No. I'm here to see Galliard."

"Oh," Dora said and bit her bottom lip. "Well. He's in his study. He's going over some accounts I think. If you wait right here, I'll go check with him and see . . ." Her voice trailed off. She raised her hand. "Just wait here. I'll be right back."

Where does she think I'm going? Della wondered. From the foyer she could see the soaring wall of glass on the back of the house overlooking an enormous swimming pool and a stone patio. Way back on the property Della saw an arbor topped with vines. Without a doubt, this place was expensive and well-manicured.

She heard Galliard coming before she saw him. When he stepped to the foyer, his face was flushed—she guessed the florid color came from his surprise at seeing her standing on his turf. He put his hand out and took her hand into his. "Della. Good to see you." He cleared his throat. "What brings you out this way?"

"We need to talk. I've got a few things I need to say."

His color was almost magenta now. "Come on. Let's go to my study." Galliard led the way.

The large room, paneled in dark wood with massive crown molding, had an entire wall of bookcases. It was not at all like the little add-on room at the side of the white chapel where she envisioned Reverend Stevie Knight sitting. This office shouted affluence—an abundance of money earned in the gathering and disposal of garbage.

Galliard seated himself on a small, elegant sofa upholstered in a red and yellow oriental print. He motioned for Della to sit in a tall, red-silk, wingback chair.

"Okay," he said, "what's your beef?"

"The beef," she said softly, "is this—we need to talk about Josie."

Galliard slapped his hand against his knee. "Not again."

Della leaned forward in her chair. "Again, Galliard." She was angry now, but she remembered Stevie Knight's warning. She prayed the brief prayer Stevie Knight had told her: *Dear Lord, keep my lips from senseless flapping, and my head screwed tightly to my shoulders.*

Then, she marched forward.

"Josie has a drinking problem. You know it, but you want to pretend you don't."

Galliard too leaned forward, his face as florid as when he entered the room. "So what? She drinks a little. She'll get it under control." He clinched his jaw, ready for battle.

"She won't get it under control unless we address it. And, she won't get it under control unless she admits it and sets out to control it. It's that simple Galliard. Pretending you don't see the problem won't make it go away."

"Look," Galliard's hands flew into the air. "I've raised the children these past few years while you've been over in New Orleans. I'm doing the best I can here. What specifically do you want me to do?" His voice was acid with sarcasm.

Della sat on the edge of her chair. "Specifically, I don't want Josie to go to that dance tonight. If she does go, I don't want her to drink a drop. Specifically, I want you to talk to her about her drinking. And specifically, I want you to get counseling for her." She spoke rapidly, her voice as pinched with acid as was Galliard's.

321

"But I want her to go to that ball tonight," he said. "She's a debutante. I don't want her to be blackballed. I've worked too hard to make all this possible."

"You have worked hard. It's paid off. But you can't sacrifice our daughter to boost yourself up the social ladder."

"What the hell are you accusing me of? I was raised dirt poor." He spread his arms wide, encompassing the room. "Look what I've provided for my family. Little help from you, I might add. Sure I want her to go tonight, and a little drink won't hurt her."

"Galliard, I'm here begging for Josie." Fear was in Della's voice now. "Don't let her drown. Address the problem. Work with her to solve it. I'm living proof a drinking problem can be overcome. I'm also living proof it can bring you down."

"Now you're throwing it in my face. Look at you. You got a big law degree from a fancy university. You're back in town and everybody will be saying, look at that Della Boudreaux. Boudreaux," he added, "not McElhenney. Look what she's accomplished. Well I'm here to tell you old Galliard McElhenney has accomplished a few things too. It's time folks stood up, and took notice."

Della realized the situation could not have been stated any more clearly—Galliard McElhenney needed recognition, and he was willing to use whatever means necessary to gain the admiration he so desperately sought. *Lord, keep my head screwed tightly on my shoulders.*

She took a deep breath and decided on another route to her destination. "You've done a fine job, Galliard. Look at our children. They're first rate. Josie's a wonderful girl and Kevin's kind, and good, and hard working."

"He's leaving. You probably already know that." Galliard shot the words at Della. "Did you put him up to it?"

Della wanted to protest, but Galliard leaned forward in his seat and spoke rapidly. "He'll earn cents on the dollar compared to what I pay him here. He'll look ridiculous walking around in boots and a cowboy hat."

Della wanted to tell Galliard that Kevin would look far less ridiculous in boots and a cowboy hat than he did in his lavender knee britches trimmed in fake fur and sequins. But on this, she held her tongue.

Galliard looked toward the tranquil backyard as he contemplated his son and the dollars and cents of Kevin's decision. He had finally run out of steam. He folded his arms across his chest and sat back on the couch.

In the quiet that settled between them, Della had time to regroup. The steam and acid were all used up in her too. "Galliard," she spoke softly now. You've done a tremendous job. Look at all you've accomplished." She waved her hands around the room and lifted her open palm towards the beautiful landscaped stone patio and pool. "You deserve respect. You've also done a wonderful job with the children."

She didn't tell him how he had been a major contributor in her own dive into the world of excess drinking with his insistence on making her into someone she wasn't—the look, the dress, the maraschino red nails, the right clubs, the proper social events. Try as hard as she could, she had been unable to transform into his image of her, unable to keep herself afloat and incapable of raising Galliard above his own self-doubts. She was inadequate—never enough. But there was no reason to say any of this. Proverbial water under the proverbial bridge. They were discussing Josie. Josie was the one in peril, the beloved child whose feet dangled over the precipice.

Della's head still felt screwed down tightly, so she continued. "I know how much you love our children. I think what you're really saying is that you'll miss Kevin when he's gone. You love him, and you'll miss him. You want the best for Josie too. She needs help and you can provide that help. That's all I'm asking you to do. Help Josie."

Galliard was silent for a long, long minute. The florid color drained from his face. He rubbed his fist across his mouth. "I've tried to make everything right for everybody," he said. He sounded tired. "All I want is respect for me and my family." With his fist, he thumped his chest. "I got a big heart. I love Josie, and I love Kevin."

They looked at each other, really looked at each other—eyeballs locking with eyeballs.

"Okay," he said. "I'll talk to Josie, but I want her to go to that dance tonight. I'll be sure she doesn't drink anything stronger than a Coca Cola." He paused, his eyes not focused on anything now. "I'll get her some counseling too." He raised both hands in front of him like a shield, but still establishing eye contact with Della. "Although I'm still not convinced it's necessary."

She started to protest, but Galliard continued. "I'll do it anyway as a precaution."

Della saw Galliard's shoulders relax—no longer battle ready. She drew a deep breath. She was proud of herself. Instead of flapping senselessly, her lips had spoken meaningful words. Where there had been anger, she had brought peace, and her head was secured as tightly to her shoulders as was the head of a wise old owl. She thought of Mercedes when she envisioned the owl.

When Galliard opened the door leading out of his study, Dora nearly fell inside the room. "I was polishing the door. I noticed the wood was a little dull." She held a dust cloth in one hand and raised the can of furniture polish in her other hand. Della stifled a laugh when she saw the pattern of small rosettes from the heavily carved door imprinted on Dora's cheek.

Josie came down the stairs just as Della reached the foyer. She looked at her mother.

"Your mother's just leaving," Galliard said. "We've had a nice little visit."

Josie stepped forward and kissed her mother on the cheek. The first kiss they had shared in several years. "Thank you for staying at the hospital with me," she said. "You're leaving?"

"Yes," Della answered. "Don't forget I want to have lunch soon, and I want to show you my office."

"We'll do it," Josie said. "I want to meet that detective who works for you too."

Della hugged her daughter. "I love you."

Outside, the old Dodge turned over several times, but the engine wouldn't engage. Della stroked the dash. "Come on," she said. "I'll get you out of here, but you've got to cooperate. Come on, baby," she begged.

The old thing groaned. The engine sputtered, but then it came to life.

37

Around the corner from Galliard's house, Della pulled to the curb and telephoned Candy Sue. "I'm ready. Where are you?"

"I'm at the docks where the shrimp boats come in. Miss Della, I might be on to something. One of the shrimpers, an old Asian fellow with about half his teeth missing, told me a commercial fisherman named Johnny had a new man with him. He thought the man's name was Billy, but he didn't know Billy's last name. I got an address for Johnny."

"I'll be there in fifteen minutes," Della said, pulling away from the curb.

"You had lunch?" Candy Sue asked. "How about I buy us a couple of oyster po-boys and a couple of diet cokes? To go," she added.

The air in Bayou La Batre smelled of fish — dead fish and fried fish. Seafood processing plants, where oysters were shucked, fish gutted, and meat pulled from crab legs, dotted the landscape. Della met Candy Sue at a little carry-out seafood shack near the water.

Candy Sue held the oyster po-boys in a plastic bag. In her other hand, she carried the Coca-Colas nested in a cardboard tray. "These are hot," she said, lifting the plastic sack when Della was within ear shot. "I waited to place our order. Got some French fries too and a small order of onion rings."

Della glanced at Candy Sue — thin as a shadow. She knew she'd gain a couple of pounds just inhaling the fries and onion rings, but not Candy Sue.

"Thanks," she said. "I'm hungry." She glanced at her watch—well past noon. The wind coming off the water was so cold she shivered and headed toward the old Dodge.

"Excuse me, Miss Della. If you don't mind, I think we'd better take my car. No offense, but if we need to boogie, my car knows all the fast moves."

Candy Sue's canary-yellow Firebird looked like it clocked a hundred and ten sitting in the parking lot. Della patted the hood of her old Dodge. "It's okay, baby," she whispered, and stepped toward the sleek, young Firebird.

"Guess my car's not exactly the right color for undercover work, but it's what we've got. We'll make the best of it," Candy Sue said.

Della took the cardboard tray that held the Coca Colas, opened the passenger door, and slid inside.

"I've checked out the location already," Candy Sue said. "I know exactly where we're going."

They drove to a residential area of 1950s era houses and parked beside a small Catholic church with a large plastic statue of Mother Mary, her eyes cast heavenward and her hands clasped in front of her lips in the universal gesture of prayer.

"There's the place we need to watch." Candy Sue pointed across the street, three houses in front of them.

The women placed the oyster po-boys in their laps and unwrapped the waxed paper. They placed the French fries and onion rings on top of the console. Candy Sue pressed a button on the dash and drink holders slid out.

"Pretty good," Della said, when she bit into the sandwich dressed with lettuce, tomatoes, ketchup, mayonnaise, and dill relish. The oysters were still hot and fried to a golden crisp.

They watched the house as if it might take legs and walk away. An old, white Econoline van was parked in the driveway. The curtains were drawn in the front room.

Oliver's Song

"Guess if we sit here for a while and don't see anything, we should go to the door and ask for Billy Wong," Candy Sue said.

Della winced. "Let me think about that." She took another bite of her oyster po-boy. "We'd better go light on these drinks. Finding a bathroom around here might not be easy."

"Good point," Candy Sue said, her eyes still watching the house. "No gulps."

For some minutes, both women ate in silence.

"A stakeout's tough work. If we get tired, one of us can spell the other one. A short nap might be good after lunch." Candy Sue spoke without taking her eyes off the house. She took another bite of her sandwich. "You can take the first nap."

"I'll be fine," Della said, munching an onion ring after a bite of her po-boy. "If we need it, I've got this little canister of pepper gas on my key chain," Della said, bending down toward her purse to withdraw the pepper gas and show Candy Sue.

"I got us covered, Miss Della. Don't you worry." She tapped the console without looking down.

Della sat up, leaving the small tube of gas in her pocketbook—it was, no doubt, tiny potatoes compared to what Candy Sue stowed in her console.

The lettuce and tomato slid out of Della's po-boy, landing on the waxed paper in her lap. She looked down at her sandwich, retrieving the condiments.

Several cars passed on the street. But no one looked twice at the Firebird. "We got a pretty good place," Candy Sue said, "in front of the church. Probably looks like we got church business. Maybe a little counseling."

"Right," Della said.

That's when Candy Sue, who had just taken another bite of her own sandwich, slapped Della's arm, knocking the tomato and lettuce out of her hand, and onto the waxed paper again. Candy Sue pointed toward the house. "Uuuum," she hummed, her mouth full.

Della looked up and saw two men, both Asians, one slightly stocky, wearing blue jeans and a tan sweatshirt, while the other man was distinguished looking, tall and thin, with black-framed eyeglasses. The tall, thin man was well dressed in a blue dress shirt under a good-looking sports jacket. The men walked toward the Econoline van. The tall man opened the back of the van and placed a suitcase inside. In his left hand, he carried a violin case.

"That's our man," Della whispered. "He's got the violin." Without taking her eyes off the men, she lifted the waxed paper from her lap and placed it on the back floor of the Firebird.

Candy Sue swallowed hard and also lifted the waxed paper from her lap, keeping her eyes on the two men. She reached behind her, dropping the sandwich on the car's floor. The French fries and onion rings joined the sandwiches.

Della flipped open her cell and punched in the number for J.J. Ernest. While J.J.'s number was ringing, a small boy ran from the house and wrapped his arms around the waist of the man who carried the violin. The man's short black hair was neatly parted and combed to the right. He smiled down at the boy.

Della and Candy Sue slid low in their seats, only their eyes showing above the dash. The stocky man looked toward the yellow Firebird, but turned back to speak to the boy. He patted the boy on his back and pointed him toward the house, but the boy did not move.

The boy and the tall man talked. Then the man sat the violin case at his feet, opened the case, removed the violin, and allowed the boy to look at it.

"J.J.," Della said when the Attorney answered, his voice barely audible above the noise around him.

"I'm at the Athelstan Club," he shouted into his phone. "Let me step over by the window." Della heard the chatter and the laughter at the club, everyone there celebrating Mardi Gras.

J.J. was silent for some seconds. Della and Candy Sue never took their eyes off the two men. After allowing the boy to look at the violin, the tall man sat the violin in the case, and he too pointed the boy to the house. The boy gave the man a thumbs-up, and took off running toward the house.

The tall man lit a cigarette, took several puffs, then he threw the butt on the cement driveway and stepped on it. He squatted on the driveway and lifted the violin from the case. He tucked the violin under his arm, opened the back doors of the van, and placed the violin case inside, still holding the violin. He brought the violin to his chest and carried it like a baby as he walked to the passenger side of the van.

"Better." J.J. said. "I can hear you now."

The roar of voices and laughter was reduced, but not muted.

"We've located Billy Wong," Della said. "He's in Bayou La Batre. We've got eyeballs on him right now. He's carrying the violin."

"You serious?"

"Listen, J.J., I need help now." Her pitch was steady, low, and all business. J.J. could not mistake the mettle in her voice.

"Go on," he said, "give me the information."

"He's getting into an old, white, Econoline van. A stocky Asian man is driving. We'll stay with him," her voice was still low and steady as the van backed out of the driveway."

"Can you see a tag number?"

"Can't read it," Della said. "We need backup—the police, the sheriff, state troopers. Whoever owns this jurisdiction out here and whoever can locate us fast. We'll be following in a canary yellow Firebird."

"Neon Firebird?" J.J. chuckled.

"No time for that," Della shot back. She hesitated a beat while she watched the van head toward the intersection. "I'll get off the phone. Have the police dispatcher call my cell. We'll keep eyeballs on the van. I'll keep the dispatcher up to the second on our location. Got that J.J.?"

"Got it. Hold tight. I'll have backup in minutes." With that, Della flipped her cell closed.

38

Candy Sue turned the key and pumped the gas, but her left foot remained on the brake. The Firebird begged to sprint away from the curb. Both women kept their heads low, their eyes barely visible through the front glass.

"You strapped in, Miss Della?" Candy Sue asked without taking her eyes off the van.

Della pulled against her seatbelt. "Ready," she said.

They watched the van ease down the street and turn left at the intersection. That's when the Firebird bolted from the curb, and Della's seatbelt nailed her in place. "Holy moly!" she shouted. "This thing's wrapped around me like an octopus." She pulled hard against the seatbelt that held firm.

"It'll let up," Candy Sue said and turned at the corner in time to spot the van two cars ahead of them. "We don't want to be too close and we don't want to be too far away," she said.

The SUV, directly in front of them, turned left and now the Firebird cruised one car behind the Econoline van. "Great spot," Candy Sue concluded. "We'll ride here as long as we can."

With the Firebird holding a constant speed, Della's seatbelt relaxed its death grip. She sat up, took a deep breath, and watched the van, which made a right-hand turn ahead of them, while the Firebird caught a red light.

"This is totally illegal," Candy Sue said, as she steered severely to the right.

Della suddenly realized what her secretary, turned detective, was about to do.

"No. No!" she shouted. "We don't need to do this."

"Got to, Miss Della. We'll lose 'em if we don't."

Candy Sue slid the Firebird halfway into a ditch and pulled around the car in front of her. She glanced in both directions, and then she ran the red light. Both the driver in front of the Firebird and the driver behind the Bird honked their horns. The man in the front car raised his fist.

"We can wait!" Della shouted.

"Miss Della, there was nothing coming. We need a police escort anyway."

"We'll get one for sure," Della said and tugged on her seatbelt, which had tightened around her again. In front of them, she saw the van turn onto the I-10 ramp.

"Just what I expected. We got to stick with them. Those two are on the move." With that, Candy Sue put her foot to the pedal, and the Firebird ate up the road, galloping until it drafted wind immediately behind the old van.

Della's cell rang. The police dispatcher. J.J. Ernest had done his job.

"We're behind the van," she told the woman. "Hold on," she said when the dispatcher asked for their exact location. When the Firebird passed a mile marker, Della called out the number.

"We got you tracked," the dispatcher said. "You'll pick up a police escort soon. When you see our car, drop back. Let the police handle it from there."

Della conveyed the information to Candy Sue, who followed close behind the van.

"Hold on the phone with me," the dispatcher said, "until our cruiser catches up with you."

"You got it," Della said, and kept the phone pressed to her ear.

"We'll see this whole thing come down," Candy Sue said. "With Billy Wong in custody, Ollie Fitzsimmons should be released."

"That would mean—first case handled nicely," Della said with her hand over the cell phone speaker.

"Oh no! The driver just spotted us," Candy Sue said. "I saw him look in his rearview."

The van speeded up, and so did Candy Sue.

Oliver's Song

"He must have seen us parked by the church. Now he knows we're behind him."

"Mile marker?" the dispatcher asked. Della gave her the number on the sign as the Firebird flew past it. She glanced at the speedometer too. Eighty-five and edging up.

A considerable way behind the Firebird, Della spotted a blue light flashing. "Help's behind us," she told Candy Sue. The needle on the speedometer now topped ninety.

The driver of the van must have spotted the blue light too. He speeded up, and Candy Sue fed the Firebird more gas.

Della saw another vehicle, blue light flashing, enter the highway from the ramp they had just passed. "We got two coming," Della said to the dispatcher.

"You got more on the way," the dispatcher answered.

Another police car flashed by them headed west. "He'll turn at the next median," Candy Sue said. "That makes three."

The two patrol cars in the rear were nearly on them when the driver of the van pulled a surprise maneuver. He made a sharp right hand turn onto the exit ramp.

"No way!" Candy Sue shouted.

"That's a hairpin turn!" Della twisted in her seat, facing the window.

Candy Sue was already slowing the Firebird.

Della saw the Econoline's wheels leave the pavement when it hit the curve. As the van skidded, it rammed the embankment. Della now looked through the rear window to follow the van, which was completely out of control.

The van flipped. Once. Twice. Off the ramp.

"My God!" she whispered.

"What?" Candy Sue asked. She took a quick glance in the rearview mirror.

"Flipped!" Della shouted. "Rolled and flipped." She released her seat belt, turned around, and hunched in the seat on her knees, looking behind the Firebird at the unfolding catastrophe.

"Put that seatbelt back on, Miss Della. Won't do anybody a bit of good if you get hurt too."

Della turned in her seat and locked her seatbelt around her again, still looking over her shoulder at the accident behind her.

Candy Sue took the next exit, circled around the cloverleaf, and now headed west on I-10. Back to where the van took the hairpin ramp, skidded and rolled.

Traffic slowed. Drivers on both sides of the interstate gawked at the accident.

The Firebird slowed to twenty-five. Candy Sue took the exit. She pulled off the ramp, parked, and the women got out of the car.

The two patrol cars that were behind them on the interstate were at the scene. One officer glanced in the direction where Della and Candy Sue parked and shouted, "Get back!" He pushed the air with his hands as if he pushed the Firebird. "Get that car out of here! Now!" He ordered.

Flames shot from the rear of the Econoline Van. The occupants of the van were now in serious peril.

Both women stopped in their tracks and stood for a split second on the grassy shoulder off the road. Then Candy Sue and Della got back into the Firebird. Candy Sue pulled the car several hundred feet away from the Econoline that rested on its roof— wheels in the air, fire shooting from its rear.

A Highway Patrol had joined the two police officers. The trooper backed his car up the exit ramp and parked in the middle of the lane, blocking any additional drivers who might consider taking the ramp.

Della and Candy Sue walked toward the van, but the police officer shouted at them again. "Stay back!"

Now, flames shot from the rear windows of the van.

"Two men are in that van," Della shouted. "You got to get them out."

She didn't want to witness this. She didn't want to see two men burned alive. Nothing in her entire life had prepared her for this. She wanted to turn her back. But she could not. She would not allow herself that luxury of turning her back. Her eyes remained on the van, her breath shallow, her nerves unstrung.

"One's coming out!" Candy Sue shouted and grabbed Della's arm.

As the two women watched, the stocky Asian, his face and tan sweatshirt covered in blood, crawled through the shattered front window. He remained in the grass on all fours, like a wounded and suffering animal.

"He's out!" Candy Sue shouted and pointed at the man in case the police failed to see him.

Two of the police officers ran to the man, pulled him away from the van and lifted him. They wrapped their arms around the man's waist, and walked him away from the flames. The stocky man leaned against the officers, his legs wobbly.

The officers crossed the street, still supporting the man. They walked him a considerable distance in the opposite direction from where the van burned, and eased the man down in the grass.

Della looked again toward the van. That's when she saw him—Billy Wong with the violin. He stumbled around the far end of the vehicle, his hands clutching fire to his chest.

"Oh my God!" Candy Sue shouted. "That violin's on fire."

"Put it down!" Della shouted. "Put it down!"

"Drop and roll!" the officers commanded. "Drop! Roll!"

The tall, thin man held the flaming violin. The body of the violin was on fire, but still Billy Wong held it. Flames edged up the neck of the violin, up the beautiful scroll. Billy Wong staggered, but he clutched the violin as if it were a baby he held next to his heart. Small tongues of fire now licked his chin.

Too painful to watch. But, Della could not turn away.

"Drop it!" she shouted. She took several steps toward the man clutching the flaming violin, but a trooper threw his hand up.

"Stay there!" he ordered. "Keep back!"

"Drop and roll!" the officers shouted.

Never could she have imagined a sight like this. She had seen newspaper pictures of monks during the Vietnam War, monks who immolated themselves, incinerating their flesh—their robes in gossamer flames, rising above their stolid faces. She had only glanced at these pictures, not wanting to see the agony in detail.

Now, before her own eyes, the man's expensive looking sport coat caught fire. The front of his chest in flames.

"Drop it! Roll!" Della yelled. Tears wet her face. "Roll!" she shouted. "Drop and roll!" She pounded her fists in the air as if they could force the man on fire to roll in the grass.

The man still held his arms around the flames as if he held the violin.

"No!" She screamed. "No! . . . No! . . . No!"

Two officers ran toward the man, knocking him down and kicking him into the grass, rolling his body over, and over—and over again.

When the flames were extinguished, they grabbed the man under his arms and dragged him across the street, pulling him away from the flaming van and resting his body not far from the man in the tan sweatshirt.

An ambulance, its siren squealing, pulled around the State Trooper's vehicle and parked on the grassy shoulder where the two bodies rested.

At that very moment when the ambulance parked beside the two men, the van exploded, sending a ball of fire and flames thirty feet into the air.

Later, Della would swear that moment in time slowed down. Slow motion—not regular speed. She felt, and heard, and saw everything with perfect clarity. The explosion that nearly deafened her. The heat that felt as if it singed the tiny hairs on her arms. The ball of fire—at first, a nearly perfect sphere of orange and blue. Then the fire charged forward engulfing the van in random flames that cavorted and danced around the wheels, past the doors, across the upended hood.

Della had to avert her face to keep her eyes from searing in the heat and light from the fire. Through the smoke, she saw the ambulance driver back away from the flames. Gurneys out now. Both the ambulance crew and the officers ran. Lifting the men onto the gurneys. Covering them. Rushing to the ambulance. Everyone rushing! Rushing to get away from the van—a blazing inferno.

Candy Sue wrapped her arm around Della's waist. The two women watched for another second. "Dear God in heaven," Della whispered.

Another explosion from the van. Another fireball. The two sprinted for the yellow Firebird. They scrambled inside and Candy Sue pulled the car even farther away from the van before they stopped and got out of the car once more to witness the last of the fiery cataclysm. The van shuttered and popped in small explosions as it continued to burn down to what would be a scattering of metal bones—a charred and smoldering carcass.

Della did not see J.J. Ernest and Sidney Winfield pull their car in front of the Firebird. The men simply appeared. They stood beside Della and Candy Sue, lifting their arms to shield their faces from the heat and light of the fire.

J.J. whistled between his teeth. "That is something else!" With the backside of his hand, he wiped his forehead. "I'm sweating from way back here."

The siren squealed as the ambulance roared up the ramp headed toward the hospital.

"Billy Wong held that violin until it burned up," Candy Sue said to J.J. Ernest and Sidney Winfield.

"It's gone?" Winfield asked.

"Gone," Candy Sue said. "And, it most likely killed the man who held it. His whole chest looked like it was on fire. He held on to that flaming violin, though."

"I never thought I'd see a thing like that," Della said. "I hope I never see anything else like it. Never. Ever."

"He must have been in shock," Candy Sue said. "Who'd hold on to a flaming violin?"

"Crazy," J.J. Ernest said. "That's just crazy."

To steady herself, Della placed both her hands on the trunk of the Firebird. She knew she would spend the rest of her life trying to forget what she had seen—the tall, thin man clutching the fire-eaten violin to his heart.

39

Billy Wong remained in the burn unit at the university hospital for a solid week before he succumbed to his injuries. Both Della and J.J. Ernest regularly checked on him. When he died, Sidney Winfield spearheaded the effort to return Billy Wong's body to his elderly grandmother in China. She lived in Hubei Province at the foot of the Wudang Mountains.

"Supposed to be beautiful in the Wudang Mountains," Winfield said. "Lots of monasteries there. I have a friend who visited China last year. He said the people believe spirits live in the Wudang Mountains. Funny how legends like that get started."

Winfield's obsession with the violin abated slowly. He interviewed Della and Candy Sue several times. *Did you get a look at the old violin? Color? Any ornamentation? Size? Fancy work on the scroll?*

"The pegs?" he asked. "If you saw the pegs, that would tell me something."

"We weren't that close" Candy Sue said. "It was reddish brown," she added. "I did see that much. Kind of a honey-brown. Billy Wong took it out of its case and let that little boy see it. That's when I got my best view of it. But, it was at a distance. The next time we saw the violin, that thing was on fire."

"Please," Della begged. "Let's not picture it again."

"It was something special," Sidney Winfield said, "I know that much. Could have been Stradivari's Le Maurien. It had to be something extraordinary. Something Billy Wong couldn't let go of. Even if it destroyed him."

Winfield collected ashes from the violin, hoping scientists somewhere could work their magic and determine if the ashes were indeed a Stradivarius. For now, he had encountered only dead ends. He still had the ashes though.

Johnny, Billy's cousin, had recovered from his injuries and had not been charged with any offenses. He claimed he didn't know Billy Wong was sought by federal investigators. He was considering filing his own lawsuit against the Mobile P.D. for chasing his van. According to Johnny, he exited the interstate to get out of the way of the racing patrol cars driven by reckless drivers.

The Mobile P.D. claimed Johnny knew exactly what he was doing—transporting an illegal alien with false documents. He aided and abetted a man who was somehow involved in the drug trade. Neither the P.D. nor the U.S. Attorney had yet come forward to provide all the particulars of that scenario. To date, Johnny had not filed a suit and no law enforcement agencies had filed any charges against him. All parties remained in a holding pattern.

Ollie Fitzsimmons was out of jail—but his release had been nothing short of dicey. Della was still a little uncertain of the forces that had come together to gain her client's release. J.J. Ernest had come from a court hearing to Della's office with FBI agent Sidney Winfield in tow.

"I brought the FBI with me," he said, "because Winfield here can bring you up to speed on what's been going down."

What has *gone down*, Della wondered.

"We'll give you the chance to talk first," J.J. said in his usual drawl. "Tell us what you've got."

With the men seated across from her desk, Della proceeded to tell them about the two witnesses who corroborated Ollie's story. The student who had heard Billy Wong ask Ollie to transport his bass to Mobile. The student heard Wong tell Ollie he would come through Mobile and get his bass for an audition in Texas. Then she told them about May Lin, Billy Wong's scorned lover. May Lin had been promised a big ring, a fancy car, and a honeymoon when Billy came into money. But . . . he disappeared.

The men listened politely. Occasionally sipping their coffee and occasionally nodding their heads. When Della finished, J.J.

Ernest grinned at her. "Della, don't for a minute think you're the only one who knows the ins and outs of snooping. We got good noses too." He tapped the side of his nose. He turned to Sidney Winfield. "Sid, I think you'd better tell her."

Sidney Winfield looked uncomfortable. He shuffled in his chair and sat up straight. He cleared his throat. "We had a tap on Billy Wong over in Florida. We got your boy on tape."

My dear God, Della thought. *Have I been deceived?* She too sat up straight and leaned in toward J.J. Ernest and Sidney Winfield.

"Wong had ties to several major drug cartels operating in Florida. We knew this." Winfield cleared his throat again. "In one of Wong's phone conversations we heard him discuss transporting the bass to Mobile. Must have been after the student overheard the conversation—after Fitzsimmons agreed to bring the bass to Mobile. Wong arranged a time for them to meet close to the music buildings. He told Fitzsimmons he'd come through Mobile on his way to Texas and get his bass."

"See, I told you," J.J. said. "We got good ears and got good noses too."

"Wait a minute," Della said. "You knew all along Ollie was telling the truth and you let him go to jail?"

"I wouldn't say we let him go," J.J. said. "Your boy had the stuff in his possession, and he was transporting it. A substantial amount too. We can still nail him down tight."

"But you knew he was telling the truth," Della insisted. "He was not involved in any drug ring. He did a favor for a friend and then decided to move that case so it wouldn't be at the fishing camp when his little nephew arrived. You knew that, and still you let him sit down at the jail. You let him get beaten too. Beaten badly."

"He made a stupid mistake," J.J. said. He shrugged his shoulders. "Not our fault. Those drugs were in his possession and he was transporting his load on the interstate highway. How do we know what he intended to do? For all we know he intended to sell his haul. We could make a powerful argument in court."

J.J. slid the nail on his left index finger under each nail on his right hand, grooming his fingernails. Challenging Della to counter what he had said. Waiting for her response.

A heavy silence filled the room before Sidney Winfield spoke. "We also thought he might give us a little more information. We figured anything he could remember would help crack this whole thing wide open."

"You let him stay in jail and you didn't tell me about the tap?"

"There would be a time and a place for that," J.J. said. "The time's come." He raised his shoulders again in another shrug that said *so what? We're telling you now*.

"Ollie Fitzsimmons lived in fear down at the jail. He could have been killed."

Della was hot now. She didn't like deceptions in criminal justice any better than she liked deceptions in families. "I want to know everything you know," she said.

"Tell her the rest," J.J. Ernest said to Sidney Winfield.

"Billy Wong and the Asians down at the jail were tied to a man named Chang Wu. He was the man found dead by the water in Bayou La Batre. Multiple gunshot wounds through his chest."

Della nodded.

"The Asians were starting a new drug operation in the southeast, from Texas, along the Gulf Coast, and on into Florida. From the southeast, they planned on using the interstate highways and establishing their trade in the great heartlands. Their product was heroin."

"We stopped the Asian cartel in its tracks," J.J. Ernest said. "We don't want heroin down this way. We won't have it. Those men at the jail will be shipped back to China." He brushed his hands as if liberating them of crumbs.

"What else do you know?" Della asked.

"The fat boy who tried to pick your lock on Monday decided he wanted to do some talking too. That boy loves to talk," J.J. said. "He was tied to a South American operating out of New Orleans. The reason I say *was* is because the South American is the man found shot in the French Quarter, shot with what appears to be the same kind of weapon used to kill Mr. Chang Wu here in Mobile. The fat boy was looking for Billy Wong and he was also searching for that violin. Thought you might have the violin in your office. That's why he was trying to pick your lock."

Answers to many of Della's questions came fast and furious. All the pieces were now beginning to fall into place, but she had been excluded from the loop.

"I think the young man downtown is glad he was in jail when the murder took place over in New Orleans. He's not a suspect. But we got him on all kinds of other charges and he knows it. He's talking plenty to save his own neck."

Della was angry. So much information had been kept from her. Deception—plain and simple. *Hold 'em*, she thought. *Don't play your cards yet.*

J.J. smiled at her. "You see your Asian and Hispanic link," he said. "I'm here to tell you, we nailed this one. That van the Asians were driving had about five hundred pounds of pure heroin in it. Another big bust," J.J. concluded. He held his hands out in front of his face, examining his fingernails again.

Della was sure all of this would play well if he decided to toss his hat in the ring for the Senatorial race.

"But my client," Della protested. "You had every reason to believe him, yet you let him remain in jail. You didn't support bail."

"He made a big mistake," J.J. reminded her. "Why should I agree to immediate bail?"

It's time, she thought. *Put your cards on the table.*

"Because you knew he was innocent." She placed her hands on her desk, leaning toward the men. "I'll see your butts in court," she said. "I want this whole thing to come to light. You've allowed my client to be put in serious jeopardy. He's been beaten and his reputation sullied. This meeting is over."

"Whoa," J.J. said. "The U.S. Attorney's Office doesn't want trouble. We're willing to deal. That's why we're here."

"I don't want Ollie to spend any more time in Metro Jail and definitely no time in federal prison," Della said.

J.J. rubbed the backside of his hand against his chin. "We can arrange that."

"I want all charges dropped."

"Can't do that," J.J. said. "He was caught red handed transporting the stuff. You can say anything and everything you want to say, Della, but it won't change the fact that he had the goods in the trunk of his car. Million in heroin."

Della slapped her hand against her desk. "See you in court," she said. She gathered the file folders Candy Sue had given her.

"Wait a minute," J.J. said. "We can't drop all the charges, but I'll ask for only a couple of years. My office will specify he was not involved with either cartel. Not as far as we know, that is."

"We can't accept that either," Della said. "I can't let him go to prison." She was playing hardball. Her client's life was at stake. As Reverend Stevie Knight had said—there is a time to get angry. *Dear Lord, keep my tongue from flapping and my head screwed on tightly.* She stood, a clear announcement that the conversation was over.

"Sit down," J.J. said, irritation in his voice. "Tell you what I'll do. I'll reduce the charges. I'll go before the judge and argue for probation. Fitzsimmons won't spend another night in jail or in federal prison. He'll have to answer to a probation officer though." He rubbed his chin as he calculated. "How about a year to eighteen months?" he asked.

Della sat down in her chair.

"It's the best deal you're going to get," J.J. said. "We can make a powerful case. Nothing will change the fact that he was in possession." He paused a beat. "Here's the deal: you don't file suit, and we'll go away. It's the best thing for all of us, including Ollie Fitzsimmons."

Della pondered this. Probation. It wasn't a bad deal. She sat down. "I'll speak with my client and let you know," she said.

Oliver's Song

At that very moment, they all heard a scuffle in Candy Sue's office. "Right there!" Candy Sue shouted. "Spread eagle!"

Sidney Winfield was first out the door, followed by J.J., and then Della. Candy Sue stood behind her desk, her pistol drawn. Bobby Jack Arnold, Oliver Sr.'s lawyer, stood with his legs spread wide against the wall, an amused look on his face.

"He's got a gun," Candy Sue said. "It's strapped under his left arm. I spotted it soon as he walked in. I asked him politely to remove it. He laughed. This man had better learn to do what he's told when he waltzes into somebody's office carrying a gun."

"Bobby Jack, what are you doing here?" Della asked.

"You know this man, Miss Della?" Candy Sue asked.

"Kinda," Della said. "I can't vouch for him, though."

He turned from the wall and faced Della, his arms still held above his head. "I've come to discuss a small legal problem. This charming woman here," he nodded his silver head toward Candy Sue, "drew a pistol on me. Might I lower my arms?"

"If Miss Della knows you and says you're okay, you can lower your arms," Candy Sue said.

"I know him, and I guess he's okay," Della answered.

"Lower your hands," Candy Sue said, "and remove your holster. Place it on my desk. You and I'll be straight then."

"You ever think of joining the FBI?" Sidney Winfield asked Candy Sue.

"I don't appreciate folks coming into my office attempting to steal my personnel," Della said to Sidney Winfield.

"Just an idea," Winfield said. He raised his hands in front of him in a plaintive gesture. "Just an idea."

"The FBI might be a little too tight for me," Candy Sue said. "Don't most agents wear black and white?" Before Winfield could answer, Candy Sue spoke again. "No," she concluded and wrinkled her face. "I don't think that would work for me."

Bobby Jack placed the holster with the gun still in it on Candy Sue's desk.

"You get back with me on that offer," J.J. said to Della. "It won't remain on the table very long." Sidney Winfield saluted Candy Sue and the two men from the Federal Government headed toward the door.

Della turned to Bobby Jack. "You want to see me about a legal matter?"

"I have a small problem I think you might help me solve," he said. He winked at Candy Sue. "Thank you, lovely lady, for safeguarding my pistol. Might you be interested in a boat ride about the bay when the weather warms up a little?"

"I believe my calendar's full," Candy Sue said.

Inside her office, Della poured New Orleans dark roast for herself and for Bobby Jack. She eased herself into her desk chair. "So," she said, "you have a problem?"

He looked cautiously behind him. The door leading to Candy Sue's office was ajar. "Mind if I close this?" He whispered.

"Not at all," Della said.

Bobby Jack stood and closed the door. He began speaking before he fully settled himself in his chair again. "You see, Miss Boudreaux . . ." He grinned at her. "Might I call you Della?"

"Please, call me Della."

"Thank you, kind lady," he said.

Della wanted to say cut the crap. What she said was, "Go ahead please, tell me your story."

"Well, I was up in McIntosh, you know just north of Mobile."

"I know McIntosh," Della told him.

"I have a little hunting camp there with three buddies."

Della wondered if everyone except her had a little hunting camp north of Mobile.

"Nice place," Bobby Jack said. "Well, I was up there with a friend last weekend. We were at a bar. I suppose I imbibed a little too freely. The bottom line is this—someone said, 'Bobby Jack, you're so drunk you couldn't even shoot the light out over our heads.' At the time, and in my circumstances, that sounded like a perfectly good dare.

"I removed my pistol and proceeded to shoot the light out above where we sat. Then I proceeded to shoot out every light in the place. And, for no good reason I can give you, I decided I could take out a goodly number of liquor bottles behind the bar. I proceeded to do exactly that. I hit more than should be statistically probable for a man in my condition, considering the feat was accomplished in total darkness." Bobby Jack sipped his coffee and looked at Della.

"Well," he said, "the bar owner has filed charges. I've offered to pay for everything, but he's not accepting." Bobby Jack grinned at Della. He looked like a Siamese twin of the Cheshire cat—bright blue eyes, his teeth showing in a wide, forced smile. "Della," he said, "I believe I'm in need of legal counsel."

Della opened her mouth to speak, but Bobby Jack raised his hand. "One other thing," he said. "I need this held in strictest confidence." He cocked his silver head, "Della, how about it? Will you take this case—and strictly on the hush, hush."

"I believe I can settle this for you," Della said. "It's a thousand up front. I bill by the hour, and I'll charge you expenses for any travel to and from McIntosh."

"Not a problem," Bobby Jack said. He stood, removed his wallet and counted out ten one-hundred dollar bills. He placed these on Della's desk. Then, he winked at her, the Cheshire cat grin on his face again. "I got several other small legal problems that need addressing, but one thing at a time. Right?"

"Right," Della said and tucked the hundred dollar bills in her desk drawer. She'd have to wrap the bills in tissues to keep the old Dodge from smelling them and begging for a tune-up.

She suspected Bobby Jack was a goose laying golden eggs. No doubt his legal problems were extensive. But, as Bobby Jack said—*one problem at a time.*

Before he left, Bobby Jack strapped his pistol on his chest again. "Never know when you might need this," he said, and winked at Candy Sue.

Candy Sue was having none of it. "You put that pistol right here on my desk if you come back in this office again." With her perfectly manicured index finger, she tapped the corner of her desk, indicating the exact spot.

"Certainly, lovely lady," Bobby Jack said and dipped his head in Candy Sue's direction. "Don't forget what I said about that boat ride. Offer still holds. A moonlight cruise around Mobile Bay."

"I checked my calendar already," Candy Sue said. "I'm all booked up."

Epilogue

It was after five, but Della still sat at her desk and Candy Sue worked in the outer office. Della was putting the final touches on the settlement in Bobby Jack Arnold's case. The bar owner up in McIntosh had dropped all charges in exchange for a handsome chunk of change. Bobby Jack had delivered several other clients to Boudreaux Attorney at Law, each bringing an assortment of legal snafus in need of detangling. Bobby Jack would indeed be a goose laying golden eggs.

Della stood, rotating her shoulders to relieve the tension across her back. She stepped out of her office and walked to the window in front of Candy Sue's desk. "Been a long day," she said.

"Sure has, Miss Della." Candy Sue locked her hands and held them out in front of her, stretching her arms. "I'm about ready to go. I got a weekend class I need to get ready for."

"I'm about to go too," Della said.

"Think I'll freshen up my make-up before I go," Candy Sue said. "I've got a dinner date before I go home to study." She headed toward the bathroom with her cosmetic bag in her hand.

Della looked out on the street in front of the old Bankhead Tunnel. Night was settling around Mobile Bay with a little fog, like a light-weight blanket, soft and just right for late spring.

As she rotated her shoulders again, she allowed her mind to wander. Three months earlier, if she'd placed bets on how things would have turned out, she'd have been wrong on nearly every bet. Some things were resolved and other things were in various states of—how would she label it—various states of continued unfolding?

If someone had asked her to guess what her son Kevin would be doing, she would have envisioned him doing his father's bidding—winning new accounts for Galliard and establishing his foothold as a garbage magnate in his own realm. But this was not what had happened at all.

She and Moss Maple—not Galliard McElhenney—had gone with Kevin to assist him in selecting a new 4-wheel-drive Jeep for his trip to Wyoming. Kevin had chosen a silvered tan color for his new car. She had been instrumental in his selection. "It won't show dust from the ranch as badly as a darker or brighter color might," she told him.

Kevin packed light for his trip—four pairs of blue jeans, seven work shirts, a couple of pairs of brogans, two pale blue button downs for dress-up occasions, one pair of slacks, and a new sports jacket. "I'll buy a Western hat and boots when I get there," he said.

Della had walked out to the driveway to see him off, her heart breaking. Yet, she wanted him to go. When she put her arms around him, she held him for a solid minute, his heart close to her heart—flesh to flesh and heart to heart. This was her son in whom she was well pleased.

"I'll write every week," Kevin said. "I don't know how much we'll be able to talk." He held his cell phone in the air. "I'm not positive I'll have a good signal out there. I'll be in the middle of nowhere."

"You write and you call whenever you can," Della told him.

She walked into the middle of the street still waving and blowing kisses. Just before he turned the corner, Kevin leaned his head out the window and blew one final kiss to her.

The tears started then. She wanted Kevin to go to Wyoming and she wanted him to stay here, close to her. Kevin was her ally—more so than anyone else on the entire earth. Now he was headed out to Wyoming to work on a cattle ranch, and serve as a teacher's aide in a tiny rural elementary school. Della walked around the block two times, unable to go inside her small apartment. The confined space would have closed in on her, and crushed her.

True to his word, Kevin had sent a long letter every week since he had been gone. His cell phone didn't work on the ranch, but on several Sunday afternoons he had driven into town and had placed a call to her. She loved the sound of his voice—strong and confident. Kevin was earning his independence by the muscle of his back, the sweat of his brow, and the emptying and refilling of his heart.

Ollie Fitzsimmons had surprised her too. He had done just the opposite of what she would have predicted. He remained in Mobile, partially because he had to answer to a probation officer, but also because he had made the decision to mend the relationship with his father. He now worked part time for Fitzsimmons Industries, and had taken a special interest in the new townhouse development on the waterfront in downtown. He also secured the position as a low-level assistant on a tug boat, pushing barges of timber and coal up and down the Tombigbee Waterway. From his work outdoors, his hair had lightened to a sandy blond, and his blue eyes were bright as crystals in his tanned face. His leg was recovering nicely, but still required a doctor's supervision. He walked with a gold-tipped cane, but the cane would soon be a thing of the past.

One other surprise: Ollie and Josie were dating. Josie too had decided to take some time off from school and attend counseling in Mobile. For this, Della gave credit to Galliard. When she complimented Galliard, he had dropped his head and kicked the dirt with the toe of his shoe—reminiscent of a six-year-old boy on the school playground. "No big stuff," he said. Still the same Galliard McElhenney, but for Josie's sake, he had done the right thing. Della was grateful.

Josie had come to Della's office at the foot of the old Bankhead tunnel. They had gone to lunch, not once, but twice. The last time Josie came, she stood in Candy Sue's office, looked around the cubbyhole that was Boudreaux Attorney at Law and said, "It's small, Mom, but I like it." Then Josie hugged her—actually hugged her. "Thank you for sticking by Ollie," she added. "You saved him, you know." Then, as if embarrassed, she moved hurriedly toward the door. "Bye," she said over her shoulder.

And, she was gone. Della smiled. They were moving closer together, not by miles, but by inches. But those inches would turn into miles. Della knew it—she felt it in her bones.

Mercedes Magellan was changing her life too, and the change had come unexpectedly. After the funeral of her sister, Mercedes had returned to her estate in Spring Hill, but had not been the same for a solid month. She had all the outward signs of depression, and looked a decade older. She was more feeble and depended on her angel-headed cane—her girl—for every step.

That was true until something happened—Della was not sure what had happened. But whatever it was, it had come from deep inside Mercedes. A resolve. A new commitment. Della returned home from work one afternoon and found Mercedes, her pocketbook in the crook of her arm, pacing in the front yard. The first evidence that a metamorphosis had taken place was that the old woman twirled the cane in the palm of her hand like a baton, and when she saw Della, she headed straight for the old Dodge.

"I'm alive," Mercedes said.

"You are indeed," Della affirmed, not knowing where this conversation would lead.

"I'm alive and I've got to decide whether or not to survive or die." Without even a moment's hesitation, Mercedes continued. "I've decided to live and live big," she said. "I want you to take me to a sporting goods store. I want some of those tight jogging pants I see all these young women wearing. I want a tight-fitting top too, and one of those billed caps the girls pull their ponytails through."

Mercedes had been true to her word. She had begun an exercise program. In the beginning she had walked half a block, her angel-headed cane in her hand. One week later, Mercedes increased her distance and was walking the length of an entire block. Granted, the distance was short, but the progress was major. Mercedes envisioned herself forming a Port City Walking Club, complete with races. She would win every one of her races because she would be the only female contestant in her age group.

For now, she was content to strut her half mile in full sportive regalia.

While Candy Sue freshened her makeup in the bathroom, Della stepped back to her desk and placed Ollie's beautiful compositions in her new leather briefcase. She had been able to purchase the briefcase and pay her bills because of the assorted clientele Bobby Jack sent her way. Bobby Jack's friends had more legal problems than a monkey has fleas. Bobby Jack and his entourage provided steady and lucrative business.

Candy Sue, looking gorgeous, emerged from the bathroom. "I'm going on, Miss Della."

"You got a second to look at these?" Della asked as she pulled the manila folder out of her briefcase again and opened the file. She showed Candy Sue the handwritten compositions Ollie had used as pay to retain the legal services he needed. "I'm taking these to be framed. They'll look great behind my desk."

Candy Sue leaned in toward the heavy rag paper and studied the black-ink notes. "Woo-eee. Those are nice. They'll dress this place up."

"Have a good weekend," Della said as Candy Sue turned to leave, but the secretary turned back toward her boss. "Oh, by the way, Miss Della, I got a new hairdresser. Her name's Ju Ju. She gives a dynamite cut. Want an appointment?"

Della considered this for a moment. Maybe a haircut by Ju Ju would be just the ticket for launching herself into a "new you" program as progressive as Mercedes'.

"Sure," Della said, "I'll give Ju Ju a try."

"I'll take care of it on Monday," Candy Sue said as she headed out, but turned toward Della one more time. "Oh, don't let that red-eyed devil tattooed right above her left breast put you off. It does have red eyes and fangs and all, but Ju Ju knows hair." With that, Candy Sue was out the door.

Della snapped her briefcase shut, stood and turned off the lights. On Government Street, she locked the outside door and pulled against it to be certain the lock was secure. Down the street, in front of the sea wall, she heard Covey strumming his ukulele for any evening walkers who might be enjoying a stroll through Cooper Park. He had added a couple of new pieces to his repertoire *The Circle Won't Be Broken* and *When the Saints Go Marching In*. These old favorites kept the tip bucket brimming. Della wondered what happened to the money Covey collected. Did he get to keep it, or did it go to the FBI? She hoped Covey put the money in his pocket. After all, he was the one who mastered and refined his repertoire.

She still wasn't absolutely sure if Covey and Sidney Winfield were one and the same. Every time she was near one of the men, she studied his face closely. She also studied the shape of their bodies, and their hands and fingers. She had told no one of her suspicions. She would protect both Covey and Sidney Winfield, if in fact they were a one man duo.

"Look who we found," a familiar voice said from behind her.

Della turned to discover a small crowd—Ollie, Josie, and three slender black men dressed in navy blue uniforms with gold epaulets on their shoulders. Under their blue coats they wore crisp white dress shirts and on their heads they wore snappy, navy-blue billed caps with a thin band of gold around the brim. The caps matched the uniforms.

"Looks like a party," Della said.

"We got a gig," the man who carried a large bass said. "We'll be the party once we get there."

Josie stepped forward and hugged her mother, then she stepped back and wrapped her arm through the bend of Ollie's elbow. Josie and Ollie were elegant. Josie wore a blue silk dress with long stemmed gold roses running through the fabric. Over her softly draped dress she wore a knee length, light-weight, black coat, hanging open. Ollie wore a black suit and a white shirt as crisp and fresh as the elegantly uniformed men.

"This is my mother," Josie said to the men who stood around her.

Oliver's Song

"Come on. Go with us, Mama," the man who carried a horn under his arm said.

"Not tonight," Della answered.

"Don't worry," the third man said. "We're playing downtown every night this week."

"Well, count me in for tomorrow night."

"It's a deal," the man answered.

"We had to change our name," the bass player said. "We used to be the Dixie Trio. Now we're Three Dots and a Spot. Guess who's the spot?" He threw his head back and laughed.

"He don't got no uniform, but he's the Piano Man. Piano Man can be different."

"Got to move on," the third man said. "Don't want to be late for a payin' job."

The entourage began to move forward as a unit until Ollie broke ranks and came back to where Della stood. Josie and the musicians stopped and waited.

"I almost forgot," he said. "I have a check for you. I sold one of those pieces of music. I got two-hundred-and-fifty dollars. Every cent of that belongs to you. I'll bring the check by your office on Monday morning and pick up the composition." But, it is only fair to tell you that my dad has offered to pay you $10,000 for the other piece. He feels our family owes you that much and more. I can't ever pay you enough for what you did for me."

It took only a second for Della to reply. She knew she was nothing if she didn't stand on her principles. "No Ollie, we had a deal. I worked for a song and that's all I want from you. I'll take the $250 from you on Monday, but you've just sold the other composition too. I want to purchase it." She hesitated a moment. "Let's say two-hundred-and-fifty."

"No," Ollie said. "It's yours. I won't try to sell that one, if you want it."

"Good. Come in on Monday because I want you to write the title on my composition. I want it to read 'Oliver's Song.' Bring

357

that same black pen you used to notate. I'm framing 'Oliver's Song' and hanging it behind my desk."

"One last thing," Ollie said, looking down as he spoke. "You have one of the best daughters in the whole world. This sounds crazy, but something good came from this mess, and that was getting to know Josie."

"Ahhhh," Josie said as she kissed Ollie on his cheek, and placed her arm around his waist.

"Oh now . . . oh now," one of the three Dots said, and he laughed.

Della embraced Ollie. When she released him, she looked at the man who held the horn tucked under his arm. "If you're not in a real great hurry, could you play this piece for me? I've never heard it performed."

The horn player stepped forward. "Well, I guess I'll give it a shot," he said.

Ollie held Della's briefcase while she withdrew the composition. The horn player stood in front of her, and she held the paper, one hand at the top of the sheet, the other hand at the bottom. He studied the notes, put the mouthpiece to his lips, and began playing.

Sweet sounds with an aching melody filled the night air from where the little group gathered below the sign D. Boudreaux Attorney at Law, the sound floating all the way to where the city opened to the bay. The honesty in the notes brought tears to Della's eyes. The sound dipped and then swelled to a long, rambling note that wafted through the streets of downtown Mobile.

Down by the water, Covey had stopped playing his ukulele. Della thought he too must be listening.

"Ah, Mom," Josie said when she saw tears on her mother's cheeks.

The bass player shook his head. "That's a fine piece."

Della wiped her cheeks with the backside of her hand. "Tell you what," she said to Ollie. "That piece is so sweet, it ought to be played. May I keep the original, but you can still sell the music. And, you pocket the money."

Ollie grinned. "We'll split it," he said, extending his hand for a shake.

Josie slipped her arm inside Ollie's elbow again. Ollie blew Della a kiss as the group strolled toward the Convention Center. Their laughter was its own music.

She smelled the spice of his aftershave before she turned and saw him. Moss Maple stood like a preacher, his hands clasped in front of him.

"You were enjoying watching the young people," he said, "I didn't want to interfere with that."

Della extended her arm, motioning for Moss to join her. He stood beside her and they watched the happy entourage strutting toward Water Street.

"Everything worked out well," Moss said. "Your first client's going to do something important with himself."

"He will," Della affirmed. "He's already sold his first two compositions." She thought again of 'Oliver's Song.'" She knew exactly how she wanted it matted and framed.

"Miss Della," Moss said. He bowed slightly toward her, feigning southern charm. "How about allowing me to buy you a seafood dinner on the Causeway? I'm in need of a dinner companion."

"You got it," Della said.

Moss slid his arm around the back of Della's waist. "You think we could have half as much fun as those young people?"

"Let's try," Della said. She slid her arm around his back.

"Let me carry that briefcase." Moss reached across Della and took the case from her hand. They headed east where Moss had parked his car close to the water. The orange moon, big as a saucer, had risen above the horizon.

"It's going to be a perfect night on the bay," Moss said.

Della knew it would be—the mullet jumping, the moon warming the night sky, the pelicans soaring on the Gulf breeze. Night had come, but with night came the promise of a new day.

The wind blows to the south, and goes round to the north; round and round goes the wind and on its circuits the wind returns.